I AM BECAUSE YOU WERE

INSPIRED BY TRUE EVENTS

JESSICA LOVELESS

Here's to any person who has been a victim of childhood abuse.
& especially for you, Mom, with all my love.

You are not what happened to you. **We believe you.** *You are brave and wonderful, and you didn't deserve any of it. We are happy you are alive on earth with us. Your past is now a story and once you are ready to accept this, it has no more power over you.*

Live for the Bonnie that exists within your child-like heart.

ACKNOWLEDGMENTS

I am deeply thankful to the following: My husband, Corey, for believing in me, and always supporting my time to write despite our four kids. Without you always being there to listen and your patience to provide feedback any time I needed it, I would have never finished. My children, Logan, Stella, Lilah, and Luna for prolonging the completion of this novel but giving me the motivation to follow my dreams. You four are my everything; may you always follow your dreams. My editor, Bambi Sommers, for her genuine feedback, support, and wisdom. Your compassionate guidance and editing have made all the difference. My loving friend, Meagan, for continuously giving me the encouragement I needed to develop this heartfelt story into a novel. Your unconditional support means the world to me. My sweet father, David, for always loving, encouraging, and supporting me. Thank you for going above and beyond to help make my dreams come true. My writing community on 'Bookstagram,' who helped me evolve this story into everything it could be. Many thanks to my Beta readers and ARC team, I am forever grateful for your feedback. I also wanted to thank Cathryn Carter for formatting this novel. Her professional contributions were a vital asset in turning this book into everything I ever imagined. Lastly, and most importantly, to my beautiful mother who gave everything she had to give me a good life. Who taught me all the wonders and love in the world. You were the mother every child should get to experience. You lived and loved and will forever stay alive in our minds.

INTRODUCTION

My own mother dropped the three of us off like a sack of garbage. The kind you fling into the dumpster because it's too heavy to carry and you want the smell gone. Disposable. Waste. No second thoughts, never turning back to regret it. But there we stood, with tear-filled eyes, uncombed hair, and arms extended, desperately reaching for someone who no longer wanted us. As the dust from Mama's car flung behind the wheels and faded into the unfamiliar distance… I realized for the first time my brother and sister were all I had. They were all that mattered in my eight-year-old mind. I held Ralph in my arms, his body half the size of mine at just one-year-old. Emma's fingers were squeezing my hand so tightly, I hadn't realized she had dug her nails into my skin until I bled onto both of us. It wasn't until Ralph was pulled from my arms that I noticed the maroon drops of blood that lined the steps from my hand. We had been alone most of our lives with Mama coming and going, but we had never felt the kind of loneliness that existed when we were pulled apart. Ripped from each other and placed into stranger's arms. We had been so busy pleading for Mama to come back, we hadn't noticed the women who came to take us.

"Bonnie! Please save me. Don't *leaf* me!"

Emma's indignant roar made the hair on my arms stand up. Emma was only three, but she was so mighty. She was thrashing in the stranger's arms- kicking, biting and screaming so rabidly she turned into a wild animal right in front of my eyes. A woman swooped in and got ahold of me too.

"Come inside," her voice croaked as her hands squeezed my shoulders, but all I could hear was Emma begging for me to save her.

"Sissy, please- don't *leaf* me!"

She screamed just as I had taught her to do if a stranger ever grabbed her. From the day Emma and Ralph were born, I was the one who protected them. I taught her not to touch the hot stove when Mama used it to light a cigarette and forgot to turn it off. Sang her to sleep when she had nightmares. Hid them when Mama stumbled home in the middle of the night with one of her scary boyfriends. But not today. There was nothing I could do to save them. I couldn't even save myself. Why hadn't I seen this coming?

CHAPTER ONE

That morning the rain thrummed against the windows making it especially hard to concentrate. The gray skies were the least of my worries. I couldn't hear a single thing they were saying. I pressed my face tighter against the old wooden door, until my ear was completely flat against it. I held my breath until the pitter-patter matched my racing heartbeat. The coolness against my cheek was all too familiar. I couldn't even count the number of times I'd held on to hope up against this door. Wishing, hoping that something would change, but it never did. I closed my eyes, as if it would somehow make the voices on the other side louder. I had to hear something, anything so I could prepare.

Emma stood beside me, copying every move I made as usual. Her entire body was pressed against the door, but not her ears. I smiled at her with her curly blond locks and dirty face. She hadn't had a clue of what I was doing but at least she was being quiet for once. I didn't want to call attention to us, but I had to hear what they were saying. My bare feet were perched on the floor, pins and needles shot through my legs. I dreamed that we were getting a father. I always wanted one.

Finally, the rain slowed enough for me to hear Mama arguing with my grandparents. It was a typical part of any conversation they had with her.

"Ruby, I don't think that place will be healthy for the children," Ma-maw growled.

Even though I couldn't see her, I could imagine her wrinkled face all scrunched up with her brows pulled together. She gave that look to Mama often.

Mama whined back, with her strong southern drawl.

"Well, I just don't know what y'all expect me to do with them?"

What place? What place?

The wind picked up and, that quickly, I couldn't hear the response my grandmother gave. I imagined she replied that we would be staying with them until Mama got her stuff together again. That would be fine with me because summer nights spent at Ma-maw and Pa-paws were always filled with magic. The kind of magic that only existed in comfort and nature. Images flashed through my mind. Running free in the back yard. Picking fresh tomatoes and carrots from the garden. The faint taste of honeysuckles on my lips. Jumping into mud puddles and chasing after bees and butterflies. When the day finally ended, we had a warm meal to eat and fell asleep listening to the magical words of a fairytale.

The best times of my life were here in this house. Being the first child of three from Mama, I held a special place in my grandmothers' heart. This used to make me feel special, but now, it was replaced with tight knots in my stomach as I looked at my sister. It would be better if there was enough love for us all. I was once a promise to my grandmother that her daughter would change.

Mama made a promise to be a better mother with each new child. She seemed to try for a little, but after Ralph was born last year, her empty promise barely made it out of the hospital.

Suddenly, the door popped open, leaving Emma and me to tumble to the floor like dominos. Ma-maw and Pa-paw had expressions that looked like they did when they had to "put down" old Rupert, the black lab. They didn't tell us he was leaving or let us say goodbye then either. One minute we were rubbing Rupert's old furry back, and the next he was riding away with Pa-paw, never to be seen again. I swallowed hard, what would happen? Hopefully, we wouldn't be disappearing next? I steadied myself, and took a deep breath. The oxygen evaporated around me.

Mama briskly brushed by us, nearly knocking Emma to the floor again. She lifted her arms up in the air as if we had cooties. Mama always acted like we had cooties, but we didn't. I knew for sure we didn't because I once asked my doctor and he said, "no cooties" and laughed like I made a good joke. It wasn't very funny. I pulled Emma closer and swiped her curls out of her eyes. It was hard being the only one she had.

"Are y'all hungry?" Ma-Maw's voice was layered in tears.

"Yes ma'am."

I shook my head yes and straightened my shoulders. This was our cue to go inside. From the kitchen, I could see Mama out in the sunroom that overlooked the back yard filled with sagging rose bushes and a large garden that overflowed with rainwater and now mud. Mama lit up a cigarette and let out a deep breath of smoke. For a moment, I admired the way the smoke swirled around her head like a halo. She always looked so content during the first drag.

Emma's little hands slapped the table as she climbed up nearly sitting on top of me. She tended to stay close. I didn't mind and, even if I did, there wasn't another choice. I never even considered Emma not being glued to me. Her stomach growled loudly and she smiled at me. I smiled back at her. We were both happy to have food. Ma-Maw made fluffy peanut butter and jelly sandwiches, the best, with the perfect amount of peanut butter spread evenly across the soft bread. She sat it down in front of me and I poked it with my finger to watch it rise back up. The bread at home was never that soft. My grandmother patted my head as I chewed hastily, making sure to keep my mouth shut just as she often reminded us to. She had many rules. Her rules were not in place to be bent or broken. Emma's stomach let out another roar and she smiled again, this time with peanut butter and jelly smeared across her face and dripping down her arm. "My belly says thank you," she mumbled as she chewed. "I was *hunry*." I held back my laugh as my grandmother shook her head repulsively. I wanted to grab Emma up right then and run away with her. I looked away instead. In the living room, bundled up like a baby doll, slept Ralph peacefully. I could see his little toes wiggling under his blanket. Ralph slept a lot. He didn't have much of a chance to experience life yet. This was a good thing though because, for the most part, life was hard.

Once Ma-Maw stopped glaring at Emma and patting me like a dog, she turned and left the room without a glance at Ralph. Going to be alone as she had so many times before. It was almost as if Ma-Maw could only take so much company. Like she was a balloon that would burst if filled with too much interaction. Maybe that's why my own mother didn't like to be touched? I could already hear her fussing at the housemaid, Rissy. Again, my muscles tensed up. Once Rissy was caught eating leftover scraps in the kitchen, and she was made to eat in the pantry where the dogs ate. Rissy was paid a dollar and some change for her work daily. I only knew that from counting the money Pa-paw left her on the old table where she ate. I wasn't to sit with Rissy when my grandparents were home, another one of Ma-maw's rules. I followed her rules closely even when it made me feel guilty. But there was nothing stopping me when they were gone, I sat with Rissy anytime I could. This type of treatment was common for women of color, but I knew even then Rissy didn't deserve that. Rissy was my favorite adult. It was nice to have an adult treat me like a person and not just a dumb kid. We both had a clear understanding of what it felt like to be belittled and treated as if we would never be good enough. Despite the unfair treatment, Rissy attempted to show me the way of kindness in the world, at least a filtered view in which people were kind. Rissy also liked the empowerment of making sure I knew she chose to work for our grandparents and had the choice to leave if she wanted to. Rissy taught me to grow up and know there wasn't a difference in skin color. Although she was paid very little, Rissy appreciated the work because it allowed her a certain level of independence and helping care for her own family. She had a husband but sadly, her only child, James, died. Rissy was the kindest person I had ever met. I drowned out the words Ma-Maw said to her.

Left alone as usual, I knew from the prickly feeling on my skin something bad was going to happen. I didn't know just what but could feel something coming. The feeling filled my stomach, the same one I felt so many times before. It wasn't rumbles of hunger like Emma's. I put the other half of my sandwich down and propped my hand on my chin to watch Emma. Watching her eat was always amusing, the food would be anywhere except her mouth. I would count just how many places on her body would be covered before she finished. Whatever happened, she would always be my sister. I loved her with everything- even the messy parts. I continued to watch her chew with her mouth wide open, crumbs and globs of jelly falling into her lap. I couldn't help but smile as I waited for her to finish. Emma was not old enough to follow Ma-maw's rules yet. Just as she took her last bite, I stood and grabbed a towel wiping it swiftly. "Face all Queen?" Emma said smiling, her crooked baby teeth had food embedded in them. I laughed out loud at her this time, "How can one girl be so messy?" I cleared the table and wiped up the crumbs and sticky spots Emma left behind before anyone saw.

I followed Emma into the living room. I had no choice because I had to make sure she stayed out of trouble. "I *goin'* to the store today." Emma always spoke nonsense to herself. I was one of the few who could actually understand her. She told elaborate stories about alligators and her imaginary friends. Mama often lost her patience with Emma, and I had to be the interpreter. Everyone lost their patience with Emma. Pa-paw said he ain't never seen so much wild in one little girl. I wanted to shout that the poor girl was only three, but I never did. I peeked at Ralph, his cute sticking-up hair and chubby cheeks were perfect as he slept. He could sleep through anything. Ma-Maw often talked about how Ralph was ignored so much he wasn't reacting to stimuli as he should. I wasn't sure what that meant, but it made me want to fly off the handle anytime I heard people talking bad about my baby brother. Many times, I would walk by and fiddle with him while nobody was in the room, just to show them he was acting like the baby he was.

The house was mostly quiet, but I felt like my heart was going to beat out of my chest. For a moment, Emma and I just stared at each other, as the tension filled the air like smoke from Mama's cigarettes. It was hard to breathe.

"Went outside and *there* alligator," Emma said smiling- my frown disappeared. "Alligators are nice." she continued. A clicking noise became louder so we stood together, Emma clinging to my knees.

Rissy was finishing laundry in the washroom. She peeked around the corner at us and smiled. Rissy always had a smile on her face when we were visiting. Rissy was beautiful, her brown skin and dark eyes were always inviting. Rissy often went out of her way to look over us children, even when she wasn't asked to. She knew anytime something was wrong, and she knew just how to patch a boo-boo, and sing you to sleep. Rissy must have sensed the familiar anguish coming from my face. She motioned with her hands for us to join her. Rissy didn't like people to mention her son, but on occasion she would tell me a funny story about how James would bring home things in his pockets. It was usually things like bottle caps, rocks, sticks, old bubble gum, and crinkled up flowers. One day though, he brought home a salamander that jumped onto Rissy and got in her blouse. She was as mad as an old, wet hen. She never checked his pockets again. She made him empty them before her, oohing and aweing at his latest collection. She saved the collection in a box, and once she even showed them to me. I had my own collection box we kept hidden in the garden shed. Our own little secret.

I smiled, remembering the look in Rissy's eyes when she told me that story. I desperately wanted someone's eyes to glisten like that when they talked about me the way Rissy talked about James. Once we reached the washroom, we watched Rissy effortlessly monitor the wringer washer. Rissy pressed a lever that released to let the dirty water out. After the water drained, she refilled it with clean water, and pushed the agitator. As it shook the floor, she waited patiently until she sorted the clothes out of the washer, and ran them through the wringer. I stood to help and took clothes that fell below into the basket. Rissy and I didn't have to talk to communicate. When Rissy was in the room, I felt the warmth from her eyes like sunshine. One by one, we hung the clothes up on the indoor line to dry. Rissy hummed the mocking bird song. Emma stayed close, not too far from the clothesline; climbing in and out of the giant wicker handmade clothes basket. Half-way through, Ralph sounded his hungry cry. Rissy went towards him gleefully. For the next twenty minutes, me and Emma giggled together as we climbed in and out of the empty clothes hamper while listening to Rissy singing softly to Ralph from down the hall. In the small washroom surrounded by cotton and scents of soap. These were the magical moments and they were fleeting.

I heard the screen door slam, so I crept over to the window. Mama stomped through the rain and back to her car without saying goodbye. I watched her roll down the driveway, fighting back the tears building up in the corner of my eyes. Maybe if I were better, we were better, Mama would stay?

Ma-Maw came back down the hall and also watched her leave. She turned her attention back to Rissy. "Don't you have more work to do?" She barked.

Chills shot up both of my arms and I cringed to hear Ma-Maw speak to Rissy like that. Darkness closed in, as the dreary gray skies turned to blackness. "You girls are staying here for the night." Ma-Maw called, her voice cracking slightly. I wondered what horrible place Mama wanted to take us to, finally exhaled, we were safe. I watched Ma-maw smile gently as she rocked Ralph in her rocking chair that creaked with each motion. Ma-maw didn't look at Rissy like that. We headed to the bathroom and washed up for bed. I brushed my teeth, then I brushed Emma's teeth as I had always done. I taught Emma how to do *everything*. When we finished, we secretly waved to Rissy as she gathered her things to leave. She blew us kisses. Later as we were tucked into a bed that belonged to Mama when she was little, I took a deep breath and smiled at the familiar, musky smell of my grandparents' house. It was easier to breathe for now. In the room, there were not a lot of things that belonged to me, but it was my favorite place to sleep. The walls were painted a light green. It had remnants of who we imagined our mother to be as a little girl, with old flowered wallpaper, one small white and golden rimmed bed, and a table side lamp with a little ballerina on the top. Along the back wall was a tall bookshelf, filled with Encyclopedias and novels, and other things that my grandparents had stuffed inside throughout the years. I especially loved the Big Green Book of Fairy Tales. It was the only time I could escape in my mind.

Ma-maw had many rules and was very strict but somehow, she always had time to read the fairy tale book to us, and it was no different that night. She opened up to the paper bookmark and began to read. Her old voice weakened as she turned the pages. This particular story was about fairies who were guardians of a magical tree. If you took a nap under a Hawthorne tree, you could be swept away to an otherworld. I was fully immersed to the point I felt like I was inside of this fairy world. When the story was over, I pictured the thorny branches above me, hoping to be whisked off to an otherworld. Ma-maw left and I cuddled closer with Emma. "You still awake?" I whispered to her. She normally had trouble falling asleep. Just as I closed my eyes, Emma began talking.

"Alligators like other worlds too."

CHAPTER TWO

I woke with Emma's small body tangled in mine, rolled and twisted up like a pretzel. I attempted to pull my sweaty arm from underneath her. She didn't even give me space in my sleep. Even though I loved her dearly, I did need just *a little* space. I usually tried to creep out of bed in the mornings. It was the only time I could be alone. I held my breath and moved as slowly as I could so she didn't feel the slightest shift in the mattress. The sun came through the window slowly, creeping in through the open spot in the drapes. I wondered what the day would bring when my thoughts were interrupted by a loud and jangly, *'Er-er-er-ROOOO.'*

That dumb rooster, Red. Cock a-doodle-do is a universally known sound just about everyone knew, everyone- even Ralph. But not Red because he was a dumb rooster. I didn't know for certain that he was dumb, but I did know he wasn't smart. He didn't sound like a normal rooster. He sounded like a cow and a duck put together all in one. If roosters could start the day by screaming, I should have too. There were so many things inside of me that I had no idea how to get out. I dared not to though and instead, focused on the pile of poop and feathers Red left on my grandparent's porch again. He roosted there each night and each day he was chased away.

It was always funny to watch Ma-maw chase Red away. She would use a broom and jump if he came towards her. After 5 minutes, she would send poor Rissy out to get rid of him. She would then lead him out of the yard with corn. But every night he came back, fluffing his feathers on my grandparent's porch. He belonged to the Bradley's next door, but he seemed to like to call my grandparent's porch home. If only running away from home were that easy for me. It's crazy how he can just pick a home and sneak back day after day, but I'm always stuck in the same old place. I guess the world would be more fair if we could all choose where we wanted to call home.

I watched him settle in on the banister, almost like he was waiting to be shooed away. Everyone seemed to think Red was just a big bully, but I secretly admired the way he stood up for himself. The way he did whatever he wanted and stopped anyone who got in his way. Mama's old car came barreling into the driveway and my stomach sank to the floor. She didn't usually return this quickly after a drop off. Sometimes it was days, even weeks, before she came back for us. We, like Red, also wanted to call this place home but we were usually chased away too. I checked on Emma, who was still drooling on my pillow, and ran out to see what would happen.

I passed the fringed window curtains, and the smell of Listerine met my nose as I crept by the bathroom. It took everything in me not to skip through the house, but I was avoiding being yelled at. Running wasn't lady-like. Neither was screaming. Or any of the things I always wished I could do. The air was filled with a light haze of bacon grease and fresh cornbread biscuits. Dust particles danced across the living room in the dappled rays of morning sun. My stomach growled on cue- the food was another reason why me and Emma never wanted to leave. As I rounded the corner to the living room, I ran smack dab into my grandpa.

"Is Mama here!?" I asked, looking way up to meet his gaze. My voice came out louder than I intended to speak. Instantly, I shrank. *Children were supposed to be seen and not heard.* Pa-paw placed his finger to his lips and shushed me while motioning to Ralph fast asleep. He didn't answer my question but instead turned and slowly sat in his recliner. It surprised me to see him unfold a newspaper in front of his face. He never read the paper. Come to think of it, he was never really sitting inside. He usually found any excuse he could to roam in his yard, coming back home each night- just like the dumb rooster. Confused, I stepped closer to him, gently moving to the side of his view so I could see his face again. His face was steeped in guilt but he pretended to be extra focused.

"Are you reading comics?" I whispered, leaning over his shoulder. He grimaced at my closeness. I loved reading comics. In all of the 8 years I've visited here, Pa-paw had never read the paper. For a moment, I forgot about figuring out the big thing that was happening today and I leaned in even closer to take a look at what he was reading.

Page 8, Obituaries.

I turned my nose up and pulled away. *What did dead people have to do with anything?*

I loved reading comics. The ones with pictures of alive people. My mama constantly bragged about me being able to read at a young age. Not because she was actually proud of me, but as proof to strangers that she was a good mother. But she hadn't taught me to read, Rissy did.

I slowly pulled away while Pa-paw breathed heavily but said nothing more. There was no way the stories about dead people could be that interesting. I scrambled into the kitchen.

Ma-maw sniffled, there were actual tears. I stopped right where I was and watched. As the drops rolled down my grandmother's aged face, my insides tingled. It was like those knots just kept getting tighter. I felt something inside of me crying too, but I didn't dare let a tear escape.

"What are you…" I started to question, but stopped myself once they turned to face me. *That wasn't very lady-like either.* My voice trailed off and eventually their gazes too. I didn't know what to say, so I just walked up to Mama instead. She was in the corner of the bench table, and a part of me hoped she would be crying too, but her face was dry. The sunlight crept in through the back door. It illuminated the bright patterned wallpaper, Formica counter-tops and mustard yellow refrigerator. Coffee cups sat empty by the sink. It was early, and I studied

Mama's face, wondering why she would be awake. Mama had black circles under her eyes, and last night's makeup remained in bits across her face. No tears though, just a head full of tangled hair and new wrinkles I hadn't noticed before. I gently slid into her lap, hoping if it was soft enough, she wouldn't notice and would let me cuddle even if for just a moment. I felt a strong push and noticed my body shifting. That quickly, the cold bench met my bottom and my mother spoke to me for the first time that morning,

"Not now, Bonnie."

I squinted as Mama and Ma-maw locked eyes and whatever they had been talking about stopped. Ma-maw wiped her face quickly with her sleeve. My feet kicked nervously, to keep my mind off the silent stares. Mama looked so tired. Wishing I knew how to make her happy, I thought of what would make me happy. Emma and I often took turns rubbing each other's backs. I liked to have a back rub when I was tired. So, I reached over and gently ran my hand along her shoulder, smoothly and slowly over her shirt. Mama let out a deep breath, and for a moment, I smiled proudly.

Smack.

Mama swatted my hand away, it stung.

"And stop kicking your feet." She growled and scooted further away from me.

I tried not to let Mama see the hot tears that gathered in both of my eyes. No matter how many times she rejected me, it always hurt like it was the first time. I was so used to this side of her that every time I cried, I promised it would be the last. I tried to make sense of her rejection. It was almost like she was two different people. There was never a clear answer for what type of mom I would wake up to.

Emma came in stumbling over her own feet, her wild hair sticking out everywhere, and Mama jumped up and vanished from the room. I could hear her strike a match over and over again until it sizzled.

"You *leafed* me," Emma growled at me, eyes locked and angry. I was the only one who didn't correct her from saying leaf instead of left.

"I didn't want to wake you, Em." I reached for her gently and patted the seat next to me.

Emma rubbed her eyes. "Well, I not like it when you *leaf* me all alone." She climbed up and sat so close, I barely had to lean over to whisper.

"I won't do it again, I promise." I gave her a tight squeeze.

"Thank you," Emma mumbled and with that she turned and stuffed her mouth with eggs. I tried to eat but nothing tasted the same when something bad was about to happen.

"Ma-Maw- *how come* Mama look sad today?" Emma asked as she took a bite of bacon.

"Chew your food, Emma," Ma-maw replied.

I began to wonder just when the last time I saw Mama happy was? It must have been the day Emma was born. I remember meeting Emma at the hospital nursery. I peeked down into her little crib. There were little babies all around me, but none of them looked as perfect as my baby sister did. I wanted to grab her up right then and never let her go, but I wasn't allowed to. I was pulled from the room and, instead, we went to see Mama whose face was swollen and she couldn't walk. I thought she would be mad, but being stuck in that bed away from her boyfriends made her look different. I wanted to go back to the nursery, but when Mama looked happy, I radiated towards her. I knew in that moment she was the mom I used to have. She smiled and laughed and made promises that things would be different. Three years later, Ralph was born, and by that time her eyes were glazed over. There was no more sparkle, just a dull blur of who she once was.

Ralph screeched and Ma-maw set down the dishes and left the room. Luckily, Ralph slept until breakfast was over. He wouldn't have wanted to be awake anyway. Mama yelled sometimes when Ralph was screaming, and she didn't know how to make it stop, so I would go to him and rock him until he settled. I patted his little butt and noticed the calm take over his face when I held him. Mama didn't know how to do that, and I didn't know why. We made our way into the front room and tried to remain invisible. It was just easier that way. We pushed out a large box of wooden blocks. Ralph crawled in behind us and clapped as we pulled them out one by one so as not to make a lot of noise. His hair stuck straight up into the air, and his little chubby cheeks and green eyes tracked our every move. I wasn't up for listening at the door today. I figured we would be staying with our grandparents until Mama came back to get us again. Like she had so many times before. Sometimes it was a few days, or sometimes it was months. Either way, Mama always came back.

"Bonnie, build me a house?" Emma pointed as if she could control me with her fingertips. I knew instantly she wanted me to build a house so she could knock it down. I began to stack one block on top of the other, straightening Emma's blocks as we went. At the same time, I reached over to stop Ralph from grabbing hold of our house. I knew before he moved which block he would go for, and would interfere so they didn't start fighting. I had become quite skilled at watching Emma and Ralph at the same time. I gave Ralph his own little pile of blocks, and gently redirected him there. It was a constant push and pull. I had to keep them busy or an adult would yell. Or worse, give a whooping. I was so used to interrupting fights, it was like my arms instinctively knew when Ralph would reach for a block. When Mama wasn't around, my grandparent's house was pretty peaceful. The days were busy, but they went so fast we never had to worry about food or clean clothes. It was the simple things like pulling vegetables from the garden and drinking the hose water on a hot summer day. All of the delicious food and eating meals together every night danced through my head. Sometimes I even imagined Mama coming to visit and running to us, hugging and kissing us because she missed us. I pictured sitting on Pa-paw's lap as he watched the birds in the morning, and watering Ma-maw's garden with Rissy like we did last summer…

Crash, the blocks came tumbling down.

Ralph's little face lit up with a mischievous smile as he watched the blocks fall to the floor. He clapped for himself, with his 3 little teeth showing. Emma's face turned red, and she crossed her arms. Her brows came together, and she glared at Ralph. "Top it, *Walph*." I had been so lost in daydreaming, I missed this one. I smiled at Ralph and kissed his little cheek, and I reached over to wipe the one little tear from Emma's eye.

"You can't do that you silly boy." I made my voice sound high-pitch like Ma-maw did when she talked to Ralph.

Ralph giggled in return, clapping for himself again. Emma huffed and lurched towards Ralph.

She grabbed the block from Ralph's hand, and he tugged it back closer to him. Together their small bodies rolled right into the leather topped lamp table behind them in the shuffle. It was as if in slow motion, I watched the tall copper lamp, Ma-maw's favorite, with little glass serving trays wobble back and forth. Before I could reach out for them, they both started to scream. The lamp hit the floor loudly, unplugged from the wall and sent glass shards across the living room carpet in tiny slivers. My heart raced as I tried to stop it before a grown-up could hear. But it was too late. Mama's stomps were loud in the room like a flash of thunder. I suddenly was weightless- pulled up to my feet. Someone had to take the blame, and it was usually me. Mama's grasp burnt my wrist. I tried to find my footing on the floor.

"I'm sorry, I didn't mean to. It was an accident." I cried out over Emma and Ralphs screams. Ma-maw gasped as she walked in. She ran over to her lamp. "Oh no, no, no. Not my serving lamp. What did you do?"

I blinked a few times to try and keep the tears in.

"Rissy! Come in here immediately." Ma-maw stepped back away from the glass.

"This is just what I mean!" Mama loosened her grip slightly, pointing at me and continued, "It's time. Maybe now you'll under-stand they're just too much." Mama looked at Ma-maw. I felt my body shrink. Ma-maw glared over at us and I pulled free and made criss-cross steps to avoid as much glass as possible. I wrapped my arms around Emma and Ralph until their sobs quieted.

Rissy bolted into the room and tossed her broom to the side. She didn't even glance at the mess on the floor. She rushed to us, and instantly pulled us away from the glass. "You, okay?" she said, inspecting each one of us from head to toe. She kneeled to reach our tear-filled eye levels. We nodded, too afraid to say anything.

"Well of course they're okay. My lamp on the other hand will need to be cleaned immediately," Ma-maw said in that voice again. Chill bumps raised on both of my arms.

Rissy ignored her for the first time ever, she gently touched each of our faces one by one. "Mistakes can happen, baby, it's okay." She knew how often I covered for them. "Accidents happen. It's okay, baby." She held my face for a minute longer then settled Emma and Ralph on the couch.

Ma-maw cleared her throat. "Get this cleaned up." And with that, she left the room.

Rissy rubbed my cheek one more time and turned and began to gather the tiny slivers of glass spread amongst wooden blocks in her bare hands. I knew and hoped that Mama would leave. She always ran from trouble. Mama turned for the door but instead, came back towards us. I felt my feet moving underneath me. I tried to keep up with her pace. She wasn't leaving this time, it was me. How stupid could I be to let them break that lamp? I should have been watching them better.

"Let's go, give your grandparents a hug."

It was almost a blur. I heard Emma cry out for me. Ma-maw's tear-stained face felt soggy against mine. My mouth was dry, and words blanked in my mind like my lips were glued shut. I couldn't think of what to say. I wasn't even sure if Ma-maw was upset about me leaving or the broken lamp on the floor. Pa-paw shook his head and pulled me in. He smelled of cigars and vetiver.

Before I could say I'm sorry, please keep me here. I'll be a good kid- I'll do anything... Mama pushed me towards the door. "Bonnie, wait outside so you don't break anything else. I have to talk to my mother."

As usual, I did as I was told, but the air around me was still and, once I reached outside, I realized I hadn't taken a breath. The screen door followed behind my ankles with a loud snap. I gasped for air and all of the tears I held back flooded my face. I ferociously wiped them away before Mama could see me cry. If there was one thing Mama hated, it was a cry baby. I couldn't help that I felt things bigger than Mama did. Sometimes it seemed like Mama didn't have feelings at all. Just as I wiped my tears away, Rissy approached me from the side of the house. She was slightly out of breath after sneaking back here to tell me goodbye. Her once smooth hands were covered in nick's from cleaning the glass so quickly. Somehow Rissy was always there when I needed her to be. Once when I got into trouble for stealing cookies,

Rissy let me go with her to her small shack she lived in with her husband. It wasn't much but being with Rissy made everything feel better. I had stared at the pictures of her son across the tiny walls. I imagined being his friend and giving anything to have a mother that hung my picture on the wall. Rissy set the box of broken glass down and pulled me into her, hugging me so tightly I could feel the bones in my back pop.

"Listen to me. *You's* a good kid. Don't let nobody take that from you. You look after your sister and brother- you hear? Even when I *ain't witcha'* — I'll be right here. In your heart." As she held on to my elbows, I studied her face because I wasn't sure if I would ever see her again.

Rissy bent down to my level and squeezed my arm. Her dark brown eyes sparkled in the sunlight. I didn't realize how tightly she held me until she let her grip go. Unlike Mama's though, Rissy didn't want to let me go. Rissy turned and picked up the box of broken glass and took it to the shed. I watched her back heave up and down and knew she left so I didn't see her cry. Mama emerged with Ralph in her arms, and Emma ran out and grabbed my legs. I wasn't sure if I was sad or relieved that Emma and Ralph were coming with us. I had no clue where we were going. Mama tossed Ralph into the car and motioned for us to get in. Emma still sobbed as she climbed in, and Mama slammed our door closed. I sat up to see out of the window as the car lurched backwards and out of the long driveway. Rissy peered out from the shed and I waved to her slowly. Her hand was held in the air for several moments like she had forgotten to move it, like she wouldn't move from that spot until we came back. I swallowed hard, *if* we came back.

As we rolled along and down the country roads, Emma began to nod off on my shoulder. The outside was moving so quickly, I didn't know where we were going. I scanned the roads trying to spot street names, but nothing was familiar. I closed my eyes and pretended to be asleep, all the while hoping Mama would turn the car around.

CHAPTER THREE

I must have fallen asleep. Mama lit another cigarette as she drove onto a brick road. The ashes clung to the end like a burning rope until it slithered through the open window. The car slowed abruptly. I bounced in the seat and struggled to put my legs underneath me. I had to stretch my neck all the way up just to reach the window. Being little was annoying. Houses lined the brick road, and the car bounced forward. Just as I would get a good grip on the door, the bumpy and noisy and teeth-gritting movement would set me off balance. This was not a good place to be if you want to get somewhere in a hurry. It didn't slow Mama down though. Our bodies jerked forward as the sound of metal crashing into metal clanged. We were parked. "Damn guard rail," Mama hissed, looking into the mirror at herself. She studied her reflection and fixed her hair. I tried to figure out where we were but I couldn't. It was a tall brick building surrounded by a lot of other buildings, all overgrown with ivy.

Emma wavered awake. Her sleepy eyes studied our mother. Mama slammed the mirror shut and muttered under her breath but said nothing to us as she got out of the car. I reached over and patted Emma's shoulder, "It's okay, Em."

As she rubbed her eyes, Ralph began to scream. Instantly I watched the sweat gather across Mama's scrunched forehead who, at this point, was taking big breaths as if she were blowing a balloon.

That was not a good sign. Ralph's cry became louder and louder and, instantly, it was enough to make Mama run to a liquor store. She did that often but today she didn't get back in the car. She grabbed him out forcefully. "Hush now," she growled at him. As if squeezing and yelling at him could help anyone stop crying. I patted his leg that dangled from Mama's arms.

"I can take him," I said just a little louder than a whisper.

I took hold of Emma's tiny hand and helped her down from the car. By the time I turned around, Mama shoved Ralph at me. "Hold him for a minute." As if it were her idea all along, she disappeared inside the car for her purse. Ralph's cry slowed as I began to rock him. She led us to the stairs of a tall building and stood there. Mama breathed heavily a few times and rang the doorbell. Perhaps we were meeting a friend of hers? Awkwardly we all just stood, with the wind blowing and each of us too afraid to talk in case it made Mama even more angry. Mama pulled Ralph from my arms and shifted him to her hip. The buzzer went off, reluctantly we followed our mother inside.

The door creaked as it opened, and I immediately smelled the pungent odor of moth balls. I cuffed my hand over my nose and shook my head to rid the smell, but it lingered. Ralph's cries had calmed with me holding him but once inside, his cries echoed across the room. People turned and stared. I only knew what moth balls were because of the time I went looking for candy in Ma-maw's closet. I didn't actually remember eating any candy that day, but I did remember the whooping I got with Pa-paw's belt.

There was a little girl with red hair and freckles screaming at a grown-up. I couldn't move my eyes off of her. It was weird to see someone so brave and un-lady like. She jumped up and down and pushed the old lady away from her. I tried to hear what she said, but Mama kept walking in the opposite direction. I half-heartedly followed behind, turning my neck so I could see the red headed little girl. She seemed to be having a very bad day.

"Mama…. Where are we?" I asked, louder than I normally would speak over Ralph's roaring cry. Mama didn't answer. We approached a tall desk. Behind the desk there was a chubby woman wearing purple who sat up high on a raised chair and looked down at us. She looked like one of those judges who make big decisions in court. She was scary. Her purple sweater looked itchy, and she had magnified eyes underneath her glasses that slid down her nose. I glanced around the room waiting for the adults to talk to each other for what seemed like ages. Ma-maw always said that everything takes forever when you're 8. She also often reminded me I was impatient. Emma started to whine. I couldn't follow what Mama and the lady with the purple sweater were talking about. If only they weren't so loud- if only I could make them stop -then maybe Mama would love us like other moms loved their children?

Mama was doing an awful job at talking to purple sweater lady. The lady in purple kept asking Mama the same questions and staring at each of us with wide eyes. Every now and again, Mama glanced down at Emma with disgust as she wiped her wet, snotty face on her dress. It was like we were a train wreck waiting to happen or one that had crashed many years ago but kept slowly creeping along. It was almost painful to watch. For some reason, Mama just wasn't the kind of adult who could do adult things. I didn't know whether to laugh or cry, watching Mama holding my crying brother with Emma screaming and pulling at her legs. I watched her face harden and, without thought, I reached for him with an offer to take Ralph from her arms. Mama thrust him into me so hard, it made me slouch down. Ralph's crying became quieter, and he laid his head on my shoulder. As I rocked him slowly, like moms were supposed to, he became still, and I could feel his weight against me. His feet nearly touched the bottom of my legs. I sat down on the floor with him, and quietly sang that mockingbird song Rissy always sang to us. Emma crept over, laying her head across my arm. Her pudgy little fingers were wet from tears, but that didn't stop her from holding on tightly. She laid her head across my arm, and I looked around the strange room. I noticed pictures with a lot of children in them on the walls. Children who smiled but didn't really smile in the picture. I felt my chest rumble... if Mama left us here, how would we ever leave? I felt the weight of the world on my shoulders, and the weight of Ralph and Emma in my arms.

"Sign here and here. You have visitation rights on the weekends." The purple sweater lady said flatly. Mama signed without hesitation and turned to us. "Come on, follow me." For a moment I thought we were leaving with her, but I could barely stand when Mama brisked by us. We walked back through the lobby, back by the redhead who was done screaming. She sat in a chair with her arms crossed. I wonder if her mom left her too? Mama held the door open for us and I struggled to carry Ralph.

"Are you leaving us here?" I asked while shuffling down the steps. I felt the weight of Ralph and the gravel shift beneath my feet, as I chased after Mama. She didn't answer but instead opened the trunk. I saw our bags of clothes and felt the world spin around me. She was leaving us.

"I'll be better! Mama, I'll help with Emma and Ralph. I can help keep them quieter."

"Oh, Bonnie, don't be so dramatic. I'll be back every weekend; this will do you and me some good." But it didn't feel good. It felt wrong, all wrong. Mamas are supposed to love their babies and hug them. Isn't that what they were made to do? Not throw them away like they were trash.

"We ain't gonna break *nothin'* ever again, I promise!"

I grabbed onto her, pulling at her shirt, hoping she would change her mind. I knew she wouldn't like my crybaby behavior, but the idea of her leaving us for good was worse than anything I ever imagined. Mama peeled me off of her and pulled our bags from the car. She tossed them down by the steps and then she really left us.

BACK TO THE DAY

The ladies took Emma and me to an empty room. I clung to her, squeezing her sticky little hand tightly. They could not take her from me too. They left the door propped open and there was one window, one table and five chairs. This room must be the room you're left in when your mother no longer wanted you. But where was Ralph going?

The red head from the lobby was sitting at the table. Her arms were crossed, and she was facing the corner in her chair. She turned when we came into the room. We sat in the silence staring at the ladies and then back at each other. The tears had dried on our faces but inside, I was still screaming. Nobody said anything. I had this ache in my tummy that I had never felt before. I couldn't stop thinking of Hansel and Gretel from my fairy tale book. I imagined them slapping us down into a big kettle, cooking us up— never to be seen again. I wondered if the redhead was mad at her mom too? I studied her face until the strange woman in purple came up and patted Emma's head like a dog. Her sweater rubbed across my arm and it *was* itchy! She acted as if this were a normal thing, leaving your children with strangers.

"Hello girls, now that that is over… I'm Juliet. There is nothing to be afraid of, we're *gonna* take you to meet your new house parents. We have nice *lil'* cottages here at Hawthorne. Sometimes, grown-ups have grown-up problems they have to solve. Before long, you'll love it here, just like the rest of the kids." I shivered at the sound of it. *Love it here, never, in a million years.* Hearing the name Hawthorne, after the fairy tale the night before gave me chills. Was this an otherworld? The redhead turned around in her chair. "Are you serious? You can't be serious." She smacked both of her thighs with her hands. "Nobody likes it here. I should know, I've tried almost every cottage and now… here we go again."

"Well- now you do have a quiet voice after all. I would prefer if you didn't speak at all if you have nothing nice to say. As you can tell, Susan is having difficulty finding the right cottage that works for her, but she will eventually adjust." Juliet grinned at the girl. "Any other questions?"

"Where is Ralph?" I asked while scooting Emma away from her. I glanced at the door to see if I could run with Emma in my arms. She had it blocked. "He will be going to the nursery. You can see him anytime you want to," Juliet said in an unfavorable tone. In that moment I knew it wasn't only my mother who told lies. We were told to stand as she led us down a narrow hall and out onto a sidewalk trail that led to several different buildings in the distance. I was surprised when the redhead listened and stomped behind us.

I couldn't help but notice how serenely quiet the neighborhood was. The only noise was the sound of the wind- cloying and heavy and it wrapped humidity around my face making it even harder to breath. Thunder rattled in the distance. "I guess there's another storm on its way, we better hurry," Juliet called and walked even faster. Juliet talked about as fast as she walked. She mumbled things loudly. "Over here is Johnson's cottage, there is the Brown's Cottage, here at the home and school for children..." She pointed as she talked, but none of it made any sense.

"Is this an orphanage?" I managed to ask, my voice louder than I intended to be. It sounded like someone else's voice. Maybe this was someone else's life, someone else's mother who didn't want them...

"No, child, you're not an orphan. I said *home* and *school* for children."

I blinked my eyes at her. Clearly it was an orphanage if we lived and went to school here without parents, but I didn't respond. "My parents are dead, so I am an orphan." The redhead rolled her eyes at Juliet.

Juliet blinked back at us and continued. "You should feel lucky, these family-style living homes are new for Hawthorne and replaced the traditional dorm style rooms. The cottages, as the houses are quaintly called, were designed for 6-8 children to live with a set of house parents." Juliet was sure to emphasize house parents and proudly smiled. "This big change is new to the times, and especially new in the South, and it is to help children feel like they have a fami-ly..." She paused to correct herself. "Like they are a family." I knew I had a family as of yesterday, but the idea of having a house father made me listen closer. I never got to meet my dad, and Mama told me she didn't know who he was. I couldn't ever understand how one could lose their kid's father but if anyone could, it would be my mother. Emma and Ralph had the same father, and while they got to do fun things with him, I was stuck with Mama on my own. Juliet's droning voice pulled me back to the conversation. "Each cottage was donated in honor of other kids who lost their parents too." *Is this supposed to be making us feel better? I know where my Mama is. I didn't lose her, she left me. She. Left. Me.* Emma squeezed my hand. *Us. She left Us.*

We reached a tall brick house that didn't look like a cottage. "Susan and Bonnie," Juliet mumbled as she read our names off her clipboard. Emma looked up at me with big eyes.

"What about Emma?" I cleared my throat as she went to knock on the door. Juliet acted as if she didn't hear me. I glanced at the redhead who shrugged her shoulders. Juliet pulled the door open and we followed her inside. The large windows that could be seen out front were covered with heavy drapes, the house was tidy, but old, and murmurs could be heard from the other room.

"Mara- new guests," Juliet called out. Her words flowed in a way that made it clear she had said them a thousand times before. She turned into a recording that just effortlessly repeated. I squeezed Emma's hand again.

The wood floor creaked and a woman appeared followed by a trail of lavender, chocolate and mint. The light from the window illuminated her tired, worn face, and wrinkles that bore deeply down into her neck. She was older than Mama, but not as old as Ma-maw.

Juliet stepped forward. "This will be your house mother, Mara. Mara, this is Bonnie and Susan." I looked up, a *long* way up. Mara was tall, her body thick. I saw the same look in Mara's eyes that were in my own mother's. That should have been comforting, but the emptiness gave me goosebumps.

CHAPTER FOUR

If I could get a penny each time Mara had to say, 'Bonnie, SHOES!' then I would be rich. She said it in the morning before church when I wasn't yet awake and almost left barefoot. She barked at me on the days I was running late for school and bolted out the door. My feet barely touched the dew droplets on the grass when she'd holler at me to come back and put my shoes on. She even yelled whenever I just simply wanted to feel the grass beneath my feet on a sunny Saturday afternoon. Or on a rainy day when I let the grass and mud squish between my toes. Or basically any time I tried to leave because I hated wearing shoes. Over the weeks I hoped it was something she would forget about or let slide, but as soon as she found I enjoyed not wearing shoes, it was like she made it her life mission to ensure I was wearing shoes at all times.

Life was nothing like it was before. At this point, I didn't know if it was a good or a bad thing. Our days had the same routine every day, and in each scenario, shoes were required. Life felt odd and very boring. I didn't have to wonder when Mama would come stumbling home, and I didn't have to worry about what food we would have for dinner. I didn't have to care for my sister and brother- I kind of just became a kid again. Just one of the others- the others whose parents didn't want them too. If you pretend long enough everything is fine, it becomes harder to face the truth. But it wasn't being there at Hawthorne that was actually the worst. It was that feeling inside of me- the confirmation I had always avoided. The hole in my stomach that kept me awake at night.

My mother *didn't want me.*

Unwanted. Unlovable. I wouldn't dare speak these words out loud, but I carried them with me each day. Hidden down deep in the place where I kept all of the things I didn't want to think about. I just tried to put a smile on and play with the other children and pretend my insides weren't upside down like the rest of my life had been. Sometimes, I would get so focused playing with dolls, I would actually forget where I was. Mara constantly told me I needed to pay attention, to be patient, to use my manners. I tried to, but I wanted to tell Mara she wasn't really living if she never had fun, I would know. Each thing Mara pointed out just reminded me more of how bad of a kid I was. 'Don't cry, it's not lady like, don't go barefoot outside, you'll get sick.' Every adult just wanted me to be quiet and perfect and avoid anything negative. It made me want to scream. But no matter how unraveled I became- like a ball of yarn being pulled- I never let it out. I missed Emma's constant talking. I missed the sound of baby Ralph's cry. The way it felt to sleep curled up next to Emma. The smell of Mama when she came home and finally allowing my eyes to close because I knew she was at least alive. All of the things I thought I would never miss. All of the things I didn't even know I had to hold onto in those moments. It was those images that would come to mind as I waited for Mama to pick me up. A mixture between joy, and fear, and excitement.

One by one, I watched all the other girls leave with their parents as I did the past four weekends. Down the steps into an array of different colored cars. 5 Red. 2 green. 3 white. I would count them so I could think of anything other than my mother not coming to get me. I stayed away from the crowd that loudly chattered at the table. My small hands were sweaty and my knuckles were white from holding on so tightly to the chipped window sill.

With each new car, I whispered, "Let that be Mama, let that be Mama." My heavy bag tugged at my shoulders until they were numb.

The weight was the only thing keeping me from toppling over out of defeat. I was afraid if I looked away from the window, I would miss her. I would miss her driving by and changing her mind... I didn't want to give her the chance to change her mind. One by one, each of the girls ran from the room and loaded into cars when Mara called their name... there was an emptiness left behind in the space that had just been so filled with excitement. I looked around finally as the sun began to set. The chairs were pulled out and drinks were left on the table. There was nobody else. It was just me. I was the only one left. The house felt still, as if it were sleeping. I watched the sun dip into the sky. A fresh swell of irritation pricked at me. The sunset on this day was particularly beautiful. The colors in the sky made you want to believe there could never be a dreadful day on earth. Like there were happy people painting the sky with cotton candy colors. The warmth from the dappled rays were so beautiful for a moment I could forget she didn't come. But I didn't want to believe in beautiful things, fairy tales and good things happening. It seemed to just be a let-down when I did. I slumped against the wall and let out a deep gusted sigh.

I'm the only one left.

If I just kept following the rules and making good grades, would I then be enough for Mama? The silent house was suffocating, and I knew since I didn't have a parent pick me up, I had to go to a church service with the 'swap out' parent who gave Mara a break from her duties over the weekend.

"Life sucks and being a kid sucks," I whispered to myself, and I freed my legs from underneath me to stand. I felt the hot tears form in my eyes, and just let them drip slowly down my face and over my lips. Mama wasn't there to see me cry anyways.

A piercing voice broke the silence. "Hey Bunny." Susan, the girl with the red hair appeared by the staircase. She drew out the ending and it sounded more like *Buuuunnnyyyyyy.* I couldn't tell if she was mocking me or trying to be nice. We had never actually spoken to each other before. She was always too busy running around yelling at everyone she could. I looked into her curious eyes and a familiar despair shined back at me. I wiped my tears on my sleeve, unsure if I should stay on the floor or get up and leave.

"Might as well give it up." Susan reached down for my hand and looked out the window.

It had been a long time since someone reached out for me. The warmth of her hand felt like the remaining bits of sunshine. I stood with her help and adjusted my bag, "My name is Bonnie," I mumbled to her, adding "not Bunny."

Susan cocked her head sideways slightly and grinned. "Well- I have an idea of what we can do." She smiled big, her eyes scanning the room.

"Let's. Ditch. Church!" Susan excitedly whispered, drawing out each word.

I didn't know if she was testing me to see what I would say. It was a bad habit of mine to try and make everyone feel comfortable- to please people. So, I froze- and we stared at each other with our eyes wide. Was Susan someone I could trust? Susan nodded her head towards the steps and crouched down on the floor. She whispered, "Follow me." She wasn't joking. I watched her crawl away slightly before I dropped to my knee's trying to balance the heavy bag on my back. I couldn't help but notice Susan wore one too. Had she packed with the intention of leaving like I did? I felt my body follow Susan and realized it was the first time I took a chance in an awfully long time. My heart sped up, faster and fuller than it had been in weeks. I worked so hard at being good in hopes Mama would come back for me. I forgot what it felt like to actually have fun. Once we reached the steps, past the kitchen where the 'swap out' parent was talking to Mara, we tiptoed up the stairs. "Watch that one," Susan nodded towards the step I was going towards. It let out a loud screech and we smiled at each other giddily. We crawled the rest of the way up and froze at the top to see if we had been caught. I counted to 60 in my head before Susan was motioning for me again. She pointed at my bag and I went into the bedroom next to hers. I had spent one month in this house one room away and I hadn't even taken the time to say hello. I buried my bag underneath my made-up bed. The empty room was filled with remains of things nobody cared about, like schoolbooks, uniforms, and itchy blankets that made you feel more cold than warm. I had two roommates, Felicity and Jane, who were both lucky enough to leave for the weekend. I took one last glance at the empty room and met Susan in the hallway. I held my hands up to ask what was next. We heard a door close, and we rushed to the window at the end of the hall. Below we watched Mara get into her car, and the substitute walk across the lawn and through the courtyard in the direction of church. Susan raised her eyebrows at me and smiled as if to say- I know what I'm doing. That smile took the rest of my worries away and, instead, I felt excited.

"We should be here alone until 8. The substitute won't be able to make her count until she gets back from church." Susan turned from the window and made her way up the second set of stairs. I had never been up on this floor. This was where some of the older girls lived... the teenagers... I swallowed hard as I surveyed the open room. Hints of cheap perfume lingered. Four neatly made beds with crocheted blankets lined the bright teal walls. I wondered if the beds would have been made if it wasn't a part of the rules. I marveled at the psychedelic patterns and splashes of bright colors. Groovy patterns lined the walls with handmade art and yellow plaid curtains. They had lived here for a while. How long was awhile?

"This is where the older girls live, they don't stay home too often. Especially not for weekend pass. Felicity told me if they can't go with their parents, they go with boys!" Susan blushed.

"Boys! Yuck." I smiled back. "Hmm- but what are we doing?" I asked curiously, tracing the flower shaped wall mirror with my finger.

"We're going to make our story better for today." Susan said confidently, her smile displayed the gap in her front teeth.

"Our stories? Better?" I asked. Susan made her way to open the window on the back wall. As it jammed, she stopped just in time, to push it left some, then right, and then the old wood slid smoothly. She maneuvered the window, as if she did it a million times. Just how many weekends had Susan spent here alone?

The window had no screen and opened facing the back of the yard. I could immediately feel a gust of wind hit my face, and the warm rays of remaining sunshine streaked through the trees.

"What are you doing?" I asked, this time in the motherly voice I used when Emma did something wrong. Susan didn't reply and climbed out of the window. The wind whipped through her hair in a marvelous dance.

"We won't make our stories better if we're dead!" I sneered, glancing at the roof underneath Susan's feet.

"Don't be a baby." Susan said quietly and, again, held out her hand for me. I hesitated, my muscles clenched, and my cheeks felt hot. It was what Mama often said to me. I didn't want to seem like a baby, I wanted Susan to like me, after all. I took hold of the window frame and placed one leg out of the window onto the roof. My knee's bucked beneath me. I was afraid of heights and the last thing I wanted to do was skip church and die. Three stories high didn't sound like a lot, but the view when I looked up was the closest to the sky I had ever been. The wind blew strong enough it felt like any moment we could be lifted- tumbling down like leaves in the fall. Susan smirked at me again, still clasping my hand, she led me even higher. I didn't have time to panic because I was so focused on not falling. I could feel my clammy palms slipping inside of Susan's tight grasp. I followed her as she bent over, one arm touching the warm shingles beneath us for balance as we continued to climb up.

"You're going to be fine," Susan whispered. "I do this all the time."

I had never seen anyone do anything like this before, but I was even more surprised when we reached the peak at the top. Susan had a blanket held down with rocks. In a small Tupperware container, she had what looked like a half-eaten bag of Pizza Spins. Susan had planned to be here all along, so why did she pack a bag?

"How did you- where did you? How often do you come up here?" I asked as we sat on the blanket. I couldn't position my feet in the right place to make me feel sturdy on the slope.

Susan laughed. "Just lie back- like this." She lied flat on the blanket with her hands beneath her head, staring up into the sky. "You see that? The clouds floating away?" She paused to look at me and motioned for me to lie down next to her. I did quickly before she saw my doubt.

"Yeah?" I asked curiously. The clouds were immense and moving quickly, faster than the wind.

"That's actually the earth rotating. Did you know we could see that?" Susan smiled. "Hmm. No. I didn't." I said, still having trouble knowing whether she was joking or not, whether this whole thing was a trick to get me in trouble. But that was the thing that didn't make sense- even though Susan did crazy things- I don't think she ever said something without fully believing it.

"We can see the earth moving and that's what keeps our moms away from us. My mom is dead, but yours isn't. We have to be extra special for us to be able to see the earth rotate. My mom won't, but I have a grandmother from London and one day, they will come back for me. Today, we don't need them to because today we have each other." Susan smiled, a heartfelt smile I hadn't seen from her before. It felt nice breaking the rules for once.

"You mean like London in France?" I asked, imagining the Eiffel Tower and glowing lights.

"No, London, Virginia." Susan laughed, and together we lied still in silence, wishing for mothers who we may never have. Grateful today, we had each other.

CHAPTER FIVE

Cloud watching kept me sane as the next few weeks were quite the blur. Tedious routines, busy work, chores, and bedtime. The only bright part of my day was my new friend, Susan. Susan had many freckles on her face, and fuzzy red hair that was cut short, and even along her face. I was so happy to have someone I could talk to. Nobody ever understood me the way Susan did. I had never actually met anyone like Susan before. She was like this big ball of energy who knew how to do everything and get what she wanted. Somehow, she convinced Mara to let us be roommates. I swapped beds with Matilda who wanted to be closer to Jane. I admired the way Susan would take risks. I had never sought out opportunities for trouble like Susan did. I got in enough trouble when I didn't even do anything. I had always just done what I thought was the right thing. I tried to make everyone happy and do as they wish. But now that everything was different, everything was strange, I didn't know what the right way was anymore. There didn't seem to be rights or wrongs at Hawthorne, just a lot of rules and pretending to be happy. I just acted the way everyone else did- as if it were totally normal to be living here. Everyone except Susan. Susan literally did anything she wanted. One night Jane dared her to steal candy from Mara's bedroom.

Without hesitation, she dropped down to her knee's. The ninja crawl-as she called it. As soon as Mara went to attend to the laundry, she slipped into Mara's talc and lilac scented room. She headed straight for the top drawer next to her bed. From that night on, she always took two, one for me and one for herself.

Not too long after we got a room together, Susan heard me crying. She called me over to her bed and told me to get under the covers. She patted my head and wiped the tears from my eyes with her sleeve. "You know you're not the only person in this room, right?" I smiled at her through my tears. "If you learn anything, Bunny, you should learn chocolate fixes everything. Ever-y-thing. At least for a few seconds anyway."

A smile extended from her eyes down into her soul as she threw the small candy right at me.

"Ow!" I squeaked.

It kind of hurt the rim of my nose. Without another word, I opened the small candy and placed it into my mouth. I closed my eyes and really tasted the sweet chocolate. I twisted the foil wrapper in my fingers.

The melting, and sugar, and creaminess.

Susan was right, in that split second the warm sensation helped make the pain go away. I sat up and smiled at Susan, and that was all it took.

"I will be so fat if I eat one every time I feel sad."

Our pure, joyful laughter could be heard from a mile away. It echoed through the halls and right into Mara's room.

Many nights, we shared a bed trying to remember what it felt like to be close to someone.

CHAPTER SIX

As the time continued to pass, Susan quickly pointed out that I was a wimp about most things. Susan had been living in a Hawthorne cottage since she could remember, it was all she had ever known. Her freckled face and over the top expressions were the only comfort I had, other than moments when a cottage parent would walk by with Ralph or Emma. I would stand on my tippy toes until they disappeared out of sight. Those original promised visits with my siblings had never happened. I never received visits, nor phone calls from my mother either... when I did happen to get close enough to hug Emma or Ralph, they would reach out to me. I would pick them up and hug them so close. Smelling in their baby smells. But they would push away from me and get down. In another minute they would extend their arms to me to be picked up again... it was like they were desperate for attention but didn't know how to receive it. Since coming to Hawthorne, we also lost every single familiarity. The new normal was trying to hide the deprivation of a parent or someone who acted like a parent. I couldn't save my siblings, so I continued to question what was it that made us unlovable- so easy to leave behind? What was so wrong with me?

What was so wrong with us?

The wind howled outside, and it almost seemed as if the old window pane would give in at any minute.

Tap, tap, tap.

Susan stuffed a pillow from over her head to under and moaned loudly. "I can't even make myself sleep. Today is so boring!" She groaned, her face still halfway inside of her pillow. I closed the book I was reading and wrapped my arms tightly around my legs. Thunder crackled through the grayish blue sky causing both of us to jump.

"Well, anything would have to be better than thinking," I said.

"What's so wrong with what you're thinking?" Susan asked, shifting her weight to her elbows and scrunching her nose.

"Nothing," I said with a half-smile while shaking my head.

"I know that look."

"What is so wrong with me that my own mother doesn't want me?" I blurted out.

Susan sat fully up. "Don't do that to yourself. Look, Bonnie, it isn't about you. I'm sorry but you just got a bad mom. Cuckoos notoriously lay their eggs in other birds' nests and abandon them, tricking other birds into raising a chick that isn't theirs. Even cute, cuddly, pandas often have twins and then abandon the one that seems weaker. And many animals, when stressed or starved, abandon their young—or eat them."

I giggled. "Hmm. Maybe I'd rather be eaten." I threw my pillow across the room, and it thudded into Susan's face. She elaborately gasped and pretended to be passed out. But she sprang up to her feet.

Her eyes lit up like the lightning outside.

"We can't just sit here. If it's going to keep raining, we need to face it."

"Face what? Being eaten?" I asked, smiling. I never knew what she would think of next.

"No. Being here. Being stuck in the rain. Do you want to go play in the rain?"

I sat my book down and leaned forward. We both glanced out the window.

Lightning, thunder, heavy rain, wind. It wasn't a good idea.

"It's better than reading. Fairy tales are stupid anyway, I don't know why you believe in them."

"You are never, ever too old for fairy tales, Susan," I said but she continued to stare out of the window. "Wait- you're serious?" I asked.

Susan came closer to my bed. "If we keep avoiding our problems, we'll be crushed. We'll just be the abandoned ones. We'll be eaten. We need to face it. We didn't ask to be here."

I couldn't not smile. I got those butterflies in my stomach, the ones that always fluttered at Susan's ideas. And then I surprised both of us. "Sure- why not? Not like anybody would care if we got hit by lightning."

"Exactly or *eaten*." Susan emphasized and grinned. "Now let's just find a good way to escape."

Outside the rain fell so heavily we had to close our eyes to make it across the soggy yard. Our bare feet slipped on the cold mushy grass. Mud seeped between our toes. The lightning was more intense outside, intimidating and a million times closer than it had been in the safety of our bedroom. I had never been out in a storm before. There were many things I had been too afraid to do- the normal child-like things your mom usually forgives you for. But not mine, she held it against me like I was the worst kid so I never broke the rules. I truly believed if I was always good then she would love me the way other mothers love their children. The flashes of light were bright enough that, for an instant, it was light as day. Then complete blackness. It was the first time in my life I learned to accept things for what they were. Instead of hating every moment, we lived in that moment, despite being left at Hawthorne. We accepted it. Perhaps it was desperation for a lesson or some meaning in life. Whatever it was, we twisted together in sync with our arms wide open. Rain pounded on our skin, washing away the days of idiocy.

"If we can't change it, we can face it!" I yelled into the rain. We raised our arms up like we had won a true battle. Each drop that hit me matted my hair and rolled down my face. I felt alive. There was something about the smell of rain and the fear of lightning and the cold, wet, earthy ground beneath me that was soothing.

"We'll wait it out and we will take what comes!" Susan shouted back. She grasped my slippery hand. With each drop of rain, I felt the sadness running through my veins, filling every part of me being washed away. For so long I had been hiding from the feelings, trying to do anything I could to avoid them. But there I was standing in the rain, breaking rules and being alive.

"Nothing could be any better...." I began to whisper until I was interrupted.

"For heaven's sake! What in the world are you two doing? Trying to catch pneumonia? Get struck by lightning?" Mara's voice echoed louder than the thunder pulling us back to where we were.

"Shoo!" She called to the other girls who had appeared behind her. They all gawked at us like we were on display at a zoo. She threw her apron down and hugged to the door, holding it open, waiting. We sheepishly made our way in. Her eyes widened when she saw our bare feet caked in mud and grass. The tracks trailed behind us until we reached a towel Mara had angrily tossed down. The whole time she was bright red, huffing and puffing and murmuring under her breath. "To think that you're going to be sick isn't the worst. You could have been hit by lightning." Susan bit her lip and looked away from me to refrain from laughing. I stood rigid as Mara pulled my drenched shirt over my wet hair. I avoided eye contact and feared if I faced Susan I would also begin to laugh and not be able to stop. "No shoes. No coats..." Mara continued. "What is so hard about putting your shoes on, child?" She thudded my head.

Susan took the towel from Mara and wrapped it tightly around her. "Mrs. Mara- sometimes, you just need to stand in the rain." Mara looked at Susan for a moment and something washed over her face- perhaps a time from her youth, but it faded- "If you're a duck. Now go upstairs and get ready for bed. And girls..."

"Yes?" we whispered.

"There will be consequences."

We bolted up to our room. Mara was not especially cruel, but she lacked basic qualities that could have made living there better. Mara was strict, and believed with rules, children could become more structured. She often said things like, 'you get what you get, and you don't throw a fit.'

Susan mocked her the whole while, her mouth perfecting the words silently. 'Productivity is a child's worth.' 'Be seen and not heard.' 'Be grateful you have a roof over your head.' I don't know if Mara always believed these things, but I couldn't imagine her as a child. Mara had this look to her, like one night she went to sleep a child and the next morning awoke and her entire youth was gone. She didn't know how to have fun. She didn't believe in getting dirty, or being barefoot, or having hobbies, or toys. She especially hated the rain.

Once we were dressed and back in Susan's bed, she turned and whispered to me. "Mara doesn't have any children because she ate them."

I chuckled. "That was the best night of my life." I had forgotten the rewarding feeling of following my gut instead of doing what is lady like.

"Her face when she caught us was priceless! We showed her how to face it." Susan paused and turned, a serious expression took over her face, and in her lady president voice she whispered, "One day, I'm going to be a weather woman. I'll show Mara. Then I can stand in the rain anytime I want." The look in her eyes told me there was no stopping Susan from achieving anything she wanted to.

I woke at the same time each morning, right before the others in the house began to stir. It was like I had to mentally prepare to pretend I was okay. We marched across the concrete to the school like ants. I did my schoolwork, passed my exams, and competed in spelling bees. I tried to belong, but there was always a lingering shadow that reminded me I was not good enough. I was unlovable and unwanted. There were only so many games Susan and I could think up. Only so many times we could pace the length of our bedroom and try to escape in our minds.

After school was really the only time, I was alone. I would do my homework quickly so I could have time to read in my bed. Susan's absence was noticeable. She had detention almost every single day for something she did at school, whether it was talking back or making kids laugh or mocking a teacher. I was too afraid to move the wrong way in class. I never wanted to call attention to myself. I usually made it through by imagining I was a part of the fairytale stories Ma-maw used to read. Sometimes I pretended if I were good- really good- that Mama would love me. *That one day she would come back, and I would show her I'm a good kid.*

It was the only time I had a chance to truly cry alone. Because if I learned anything at Hawthorne, it was that it wasn't okay to be sad, to feel things. We were taught to hide it all behind this structure. But I thought maybe I could feel things other people couldn't. Because if not, how on earth could they not talk about it? I could see it in their eyes when they watched families interact on television. I could feel it in their faces, as their parents made an excuse as to why they wouldn't be picked up on the weekend. Together we shared one thing; we were misfits, and unwanted in the world. This should have brought us together, but it made us pretend even harder to be normal.

It was like I was sinking in my own misery. I also carried the weight of guilt for Emma and Ralph. It ate me alive and pestered me throughout the day. My mind kept retracing everything I could have, should have done to save them. After being separated for almost a year, I began to shut down. If I would have watched them better, if I would have kept that lamp from shattering- then maybe we would be together. I took all of the blame. Pictures of little Emma and Ralph's sad eyes would run through my head.

If only I could have been a better daughter, sister, person?

It began to take more effort just to smile. My emotional responses were dwindling, and every day was monotonous. But with each sunrise, I started a new day.

That afternoon I couldn't take it anymore. I wondered if Emma and Ralph were happy, if they were being taken care of. One of my biggest fears was Emma forgetting me too. I closed my eyes to hear Rissy's voice. It was getting harder and harder to do. I squinted even harder to feel Rissy's warm hand inside of mine. I imagined standing in my grandparent's house.

The musky smell, cigarette smoke, the way the grass felt on bare feet with freshly covered dew in the morning. Running across the yard with Emma, afraid of being attacked by Red's spurs, and drinking the cool water from the hose spigot. The bright mornings, feeling annoyed at Red's crow that never sounded quite right. That dumb rooster, Red, would at-least keep us company, even if it was just a game of chase.

I needed to be with someone. I glanced back at the sunset. I knew I wasn't supposed to leave, but what more did it really matter anyway? Mama already made it clear she wasn't coming back for me. As everyone else settled into their bedrooms, I crept down the stairs, and out the back door. My bare-feet found footing immediately. The wind riffled through my hair as I stepped into the shadows of the old house. The moist ground connected me back to the earth. With each step, I felt recharged— perhaps this is why Susan lived in the moment? There was a sense of freedom and letting go of living up to everyone's expectations. There was nothing but my footsteps amongst the crickets and a sky full of clouds. Every once in a while, I reached down to slap at my leg, making the mosquito's waver. Susan taught me to be brave enough times that I could break the rules on my own. How exciting. I crept up to the window once I reached the Hollifield cottage. I peered in and at once my heart sank. Was it relief or a deep hardening sadness? I watched through the prickly bushes; Emma being rocked and sang to. Emma's hands clung to Meryl's shirt. She slept peacefully in her *house* mother's arms.

I wanted so badly to have a sense of relief, knowing Emma was safe. Instead, I felt like I was drowning. The tears flowed like a rapid river down my face, and as I sniffled to keep the snot from rolling into my mouth, I took a step back. I raced with all of my might back to my cottage. I was supposed to be a good sister. I was supposed to be happy for Emma, but inside I felt hot and angry. How can she get that love without me? Why did nobody love me? I reached the back door, wiped my feet on the doormat and opened it just slow enough so it didn't alarm Mara. I bolted up the stairs and didn't stop until I reached my room. I took one look at Susan, who lie waiting and the tears fell again. Once I climbed into bed, I felt something hit my face. I opened the chocolate and placed it in my mouth.

"Don't worry, detention is worse than hearing you cry."

Through the tears, I smiled at Susan across the room.

"Thank you."

CHAPTER SEVEN

The following weekend, Susan and I had art supplies sprawled out across the living room floor. The other girls had left and Mara had no substitute for the weekend. It was just the three of us in the old house. She pulled down some scraps and art supplies for us and told us not to make too much noise. Each weekend we had been working on our project.

"That's not big enough! If I'm going to be married in front of the waterfall, it needs to be huge." Susan colored over the veil I drew. Every month, for each holiday, we added a new dress to the construction paper book. It was Susan's idea of course, she dreamed of a large wedding. In the front of the book, we kept an image of Susan's mother in her fancy wedding dress. It was all she had left of her mother. She could be quite bossy when it came to the images added. I understood why, at least she had this connection with her mother. She often had me re-draw images that were too sloppy or not fancy enough. Susan definitely didn't approve of any of my stick figures. But I did like to watch while Susan worked on coloring a pearl necklace and lace, she was ridiculously good at designing puffy wedding dresses. With ease, Susan added a cream colored, lacy veil that touched the floor.

"That's more like it" she gloated.

I giggled. "You're so good at that!"

"I can't say the same for you!" Susan laughed, glancing down at my scribbled crayon dress. I had gotten better at sneaking around, but art was still not my strong suit.

"When you get married, I will design the dress. Don't you worry." Susan finished the picture with feathers and real lace she had stolen from one of Mara's old blouses. Whenever we were having a bad day, we would work together, planning out a fairy tale wedding. It was more for Susan than for me. Maybe we couldn't have fairy tales, but we sure could make believe.

Weeks changed into months, and before I knew it, I shared that bedroom with Susan for two years. Day in and day out, I had Susan by my side. It was Saturday morning, and we were upstairs in our room. By this point we just waited for everyone else to leave. We no longer packed a bag to pretend we would leave long after everyone else. It got easier to accept because we had each other.

"I want to go home." I sat up in bed and called just loud enough for Susan to hear me. Susan glanced over at me, as if she hadn't heard that a million times.

"And I want to go to the moon," she replied, grinning. "It ain't happening, Bunny." Susan crouched while she tried to build a house of cards. I couldn't help but smile at her frustration as it kept falling with every gust of wind blowing in our open window. I considered closing it, but it didn't usually help anything. Susan really wasn't good at stacking cards. "You know that day… when we went on the roof for the first time?" Susan asked me.

I sat up, "yeah, why? The day we became best friends?" I responded. She grinned and nodded at me.

"I was planning to run away that day, but you were the only reason I stayed." Susan smiled and instantly my mood shifted.

"Well, what can our story be today?" I asked. I became so used to exploring with Susan, and even looked forward to days on the roof, watching the clouds roll by. I noticed Susan was concentrating more than she usually would. Like she had something on her mind she couldn't shake. Susan had given up a long time ago, and never had homesickness like I did. For her, it was just as far as the moon was. Susan looked over at me. Sitting there on my bed, I pulled the blanket closer to my face, patiently waiting for us to do something— anything. Susan shined a smile that said she was grateful to have my company after everyone else left. She opened her mouth to respond when the door shot open.

A woman Susan had never seen walked in. She was wearing a cut off shirt, and a short skirt, and she looked like Loretta Lynn. Susan's mouth dropped open even further. I knew Susan was admiring my mother's beauty. I recognized that face, it was the same one men made anywhere Mama went. Beaded necklaces dangled from around her neck as she glanced around the small room with approval.

"Pretty nice. I mean, what you did with the place."

Was Mama complimenting me? I sat up straighter in bed, turning red at the sight of the blanket making me look like a baby. I couldn't find any words to say. I just sat there with it in my hand, staring at Mama like a deer in headlights.

Mama took a step near my bed. "I don't care if you're panicking again, just do it quickly. We have things to do." She said, a smirk covering her face.

I exhaled deeply. I had forgotten to breathe.

"I thought you forgot about me." I tried to say, but the words didn't roll right off my tongue. When they did finally, I couldn't recognize my own voice. The words replayed in my mind, on repeat, as I glanced over at Susan for help.

"Never. Why would you say a thing like that?" Mama asked.

She had a glow in her eyes that filled my cracked heart with all of the light it never had. I would follow that woman anywhere she wanted to go.

CHAPTER EIGHT

I awkwardly packed a small bag, not sure of what to bring or leave behind. It had been two years since I saw my mother. I hoped Susan read the apology in my eyes as I took my mother's hand and followed her to the car. My vision felt fuzzy, and I walked off balance. My heart leapt with each step I took.

I could not mess this up.

Is this even real? I blinked my eyes several times to see if I was dreaming.

"Are you having a seizure? Or what?" Mama was staring at me.

I looked up, mortified.

"No, just a bug. In my eye…" I quivered, wiping my face.

I didn't like the way it felt to lie. As I got inside the car, I was hit with the sudden smell of a million puffed cigarettes and Mama's tangy perfume. I felt my body sink into the cracked vinyl seat, the moment I had waited for, for so long. As I looked over, I saw two sets of eyes staring back at me. My stomach filled with glee. *Ralph and Emma!* I smiled deeply and reached out for Emma's little hand.

"I told you she'd come back."

As the car sped forward, I looked up in time to see the brick cottage I had called home. My eyes widened and my stomach churned as I watched Susan holding onto the glass window. The look in her eyes was one I had felt a million times watching the other children pull out of the driveway. Jealousy and lust for all of the things that weren't yours. The hot tears formed in my eyes, and I rubbed them away furiously before Mama could see. As we made it to the main road, and down to the highway, I thought I would feel relief. But in the backseat of the car with my brother and sister, all I could feel was Susan's empty eyes burning into me until she was just a speck in the window.

I would be foolish if I didn't consider there was a reason for Mama to pick us up. I didn't care, but the thought continued to come to me. The hopes of having Mama hold me returned to me as if they had never left. Any anger I felt for this woman was forgiven in seconds. I admired Mama as she drove, singing to music, and smoking a cigarette.

I made sure to keep the children quiet all the way home. Instantly I returned to the state of alert. Walking on eggshells, hoping to be perfect. I would prove myself this time. I took a breath of fresh air when we finally parked. I hid the disappointment clouding my mind when we pulled up to a dumpy apartment place instead of our grandparent's home. Mama got the kids out with less energy than she had earlier. Her face leaked the desire to sequester herself from the presence of children.

As we walked inside, I tried to swallow the sadness amongst butterflies in my stomach. I hungered for a normal home with a mother and a father, a big table to eat at together, with soft blankets and a fluffy cat. Mama closed the door behind us, and I felt homesick for a place that didn't exist.

It was dark and dusty in the apartment, the shades barely cracked allowing one sliver of light to shine through, exposing the dust particles in the air. Almost as if Mama hadn't cleaned since she moved in, nor did the person before her. There were cobwebs in the corner, and no kitchen table.

Where will we sleep? I thought, but dared not to ask.

Emma cried out for a juice cup and as Mama shuffled all of us in, she let out a puff of air.

"Calm down, calm down," she said more to herself than to us. It didn't look like she would have any juice cups here.

I instinctively went to the refrigerator to see what we had to work with. I drew back from the smell, but smiled when I noticed pizza spins. Susan and my favorites. There was only one beer can, on the top shelf. I hoped Mama wasn't saving it for later. Something green sat in a Tupperware bowl and soggy rice grew mold. Wasn't much to take inventory on, so I closed the door. The stench lingered like the look on Mama's face.

"Alright, ya'll look at what I got for you!" Mama called coming from her bedroom. Her face blushed. Emma and Ralph gathered around her, pushing each other to be closest to their mother. She dumped a sack onto the floor, and several toys clanked. I raised my brows, but couldn't help but smile as I saw Emma's face light up. Ralph charged towards the dinosaur. Emma swiped the baby doll with yarn hair. They all looked at me. I stepped closer, and slowly picked up the stuffed animal that was left on the floor... held it close to me, and inhaled the scent of my mother. I felt like there was a cage that would drop once I picked it up. There had to be something. Mama didn't give gifts for no reason. It was a pink flamingo and instantly I vowed to never lose it. Mama got us something.

There was a knock at the door, and Mama stood and brushed us away from her, as if it was what she was waiting for. She flung the door open and her telephone voice filled the room. "Oh Hello! Come on in,"

A woman waddled inside, she had a long nose and smelled of peppermint. Her smile was that of a person who smiled all day but never really meant it. I studied her, wondering who she could be. Mama never took her eyes or the smile off of her face. Quite a bit unusual for her.

"Y'all play while we talk for a little bit." Mama led the woman into the kitchen. She turned around and in her sing song voice called, "be good," her expression not matching her face. Her face said if we weren't good, there would be problems. My muscles tightened. I had to keep them calm. I sat on the floor with Emma and Ralph and chased them with my flamingo. Ralph chomped at me and Emma's toy rode the flamingo's back. It was like for the next ten minutes we were actually a happy, normal family. But Mama's telephone voice slipped out of the door when the woman left.

By the time Ralph started screaming, and Mama couldn't find the diapers, and 3 cigarettes later, she decided it was time to leave. Her face didn't have that smile anymore. It was back to being empty.

I prepared to be taken back to Hawthorne. I felt a sense of relief as I looked around Mama's apartment. Isn't it weird when a wish comes true? Shouldn't I be happy? I tried so hard to find the happiness that I buried deep down, but nothing came. I brushed the nerves away, and tried to savor every moment.

At least she tried.

Mama tried. She tried.

CHAPTER NINE

As we pulled up to the house, I couldn't calm the excitement within me. I didn't have to find it- suddenly I was bursting with excitement. I had imagined this moment more times than I could count. Ma-maw and Pa-paw's house. It sent an electric shock through my whole body- that feeling when you know you can just let your guard down. I huffed when I noticed my grandparent's car was not in the driveway. The sight of the old house called out to me with comforting memories, and pulled me back in. I instantly noticed Rissy out of the corner of my eye. I leapt from the car, faster than Mama could yell at me. I instantly found comfort in Rissy's strong arms, and laid my head onto her soft chest. Rissy held me tightly, with both arms linked behind my back, and we stayed that way. Longer than I had ever hugged my own mother.

"My girl. My girl. Look at how big you all are." Rissy squeezed.

"Can y'all help them get out?" Mama said with half of her body inside of the car still, she tapped her foot. Emma and Ralph sat together in the car, clearly afraid to get out. I didn't realize they may not remember the same way I did. After-all it had been two years. Two years at Hawthorne, over half of Ralph's life. Ralph made sobbing noises, and it just sent Mama into another breathing fit.

"For God's Sake!"

I forced myself to let go of Rissy. "I can help them, Mama."

I rubbed her arm softly in an attempt to comfort her. Mama pulled back, lit a cigarette with shaking hands. "Thank ya, Jesus! I have to pee."

Mama disappeared into the house, with the screened door slamming behind her ankles. I shrugged my shoulders at Rissy and reached in for Emma. Rissy rolled her eyes- and a giggle escaped my mouth. She took hold to Ralph and squeezed his dangling long legs. Together we walked inside.

"Tell me everything," Rissy purred while we prepared juice cups and a snack together in the kitchen. A smile lit up on my face. There were so many things I wanted to tell her.

"I have a friend. A special friend and Rissy- she's like James."

"Like James?" Rissy paused and pulled the lid off of the apple jelly.

"Yes, her name is Susan. She is funny, and collects things— well, mostly detention stubs, but she makes me smile the way you do when you talk about James." I slopped peanut butter on the bread, licking my finger.

Rissy's eyes filled with tears. Not the sad kind, but the kind that someone gets when they feel happy and heartbroken all at the same time.

"Well, now. James was my funny boy." She finished the sandwich with her eyes lost in memories.

"One time, when James was playing with his friends, they came inside to get a ball and one of those boys opened the door on me while I peed. I told him he needed to be fixin' up my bathroom door to make up for it." She placed the peanut butter and jelly sandwiches and juice on the table for Emma and Ralph. I smiled following right behind her.

"Well sure enough, just the next week, when I got home from work… James was locked inside of the bathroom. He said, 'I tried fixin' it Mama, I did.' Boy, did me and his daddy get a laugh out of that." The laughter and joy faded from her face as quickly as it came. I moved closer, wondering if I had done the wrong thing by bringing him up?

"Rissy, how did he get locked in there?"

"He been working over at the farmer's next door. He wanted to make sure the door locked for his Mama. So, he asked if the farmer would pay him with a door lock. The farmer ain't have no door lock so he gave him an old doorknob. He used that doorknob, but he made one mistake. He put it on backwards and locked himself in." We smiled together, and a hearty laugh filled the room.

"We stayed up with his daddy fixing that darn door. You just need a screwdriver and it can be reversed. Don't you know, when we got it turned around, the look on James' face was as proud as his daddy's."

Mama wandered into Pa-paw's liquor cabinet and gurgled down a shot of warm whiskey.

Me and Rissy's eyes locked, the warmth from the story radiated enough to ignore Mama for a moment. But she didn't leave- she lingered there as if she were waiting to hear what we talked about.

"I've got to get back to work. Your Ma-maw wants the rugs cleaned today." Rissy patted my hand softly. Her voice slightly raised so Mama could hear.

I reached for her, stopping her from leaving. "Thank you for telling me that story."

Rissy smiled big enough for me to see the gap between her front teeth. "There are only so many stories I get to tell- thank you, Bonnie, for listening." Mama stormed back outside. Rissy walked over to the sink. She ran her fingers along Ma-maw's African Violet plant that had grown taller than the window ledge this year. She traced the stem and then snapped it off, exposing the moist center. She wrapped it in a wet paper towel and placed it inside of a little bag.

"What did you do that for?" I leaned in closer to inspect the plant.

She kneeled, her brown eyes locked into my blues and she poked her pointer finger to my chest.

"Take this. Put it in water when you get back. Watch it until it grows roots. Once it does- you can plant it. Even when I ain't *withcha* I'll be in here, in your heart." I spun the single leaf in my fingers, and placed the wet paper towel inside of my pocket and patted it slightly. I smiled. I liked the idea of having Rissy with me. Her voice dropped to a whisper. "Never forget, my girl, even if you grow in dark places, you can always begin again. Loss is just something that happens to you in life. Meaning is what you make happen."

Mama returned and paced the room. Rissy disappeared out the front door. Emma and Ralph's eyes longed for their house mother's. They no longer looked up at me for their every need. Their faces were smeared with remains of PB&J sandwiches. I cleared the table and warmed a towel from the faucet. When I got it to the right temperature, I wiped their hands. I knew Ralph would fight to the death to avoid having his face wiped.

"You must have been hungry," I said, slowly and calmly raising the damp towel.

"We're going to wipe on three: 1, 2, 3, wipe."

Ralph pulled away and threw his head backwards, hitting the table. I grabbed a hold of him and bounced him. He was much bigger than he used to be.

"Oh *Walf*, it's not that bad," Emma piped in, smiling. At least she still sounded the same. She picked up the towel and wiped her own face. Ralph smiled and reached towards her. I pulled both of them near to me, their warm bodies were just what I needed.

Mama stared as she puffed on her cigarette from across the room. I silently willed her to come over, hoping for once Mama could be the haven we needed. When she didn't move, I tightly clamped my eyes shut. *I would not let it affect me.*

Mama poured another glass and waved us outside. I wrestled Emma to put the shoes on her feet. I continued to watch Mama from the corner of my eye. She picked up the glass, slammed it, and poured another one. I hoped by showing Mama I could care for the children, that maybe she would stop drinking so quickly. I just wanted Mama to see how good we could be and to show her we weren't crybabies anymore. I paraded them across the yard, sensing Mamas eyes tracking us like prey. Was she jealous? We raced back and forth. We danced with imaginary friends, went on mythical adventures and saved the world together. All of the worries were erased. For a moment in time, we were just normal kids playing in our grandparent's yard. It annoyed me that I had to add normal kids to every sentence. As if when we weren't doing these things, we weren't really people. The desire to be normal is to feel like yourself and connect when you struggle to find acceptance.

As we walked along the yards exterior, I had them stay in line, one behind the other with me following. That way no matter what, I could protect them if I needed to. I constantly made sure they were away from the road, and they were within arm's reach. The humid air, and sweet honeysuckle wafted towards us. I pointed to the flowers growing along the tree line. "Smell that?"

"Yum, smells like butterflies," Emma said.

I led them over carefully across the street and reached for one and plucked it. "You take it out like this," I explained, holding the little yellow trumpet in my fingers, the way Rissy had once taught me. "The little bells with precious droplets of suckle," I said as I pulled them out slowly, so not to rip the flower.

I held it out to Emma. "This is so good!" Emma shouted proudly.

I leaned down so Ralph could get a taste. He chomped and put the entire flower in his mouth. "Ew!" We laughed as he spit it out. Ralph wiped his tongue off.

I plucked another and let him taste the end. "Don't eat it this time," I said while studying his mischievous grin. I let them each try to have one of their own and, just as we were turning to head out, a car approached us. I stepped in front of my siblings and extended my arms back to keep them there.

I noticed the red truck, and Mr. Redner rolled down his window. "Y'all can't be in there— it's private property."

I hadn't even noticed we crossed the property line. I shook my head apologetically. "I'm sorry, sir, we were just trying some suckle."

He looked me up and down. His face was red, his lips tightly closed. "Alright. Just stay out." Mr. Redner rolled his window up and sped away, as quick as he came.

"Grumpy old man," I murmured.

"Grumpy ole man," Emma repeated. I didn't even tell her to stop mocking me. I just had missed her so much. We walked back to our property and headed towards the house. But as soon as we passed the old Magnolia tree, I saw another familiar face.

Red. The rooster riddled up to us. He started skittering sideways.

He reached us so quickly I didn't even have time to react. He launched towards us in one motion. His wings flapped loudly. He puffed his hackle out. I glanced at Emma and Ralph. I scooped Ralph up. I pushed Emma behind me. Emma stumbled to the ground. Red shot into me like a dart. His sharp spurs pierced through my skin, instantly ripping the layers. I lost my balance and fell to the moist ground.

Beads of blood ran down my leg. Ralph screamed. Emma cried. My heart twisted as I tried to comfort them. Red took off into the brush. I scanned the children. Other than the mud that covered every inch of us, nobody was hurt.

"You dumb old rooster, Red!" I cried, furiously hitting my thighs. How had I ever missed that dumb rooster, or my Mama? *Mama,* I gulped as she scanned our mud-covered clothing.

As if it wasn't bad enough, to come home covered in mud with a screaming baby, as we neared the house, I watched Mr. Redner flee from the driveway. I had always hated the way he looked at my Mama.

Rissy was still out front beating out the rugs from the living room. She looked up with rounded eyes as we came into view.

"Lordy, you're lucky your Ma-maw ain't here. What happened to you, children?"

Before I could reply, Mama stepped around the front of the house.

"Seriously!" Her eyes were huge, her nostrils flared… a smirk covered her lips slowly, and then vanished. Was she happy I failed?

"I can't believe this. You think you can just come home and ruin your clothes? Going on private property? Do you think that you could really be in charge? You're just a stupid — stupid kid." Mama's words slurred slightly.

I looked up finally and my shoulders sagged.

Here I went again, ruining everything. My eyes filled with a rush of tears that left salty traces down my cheeks and onto my mud-ridden clothes. The muscles of my chin trembled like a small child. I couldn't hold it back anymore. All of the tears I had ever kept hidden from my mother, escaped in that moment. I put Ralph down on the grass and tried to cover my face.

The flood of tears couldn't extinguish years of burning shame.

Rissy watched, painfully, and she stepped towards Mama. My body felt like it was on fire. Every inch of me tingled. I no longer felt the pain from Red's spurs.

Rissy huffed. "You're wrong, Miss Ruby. You are wrong. That ain't no way to treat YOUR child, she stopped being a kid the day you sent her to... to...that place!"

Rissy hit the rug one last time, sending a dust cloud over to Mama. Rissy stormed towards us. She lay a gentle hand on my shoulder as she passed. She took off her apron and threw it to the ground and she kept walking. My eyes widened. I had never seen Rissy so angry before.

Slowly, I watched Mama recoil like a snake who had just lost a battle. Confused, we continued to wait in the silence, other than chirping birds, and wonder what would happen next.

Mama lit a cigarette and Rissy went to tend to the garden, almost as if we hadn't seen it happen. But it did happen and it was the first time in my life I was taught how to stand up for myself.

I led the kids to the hose and hid the smile that crept along my face. I washed the dried blood from my leg. I had never, ever seen someone put Mama in her place before. The ride back to Hawthorne was quiet but satisfying.

CHAPTER TEN

That night, when I saw Susan for the first time, my entire body turned into a puddle of feelings. I suddenly felt everything all at once. I brushed the tears away with my sleeve as Susan climbed in bed next to me. She extended her palm, then placed a chocolate in my hand. "It was a drag without you, Bunny."

"You have no idea," I replied. Under the moonlight, our breathing matched. The following day was Labor Day so we didn't have any school. I looked forward to just being alone in my room with Susan.

"I'm sorry you had to leave… but I couldn't help and feel just a little bit jealous… until I worried that you would be eaten."

I smiled at her, despite wanting to laugh I was filled with an emptiness that often settled deep within myself when I saw my mother.

"What would your biggest wish be?" Susan asked, just inches away from my face.

"That's easy. I think it would be a dad." I smiled. "I would want him to be tall, and strong. He would like to play with us children, and he would be quite dirty from working with cars and machines and stuff."

"Ewe, dirty!" Susan giggled. "My dad wasn't like that at all. He was actually quite nerdy. He wore a white jacket, he had like a lab with glasses and stuff and he liked to write math."

"A scientist dad? How could I not know that! Susan, that is so cool," I said, turning to her. I noticed she was crying, and I regretted my words. I wish I would have thought before saying I wanted a dad. How selfish of me.

"I'm so sorry." I put my arm around her and laid my head next to hers. Susan wiped a tear from her cheek. I tried to think of what to say when Susan spoke instead. "It's okay. I miss his laugh, and the way he swung me up into the air. The way his clothes smelled like warm salt. The way he called 'Good morning, Suzy girl.'" Her voice cracked and the tears trickled down her cheeks. I patted her head in between the sobs. I opened my hand and slid my slightly melted chocolate back into Susan's.

"You need this more tonight. I'm sorry you miss him. I know he must have been great." Susan didn't say anything. I tried to swallow my words. I forgot I grieved for the living and Susan's parents were really dead.

"You think you have forever, Bunny. But we don't have forever." Susan cried and I continued to pat her until her sobs slowed.

"Don't you ever stop and think about how far you've come from the events you thought would end you?" I asked her.

"I think you saved me." Susan told me.

"And you saved me," I responded back to her with a nudge.

I didn't get a chance to ask Susan what her biggest wish would be. I was too unnerved I made her cry. Once she was asleep, I lie awake with a longing, but had no idea what I was longing for. I had a giant hole in my gut with no idea how to fill it.

The churning in my stomach was trying to tell me something. It lasted early into the next morning. The sun wasn't even all the way up yet when we were abruptly awoken.

Downstairs, I shifted from one foot to the next. What could it be now? I had been through so many bad times, I had this ability to sense them out right before they happened. Once we were all grouped together in the living room, we stared at each other. The older girls stole the couch seats, so we crouched down on the floor trying to keep our eyes open. Mara looked like she had been up for hours. Her dress ironed so smoothly, I wondered how she could walk in it.

"I gathered you here this morning to share the news that some of you will be moving to a new cottage. I wanted to be the first to let you know, well, because it is something you should all be prepared for. Life is hard and you need moments like this to help you adjust to change."

The murmurs in the room clearly alerted we were no longer asleep. Suddenly wide awake, I pulled at the skin on my nails. I didn't want to look up because if I looked up, I knew I would be one who had to leave.

"Anna, Sarah, and Grace will be moving over to the Gardner Cottage,"

Whispers crossed the room.

I gnawed at my nails, *don't look up, don't look up.*

"Felicity, Jordan, and Bonnie will go to the Aldrich cottage".

I looked up. I couldn't see through the tears that had gathered.

I made eye contact with Mara, hoping I hadn't heard her right, praying my ears were playing tricks on me. Wishing there was another Bonnie that could leave instead.

My mind spiraled. I didn't want Susan to forget me. In the past two years, the only moments of peace I could recall were when I had Susan, standing next to me, ready to fight with me against the world. Now my world slowly disappeared right in front of me. I had finally found a place I belonged.

Feeling sick, I ran up to the bathroom and curled up on the floor. I cried silently as I rocked back and forth holding my legs. The walls around me collapsed. There was nothing I could do about it. Normally when I was overwhelmed, I would picture hugging Emma, or singing to baby Ralph, or kissing his moist little smile. I longed for something familiar. Something that wasn't Mama. Or maybe it was? It hit me then - the flamingo Mama had bought me. I forgot it lying on Mama's floor. I bit my hand and sobbed even harder. I left behind the only real toy she had ever given me.

I returned to the room I shared with Susan. Susan sat on her bed with her arms wrapped around her knees. "My biggest wish would have been that we could stay together." Susan shrugged angrily. I didn't know how to respond so I went to her and hugged her tightly.

"Mara says I've done so well here… they don't want me to move again. But what they don't understand is that it's because of you." Susan pulled away and reached under her bed. Her cheeks were also stained with tears.

"You should keep these." She placed the raggedy book into my hands.

The book of dresses we had worked on for two years, wrinkled, and reopened so many times that the old staples were about to give out. I feared it would crumble as I flipped through the pages.

I smiled. "This is the best gift anyone has ever given me. We will be friends forever, I promise." I traced the tattered cover with my finger, and smiled at my friend.

"I don't know what I would do without you." She gently pulled the photograph of her mother from the front page and held it to her cheek.

"I'm going to miss you, Bunny."

"And I'm going to miss you, Susan."

Susan smiled half-heartedly, and pulled a piece of chocolate from her pocket.

I gathered my things with my fingers pinching my nose to trap the tears while I packed my small bag of all of the items I owned. I embraced Susan one more time, and followed the other girls down the steps. Mara waited at the end of the staircase with her usual stern grimace.

"Bonnie, Felcia, Jordan, you're coming with me."

Susan held on to me for a moment longer. Until we were separated, ripped away like strands of string cheese until we were forced to break loose. I could feel her watching as we walked outside. I knew if I looked back, I wouldn't be able to calmly walk away…

"You forgot your shoes again, Bonnie," Mara growled as the older girls giggled. I turned to run back inside but Susan stood there holding my shoes. With tear filled eyes and knowing smile, I slipped my shoes on, and hugged her once more.

"Bonnie! Let's go," Mara called. I rolled my eyes and purposely dragged behind Mara and the other girls. We walked along the path I felt I had just become used to, was finally settling in and now everything was upside down again. The distance between Susan and I was noticeable- like the force of two magnets being separated.

The once gravel path turned into crunchy dirt. My back began to ache from the large sack with all of my priceless things. The air was hot and muggy, fine baby hairs were glued to my forehead.

Cornered in the very back of the lot stood a tall brick home. The reddish brick color was rusty and contained patches of exposed mortar in the cracks. There were thick vines that slithered across the brick and around the windows. In the heat, I shivered. I didn't want to do this. I didn't want to start all the way over again.

Mara knocked.

The door creaked open and we were greeted with a dull energy, as if someone just finished a shouting match and left the room feeling jumbled even with empty walls and silence.

I had grown so used to having Susan with me everywhere I went. It felt odd, to be close to someone and then taken away. You would think I felt the same way when my mother left, but this was different. Susan was the first person who enjoyed my company just as much as I enjoyed hers. I heard footsteps so I stood taller and straightened my shoulders.

"Come on in, girls, make yourselves right at home." A voice called to us.

My posture faded once we rounded the corner to the living room. "The new house parents of the Aldrich cottage called for a group meeting in the living room," Mara whispered before we entered. I tried to avoid bringing attention to myself while it felt like all eyes were on me. When Mara turned to leave, for the first time ever, I wanted to be with her. I was the smallest out of any of them. I didn't belong here. There were five girls sitting on couches with their hands folded in their lap.

"Hello, girls, I'm Jackie and this is Dale. We wanted to touch up on the house rules as we welcome new family." Jackie smiled brightly. "Now let's go around the room and introduce ourselves."

My eyes settled on the house father. For so long I wanted someone to be a father to me. I studied his face while Jackie continued introductions. Dale's mouth was crooked like that of an old sock that had hung to dry too long. His hands weren't rough from working all day, instead, they were neatly clasped together on his lap. He was quiet and his lips were pursed together tightly. His hair was straight, fastened to his head with a glue-like substance. But his eyes were what stopped me. It was as if they were a black mud puddle that had no end. I squirmed as he stared back at me and waited for him to look anywhere else, but he never took his eyes off me.

I broke the gaze and looked down at my fingers, my chewed nails no longer than my fingertips. I couldn't stop chewing them. "And you?" Jackie asked again, motioning at me. Her voice had grown stern, and I looked around the room and realized she was talking to me.

"Bonnie," I whispered. I looked down until she finished explaining the rules. Instead of listening, I pictured the Hawthorne tree and imagined being swept away to an otherworld.

"Any questions?"

We looked around the room, everyone dodging eye contact.

"Okay, no. Ladies, begin breakfast and I'll take our new family up to their rooms to get settled." Jackie sounded as if she just came up from a long dive under water and forgot to unplug her nose. She was different. Her voice was cheerful but it was demanding. I expected everyone to scramble and to fall in line like soldiers from the way she sounded. Nobody moved, so I awkwardly stood and followed behind, down the hall and up the stairs. Maybe I could get on her good side if I followed what she said. I should have paid better attention to the rules.

Jackie stopped abruptly on the stairs, and I walked straight into her bottom. I felt my body shrinking and my face turned red.

"Well, we have a day dreamer. Bonnie, pay attention to what you're doing!" Jackie growled at me.

I exhaled strongly. "Sorry." So much for her good side. The other girls giggled at me and I wanted to find the nearest hole and bury myself in it. Once inside of my room, I turned away from my roommates and pulled Susan's chocolate out of my pocket. I cried when I placed it on my tongue, knowing that it would be my last one.

CHAPTER ELEVEN

Over the next year, I did my best to follow all of the "house rules." Jackie made Mara look like a saint. Her sing-song happy voice was nothing like her. It was a mockery of everything she was.

I made my bed in the morning, dusted the cabinets, furniture, and put the dishes away. After school I did my homework, swept the kitchen and emptied the bathroom trash cans. I minded Jackie, avoided Dale, basically did what I needed to do to survive. Which also included not speaking to my roommate or any other girls in the home. The age difference had pushed me to the very bottom of the food chain.

My roommate, Jane was nothing like Susan. She was bossy, and rude, and she left her dirty clothes spread out across the floor. When Jackie asked whose they were, Jane would point at me with a blank stare. I was too burnt out to even stand up for myself. I didn't want to cause any trouble so I picked up her dirty clothes and threw them in the hamper. Jane was obsessed with boys and make-up; she didn't seem to realize anyone else existed other than herself. She often came back to the room smelling strongly like cigarettes. It made my stomach curdle because I instantly thought of my mother who abandoned me.

It hurt even worse when I found out Mama just picked us up that day because she was applying for money and food assistance through the state. She only wanted us when we were beneficial to her and not really even then. I hid my book of wedding dresses underneath the mattress of my bed. I didn't trust Jane with my things, so I often packed them in my school bag to keep them safe. I carried my small bag of things with me everywhere.

Jackie and Dale were no more involved in our lives than my mother. Instead of support, they were there to make matters worse. We had to sit through torturous meals where we were forced to speak, passing around the food at the table and pretending like we cared about what one another said. We also had to do group activities, cleaning, and movie nights. I always just cowered in a corner by myself counting down the minutes until it would end. Any extra time I had was spent doing school activities so I could escape.

Dale often made eye contact from across the room, keeping his distance. His shark-like eyes tracked me across the room but he never said anything. Especially not to me. It was like other girls would walk in and he would greet them, smile. He made small talk and joked. He loved to tell jokes to Victoria and Lynn. They thought he was funny. It was the first time I had seen light within his eyes and the actual potential for a father figure. It made me wonder what else he was hiding. But he would see me and immediately freeze. Those invisible cooties again. I learned it was best to just stay away from him. Especially since I even failed at getting the only father I'd ever had to like me. After that, I kind of just gave up. Nobody even knew I existed. I became another shadow who sat amongst them but didn't really live there *with* them. There was nothing I could do about it.

As fall passed us by and turned into winter, I lost count of how long it had been since I last laughed. I disappeared by delving into books to escape the reality of my life. There was no book that was too big. If it had words, I would read it. I read the books faster than I could rent from the library. Even on the way home from the library, I managed to walk along the lonely path with a book pressed up to my nose. It helped me escape reality. My hunger for reading became as massive as the appetite for Mama to return once was. I enjoyed getting lost in the magical worlds where I could forget about how unlovable I was. Things weren't great, but they were okay. I wasn't happy, but I was okay. I was just living in a shell of someone I used to know. I didn't know what my purpose was anymore.

Just as the cold winter breeze crept through, on a Saturday afternoon I was able to have a visit with Ma-maw and Pa-paw. It was a special occasion, being my birthday. All of the other children but Jane and I had left. I had been so excited to see a familiar face that I literally had no words. Ma-maw thought I wasn't pleased to see her, but I was so thrilled, I literally couldn't even speak. My body shook and I could find no words to express it. At this point I had gotten so used to let downs, I rarely let myself even feel excitement anymore. I locked it away. When I sat inside of the car with Emma and Ralph next to me, it was the first time in a long time I had hope. It felt so normal- almost as if time hadn't changed a thing. But it did. We all looked older, much older than we had the day Mama left us.

"We're going to take y'all to dinner tonight." Pa-paw smiled, glancing at each of us.

"Celebrate our Bonnie girl," Ma-maw added. I smiled slightly but inside I felt like I could throw up. I was turning 11 and that meant I had missed the past 3 years of Emma and Ralph's lives. Three years had passed and Mama wasn't coming back. One whole year away from Susan and I had basically forgotten who I was. Ralph smiled more now than he used to, but he was especially shy in front of us. Emma had this lost look to her, like the wonder she used to have was missing from her eyes. We pulled into a little diner by a railroad track. I slowly let go of Emma's and Ralph's hands I'd held on the drive. We walked in and found a table. I was jittery and nervous- I wanted to be perfect so they would take me back home with them. But I realized Emma and Ralph probably couldn't even remember our days spent with Mama. For a moment I pinged with jealousy because if I could forget- I probably would too. The late nights, the smell of alcohol, finding Mama throwing up in the bathroom. The scary boyfriends who sometimes punched holes in the walls. "Bonnie?" Ma-maw asked me something. I looked around to feel everyone staring at me. The server pointed to drinks. "Just water, please," I whispered.

"And I'll take a rum and coke," Pa-paw said. Ma-maw glared at him. I focused back and forth to Ralph and Emma.

"My oh my- how y'all have grown," Ma-maw cheerfully stated. We smiled uncomfortably. It was in that moment I realized my dreams of returning and things being the same were as good of a chance as Mama coming to celebrate my birthday with me.

There were so many choices on the menu I didn't know how to choose. We just had to eat what was given to us at Hawthorne and I hadn't chosen a food in so long, I wasn't even sure what I liked. I settled with a plain cheeseburger with ketchup, grapes and fries. When the plate was set down in front of me, I just smiled. It was one of the other things I had forgotten about, the freedom to choose. I slowly prepared to eat and looked to see if Ralph or Emma needed help. Ralph barely spoke but he let Ma-maw put ketchup on his plate. I went to put some on Emma's and she held her hand up at me. "Ew, that is disgusting."

"You don't like ketchup anymore?" I shook my head at her. She used to use it on every single thing, even apples. Emma giggled, shaking her head. "I still like alligators though." Emma shrugged with a light in her eyes. She still had pieces of her old self in there. It was almost like she wanted to please me too. To prove she was lovable. Like all of the unfamiliarity had caused us to forget ourselves even.

By the end of the visit, I didn't want to leave. The warmth from Ma-maw's hand clasped over mine while she sang happy birthday had recharged me. But once we were parked outside and they told us it was time to go, fury roared through my mind. Ma-maw promised they would visit more. I didn't listen. I just got out and stomped inside. It was like they came back to just remind us of what we had lost. As I watched them drive away from me, I instantly regretted even eating the food they bought. It was like a cliff hanger at the end of a book. You have a little peace, a little closure and then it was jerked away again. If we were a normal family, they would have taken us home. Regret boiled within me. *I would never feel happy again.* I held it back as long as I could. But when I let it all out, I realized just how much I hated everything.

Inside the house I kicked my shoes off. When Jackie passed by me, I hated the scent of her. The fresh powdery smell, the sound of her voice as she hummed.

"Oh hello, Bonnie," she said as she rushed by me. I wanted to scream at her, break the house down. I wanted to run and never come back. Instead, assuming she was headed to the kitchen, I followed behind her. Like a soldier, I had been taught to obey all of the rules. But Jackie turned and went into the restroom. The rest of the house was quiet. I knew Jane would be the only one here. Suddenly, I found myself standing in Jackie's bedroom.

What did it matter anymore anyway? If I followed the rules or not? The powder particles danced in the setting sunlight that crept through the open window. I held in a cough. I looked both ways to make sure nobody was watching me. I pulled the drawers open, looking for chocolate, anything to help me in this moment. One drawer after the next and there was nothing. Then I saw it. The words Diary. The silver tint to the book called me over to it. And I knew I shouldn't, but I couldn't hold my hands back from taking it. My heart lurched- I shouldn't be in here. I glanced around once more, my breathing slowed, and there was nothing more important than knowing what Jackie was hiding from the world. In an instant the pages were turning in my hands. The leather cover felt smooth beneath my chewed finger-nails. Only a page or two wouldn't hurt.

The indentations on the page were deep. As if even in her writing Jackie barked orders at the paper.

Date: 01/01/1975

I must be obedient and structured.

Despite what these children need, I have to teach discipline. When ornery children react with stupid decisions — they need to be met with resistance. I was a girl once, and I was taught that children should be seen and not heard. Now look at me, I'm a role model in the name of Jesus, Amen. Dale keeps raining on my parade. He's so controlling. I've gotten used to Dale's method of asking rather simple questions as a rhetorical device. Like he's a quiz show, trying to always be the first to the buzzer. Well, I've had it. He never even glances my way anymore. I'm beginning to wonder if he is up to something. I started to wonder if it is Jules. He has come further along than anyone else in his journey with the Lord and teaching Youth but he has completely forgotten about me. He is an inspiration to the church. While waiting in line at the bakery- I ran into Jules and she couldn't help but gush about the impact Dale's making with the youth group. I just wanted to stuff her big mouth full of pastries so I didn't have to hear her talk anymore. Some people. And Dale won't even look my way. Lustful women always come first. I tell you that anyone who looks at a woman lustfully has already committed adultery with her in his heart. Won't I ever be enough?

My eyes widened. For the first time ever, I realized Jackie was just a person like myself. I almost pitied her begging for attention just like I had been my whole life. What had I thought she was before? Alien? I smiled to myself- she did kind of fit that category. Perhaps her cheerful voice was just a version of who she once was?

I closed the diary, suddenly remembering I was still in Jackie's room. I wondered how I would get out without being noticed. I paused at my reflection in the mirror by her bed and smiled at myself for being mischievous. These moments had been missed most of my life. I tried too hard to be a good kid that I forgot to take chances.

I turned to place the book back on the shelf. As I reached up, I heard the door bust open. He stared into me so intently without uttering a word, for a moment I wondered if I were actually invisible. Instead of yelling, a smile curled on Dale's lips, and I swear my heart stopped beating.

CHAPTER TWELVE

"Do you want to play a game with me?" Dale whispered. I froze with my hand, stalling mid-air with Jackie's diary. I glanced at the book, to the shelf and then back to Dale. I wasn't sure what I should say. I slipped the book back into its place, hoping he didn't notice. But his eyes tracked my every move. Fire trickled to my cheeks. My mind instantly shot to the time I was caught stealing money from Pa-paw to give to Rissy and I instinctively placed my hands behind my butt as if it could block the blow.

"Follow me," Dale whispered. His eyes directed me to the door.

So, I did. My feet felt as if they had been left in cement all day. Like it soaked into me, hardening my every move, and crept up past my knees making my legs heavy. Then into my chest. I could hardly breathe. I cleared my throat to rid the frog that was suffocating me. Once we reached Dale's office he closed the door quietly, perfectly enough so it didn't even click loudly into place. I had never seen his room before.

"I know you're a very smart young lady," Dale began.

I waited for the blow, *Stupid, I'm stupid, I'm so stupid.*

"But I feel there's something special about you." I perked my ears up and lifted my chin slightly. I looked into his eyes frantically searching for connection. *Did he really just say that?*

"Now, I know you like to read, but this is unacceptable behavior. Jackie's deepest thoughts are not for a little girl. I can barely keep up with that woman as it is." He shook his head gently almost as if he was also curious as to what Jackie would be writing about. "I can only imagine how she might feel... well, if she were to find out." Dale paused, he studied me from head to toe.

My lip quivered. *I'm so stupid.* The hot tears formed in every corner of my eyes. I refused to blink. I would stand there with eyes full of tears all day if I had to.

"Now- there. It's okay. It will be a secret, safe with me, okay?" Dale's voice softened- just enough for an overflow to roll down my face finally. I exhaled.

How did he know that I liked to read? Did he pay attention to me?

Then suddenly I was being pulled towards him- inside of his arms. His chest felt hot, fuzzy. The hair that trickled out over his shirt, itched my face. I wanted to push away, but it was nice at the same time. Much better than the whip. A smell of spicy wood and cinnamon lingered on my clothes long after the hug was over. Something in me felt funny. The attention was wrong but I liked it. I starved for it. I should have been punished for being bad, but this was a new kind of attention. What harm could one secret cause anyway? Dale had called it a game. He wanted to play a game with me. Games were supposed to be fun. Fathers play games with their daughters.

"I will keep your secret if you keep our game secret." His smile was reassuring.

That's it? That's all I had to do?

"Deal," I said smiling brightly.

"It's a deal."

CHAPTER THIRTEEN

J ust like that, I found something at Hawthorne that I looked forward to. Over the next two weeks, I no longer avoided Dale. I anxiously waited for our game to start. I found myself going out of my way to see him. To joke with him. I gravitated towards him. He was funny, he liked many of the dumb 'kid' things other adults didn't. And as the months passed, he held true to our secret.

To think that an adult man would have an interest in little me. The girl nobody seemed to love. Well, it made me feel special. Lovable. Important. I trusted him and he was exceptionally kind to me. He became the father I always wanted.

I would purposely forget my book bag at the back door some mornings just so I could say goodbye on the way out. Sometimes he might set the newspaper down and share a comic with me. He never read the obituaries. I would stumble upon him laughing at a comic and, on occasion, he would tear the comic out and pass it to me smiling. His eyes twinkled with our secret. I thought I finally saw the vividness that lived underneath the dark shadows of his eyes. For the first time, I felt special. I felt seen.

I found myself focused less on Mama and more on how I could spend time with Dale. Church, after school, all of my free time was spent on a chance I would get to be with him. Somehow, my world began to revolve around him. I actually had the father I always wanted.

One evening, I returned from school and found the first book in the series of *The Little House on The Prairie* on top of my bed. I picked it up and held it tightly in my hand. It was one I had only dreamed of having. Slowly, I checked the other bedrooms. I wanted to see if they all had books too. I considered the possibly that Christmas had come early. But there were no books on anyone else's beds. *Just mine.* It was only me. It gave me hope that someone in the world actually cared about me. *Just me.* My heart could have exploded. I climbed into bed and indulged in the book. I lie awake that night with a flashlight, barely taking my eyes off the pages until I was finished.

It wasn't until the last leaf fell that winter that I got to stay home from school for the first time. Usually, we were made to fight through a cold and still go to school. But Jackie had said I looked like a disaster and told me to go back to bed. I weakly made my way upstairs but as I rounded the doorway, I found Dale placing a book on my bed. I jumped. I had to double take what I was seeing. *Was this somehow a part of our game?* While I considered it a possibility, him delivering books all along— seeing him in my bedroom was odd. I felt small, almost invaded.

Dale looked surprised, but smiled at me, and it made my nerves calm. I was finally seen by someone, and if he went out of the way to bring me a book, I wanted him to know I was thankful. Even though my stomach told me otherwise, I smiled excitedly at him.

"Thank y…" I began, but he interrupted me.

"Shh, Shh." he said, with his pointer finger to his lips. "It's our little secret." I nodded in agreement, understanding that the only person in the house was Jackie and she wasn't to know either. *Surprises weren't supposed to be secret.*

"Have a good day, my sweet," he whispered, resting his hand on my shoulder and disappeared down the hallway. I climbed into my bed, pulled the blanket up close to me and looked at the book. I had been waiting for it. I ran my finger along the spine of the book- it smelled wonderful- the crisp aroma of new paper and freshly printed ink. It was the 6th book in the *Little House on the Prairie* series, *The Long Winter*. Typically, I was able to forget everything when I read one of Laura Ingalls Wilder books. Just as they were about real people, they made me feel alive. Life on the prairie was so different from the life I knew. It felt off, knowing Dale was giving me the books. Nobody ever bought me things like this before. But I couldn't place the feeling. Like I owed him something? I didn't like owing people anything, but did that make me ungrateful? Confused. I was confused. I set it aside, not understanding why I didn't want to read it. Instead, I lie back with my eyes closed.

I enjoyed the empty house. The way the walls echoed and the floor-boards creaked, and absence of whispers and laughter. I dozed off.

When Jackie called me to eat bland soup, I walked down the hall-way, running my fingers along the wall. The feeling in my stomach had left. I thought maybe because I was feeling a little better. Smiling, I made my way downstairs. Having surprises waiting for just me felt so much more special. I couldn't remember the last time an adult had paid the slightest bit of attention to me. Dale treated me like an equal. Like I mattered. Of course, he was just being nice. Fathers bring daughters books. I returned to my bed and spent the entire afternoon savoring every page of the book.

That night I heard sobbing in the hallway. It wasn't uncommon to hear other girls crying in the night. But this cry was different. It reminded me of Emma. The kind of cry when you just need a hug. I tiptoed out into the hallway and approached the shadowy figure that sat hugging her legs. It was Felicity. She wouldn't look at me, but she didn't tell me to leave either. I crept towards her, and her cry became quiet. So, I slid down next to her and offered her my hand. I thought maybe she would make fun of me or push me away. But she reached back for it and grasped my hand with her clammy fingers. Together we sat in silence for what seemed like hours. She made eye contact with me and smiled gratefully. It was the first time she ever smiled directly at me. In the dark I smiled back and we stood and went to our rooms.

It was like that a lot at Hawthorne. I tried to be there for anyone I could because I knew all too well what that never ending pit in your gut felt like. Empty and alone.

By the time I finished *The First Four Years*, and completed the series, it was mid-spring and, by this point, I had isolated myself from almost everyone. I still met with Susan at lunch but I didn't tell her where I got the books from or why I liked my new cottage so much. I couldn't bear to tell her that I finally got a father when her father was dead. Another part of me knew I couldn't tell anyone or what we had would be taken away. I also knew that Dale had told me to keep it secret, like he kept my secret. That was the first time I felt torn about the attention. Dale had told me not to tell so seriously, it instilled an enormous fear in my mind even when I thought about telling Susan. She asked a lot of questions and I tried to avoid them, but it ate me alive. Why was something good so secret?

"Did you hear me, Bunny?" Susan asked again, closer to my face.

"Yes, yes. I'm sorry- I'm just worried about my math test," I replied to her. We were almost finished eating lunch and I did have math next.

"I know you were daydreaming again, but this is important... Do you think we will ever be in the same cottage again? Mara says I may be moving!"

"I sure hope so!" I replied, even though I wasn't sure I wanted to share my new father with her. Then I hated myself for that thought. Of course, I wanted to be with Susan.

"Maybe we can even be roommates again!" My eyes widened.

"I would love that so much." Susan smiled. The bell rang so we stood and threw our trash away. I hugged her like we always hugged when we left lunch.

"Me too, Susan, me too."

After I finished my math test, I quietly waited for everyone else to finish. I heard pencils scribbling and papers moving. I replayed our conversation in my mind. I did want Susan to be with me, there was no doubt about it. But the idea of sharing something so secret with her made me uncomfortable. I used to tell her everything.

If I was going to stay friends with Susan, I had to tell her about Dale. Especially if she would be moving into my cottage. I knew deep down she would be happy for me, but she might even be upset I kept it from her for that long. I decided I would tell her at lunch tomorrow, no matter what.

Once school was over, I headed back to the cottage. It was a dreary day. Having rained for most of it, I avoided large puddles on the path back home. I was by myself as usual and groups of kids were passing by. I heard bits of conversations about summer break. I wasn't sure if Mama was going to get us or not. In fact. I hadn't even thought of summer break one time. My shoes were muddy so I entered the back of the house. It had more room to hold shoes and a large mat. The last thing I wanted to do was get yelled at by Jackie for tracking mud into the house. I kicked them off slowly and passed Felicity and Jane in the kitchen. I waved to them but they continued their conversation. It was Friday which meant almost everyone would be leaving. I looked forward to having a quiet house over the weekend, and especially an empty bedroom. It was the first time Jane would meet her grandparents and after hearing about it all week, I was glad to have a break from her. Jackie was in the front room on the phone so I quietly crept up the stairs to my room. I let out a sigh of disappointment. There were no new books waiting for me. I tidied up until it was time to eat dinner. It would be quiet without Jane.

Downstairs there was just Dale, Jordan, and a new girl I hadn't met.

"Where is Jackie?" I asked, confused.

"She had to leave, family emergency," Dale said seriously.

Jordan sighed and added sarcastically, "Oh no. We will miss her so much."

Dale raised his voice. "Enough! Don't disrespect your elders, Jordan."

I wanted to laugh like the new girl did, but the four of us ate dinner in silence. I glanced at Dale a few times daring him to speak to me. He wasn't the same person in front of other people. He was more serious and adult-like. When we were alone on school project nights and church walks home, he would patiently listen to me complaining about not being selected in gym class to play dodge ball. Or even how ridiculous my roommate was. In front of everyone the nicest thing he did was give me the easiest chores- dusting, and shaking out the mats. I starved for affection from him and grew confused during times he avoided my gaze. It made those moments so much more meaningful when we were alone. Like a dog feels when his owner gets home. I began to feel that if I did things wrong, he wouldn't like me anymore. So, I tried to make sure he always saw me happy. It was hard to be happy all of the time, but I tried.

That night my room felt bigger than ever. Jane wasn't there to roll around and complain about things. For a few moments I considered what her grandmother was like. Was she enjoying it or was she missing our dump of a room? My door suddenly creaked open exposing the hallway light. I feared it was a monster until I was relieved to see it was Dale. But he didn't have a book in his hand. I sat up slowly and, in an instant, that relief was stolen in the night, like everything good in my life had been. Dale closed the door and sat on my bed right next to me. So close. I pulled my legs away under the blanket, not wanting to touch him with my feet.

"What are you d...?" He placed his pointer finger on his lips and moved closer to me. I froze and stars filled my eyes. It was almost like I was running but my body stayed behind.

"Nobody can know about our games; you are special to me. You've been a very good girl," he told me. I felt my body tense, but for some reason I couldn't move. He reached for me with hunger in his eyes. Dale was the only adult at Hawthorne I trusted. The only father I ever knew. He would never hurt me. So why did he touch me that night in places that were only supposed to be mine?

CHAPTER FOURTEEN

The next morning, I got into the cold shower and scrubbed Dale's scent off me. No matter how hard I sponged, I couldn't get the dirtiness off my skin. I just stood there, unable to feel the droplets of cold water touching my skin. Goosebumps raised on my arms and still, I felt nothing. No warmth, no cold, I was just small, insignificant and dull. My mind was distant, foggy. Each thought I had bounced off of the other like little bouncy balls all over the kitchen floor. I knew that adults weren't supposed to touch you in places that were private. Rissy had told me that. But I had nobody to tell. I couldn't bear thinking of it, let alone telling someone. Was what he did to me wrong? Nobody would believe me. I won't tell because I don't want to be blamed. This is my fault. Is this my fault? I sobbed into my hand and fell to the shower floor letting the water flow right into my face.

A part of me died that night. The little girl who only ever wanted to be loved. I said goodbye to her. I didn't know what I wanted to be when I grew up anymore. I didn't even know what I liked or what happiness felt like. It was like all of the lights inside me flickered until they were so far burnt out there wasn't any more flames left. I got dressed and went to school. When it came time for lunch, I met Susan as usual.

"Hey Bunny! I wanted to tell you that Mara was going to look into what Cottage I transfer to."

My mind snapped back from the fogginess. Susan could not be hurt by Dale. She couldn't ever believe a father could do such a thing after already losing hers.

"What… what's wrong?" Susan asked, staring at my face.

"I just don't think you should come to my cottage." I blurted out emotionless, flat. As if it wasn't even my own voice. I stared at my feet to hold back the tears.

"Wait… are you serious?" Susan's brows came together in worry. She rested her hand on my arm and I jerked it away from her. Her touch felt foreign, it filled me with anger.

"Yes. I don't want to share a room with you anymore."

Instantly I regretted those words, it wasn't what I meant. Tears rolled down Susan's cheeks and it pained me to know I put them there. I hated myself. I hated who I was and the things I caused. I pushed my tray and ran from the lunchroom. I wanted to disappear, become invisible, find a hole in the ground and crawl in it and die. Instead, I ducked into a bathroom. I climbed up on the toilet so nobody could see my feet, cupped my head in my lap and sobbed like a baby until lunch was over. Guilt washed over me thinking of Susan. She was the only real friend I ever had. What a terrible person I was. But she would be fine without me. I only brought out the worst in people. I couldn't ruin her too.

Over the next month, as flowers bloomed and the earth warmed, it seemed like everything I did was wrong. Suddenly, I was dropping my grades, letting my food get cold, and not sleeping. Like I desperately wanted attention, but I pushed everyone away. Susan didn't even try to make eye contact with me in the hallway anymore. As soon as she saw me, she would look away. I could feel her eyes land on me when she was in mid-conversation and immediately face away. She already had new friends. It's the worst feeling to look at someone you knew so well and feel like a stranger to them. My heart was crushed the first night Dale touched me. *Did all fathers touch their daughters like that? If they didn't then what had I done to cause it?* I wanted to hide myself from everyone. Fold myself up inside of myself to never let anyone know what I had done. I was wrong and dirty.

The secret part, that kept me awake during the night was what didn't make sense to me. After the first time, it kept happening even after Jackie came back.

After two years passed, I heard from Jane Jackie filed for a divorce. I felt like it was my fault. Over and over, I closed my eyes and silently begged for it to stop. I held back the tears as Dale told me I should never speak about it to anyone, ever. He would whisper, "This is how love works. It's a secret between two people, a game. A love game. If anyone found out they would hate you. Nobody wants other people to be happy. They will ruin everything. Just like your mother left you here because she didn't want you. Nobody else wants you- they will hate you even more. You are lucky to have me."

I didn't want other people to hate me.

I tried not to think about Susan. I battled every urge I had to run up to her and tell her everything, to beg her to be my friend. But it was too late. I was pathetic. I wished she would read right through my pale face and dark circles and know I needed her. Of all people, I couldn't bear for Susan to hate me too. But each day as we passed in the hallway, I did nothing to change it. I just watched her red hair fade into the distance like everything else. I locked her out when she was the only one that ever let me in.

During the sunlight, Dale was a different person. I sometimes wondered if anything truly happened during those nights. Over the years, when he came into my room, I learned to "go away" in my head. I distanced myself from my body when he touched me. When he made me touch him. I distanced the sensations and pain. Then Dale would bring me gifts from outside of the shadows of our cottage, mostly books and small toys. My favorite gift was a Cathy Quick Curl Doll. Dale made everyone believe my grandmother really mailed her to me. I would spend hours playing with her. For so long she was something I dreamed of having. She was my only friend for months.

Over time, and I couldn't be certain of the last time, but Dale stopped being sweet to me. He no longer spoke to me with kindness. He was stressed about the divorce, worried he would no longer be able to stay at Hawthorne without being married. I could tell he no longer had to worry about me telling his secret. He had instilled so much fear in me I questioned myself.

His attitude towards me shifted. Like the patience for my childish complaints evaporated. It was all my fault. The entire situation could get him fired, or worse put in jail. He told me I shouldn't have looked at him the way I did. He smiled as he said this. I didn't think it was funny. I literally melted away right in front of him. Did I lead to their divorce? I never wanted to look at anyone ever again. How had I done this? Why did I feel so bad for him? I had a stronger inkling something just wasn't right and I longed to tell someone. I just couldn't let anyone get close enough for fear of them finding out my dark secret. And to make matters worse, the weight of carrying around this secret isolated me from everything I loved. Somehow, I still wanted Dale to be happy with me. To treat me like his daughter and listen. I hid in fear of my secret being exposed. And I lived solely to make him like me again. I never looked others in the eyes for fear they would discover who I really was and what I had done. I truly believed Dale was literally the one person in the world that I had. I had to make myself believe he would never intentionally hurt me. He even bought me a ring. It was golden and scalloped and had the tiniest little flowers etched into it. I loved that ring. It reminded me to be good. That someone actually loved me.

I desperately wanted to be good and to be loved. A good, lovable kid that nobody hated.

I had enough hate for myself.

CHAPTER FIFTEEN

The smallest things would set him off. Dale became increasingly paranoid he was going to get caught. It put him on edge, and he became moody, unpredictable. Each day I added another thing to my list that Dale didn't like. Suddenly, I had difficulty remembering any good times. It became more and more difficult to pretend I was happy. I had no idea how I got myself into this. Dale said extremely hurtful things. He instilled fear so deep, I completely blocked out memories of anything that happened to me. If I told anyone, the world would know what a bad kid I was. My grandparents would hate me. He had me believe that he was the only one who understood me.

I went back and forth with trusting him and hating him. I debated telling someone, but I didn't know who. I felt like if I turned my back on him, my entire world would collapse around me and then I would be all alone. Every time I even thought of having to explain what happened, I could hardly breathe. While in class I studied my teachers, wondering if they would believe me. Who would believe an orphan girl over a grown man?

Dale no longer complimented me. He didn't want it to 'go to my head.' But later, when he apologized for being mean, I believed him when he said he was just stressed out about our secret. As if I was the one who caused all of this to happen. *'When people find out you're happy they want it to stop.'* He had moments where he broke down, and he needed me to be the strong one. About how his career could end with the divorce.

Dale was particular about the people I hung out with. He always seemed to know where I was going and who I was talking to. I began to resent him for monitoring my where-abouts, and my lack of privacy. Never having someone love me in that way, I believed that maybe I was too broken to understand love. It wasn't what I had been longing for after all. I missed having fun with kids my age. I watched them all around me, sneaking out and breaking rules and playing tag. But I stopped speaking to them and I stopped trying to fit in. My motivation was somewhere else, just like the fire to my soul.

I found myself becoming upset over the smallest things. During school when I received less than an A, I truly believed I was the worst person. I hated myself. Why couldn't I do better? Why wasn't I a normal kid? I couldn't bear to have to explain to Dale why I wanted to play with kids in my grade. He made me believe I was older and more mature. Sometimes I would catch myself admiring Dean, the most popular boy in school. Fantasizing what it would be like to have a boyfriend. I became upset because I wasn't supposed to feel that way towards another person. But I was experiencing normal 13-year-old feelings and shoving them down, deeper, until I felt nothing but numbness. Although the fear was one thing that never left, constantly, it felt like I was walking on eggshells in every aspect of my life.

The other kids continued to pull away from me because I never wanted to do things. I was often getting in trouble for slamming doors, and Dale said this kind of "aggressive" behavior was unacceptable. It was like in every way every time I tried to fix something; the problem just expanded. Every time any of my feelings escaped, I was told to shove them back down again. I watched Dale talk in church, in front of large groups, smiling and talking in ways he never used when he spoke to me. He was polite and kind, and never touched anyone the way he touched me when he was in church. He stood there smiling, hiding behind a curtain of lies. I tried to block the images of him touching me inside of my bedroom, or on his office floor. I glanced around the room, wondering if he was the same person who came into my room at night. I began to question my own sanity. Nobody saw the other side of him, and the moments of anger that came out of nowhere, his temper, or the secrets he made me keep. I just figured it had to do with me being so stupid. Then I would be alone with him and it all would rush back to me, like a wave that pulled me under water. It was real. It was happening and I wasn't crazy.

It was Sunday morning. We left church early. During youth group, it was mentioned that sex was taboo. Dale was particularly angry after that and I didn't understand why. I covered my ears until I couldn't hear him cursing under his breath. I wasn't sure why he said those bad words to me as soon as we left. It was scary. It was like he was two different people, with two different sides, but both of them were repugnant to a point that I actually felt bad for him. Why did I always force adults to behave that way around me?

He was on edge, always looking over his shoulder. Anymore he hardly looked my way during meals. He chose the seat furthest away from everyone and hardly contributed to the conversations. Slowly, even while in front of others in the home, the anger came more frequently, and it led me to believe I really did destroy people.

After we arrived back home, I began my chores. I could hear Dale muttering as he slammed the kitchen drawer shut. I looked around to see if he caught anyone else's attention. Everyone else seemed pretty preoccupied. So, I sat my duster down and went into the kitchen. I patted his back the way I would Emma's. The same way I tried to console my mother. I longed for the connection I used to have with Dale. With anyone. Sadly, he was all I had left. Dale was often charming until he was enraged, so I tried to comfort him like an adult would console a crying baby.

"Go to your room," he growled at me while stepping away, nervously glancing around to see if anyone saw the embrace. His arms extended into the air, the same way my mother's used to.

Cooties.

"You said you wouldn't be mean again!" I stepped back, and the words escaped me. Before I could duck, Dale raised his hand to me. I hadn't meant to say it out loud.

"I never said such a thing!" he snarled down to me, as if I meant nothing. It happened so suddenly; I wasn't even sure it happened. He smacked me the same way Ma-maw would punish her dog. My cheek burned from where his hand had just been.

I looked up at him through the tears in my eyes and I ran. I shot for the front door and passed by Felicia who was coming down the steps. She called out for me, but I didn't hear what she said.

Had the other girls heard? The ground crunched beneath me, and I struggled to get air in my lungs. The spring humidity hit me, but I kept running until I couldn't feel the grass on my bare feet anymore.

Numb, like the rest of me.

From the moment Emma was born, I was taught to put others before myself, so why was I so bad at it? Why couldn't I just be a normal kid? I could feel my heartbeat inside my head with every step I took. I slowed to catch my breath and gripped the ledge of a metal bench. The coolness was refreshing to my sweating hands as I hunched over.

"Inhale, exhale, you stupid, stupid girl" I told myself.

"Oh my God. Are you dying?"

The voice came so suddenly, I shot up in the air, kicking my legs. I twirled around until my scared eyes locked onto a familiar face.

"What? You scared me, Susan!"

"Well, Bunny, I am naturally frightening."

I smiled at my old friend. Just seeing Susan's face brought me an immense sense of relief, but I tried to hide that. I no longer liked to let people know how much they meant to me because then they would leave.

"Are you following me?" I asked as I arched my back straighter and paced my breathing again.

"Maybe."

Susan moved her frizzy hair out of her eyes and surveyed me from head to toe. I saw a smile cross her lips when she saw my bare feet.

"What's going on?" She asked, taking a step closer.

I bit my tongue, a little too hard, the metallic taste in my mouth made me swallow loud enough to hear.

Gulp.

I so badly wanted to unload, explain to Susan the bad things I had done and that I had to get away. I wanted more than anything to confide in her, but I was too ashamed. What would she think of me then?

Repulsive, disgusting? Or that I was just like my mother? Dale's voice replayed in my mind- *Nobody will like you if they know. Stupid girls do stupid things.*

"It's okay if you don't want to talk about it," Susan said, pulling me back from my thoughts, I clenched as she continued, "Just trust your gut."

I looked her in the eyes, angry at myself for not speaking up and for feeling relieved to keep my secret for another day.

"My gut is telling me to run." I wiped the tears with the back of my hand. Hoping she could see the terrible things through my eyes and help me fix it.

"We'll then, say no more. Let's run!" Susan's green eyes shimmered like emeralds in the setting sun. She leaned over slightly in stance, one foot in front of the other. Feeling how much I had missed her made me realize just how much I missed myself.

Together we took off running, shooting down the path in sync like we did so many times before. I thought of the long hours spent playing in the backyard free of worry, the wonder in our eyes as we climbed the rooftop without fear. The nights we lie awake talking because there were no limits to the things we believed we could do together. I wanted it back, my happiness and my ability to see the world through curious eyes and the way we could find inspiration in everything. There had to be a way to get it back. Then it hit me.

"Would you run away with me, Susan?"

The humid air filled my lungs, as quickly as the ideas sprinted my mind.

Susan stalled, for once she had nothing to say. Her brows pulled together and she drew in a long breath before she spoke.

"We will need to pack chocolate and," Susan flipped her hair out of her eyes with a smile. "We can go to London!"

"London," I repeated with tears in my eyes. I reached out to touch her arm. "I would go anywhere but here…and Susan, I'm so sorry for how terrible I was to you. You have no idea how much this… "

"Listen, Bunny… we all go through things. The past is in the past for a reason. We can do this together. This is our chance to make it right…We will do this. I can't stand another day of Mara nagging me." There was no turning back now.

"But when?" I asked curiously knowing that Susan always had a plan.

"Hmm... how about August 22nd? That gives us 14, 21, 24-" Susan counted with her fingers- "31 days."

"Thirty-one more days, then we will start anew."

Thirty-one days. Thirty-one more days.

Could I make it?

CHAPTER SIXTEEN

It took me a moment to really feel what we were doing. It was like my body moved quicker than my mind. My feet couldn't quite feel the solid ground underneath me. For the past 31 days I'd done nothing but escape to this moment, and there we were. We trudged dejectedly down the sidewalk just as we had planned. We kept our eyes on the pavement so as not to see people's faces as they passed, twisted into expressions of contempt, and occasionally fear.

"This might get us killed!" My second thoughts raced out of my mouth.

"Let's get on with it then!" Susan charged ahead. Her red, frilly hair blew in the wind and the sun exposed her freckles.

I smiled and fearlessly made my pace match Susan's. As we continued without looking back. The tree's that lined both sides of the sidewalk offered a nice shade from the sun. We came to the first turn, when Hawthorne was long behind us, just a tiny dot amongst the other buildings, we paused for a moment.

"I just want to shout and scream at everyone who passes! Make it known that we're free, we're alive!"

I raised my eyebrows at my friend, but I sensed it too. Things were clear, lucid, crisp, beautiful. As if I saw the world for the first time. I realized how powerful I could feel when I wasn't blaming someone else for my sorrows. When I was an individual and not just another child at Hawthorne. I felt nothing- no pain, no sorrow, just alive. For the first time in a long time, I felt alive with the hope to live. It was the only thing that I felt.

We dared to keep going. Together we looked back and linked hands. Then we charged forward, our heavy bags with our most valuable things sagging down past our butts. The cars passing by didn't seem to slow down, we just made sure not to make eye contact as we marched ahead. We hoped we looked just like any normal kid, walking home from school.

There was no set destination in mind. We didn't care about money, or strangers or even nightfall. We had each other and that's all that mattered. The first few miles were easy. The adrenaline carried us forward like we were blowing in the wind. By the time the sun sank in the sky and the last rays shined brightly on our faces, making it hard to see without squinting, our bodies began to ache. Beads of sweat dripped from us, and our drenched shirts stuck to our backs. It was hot. I was so thirsty I could drink from a mud puddle. My dry tongue rubbed against the roof of my mouth. Susan's march had turned more into a sideways trot. The air felt like it evaporated with each breath we took.

"I'm tired." Susan yawned loudly.

"Me too!" I slowed.

Maybe we hadn't planned as much as I hoped.

"It will be fine, Bunny. We just need to follow the plans..." Susan had that look in her eyes when she knew I was afraid. "Just keep thinking about the lives we can have..."

"The only thing left for today is finding a shed to sleep in tonight."

She lowered her voice as a tall man wheeled his trash to the curb.

"So, calm down, we will start our journey over again tomorrow." As we neared the corner, we saw a For Rent sign on a little yellow house and our eyes locked. "Even better." Susan glanced up and down the street, before she opened the rusty metal gate. I leaped into the air as it clanged shut behind us. My heart raced as we inched towards the shadows of the tall willow trees that lined the yard. The house was small and yellow, and there was an inviting light on inside.

"Do you think it's empty?" I whispered.

Susan shrugged once we were out of sight from the street. Together we crept towards the window to take a look. As we neared the window, a shadow came into view. Quickly, we backed away and ducked beneath the willow branches and inched towards the trunk. We settled into the overgrown grass and took our heavy bags off. From this view we could see someone moving inside of the house.

"It's not empty," I whispered tucking my chin down.

"Well…obviously, Sherlock." Susan rolled her eyes at me. I grinned.

We watched the guy paint the walls in silence, the roller moved effortlessly. Up and down the walls, making them new again.

"After he leaves, well make our move," Susan said then glanced at the setting sun. I went digging in my bag. handed Susan a water and pulled out the old dress book and Susan's eyes lit up.

"You kept that old thing?" She ripped it from my hand, and cautiously flipped through the pages. Smiling, reminiscing. She looked just like the little girl I thought of so often.

"I can't believe it." Her eyes glistened.

Only two hours passed and yet I felt like it was a lifetime. I had never sat underneath a tree that long. Between the heat and bugs, I fought to keep my eyes open, and continuously itched my legs. With the sun setting, mosquitoes hovered.

Finally, as the young man left, Susan began placing her things back into her bag. She sat like a leopard ready to pounce. We watched him hide the key underneath the mat in the backyard and then we waited. He walked slowly, past the creaky gate to his car. As he drove away, we darted for the key. Susan got a hold of it and slid it into the backdoor and we smiled the first smile of success as we closed the door behind us. We had made it to safety for tonight. We crept across the brand-new carpet, past the freshly painted walls and into a room that faced the back yard. We kept the lights off and used the streetlights to guide us.

The air conditioner kicked on and startled me.

"Still a wimp huh?" Susan whispered, smiling. I smiled back and didn't tell her I had a real reason this time. A monster who came into my room. I breathed out heavily instead. The strong odor of paint fumes and fresh wood filled the air as I breathed back in. At least I didn't have to see him ever again.

"I'm so happy we're friends again." I reached over to touch her shoulder.

"Don't be sad, Bunny, we will always be friends," Susan replied while digging into her pocket.

She aimed perfectly, and the melted piece of chocolate hit my face.

I felt the tears come, but they didn't escape. This time they were tears of happiness. I longed to tell Susan my deepest and darkest secret, but the words wouldn't come. We counted to three and placed the chocolates in our mouths. For a few fleeting seconds, it was just like we were kids again.

CHAPTER SEVENTEEN

The house was more welcoming with the dappled rays setting a golden hue in all of the freshly painted rooms. We should have been at school at that time. My stomach twisted when I thought about the spelling test I was missing.

I sat up and stretched. Susan lie right next to me, glancing around the empty room.

"How will we ever be able to finish school?" I asked her.

Susan laughed. "Who would ever want to finish school?" she snickered. "Just kidding... But really, we're free for now. Once we start a new life, we'll finish. One day I'll be a weather woman... one day."

"I don't know what I want to be, but I do want to finish school." I yawned, she was right- all I needed to focus on was right now.

"I'm starving."

"Me too."

"Susan, we better get out of here before someone comes."

Susan nodded her head in agreement and pushed her blanket away. She stood and checked out of the window while she wiped the sleep from her eyes. We began to gather our things and were almost ready when we heard the squeaky gate open. My eyes widened in fear, and I froze. For whatever reason I was terrified it was going to be Dale.

"Did you hear me?" Susan was suddenly close to my face. I blinked and nodded and slid my bag on. "No, I'm sorry," I whispered.

"Okay— let's go out the back door, hurry." We ran with our things. Susan closed the door quietly behind us and dashed to the wooded area in the backyard. Through the window we could see the painter. Today he had a tape player attached to his jeans and did a goofy dance as he prepped the paint. We perched behind an old shed in the back yard. It would be a long day. The back yard was quite over-grown and the air was already humid. Behind the small shed was an open space to escape to the trees. I laid a blanket out on the tall grass behind the overgrown brush. We both opened our bags to survey how much food we had left.

"That was close," I whispered, knowing I didn't have to whisper but being too afraid to use my voice. Susan pulled two bananas out of her bag enthusiastically.

"Bunny, I wanted to ask you something." Susan passed me a banana.

"What?" I gnawed at my nails for comfort before opening the banana.

"Have you kissed a boy yet?" I took a deep breathe, relieved my secret wasn't exposed.

The answer was simple. "No."

I had never kissed a *boy*.

"I don't think I want to get married anymore." I told my friend, blushing. I twisted the golden ring on my finger unintentionally. I wondered why I still kept it on.

"Well, that's absurd. That's not what we planned." Susan giggled and her cheeks turned red. "I kissed Jake!" Her eyes gleamed.

Jake, the popular, cutest boy in school. For a moment I was envious, but I realized I never wanted to be kissed by anyone ever again.

"How did it feel?" I asked curiously, avoiding the thoughts of Dale kissing me. His lips so moist against my skin. I shuddered.

"It felt like… like love. It felt like love!" Susan exclaimed.

I inhaled, and pulled my fingers away from my mouth. I had bitten too far down again. The blood beside my nail trickled slowly, but not enough to be noticeable.

"I don't think I know what love feels like," I said while peeling my banana. Love was the one thing I had always wanted more than anything.

Susan brought her face closer to mine.

"It was magnificent, raw, pure, and ever enduring." I paused, and smiled at the way Susan glowed. I found myself completely overwhelmed at the idea of never experiencing unconditional love... Is it something that is taught, or is it a perspective that people have once they reach an age of understanding the complexities versus the word?

Susan's smile turned to disappointment. "It lasted for one week and then Jake kissed Felicity." She busted out laughing and for whatever reason I did too.

"Well, I'm glad you got to feel it. Aren't mothers supposed to teach love? Why didn't my mother show love?" I knew I was asking a question that was impossible to answer.

"Bunny... have you met her?" We both laughed until I had tears again. My laughter had released a bigger emotion that hid inside of me. The secret I kept chained down to all of these unwanted emotions I never wanted to feel.

Suddenly it hit me like a punch in the gut... the feelings I've tried to forget. The overwhelming drowning sensation and realization that I was unwanted and unlovable...The longing for my mother, had caused a never-ending, gut wrenching, uncertainty. In every move I made, I questioned myself.

At school I could see couples kissing, holding hands so tightly and rushing across traffic together. I could see the mothers soothing their babies while trying to finish grocery shopping. A kiss on the forehead, laughter that filled the room, a hand grasping tightly to the child's as they crossed the road. I could see the love in my grandmother's eyes as she looked down at me. I could feel love when my siblings stared into my blue eyes. I knew they felt it too, that longing for love. The desire of belonging, of being "normal" or being a part of the rest of the world. I knew that feeling all too well. On nights when Dale would creep into my room, I began to recognize that this kind of love that he said it was, was different. It wasn't real. I didn't feel any love towards Dale. I felt confusion, and hatred, but also believed from what he had told me that he was the only one who loved me since my mother abandoned me. I loved the *idea* of him being my father. I wiped the tears hoping Susan couldn't see, but she did.

"It's okay." She reached out for me and squeezed my hand. "The sun always rises."

The birds chirped loudly as we ate the rest of our banana in silence. Susan played with her peel once she was done. "My grandmother used to say that to me," she added, "You're going to find the best love one day, Bunny. I know it."

We played I Spy, constructed flower crowns from weeds and grass, and squatted embarrassingly to pee outside in the woods for the first time in our lives. Good thing we packed tissue. The time passed slowly in the heat. Like we were slowly melting and each hour our stomachs growled a little louder.

"How much longer do you think?" Susan sat up from her position on the blanket. All of the constant waiting over the years caused me to be patient. We couldn't really see the house from back here, so we wouldn't know when to leave.

"I don't know, but this is boring," I replied while yawning.

Susan glanced at the large tree we hid behind. "Let's go for a climb?" I nodded my head in agreement despite saying no in my mind. It seemed like every decision was made that way.

We crept back closer to the yard, in the tall pink tree that would give us a good view to know once the painter left. I hadn't climbed a tree since I lived with Susan. I felt the rugged bark on my hands and legs as I climbed up. It took more effort than I remembered to climb to the limbs while keeping my balance. I sat unsteady in a V-shaped section of the Cherry tree. Of course, Susan went a few branches higher than me. We could also see the neighbors back yard from up there. For a moment, we watched an old woman attend to her garden. She pulled weeds and plucked carrots and hummed happily to herself. I instantly thought of Rissy and wondered if she still gardened at Ma-maws without me. I wanted to be like the old lady in blue when I grew up. Happy and content in my own garden. It was the first time in a long time that I had good thoughts about the future. The leaves sparkled in the sunlight and the wind blew the floral earthy scent in my face. It all connected me back to nature. I could get used to this new way of life. All of the beautiful things that we take for granted. I lie across the branch and held on tightly. I didn't flinch at the ants that walked around me, nor at the roughness from the bark on my skin. I had the feeling things were finally okay, and were going to be okay. The only thing that was in the way, was the gurgling of our stomachs.

"If we can just get into her garden, we could at least have a bite to eat." Susan climbed closer to me.

"That would be stealing." I ferociously shook my head.

"We'd just be borrowing if we replant the seeds." Susan said smiling. I ignored her and continued to watch the woman until she disappeared inside. No sooner had the door slammed then Susan climbed down from the tree and was headed right towards the garden. She crept through the white picket fence and made her way in. I watched with my fists clenched to the tree. Susan grabbed two tomatoes, then filled her shirt with strawberries. She hopped back over the fence with a haughty smile.

She was back so quickly I didn't have time to panic. First, we ate the juicy strawberries that were either really sweet or really tart. I watched Susan bite into the ripe tomato- with seeds dripping down her chin.

"I'm imagining mine is pizza," I said, feeling noticeably goofy as I bit into my tomato like an apple. Every little success suddenly meant so much to me. When we were finished Susan collected three seeds that rested on her pants in a gooey puddle. She smiled at me. "Dare me?" She asked, beginning to crawl down again.

"Susan! No, don't!" My voice stalled in the air and she was gone.

Susan made her way back into the garden, but I could see the old woman behind the door. I blinked twice to make sure I was seeing it. The old woman stepped out and studied Susan from her porch.

"You're a thief! What are you doing in my garden? I *outta* whoop you with a stick, child!" the chubby woman spat and moved near Susan who was now crouched in the garden. She held a long walking stick in her hand.

I skidded down the tree, not sure how to protect her. I felt a crack in my ankle when I met the grass, but I kept running. In my mind I pictured her killing my friend with a stick and it all being my fault.

"Wait, please... wait!" I called as she neared my friend. I wouldn't survive without Susan.

The woman took a step back and shook her head. "Well, I'll be, there's two of you." Her brows were knitted together and she glared unblinkingly. Susan and I looked at each other and back to the chubby lady. Her finger still pointed at us. The stick still held tightly in her hand.

"Ma'am, I promise we were only borrowing your tomatoes," I called taking a step closer. Even I knew how foolish that sounded.

"Borrowing? Hmmm." The chubby lady put her finger down, interested. "Please explain."

Susan lifted her hand and showed the freshly planted gooey seeds with a tilted smile.

The woman leaned down, closer to the dirt and placed her glasses on. I was afraid she would tip over. But she stayed like that with her forehead furrowed. She inspected the seeds as if she could make them grow right there on the spot.

Her voice was different, softer. "Well, I'll be. You were just borrowing." A tremulous smile covered her face. "You must be hungry?"

Susan crouched next to her, slightly confused. I took a step closer, the pain in my ankle shot up my leg like flames.

"You even removed the sacks," the woman said, motioning to the tiny seeds that had been removed from the goo.

Susan beamed. "My grandma from London taught me how to...but Bonnie— we didn't want to steal from you. We were just so hungry. You have a nice garden, ma'am."

The woman surveyed us and the leaf particles in our hair.

"What are you doing all alone back here?"

She gawked at my swollen and scraped up leg, I hadn't even noticed it was bleeding. Susan and I locked eyes. I hoped she would answer. We froze and Susan's eyes narrowed.

We certainly couldn't tell her we ran away from an orphanage.

"I'll tell you what, you tell me what you've been doing, and I'll let you have dinner with me."

"Ohhh." Susan turned to face the yellow house and glanced back at me.

I turned as red as the tomato I devoured earlier. I had no idea what to say. All I could think of was the look on Dale's face if she called Hawthorne to come and get us.

"We're just on an adventure," Susan replied standing up. The woman stood as well, suddenly seeming more fragile than she had before.

"Fine. So be it. You can tell me the details over dinner… Come on in." She turned and hobbled inside, still talking. "I ran away once when I was about your age. It didn't last long because it was winter and there were no gardens to steal from…borrow… from." She smiled. We reluctantly followed behind her, knowing we weren't supposed to trust strangers, but also in our hearts we knew we came from a home for children that was full of strangers. Some are good and some are bad. I had found that out the hard way. Maybe we liked taking chances, or maybe we never had a choice. I tried to keep the weight from my leg, but with each step, tears flooded my eyes.

Once inside, the smell hit me immediately. I had never smelled anything quite like it. Chicken broth, fish, and musky cat fur. I twitched my nose. There were cats everywhere I looked. Susan sneezed and widened her eyes towards me. It wasn't the nicest smell I had ever experienced, but it was better than Hawthorne. Despite the smell, the house was cozy. I counted at least 5 cats. There was an orange one swirling on the tabletops and two cream-colored cats on the counters. A small tv was on in the living room and a black cat curled around the cords below. The final one caught me off guard as he retracted his claws into my leg playfully as we walked by. The woman immediately began digging for bandage supplies. She took down a roll of gauze, a pair of sharp tiny scissors, and bright blue tape.

"This is Bartley, and Paddy, and Fern and Gypsy," the woman called out sweetly introducing each of her very fat cats. I waited for her to name the last one. He wasn't as fat and didn't have nearly as much fur. His tongue hung from his mouth slightly like a dog. "What's this one's name?" I asked, pointing to him. "Oh! That's my husband's cat, Doofus."

I laughed with Susan at first because of his name, but the idea of a man in the home scared me, sent chills down my spine. I took a step back, blinking and surveying the room for darkness as they continued to talk.

"I'm Susan and this is Bonnie."

"You can call me Mrs. Ima. My husband is Mr. Harvey, he should be back after a bit. Do y'all know how to cook?"

We shook our heads no and looked at each other curiously. Hansel and Gretel always came back to me at the worst moments.

"Come on over, Bonnie- I don't bite." Mrs. Ima had a smug grin.

She bandaged my leg up quickly. The pressure took away most of the pain.

"I'm sorry if I startled you. I just don't like people going near my garden. Last year kids came through and destroyed my peppers… they thought it was so funny to try and eat them."

"It's okay, I understand- I don't like when people touch my— my stuff either." I shrugged. Susan studied me.

Ima washed her hands and told us to wash ours. She pulled out all of her ingredients and laid them across the counter. I was actually excited to help in the kitchen.

"Roll it and pound it just like this," Mrs. Ima said, flipping the dough with ease. Together, in a kitchen filled with cats, we helped her roll the pieces of dough. Mrs. Ima started chicken, then sliced carrots and onions. The savory smell wafted across the room. My mouth watered with anticipation. Mrs. Ima added chicken and vegetables in the chicken broth. Lastly, she added the mismatch sized dumplings, and the starch as a thickener to the broth which made it more of a gravy. Every now and again, Doofus would chase his tail. Mrs. Ima had lived in this house since she was a child. She seemed like she hadn't had anyone new to talk to in a very long time.

Ima taught us about dough, and the proper way to boil chicken. She showed us how to carefully slice carrots, and even showed us a trick to cutting onions without burning your eyes. She stored hers in the freezer. Her voice was soothing. She looked us in the eyes when we talked. We hadn't had an adult talk to us in this way in a very long time.

"Get the bowls from the cupboard, it's time to eat."

We collected four bowls and placed them on the counter. "Harvey can eat when he returns, let's get you girls fed."

Ima filed our bowls to the rim and together we sat at the table.

We didn't talk, but instead scarfed the food down faster than ever before, onions and all. I could feel my stomach bulging out and I let out a deep sigh.

"Thank you, Mrs. Ima." There was never a bigger appreciation I ever had for an adult in this moment. "You're very wel—."

The sound of a man clearing his throat startled all three of us. "Ima, come on now! What have I told ya about strays?!" His voice carried across the room like a loud trumpet. I immediately wanted to cover my ears, but I didn't.

"Now, now Harvey. These girls are just staying for a little bit."

"That's what you said about Bartley, and Paddy too… Ima, we don't need no more mouths to feed. What'd ya do, kids? Did ya run away?"

His stern face silenced us. My heart pounded.

Ima sat up straighter. "Don't let him fool ya, Doofus is a stray too!" She cracked a smile and then her and Harvey let out a cackle.

"Now, now. My sweet Doofus boy is the *bestest* cat in the world." Harvey spoke in baby tone to his cat. Susan and I perched our lips together to hold back a laugh.

Ima fed her cats while Harvey fed Doofus. They had a weird routine, of mixing rice with chicken stock and speaking to them the whole while. When they were finished, they each got a piece of warmed fish.

"No wonder they're fat," Susan whispered in my ear and chuckled under her breath.

"Always bringing in more strays." Harvey chuckled as he moved, with a light shining in his eyes. His trumpet voice was softer now, and had a friendly jingle to it. I still didn't trust him. I didn't trust any man. We got to sleep on the couch, at different ends with our feet meeting in the middle. We got used to the smell after some time. While they were watering the garden, we decided to take shifts sleeping. That way if Ima and Harvey decided to turn us into cat food, we would be able to escape. There was no use in trusting adults fully these days.

I awoke the next morning with Doofus curled up on my hip. Susan was fast asleep still. So much for taking shifts. Each time I scratched his head, he stretched his claws deeper into my skin. The skinny cat's warmth and soft purr was comforting. As the sun slipped into the sides of the curtains, Susan sat up and whispered.

"Well, we survived!"

"Barely." I grinned holding up, my bandaged ankle.

"We have to figure out our next plan."

"What's all that whispering about?" Ima said. I shot up, startled, and Doofus darted from my lap.

"Sorry to frighten you, dear." She walked from her bedroom with her nightgown touching the floor. Her face looked tired, but she had a smile on her lips.

"Thank you for letting us stay here. We better get to going." Susan folded the crocheted blanket and brushed the cat fur from her shirt. I stood to help.

"Girls. We need to talk," Ima said. "But first I need coffee."

She disappeared into the kitchen. Susan and I stared at each other uncomfortably. I wondered if we should run for it despite my bandaged leg. But I didn't know where to go. We had gotten this far and there was no way I was giving up.

Ima came back with her coffee and set two cups of sweet tea on the coffee table for us.

"If y'all are in trouble, we need to know that." Ima had a serious tone like the first time we had met her. I wanted so badly to tell her. I wanted to confide in this silly cat lady and never leave. I just wanted to escape my dark secrets and feel safe. I looked over at Susan for guidance. But not even Susan knew about the terrible things I'd done.

Shame suffocated me.

No words came.

My mind froze, and I stared blankly- rooted in place.

Stars filled my eyes and a strong tingle warmed my cheeks.

My heart rate grew faster, and my palms were clammy. I was ready to tell whether they believed me or not. It was my chance. But as soon as I opened my mouth, Susan cut in.

"We are not in trouble. We're orphans. Well, I'm an orphan, Bonnie's mom is alive but she's basically an orphan too. We left our homes because we're trying to...."

Ima pulled her head back slightly, and just stared with her eyes wide.

"We're trying to get away from bad people," I added.

Susan stared at me inquisitively for a moment and she nodded her head.

"I see... that makes a little more sense to me. So, where do y'all plan to go?"

"Not sure yet."

"You're not thieves after all." She clicked her tongue and smiled with every wrinkle telling a story of her life.

I exhaled. So close, again. I feared she would call Hawthorne immediately and, in my gut, everything told me to run like always.

CHAPTER EIGHTEEN

I started to think there wasn't an adult left in the world that I could trust, but Ima proved me wrong. Some adults could follow through with their words. Not all adults would play games but turn into a monster at night. I fought the nightmares, tried to black out the flashbacks, but each day Ima was there with a homemade bowl of oatmeal or sunny side up eggs and a good story. Ima shared part of our secret with Harvey, but she also gave us hope.

Ima told Harvey that our mother had went out of town. Though it wasn't completely a lie, Harvey didn't bat his lashes at it. She asked Harvey if he would mind some help around the house for a week or so until our mother returned. That week was blissful. Such unstructured freedom belonged to pure nostalgia that existed long ago. I finally had a glimpse of what it would be like to have a mom and dad who loved each other.

It was a safe environment. I tried not to think about what would happen if we got caught. I couldn't even imagine the way Dale would react, thinking I exposed his secret. I couldn't even bear the idea of sharing *the secret*. We were treated with love and we, in turn, reciprocated. I often had a hard time making decisions. I still felt dirty and unworthy of love. Susan and I were inseparable, sticking to each other like the fur that lined the couch. But still, I didn't have the nerve to tell her the secret I kept inside.

During that week, we were taught the basic necessities of life. The things your mother is supposed to teach you when you're a pre-teen, like sewing. The things a real father was supposed to teach you. The gentleness in his eyes and the way he looked at us with pride and not hunger. I couldn't believe Dale had tricked me. He tricked me into losing a part of myself that I forgot I had.

We learned how to cook, how to take care of the garden, and how to feed the cats. Each day Ima put a new bandage on my leg until it healed. We knew we had to figure out a plan, but we didn't want to leave. It was that kind of motherly love we longed for. We stayed away from the calendar in fear they would realize how long we've been there and send us on our way. Each night as the moon came into view, we whispered on their little couch, dreams of staying with Ima and Harvey forever.

We watched in awe the way Harvey's eyes glistened when he talked to Ima. In a way that only two could look at each other after 50 years of marriage. I learned how couples could be a team. How important trust was. I learned that a father would teach his daughters how to garden, how to catch a ball, and how to build a side table. I learned what a father wouldn't do. He never touched me in inappropriate places. He never accidentally came into the shower room when I was fully exposed. He took the trash out and carried the groceries in on his own when it rained. We wondered into the backyard and never went out front. Each night we fell asleep with full stomachs and, after long days in the garden, our eyes grew heavy quickly. I didn't wait up for the monster to come. Instead, at night, I sometimes saw him in my dreams. I knew what he did to me was wrong now. I began to believe in myself again. I wasn't crazy and those things did happen to me.

It was like a sanctuary that I needed to awake me from those nightmares. All of the attention we could ever need. Susan designed two dresses for us. One day, Ima surprised us with material and taught me how to sew because Susan had little interest. The dresses didn't have the straightest stitching's, but we were proud. One evening we heard them whispering.

"You know we can't keep them forever right, Ima?"

"Oh, Harvey. It has been like a dream. You know I've always wanted daughters." We smiled at each other because it was someone who wanted us just the way we were. Susan and I played pretend under the cherry tree like we were small children, with flowers in our hair and laughter in our hearts. We didn't leave the house very often. We only helped bring out the trash cans and stayed mostly in the back yard. Harvey went and got what little groceries they bought each week. While we stayed amongst the garden and in the kitchen with Ima. It didn't take long for Harvey to figure out we didn't really have parents, and Ima eventually told Harvey, and although he was uncomfortable, he didn't have the heart to make us leave.

We were too close to Hawthorne, we didn't know at this point who would even be looking for us. If my grandmother would be notified. If my mother would hear and never speak to me again. But I didn't care because in this moment it was all worth it to me. It never came to me how this was my chance. This was my first chance of freedom, and I was too afraid to tell anyone for fear they wouldn't believe me. For fear they would hate me. For fear I would truly be the bad kid who caused these terrible things happen.

As the sun slipped away, we began to clean up when we were called in for dinner. Each night before washing up, Harvey would say, "Every day- rain or shine, when you come in to eat you should smell like dirt."

We sat down with our forks and when Ima started the prayer, there was a loud knock on the front door.

Harvey chuckled and began to walk towards the door. "It ain't *nothin'* to worry bout, girl...." he stopped mid-sentence.

Flashing lights lit the walls blue and white. Everything around me disappeared. I couldn't go back to that home. I couldn't go back to that life.

Harvey answered a few questions that I couldn't hear over the pulse beating in my head. It all felt blurry, distant. "There was a sighting of some missing children" ... He saw us sitting at the kitchen table. The officer approached us, his shiny shoes made a sticking sound on the floor.

"Do you know you've been listed as missing children?"

Susan and I looked at each other as the joy was sucked out of life.

"No, sir. We are right here." Susan said matter of factly.

I wanted to laugh but I wanted to cry. Why had I been so stupid not to tell anyone? They certainly wouldn't believe me now. I didn't know what Dale had done to me, but I knew a grown man wasn't supposed to touch me like he did. I didn't know what to call it or how to tell them. But while my thoughts spiraled out of control, I didn't hear anymore words that were said. It all went blank- my ears rang, and my head was spinning. Ima stood in the corner, tears filling her eyes. We weren't the only ones who lost a friend that night. I fell to my knees when they made me walk to the car. I couldn't, I wouldn't go back to it. But my mouth didn't open, and my voice didn't speak up. Once again, I had failed myself.

CHAPTER NINETEEN

More than one good thing came from Susan and I running away. Other than meeting Ima and Harvey, my grandparents had been called. They were made aware of how we ran away and, after being listed as a missing person, Ma-maw cared more about my whereabouts.

For the first time in five years, we would all be going home for Christmas! That feeling of joy lit and sparked inside of me once I climbed into my grandmother's car. I was surprised to feel excited-excitement hadn't existed since returning. The familiar smell of cigarettes, vinyl, and the earthy scents of patchouli greeted my nose and I sunk down into the seat, feeling like I would be able to breathe again. The entire world was on pause for a moment. The sky was dark, the wind blew briskly, and tree branches sat on the long winding roads back to Ma-maw and Pa-paw's home. I wouldn't have cared if I saw a tornado coming right at us, being in that car was the best feeling I had since running away.

Once the car pulled in the long driveway, Ma-maw huffed and we all just sat there in silence for a moment, as if we could pretend nothing had ever happened, nobody had ever abandoned us. I could hardly recognize Ralph as he quietly glanced around at his surroundings. Ralph was now five, and his cute little voice muttered words that were quite comprehensible.

I smiled with wonder watching him point at the house.

Did he remember? Did this feel safe for him too?

Emma slid down off her seat and trailed behind me. She was uncertain of this trip and mad she had to leave her friends behind. Emma was no longer her guileless, happy self. Instead, she stared at her feet as she followed me inside with her arms tightly crossed. As I rounded the corner, I couldn't believe it. Mama was sitting on the couch. She looked like she had been awake for days, make-up was smeared underneath her eyes, and her long brown hair was disheveled and messy. The clothes she wore were unusual, not nearly as elaborate as her normal attire. There was no dramatic greeting, she almost seemed to be bored at the appearance of her own children, yawning dramatically. It wasn't until I noticed the large beach ball sized bump underneath the shirt Mama wore that she spoke.

"Well don't look at me like that," Mama said, her southern accent extending each word as she glanced down at her pregnant belly, a half smirk covering her face.

Mama is pregnant.

My mind raced and I took a seat in front of the fireplace, my insides were burning with jealousy instead of wood. We all just sat there, staring at each other in silence. Emma sat away from me and Ralph just kind of cowered on the floor where Ma-maw's favorite lamp used to be. *This is not good. This is not good.* I heard a familiar noise- that of clearing one's throat. I looked up into Rissy's loving eyes and charged into her arms inside of the wash room.

"My girl. My girl," she said, lovingly squeezing me. "You have to tell me all about Hawthorne," Rissy said quietly so Ma-maw couldn't hear. I nodded my head slightly and looked up at Rissy with regret in my eyes. In an instant, I realized that for the first time someone understood the pain I usually hid so well. But Rissy was like my breaking point and my safety net all at once.

Rissy's eyes filled with tears. "Dear Lord, child."

Rissy leaned down to pull me in closer. My heart filled with gratitude. I heard without words because Rissy saw right through to the darkness and instantly knew. Together, on the floor of the washroom, Rissy fell to her knees embracing me, and we silently sobbed in each other's arms. Rissy cried for me as she had cried when she lost her own son. She knew a part of me had died. That was one of the moments in time I always held onto, not the hurting in my little heart, but the love in Rissy's heart.

It never seemed to get less awkward. I kept waiting for the moment when this place would feel like home again, but it didn't. I guess it's hard to fix it in your own mind once you've been abandoned. There may never be a feeling of safety ever again. I tried to spend as much time with Emma as I could. But she was older now and she liked to push me away. I wanted to squeeze her and tell her how much I always loved her, and how I tried to save her. But like always, I just kept it all inside. I did, however, ask Ma-maw if I could cut my long hair. She smiled at the idea as she drove us to the grocery store. It was just me and her and the windows were all the way down. The wind wiped my long hair in waves. I was excited to get out of that house and it was nice to be alone with Ma-maw where I didn't have to worry about anyone else being treated equally or making everyone happy.

While I enjoyed the break from Dale, and pushed the monster out of my mind as often as I could- this was all unfamiliar now. If I did one bad thing, I feared I would be judged and sent away and never have another chance to prove that I was worthy of love. If I faced the car window just right, it would take my breath away, and I kind of liked that feeling. Not being able to worry about anything other than breathing and staying alive. I began to think of all the ways I could tell my grandmother what had been happening to me. The idea of mentioning it sent an overwhelming wave of disgust with myself through me.

Stupid girls do stupid things.

I knew that if they didn't believe me and Dale were to find out, I would be in big trouble. The fear grew into stomach pains as I pictured everyone knowing what I let happen on those nights. I didn't know if Ma-maw would believe it was my fault. Why was I such a shame, and so disgusting? Nobody would ever love me if they knew. I already believed that nobody loved me now so I don't know how much worse it could have been. But over the years, Dale told me many different things, and threatened how my life would change. I would be shunned from church and Ma-maw would never pick me up from Hawthorne again. I just didn't know how to speak of these terrible things. Because of Harvey, I knew it wasn't the way a father should treat a daughter. I shriveled, imagining the words Mama would speak of me, and how bad I had always been. How it would justify my mother's actions that I did truly deserve to be sent away. I was divergent, angry towards myself, and discarded. As Ma-maw pulled up to the grocery, she called for me several times.

"Bonnie... Bonnie. Okay this isn't funny..." Finally, she reached over and touched my arm, and I jumped about out of my seat with my heart racing and face flushed.

"Are you okay?" Ma-maw asked, studying me.

I nodded my head as I followed Ma-maw into the store, unable to utter a word. Ma-maw hurried through down the aisles, distracted. I saw myself in the refrigeration glass reflection. I was pale with dark rings around my eyes. I looked like someone I didn't even know.

On the way home, Ma-maw decided to take me to the local salon. Once I was in that chair, I chose a Pixie cut. It took away all of my long brown hair, but it helped light my face up a little. My blue eyes with brown speckles seemed to shine with more confidence than before. I continued to run my fingers over my short hair. I didn't care if I looked like a boy, I didn't want to be inside of my usual self anymore. The freshly cut strands felt comforting to my small hands. I wanted to take hold of any little grip of freedom I could get. On the way home, my hair just blew slightly from the wind in the window. Almost as if I had left pieces of my innocence behind with those long locks on the floor of the salon.

Sometimes Rissy would poke me awake or hug me after I jumped awake startled and with terror in my eyes. Rissy would smile softly, giving me her hand and leading me to get a jacket. After slipping on shoes, we tiptoed out the back door to garden in the morning before anyone else woke up. Out in the garden Rissy showed me how to pick carrots. She had this procedure down and as we knelt together in the damp soil, with the sun rising, she showed me how to first loosen the soil with a garden fork. By doing this, it saved the carrot from breaking off of the green foliage as it did my first attempt. Rissy laughed out loud, and said, "Here, child." Her eyes filled with admiration. I mimicked the way I saw Rissy carve the fresh dirt from around the top of the carrot leaves. This time, the carrot came out nicely. "Perfectly imperfect just like you," Rissy told me that morning. We didn't speak a lot, but there was something special in the way I could communicate with Rissy without words. By the end of the visit, I showed Rissy all of my new gardening skills. I also knew how to identify a white-throated sparrow's song, whose leisurely whistle made the garden feel even more magical. Listening didn't always have to involve words and I learned there in the garden at the break of dawn, to enjoy the small things that could easily be unnoticed and taken for granted every day.

On occasion though, we did get to talking. I admired Rissy's bravery. "I hate the world, Rissy." I looked up into her sparkling brown eyes.

"Why is that, child?" Rissy responded, leaning closer to me.

"Because, why couldn't I have a mother like you?"

"Well, child, you *is* white and I'm black, but that's not the reason why."

I looked up at her confused. "Then what is?"

"The world ain't a fair place. To make it a better place, we have to be better than those who try to destroy us."

I could swear Rissy's gaze went to Ma-maw's bedroom.

"You see, Bonnie, we don't get to choose everyone that comes into our life, but we get to choose who we keep in it. That's the part that matters."

"Then why do you let Ma-maw treat you that way?" I asked curiously, not understanding why skin color should matter, I loved Rissy all the same.

"Bonnie, I am a hard-working woman, and I don't care if your grandmother ever gave me the time of day. She was raised differently, and you, my sweet girl, were born with a different kind of heart. Not everyone is born or raised the same, but when a person cares about the happiness of others, she will be the one who makes a difference in the world." She called down to me smiling, "and when we can't find the good in others, we must be the good. That's what humanity is."

I still didn't understand. I just looked up at her, smearing the dirt across my forehead.

"I love you, Rissy," I said, and as Rissy's eyes filled with tears, the wind whipped through leaving behind a sweet honeysuckle scent.

"I love you too, my girl."

In the distance, a white sparrow sang a loud song, and we continued picking vegetables from the garden together, in silence. I decided right then I would like to make a difference in the world.

CHAPTER TWENTY

The break from Hawthorne actually ended up being a few days shy of a month. Over time, I was able to block the monster from my mind, but at night I would often awake in a full sweat, racing thoughts, and feeling as if an elephant sat on my lungs. I found comfort in Emma snoring next to me, it was the closest she would get to me. She had gotten so big, we could barely fit in the twin size bed anymore.

Mama was rarely around, coming and going with her new boyfriend, she didn't acknowledge any of us. It was easier to pretend like we didn't exist. Eventually Mama left and just never came back to see us. She took her pregnant belly with her and I felt sad for that little baby who was going to be born to a mother who didn't love her. Ma-maw didn't talk about the baby. She just stared into the distance, pretending things were normal for us.

I wondered if Dale worried I would tell. I wondered if I did tell if I would be kept safe from him. It seemed like a bad idea to tell Ma-maw and be sent back to live with him. If only I were braver, maybe then I could make a difference in the world. The day we went back, I felt my muscles tighten. It was like my entire body hardened to prepare me to be in the same room as him. On the drive back, I imagined telling Ma-

maw everything. I imagined she would believe me and I would be safe. But I saw myself reflected in the dirty car window and it reminded me that it was my fault. I would never see my family again. Once Ma-maw found out she would surely never see me again. I just couldn't get the words to come out. I feared the consequences would somehow be worse than what I already went through. As if speaking the words out loud made them really happen. I couldn't admit that I had done terrible things. I couldn't admit I was this broken little girl with no idea how this happened.

The first day back, I tiptoed around. The smell of the cottage made me physically ill. I didn't miss it. The musk and dusty cabinets- the smells of everyone's house scents all combined into one. Like pepper mixed with cotton. Strange fragrances filled the air. The voices were loud, excited. Almost every single person got to go home. The noise was too much, but I tried to fade into the room but then I saw him. Dale smiled at me from across the room.

I tried not to look at him, but he came directly towards me. It was like he could smell my fear, and bits of my renewed bravery.

"Bonnie, can you help me pick up some supplies from the office?" In my mind I shouted no as I crossed my arms to cover myself from him.

"Yes, she will." Jackie answered for me and motioned for me to follow him. "Make yourself useful," she called after me with a little shove. She seemed to be less stressed now that the divorce was almost finalized. I picked my feet up and slowly made my way across the spinning room. Every muscle in my body tensed, and suddenly I was on fire. When my body needed to react, I froze instead. I still followed him out the door and shut it behind me. Sometimes it's like that- you just shift right into autopilot and move without a thought. The last thing I wanted was to be alone with him.

"Hi Bonnie, how was your break?" His voice sounded like he cared but I know he only wanted to know one thing. Did I keep the secret?

"Good," I half whispered- he studied my hair.

"Wow, what did you do to your hair?" He reached for me and I jumped.

I shrugged my shoulders and backed away. "It looks… good." He lowered his voice so nobody could hear. But his words didn't ring true. He was angry that I cut my hair. He spat the next words out once we were further down the path, the humidity already causing sweat to gather along my hairline.

"I heard your mother barely visited with you. I guess she wasn't all that happy to see you."

I nodded at him, afraid that I would actually show he got to me. It was like he wanted to erase every single bit of confidence I had gained back outside of his control.

"I did see her. She's having another baby."

"Wow… such a shame… Your mom keeps having children because you weren't good enough for her. I don't really know what we're going to do with you."

I tried not to let it hurt, but it did. It only reinforced my belief that I would never be good enough. He knew this of course. That's what fueled him. He was filled with so much evil he only knew how to focus on the worst parts of everyone else.

"Do you remember when you said you would tell someone?" We walked through the pathway and for a moment I could see nothing but trees surrounding us. Fear shot through me. We were completely alone.

"I didn't." Tears filled my eyes- he thought I did.

"You shouldn't be so upset. You're overreacting again. Don't worry- I'll still be here for you." Guilt shot through me but that's exactly what he wanted. I questioned myself in his presence. It's like every single thought I knew about him could be erased automatically. He had brainwashed me to believe in him and not in myself for so many years, it was automatic. Why did I even want to be on good terms with him?

"Just remember… this has all been you. It's all been you and I have done nothing wrong."

I swallowed hard and looked up at him as he opened the door. He used that voice he did in church to greet the office women. The soft one. Once again, he made me question my reality. I watched a curtain lift and his show was on again. Smiling and chatting with the other adults. I always had to defend my reality around him. Could he truly be that evil? We grabbed the cleaning supplies and I stood quietly watching. I could feel myself disappearing again. On the walk back he talked about the sunshine and the flowers. How could beautiful things exist in a world with him? Returning had been even harder than I imagined. The same four walls of my nightmares waited for me, closed in on me, magnifying the bad dreams until all I could see was gray. The walls, they looked even more gray than they had before. It was all too easy to fall back into the place Dale needed me to be. Dale manipulated me into turning against my own emotions. He tried to make me believe nothing really happened. I wanted to believe it too, because allowing the worst moments of my life to be true was harder than denying my own reality. He emotionally chopped away my ability to stand up for myself. I truly believed I would never be good enough.

Each time I thought I would give up; something was there pulling me forward. It didn't have to be anything huge. Just the tiny glimpses reminding me that I wasn't crazy gave me hope. My new haircut allowed me to be brave. When I remembered how Harvey treated me. When I remembered fathers didn't touch their daughters in the darkness. The image of Rissy holding me on the laundry room floor. These moments were small, but they meant everything to me. Dale defined my own reality for so long, I had to learn how to sort out truth from distortion. I had to tell someone before I ran out of time. So, I made up my mind. No matter what. I had to escape this.

It was a chilly day, the kind where the sun hid behind the clouds and the wind sent chills down my arms and legs. School had just ended, and I was trying to find Susan. I hadn't seen her after the long break, nor since we returned from running away. I would find her, tell her, and beg her to help me. I couldn't bear another day in this life. The night before would be the last night Dale ever touched me. I pulled my shirt tighter against my body. I could have worn a jacket, but I decided I didn't deserve to be warm. There were little decisions I made each day- to torture myself because of the things that I had done. I stood on my tippy toes to find her red hair, but someone called out to me.

"Bonnie!" It was Emma. I was surprised Emma talked to me in front of everyone. Typically, she pretended like I didn't exist in public. It was weird sharing a bed with someone and then returning like we were strangers. Almost like we were never sisters. I always had a hard time believing the good things were real.

"What's wrong?" she asked, reaching out for me.

"Nothing. Just looking for Susan." I crossed my arms.

"You're always looking for Susan…" Emma muttered.

"Can you believe Mama? Going out and getting pregnant again? I'm so glad we got to come here instead of being with her." She smiled, brushing her curly locks out of her face.

"Yeah," I halfheartedly agreed. "What do you want?"

Emma scrunched her nose at me. "Wow, really? That's how you treat your favorite sister?" Emma laughed. I didn't smile, I was just destroying everything again. "Fine. No, I just wanted to tell you, Meryl, my house mother, wanted to see us."

I followed Emma back to her cottage. On the front porch there was a bench with cushions and flowers lining the steps. It felt more like a home than any other cottage. Emma had been with Meryl since the beginning. She moved with Emma from the Hollifield nursery over to the Jones cottage when the position opened up. Meryl always allowed me to visit, she was one of the good ones.

"I'm here for both of you," Meryl said as she knelt to embrace Emma.

"Did somebody die?" I asked.

Emma laid her head onto Meryl's shoulder and laughed.

"Mama had her baby today," Emma said, spinning around. She had a slight smile, that of someone who finds something funny but inside wants to cry.

"Oh," was all I could muster.

Mama had her baby. Her baby that was also my sister but by this point it felt nearly impossible to be close to another human. I wished I could just run until I couldn't anymore. Maybe it was easier for Ralph and Emma to grow up not knowing what the rejection felt like.

"You know, I always wanted to have my own children. I wasn't able to, but then there's people like your mother… she just doesn't know what a blessing it is…" Meryl's voice trailed off as she walked. Emma and I followed Meryl into the den. I nearly tripped over the shag carpet that lined the floor. My mind was so occupied lately, I couldn't focus, I scolded myself quietly, 'stupid girls do stupid things.' A new unhealthy routine of mine. I had watched Meryl love on Emma in bits and pieces over the years, and deep down I knew Emma was safe. I pushed away the tinge of jealousy towards having Meryl as a house parent.

"She's keeping the baby for now," Emma added and reached for me. Her petite hand landed on my arm, and it took everything in me not to fall into a puddle on the floor.

Then it hit me. Not about the new baby or lack of Mama's love. But instead, as I stared into Emma's sparkling eyes, I realized she was the age I was when Dale started coming into my bedroom. The sadness trickled through every cell in my body. In that moment, in seeing my own reflection in Emma's childish face, I understood the depth of pain that had been sitting below my skin all these years.

Meryl touched my shoulder.

I jumped into the air, and nervously began to shake. I couldn't make my eyes focus. Flashes of myself as a little girl in that gray bedroom burned into me.

"Did I startle you?" Meryl questioned.

"I'm sorry, Miss. Meryl, I just… it's just a lot to think about," I whispered while trying to hide my shaking hands. Meryl looked me over, with her brows up high and her curiosity lasting moments.

Would this be my chance? Would Meryl believe me?

I opened my mouth to speak but couldn't find the words. Instead, Dale's dry whisper filled my mind, drowning me until there was no more air left, only his voice.

'Child You're so very broken that nobody even cares to notice. They wouldn't believe you anyway. You'll never see your family again. It was you— all you.'

"Bonnie?" Meryl called again.

"Bonnie you are as white as a ghost, honey, are you feeling well?" she asked with a concerned look across her face. I blinked. It took everything to manage to shake my head up and down.

"Yes ma'am."

I cleared my throat and placed my shaking hands behind my back.

Meryl reached out and placed her hand across my forehead. She leaned down and kissed it gently. I shuddered.

"I better call over to Jackie and have her watch you tonight." She walked towards the phone.

Panic rose again in my chest. "That won't be necessary, Miss. Meryl, please don't! I think I am just tired today." My voice croaked.

I wanted to say more but the words were too heavy on my tongue.

It was too late, Meryl already had the wall telephone to her ear, and I could hear Jackie's careless, loud grunts on the other line.

My stomach burned. *What punishment Dale might offer if he thought. Oh God, if he thinks…* my thoughts trailed off. Meryl hung up the phone and Emma stared at me.

"Go on back home, dear. Jackie said she would check your temperature when you get there. Take care, sweetie, and Bonnie, if you need to talk to someone, I am here." She called behind me hurriedly as I shot for the door. My lungs gasped for air that I couldn't find. I didn't take the time to say goodbye. My body knew what I had to do, with my thoughts spiraling, and hands going numb I jumped down all of the stairs at once. I ran and ran across the freshly cut grass all the way back to my cottage. Who knew what Jackie would tell Dale before I got back.

CHAPTER TWENTY-ONE

I opened the heavy door and attempted to quietly sneak inside. It was three times as big as me and thudded shut. Laughter and conversation from down the hall greeted me. I hoped it meant that Dale wasn't around.

Jackie met me in the dimly lit kitchen, and her strident voice filled the walls as she barked about me being over at the Jones cottage again. I drowned out her unpleasant voice and, instead, wondered if she would have a worse punishment. I glanced around, grateful he hadn't appeared yet. My temperature came back perfect, and that gave Jackie something else to bark about. Her cheeks were bright red, and her fat fingers felt uncomfortable being that close to my mouth. She couldn't bare the idea of allowing us to have feelings- to her it had to be a physical illness.

"Yes, ma'am," I agreed once I could speak. I was about to be dismissed when Dale stepped into the kitchen. Dale had a smirk across his face, illuminating the dark side that existed behind his shark eyes. Instantly, it felt as though my mouth was full of pennies. I tried to shake the images of Dale's face smiling after making me put pennies under my tongue to make my fever high enough to stay home from school. The taste of the penny lingered. The pain that came after when nobody was in the home except for the two of us. I shuddered.

"Now, Jackie, is she trying to get out of school again tomorrow?" Dale asked in a child-like voice. He had been nothing but nice to her since she filed for the divorce.

I hated the way he spoke of me in front of Jackie. Jackie's cheeks blushed when Dale spoke to her. I don't think she knew his dark secrets.

"She was just over at the Jones cottage again. I keep telling this girl those ladies have enough to worry about. They don't need to be looking after another young'un' who is begging for attention." Jackie said staring back up at Dale, her lashes flickering. I didn't move, I didn't utter a single word.

If she only knew. But she wouldn't believe it either. Who was I to say those things? I hoped if I stood there long enough, I would just disappear. If they could hear my heart, then they would know I was about to explode. I might even die from a heart attack right there in that old kitchen. I hoped that Jackie wouldn't use the belt on me. It would make me uncomfortable with Dale watching. I hoped Dale wouldn't re-question my motives for talking to Meryl today. The last time I had the belt, the welts stayed blistered and sore on my behind for two weeks. The sound of it was enough to make me wince in itself.

"Well, we will keep an eye on her," said Dale in an edgy voice, his brows lifted. He smiled down at me as he knew he had just saved me from the belt. What would I owe him in return?

I managed to thank Dale. While walking out of the kitchen I could feel Dale's dark eyes watching me so intensely that I felt I may actually melt. Once I hit the stairs I ran and didn't look back- upstairs to my room. If I had a lock, I would lock it. I considered piling my bed up against the door.

"Damn it Meryl," I cursed.

I couldn't imagine Jackie would ever stop beating me if she found out our secret. That was close, way too close! If anyone ever found out I would die.

I sunk against the wall in the corner of my room. My thoughts moved so quickly I felt queasy.

I just sat there, on the floor in the darkness, trying to catch my breath again. I stayed there until nighttime surrounded my window. I skipped the shower, as I couldn't bear handling another one of Dale's accidental drop-ins to the bathroom, whereas he acted like he hadn't heard the water running. Being bare in the light was even worse than the darkness. Only if Jackie wasn't so blind and could see what his real intentions were. I stared at the ceiling, waiting for an answer. The white ceiling stared back at me. No answers were to be found.

A loud thud came from Dale's room downstairs, and I knew it was time. I could hear the creaking of the steps, and soon the monster would unveil himself. I braced myself for what was going to happen. This routine had become all too familiar. My breathing slowed as I managed to shut down, so I didn't have to experience the horror of it once again. As his shadow appeared, I imagined being on the roof with Susan, seeing the puffy clouds.

No matter how much darkness I endured each night, with each morning came the sunrise. I always appreciated the sunrise for a number of reasons. One because it was a new day, and two because I would try to pretend each day would have a new beginning, and that maybe something good would happen for me. Thirdly, I liked to imagine my time with Rissy in the garden at the peak of sunrise.

Since having my own room, I was able to collect colorful bottles that sat in the windowsill. Each bottle was filled with plant clippings from any plant I could sneak. In the middle, tall green bottle, I had the clipping of the African Violet Rissy had placed in my pocket from my grandmother's house. It was bigger now and sprouted roots that tangled together in the bottom of the glass bottle. Rissy had instilled her love of the garden and living things within me. No matter how dark the nights inside my bedroom were, life still blossomed each morning.

CHAPTER TWENTY-TWO

I didn't eat. I didn't sleep. I just somehow made myself get out of bed, go to school, and come home. It had been months since we were pulled away from Ima and Harvey's house and I had no fight left in me. I had finally given up. Jane was moved from my room and in place I had a locked bedroom door at night, the worst part of it was that both Dale and Jackie had the key.

The first time I was alone with Dale, I cowered in the corner. "Stupid girls do stupid things," he spat at me. I wasn't sure if he was more upset about me leaving or him not having control over me. I tried to tune out his signature low pitch rumble and generous use of profanity towards me. I realized for the first time it wasn't ever his love that I wanted. When I went along with him and did everything on his terms it was easier to pretend. It was easier for me to pretend I was happy when I was at least treated like a human. His behavior had me doubting my worth.

"I could go to prison for a long time because of you."

I tried to look at him, see through him. Anything to make it stop. Why had I ever listened to him, and how could I get away from him? Running away only made everything spiral out of control. I studied him from across the room while I did my homework. With people around I was safe. I stared because I wanted to see if he would turn into a monster right before my eyes. This person that I once trusted. He wasn't the same person who saved me from trouble or told funny jokes. He wasn't the same person that spoke in church. How could one person be so many different things? I decided from that moment that I would fight back and try to save myself since I couldn't run away.

The next night he unlocked my room and came inside. The frogs chirped outside my window loudly, and I wished for a second that I could turn into a frog and hide instead of face him.

"We need to talk about this. I'm sorry if you think that I hurt you," he whispered and reached towards me. I flinched. "I would never hurt you. I just think that lately you've been making rash decisions and well… your mind.. it seems off…a lot of other people are talking about how crazy you are too…" He paused, his eyes reflected the light from the window.

I wanted to kick him, to scream, to tell him to never touch me again but my body froze. I couldn't move, and perhaps I had really ruined his life like I had everyone else's…as the doubt sunk in, Dale continued.

"You really scared me running away like that. I don't actually think you wanted to run away. Maybe you're being too sensitive about all of this? Maybe you're feeling bad because it's all your fault for looking at me the way you did?"

I lie there as still as I could. I wondered why I had ever done this. Why I was the worst person on the planet. I made everyone leave. And the words escaped me.

"If you touch me again, I will tell." My own voice sounded unfamiliar. It came from deep within and escaped me. I expected Dale to be angry, to lash out at me. To hit me. But instead, he held his hands up to his head and began to sob. I sat slightly confused. I had never seen him cry before. Maybe he was opening up to me? Had I really caused all of this to happen? Was I wrong? I needed to be strong. I needed to figure this out.

Dale wiped his face and sniffled. "People will be so disappointed in what you've done with me. I can't believe you think this is my fault. They won't want you anymore, once they know…and I… I hate that for you." My heart tore away from my mind- the things that I had known were so wrong were now questionable to me. I couldn't even begin to imagine how terrible people would think I was. I ruined his entire life. I ruined my entire life. Then I made him cry, this person who said he only tried to save me.

"I'm sorry," I whispered. And just like that- I let him back in because I truly believed I was the worst person on the planet. I couldn't be exposed and let everyone know what I had done. Maybe I really was crazy. Each day it felt more true.

Dale didn't touch me at all that week. He hardly looked at me. I found myself wishing things were right again. That I could be happy with the make do father I had. I began to feel as though it were over, and I tried to focus on moving past it as if it had never even happened to me.

CHAPTER TWENTY-THREE

Weeks passed, as winter faded into spring it soon turned into pollen season and humidity spread just as quickly. Spring also brought rain. Nothing changed the way I wanted it to. It was like an endless loop, waking up and reliving the nightmare every day. I faded away too. The green sprouts that lined the trees were refreshing, almost as if the entire world got a second chance. I waited patiently for mine. I did as I was supposed to, no more breaking rules. Somehow believing that if I did everything right it would make me a better person. Sometimes when I felt tempted, I rubbed the scar on my leg that marked the memories of Ima and Harvey and all of their cats. I shuffled back and forth to classes and meals. I kept my eyes down and stayed away from everyone. I never found Susan, I never really looked. In some way I knew the moment I saw her I would break and I might not ever be able to pretend things were okay again. It was just me again, alone in the world.

I walked along the path from the dining room. It had been my turn to help clean in the kitchen. My dress was soaking wet with dish water, and I shivered as the sun began to set. I pulled my jacket tighter to me. It felt like someone was trailing behind me. I whipped around, confused when I didn't see anyone. Just as I faced forward again, Susan popped up beside me.

"Gotcha! Bunny! You should have seen your face."

Susan's laughter sparked a light in me that had been broken for quite some time. Her voice sounded as if the world could be a happy place again. She had that natural ability to just be, and I wanted that so ruthlessly.

I smiled to see my old friend. Dale made sure we stayed separate. He knew how close I was to breaking, so he threatened to take me away where I would never see anyone I loved again if I continued to be her friend. Over the past few months, I stayed away from her, purposely dodging her in the halls and eating lunch alone. I reached out for her and as we hugged, I found myself falling into Susan's arms crying, nearly toppling us both to the ground.

"Are you okay?" Susan asked, glancing at her friends who waited up ahead. I shook my head no, instantly cursing myself for being so pathetic.

I pulled away from Susan, ready to flee. But Susan gestured for her friends to go on without her. She reached her hand out to me, like old times, and I held on. For a few minutes, with the sound of the crickets surrounding us, we just walked in silence, as if time didn't change a thing.

"I just wish we could go back to when we were little. With Mara and her rules... I wouldn't hate it so much. I would have loved to stay in that house with you."

My crushed voice broke the silence.

"Well Bunny, the real treasures were the memories we made. Like when we ran away!"

"I almost died in that tree, Susan!"

"Ah, yes that was my fondest memory."

Together we laughed, letting go months of tension between us with each gurgle in our stomachs.

The laughter had sparked something inside of me—feelings? I didn't think it was possible to feel happiness again. For so long I made myself feel nothing at all. It was like something inside me clicked back into place. The part of me that was broken. I had an urge to release all of those evil things inside of me, but as I opened my mouth, Susan nudged me. I followed Susan's pointed finger up to the starlit sky. We both just stared into it. Anything was possible when you remember how small and insignificant you are in this world.

"Bonnie, you were the one who stopped being my friend? I've barely even seen you since we got back?" The look of puzzlement crossed her face. She stopped walking and peered intently at me.

"I miss those days too but it's like we were the best friends and then I run away with you and then you just abandon me whenever you want to."

"I have to take credit for that and I'm sorry." I avoided eye contact.

"You mean blame?" Susan smirked.

"Yes. It was me but… but…if only you knew…" I muttered.

"Knew what? What have you been keeping from me? Like really. Why do you avoid me like this… it's really confusing. What is really happening?" I froze and stared into her eyes… it was rare to see Susan so frustrated but she ranted on,

"It's like you're not even the same person! Say something! I don't understand." But Susan stopped and paused for a moment…

"That's why. I knew I couldn't keep it from you if you… if you asked me. I've kept it from everyone even myself. Something bad has happened. I've done something terrible," I whispered, glancing around. Fireflies lit all around us or perhaps it was my vision fading away.

"Keep what? Bonnie?" Susan sounded like a concerned mother. She even used my real name and shot me another quizzical look.

I paused— Should I? I opened my mouth again and took a deep breath. The chilly night air settled deep down into my lungs until it burned.

We reached a bench under the trees. After all the years of not being able to find the words, I began to talk about my experiences in the Aldrich cottage, the experience that had become my truth. My words flowed and I could hear them. It was as if I was the observer and I had somehow separated myself from the things that happened to me in the darkness. I had separated myself from the lonely little girl who only ever wanted love. And when I stopped, I thought I would cry. I thought finally I would feel a sense of relief. But I felt even more numb and horrified than before. It was like, even though the words were spoken, my body continued to hold in the pain, like thousands of knives and secrets I kept jabbed inside for so many years.

I hid my face in my hands when Susan patted me. I feared she would never speak to me again. When I finally got the nerve to look at her face, tears welled up in her eyes. She breathed heavily and clenched her fists.

"We have to do something," she said with murderous eyes.

"Susan, I don't know what to do… please don't tell. Pinky promise me."

"Promise you what?"

"You can't tell, please. Please Susan. I don't know what I'd do." I paused and pulled at my shirt collar. "What he would do."

Susan closed her eyes and, almost as though she was meditating, slowed her breathing. An overflow of salty tears trickled down her cheeks and neck, and even right down into her shirt.

"Bunny, oh, Bunny." Susan just sat there, under the stars and cried for me.

"You were just a little girl… A little girl. I hope you know that."

I nodded, truly appreciating her but nothing could erase the intense amount of humiliation. She reached her pinky out to me, and we linked them together.

CHAPTER TWENTY-FOUR

On the last day of 7th grade, I met with Susan at the Macdonald Cottage. She made me promise that I would tell someone by the end of that day and I was out of time. She looked at me with pity in her eyes. Even though we felt so much more "grown up," that afternoon we took a time machine back to the days of being little children. Adrenaline pumped through me while we climbed the rooftops again and ditched church. We could maneuver the steep roof standing straight up. We scuffed our knees and the wind whipped through and tangled our hair. It was like I could forget about all of the hurt when we were together breaking the rules. From the edge, the grass beneath us became a delicious blur. The clouds above whisked by, showing the blue amid the whimsy cotton clouds. It was funny how time worked- how years ago we believed we could see the world spinning above us. That day we were reminded that if we focused on what was right in front of us, in that moment, whatever we had would be enough. I wanted to stay in the moment and never tell. I was certain nobody would believe me. I often went back to it. As if in a dream-like state, remembering those last precious moments I had with Susan.

"It's time," Susan said, checking her watch. She nodded towards the door. We could see people trickling back from youth group. It was our plan to tell Mara first. If Mara could believe it then anybody else on that campus could.

As we stepped inside, the smell that met my nose about made me cry. It was a home smell that I had long forgotten, of a time when I still had my childhood. But there were so many people. Chatter, conversations, and I felt so out of place. Unfamiliar faces that lived in the same home I had once lived in. It was no longer safe. The smell reminded me of safety, but the noise made my head spin. I had a burning sensation in my stomach.

"Just who I was looking for." Mara chuckled and then she saw me.

"Bonnie, my heavens. Boy have you grown, how are you?"

I nodded my head at her while smiling.

"Good," I whispered.

"Does trouble still follow you girls wherever you go?" Mara smiled and it was the first genuine smile I ever noticed from her. Perhaps all those years ago I had villainized her to make up for my mother abandoning me.

"Like the rain it does!" Susan laughed and lowered her voice. "Mara, we kind of need to talk to you though. It's something important." She glanced around at all of the girls loudly fighting over popcorn.

"Step inside my room. And Susan- no chocolate games." She pointed her finger at Susan with that same smile. I took a deep breath, and followed them inside. I remembered all of the times I cheered Susan on while she stole us chocolates from this very room. I wanted to smile at the memory, but my thought blurred. Every nerve in my body was screaming. Could this really be it? The first step I had to take to get to freedom? I knew with Susan it would happen the way she made everything happen. We made it, and there we were inside of Mara's bedroom. Chocolate and mint and perfume flooded my nose. Susan trusted Mara and I trusted Susan. I clenched tighter and looked up at Mara. I was ready.

"Girls, what is this about? You're making me nervous that something bad happened..." Mara questioned us, but I didn't get to answer. Instead of words, vomit flowed out of my mouth uncontrollably all over my shirt. Onto the floor. All over Mara's shag rug and our shoes. Mara shrieked, Susan's eyes grew wide, and I just froze as sweat flooded my face.

"I'm not well." The commotion that followed was blurry. I was so sick I couldn't focus on anything. Not the mess on the floor, or Mara's questions. Not even Susan nudging me to see if I was okay.

I awoke inside of a medical room. There were little beeps that tracked my heart. I watched it rise up and down for a minute. Then I remembered vomiting all over Mara's bedroom. Embarrassment filled my entire body. Once again, I had sabotaged myself just when I was about to reach freedom. I blinked my eyes a few times and looked over to my right, hoping Susan would be there. But it wasn't Susan and it wasn't Mara. It was Dale. Black dots crept into my vision. I felt as if I were shrinking.

"There you are. You had everyone worried." His voice made me alert.

I looked for signs of betrayal in his dark eyes. But the whole day at the hospital, I got nothing. Dale was anything but mean to me. He brought me my favorite lemonade, and talked to me in his church voice. I wavered in and out of sleep but my entire body felt heavy. Almost as if I couldn't even lift my feet.

"They're running tests to see what is going on with you," Dale said, reaching over to pat my hand. I flinched before he even touched me. I spent the rest of the day sleeping to avoid him. My body felt too heavy to lift up. There was a sour feeling in my stomach that I couldn't shake. I still didn't feel quite right, something was off. The only comfort I had was lying still with my eyes closed. But even then, it felt like I was floating, and couldn't find solid ground.

A nurse came in to give me nausea medicine. "This is probably making you drowsy too," she said as I swallowed it.

The nurse looked over at Dale. "Are you her father?"

She asked with her hands on her hips and her lips pulled up slightly.

"Yes. House father- she's at Hawthorne." He answered. It was his way of saying that I had nobody that cared about me. It was also the first time someone admitted I have a father. The idea of it threw me into another bout of throwing up. The nurse calmly grabbed a bucket and patted my head. Dale just stared on. I sensed he was nervous when the nurse was around.

I stared at the nurse and pleaded with my eyes that she make him leave. But apparently, she wasn't a mind reader.

"Okay. Well, I hate to discuss this in front of you, but you're the only person she has on the list right now."

I didn't understand where she was going. Did I have cancer? Was this my last day to be alive? A brain tumor? I was dying. I had to be. I was certain of it.

She turned back to me. "Bonnie... is there any chance you could be pregnant?"

I stared at her and then I stared at him. For the first time in my life Dale stayed silent, his eyes shifted around the room.

"Are you sexually active?" The nurse tried again, this time she reached for me.

"Darling we just need to know." I shook my head no vigorously. It wasn't a fair thing to say. I wasn't by choice.

Dale sat up closer in his seat, he leaned in and spoke quietly. "Bonnie... if that's what is happening. That you've been with *boys* you need to speak up." He emphasized boys.

He chuckled a little and looked at the nurse. "You know how it is when you're young,"

The nurse patted my arm again. "It's okay, darling. We will figure this out. Sir, do you mind stepping outside for a moment?"

"Sure. Sure thing. I'm sure it's just a teenager kind of thing you know... to be young and wild again." He leaned down to me. "Tell the nice nurse the truth, Bonnie." But his voice was no longer chipper. It was threatening. It sounded more like tell the nurse the truth and I will kill you.

Once the door closed behind him, the nurse pulled something out of the drawer. "You don't have to talk about it if you don't want to. It's normal to be curious about sex at your age." The nurse's voice was sweet and understanding. The kind of voice you imagine your mother to have. I wanted to tell her but knew Dale was just outside of the door. If he were alone with me in this room, who knew what he could do. I hadn't been curious about sex, and I hadn't known I was sexually active until now. It never registered to me that the things Dale did to me over the years had progressed to sex.

"Go on in the bathroom. Get a little urine in here... once we test this, we can find out within two hours if you're pregnant."

Everything blurred even more. I took the pregnancy kit from her and went inside the bathroom. I cried to myself holding on to the tiny cup. How many times had I watched Mama do this at her appointment? How could I have been so foolish to not realize I could get pregnant. *Pregnant- me?* The idea seemed more bizarre than puking on Mara's rug. I couldn't have a child- I was just barely a teenager. I took the stupid test and put some urine inside of it. I handed it back to her and climbed back into bed. The medicine had made me drowsy.

"Try to get some rest," she called out to me and I could hear her talk with Dale briefly in the hall.

I closed my eyes when he re-entered. I was angrier than I had ever been and hoped we could avoid a conversation. But he cleared his throat until I opened my eyes.

"Now what?" I asked angrily, crossing my arms over my chest.

He glanced around the room again and sat down in his chair... "What did you tell her? That sounds like the better question right now." He demanded, his voice growing in intensity.

Chill bumps shot up my arms and down my legs.

"Nothing. I told her noth—" I began, but he pounded his fist on the wooden side table and stood up. I jumped backwards, wishing my door had remained open.

"Nothing," I said again.

Dale sat back down and leaned in close to me. I could smell garlic on his breath and it made me want to throw up all over again.

"You put my life in jeopardy, and you better not say another word. Got it? Not a single word." He growled. I considered that it was more-so my life in jeopardy right now but I was too busy trying not to throw up to say anything. He stepped towards me and droplets of spit shot out from his mouth like a thunderstorm. He reached over and took my arm. He squeezed it so tightly when I tried to pull away, I felt my skin rubbing off.

"You told her, I know you did. I saw the way she looked when she came out there… nobody will believe you," he roared at me just higher than a whisper. I was certain he would choke me to death right there in that hospital bed. I tried to look at him, to see through him… anything to make it stop.

He pinched my arm even more tightly and pulled me closer to him. "Don't say a single word… or else." He pulled even tighter. Pain surged through my arm and shot into my shoulder. I stared at the grip on my arm. In that moment I realized for the first time that no matter how much pain I endured, Dale could never take over my mind. I stayed still as he twisted and squeezed my arm until it was numb. I don't know how long he did that to me. I just remember once he let go, I had dried tear marks caked to my cheeks. The start of bruises lined the underside of my arm like soldiers in camouflaged places nobody could see. Later I would laugh at myself for actually thinking that was the worst of what was to come.

Two hours later, the nurse reappeared with a doctor. I could hear the echoes from the doctor and the nurse from behind the flimsy door. Their voices faded in and out, and suddenly my ears alert like a rabbit I heard the words "teen pregnancy." My head spun out of control. They had to be talking about someone else. It couldn't be me. I buried my face into the crunchy blanket and tears of hopelessness flowed down my cheeks. How had I become just like my mother? I would have rather died.

CHAPTER TWENTY-FIVE

In my thirteen-year-old mind I was more upset that Susan broke her pinky promise at first. Then I realized how ridiculous that sounded on a scale of things. I had a baby living inside of me. Oh, and my secret was out there alright. The most surprising part was that it didn't happen like I imagined. I imagined when my secret was exposed something colossal would explode. That it would be the best and worst day of my life. A magic fairy would swoop in and everything would be solved with the flick of her wand. Even though there were so many times that I almost told, the one thing that held me back rang true. That nobody would believe me.

Susan told Mara that same day I threw up on her rug. I don't know what words she used and I don't know what Mara said back to her. All I know is after we left the hospital, I was sitting inside of an office and there were a lot of adults whispering. When Dale got there, I melted into the chair. He had his singsong voice and smoothed back hair. He didn't even look at me. I thought I would never have to see him again. Wasn't the baby proof of what he did?

"Oh hey there, Dale, come on in- close the door."

A group of them went inside. They went inside to discuss how Dale had molested me since I was 11 years old. From what Susan told them they knew it had been happening for years and they still were smiling at him. My stomach churned. It took everything in me not to throw up lately.

Voices raised inside of the room. I remember thinking I shouldn't be there. I needed someone to protect me. The secretary glared at me from across the room. As if I really were the one who caused all of this to happen. Me, a thirteen-year-old girl, and not the grown man inside the office. That I was morally in the wrong and he was the noble one.

"Do you know what could happen? If this were to get out? We could lose state funding, be closed down."

So, they did believe me... hope filled my chest. Would my nightmare finally be over?

I never had to explain myself again. Perhaps he would be taken to jail and this could all be put behind me. Well then there was the baby but I didn't want to think about that. I hated to think that parts of that monster were living inside of me. I looked away from the secretary who peeped at me from underneath her glasses. The way she looked at me was gut-wrenching. It was that same look Ma-maw gave to my mother. Instead, I stared at the floor. The same floor Mama walked on to abandon us. As they sat in the same room, I sat in with Susan for the first day here. Time changed so many things, but then everything seemed to be the same. The same rooms, the same people, the same nightmares but I wasn't the same little girl. I would never be the same. At that time the shame was so immense I wanted to hide inside of my broken soul. Minutes passed, and passed. I watched the hands on the clock tick by slowly. I fiddled my thumbs; I did everything I could to not run from the room. But then they called out to me and for a moment I imagined being free. But when the meeting ended and Dale came out, he still carried a cocky smile across his lips, and it made me want to throw up all over again.

Not one of the men in the meeting would make eye contact with me. Not the president, the director, nor the guidance counselor. It was as if I were discarded, trash. Once again, I had cooties. I stayed in my seat for a moment and Dale walked up to me.

"Let's go, hurry up."

"But... I don't want... I don't want to," I whispered.

He turned around to face the president of Hawthorne. He looked at both of us disapprovingly and waved me on. The secretary cleared her throat but continued to write in her notebook. They weren't going to save me. I stood and followed Dale outside. Because what else was I really supposed to do? I replayed that moment over and over again and, if I could go back, I would have run.

I had never been in the car with Dale before. Until that day- our relationship only existed in the darkness. Even though I felt older, I could barely see out of the windshield. I put my hand across my stomach still not believing there was an actual— live creature in there. My legs shook as we sped down the bumpy brick roads. I looked back at Hawthorne in the mirror. Where was he taking me? Dale was angry, but he was also happy. I couldn't read him exactly and I didn't have enough mind space to figure it out. Everything inside of me was screaming. The sunshine was bright but I stared right into it and I wondered if it would be the last time I ever felt that kind of warmth.

CHAPTER TWENTY-SIX

For hours we drove in silence. At times Dale turned the radio on just low enough for it to be more annoying than anything. I strained to hear the words, but could tell it was Elvis. I busied myself by reading signs of each town we passed through. I fidgeted with the fray on my pants.

I liked it better when Dale was quiet. Sometimes his voice brought me back into the darkness, afraid and exposed.

The roads narrowed, with no shoulder and one lane roads, through the straight and curvy sections. The blinding rays of sunshine came right through the windshield of the old green Datsun. By this point I was convinced he was taking me somewhere to die. His hands traced the steering wheel and shook slightly. His listless eyes stayed focused on the road and the rear-view mirrors. Finally, we slowed.

He tried to put the car in park two times but accidentally put it in neutral. We sat on a rural road with 3 old buildings. It was creepy. The rest of the street was lined with corn. The brick building looked as if it would collapse at any moment. From the front there were two large windows, the white frame cracked and faded. *Where was the door?*

I turned back to face Dale and scooted in a little closer, trying to read his face. A drip of sweat rolled down his temple, he looked like I had when I gave my first speech in front of the entire 5th grade class. His voice came out weak, and his eyes darted around as he surveyed the parking lot. He had manipulated me for so long, for a moment I felt sorry for him. How could I have told? Was his life ruined? Would the police be here at any moment to grab him? So I mustered up the courage to speak,

"What are we doing here?" I pulled the lock button up to release it. I considered bolting into the tall corn that rested beside the car. I didn't know how to deal with my own nerves, so seeing Dale like this left me feeling helpless. Dale stared at me. His mouth was smiling but his eyes were nervous. And then I saw a shape from the side moving closer. The movement and flowing dress snapping in the wind caught my eye. As I turned, the whole world slowed as my heart rate rocketed.

I hadn't seen Mama in years.

Holding Mama's hand was a little girl. The sight of them together burned a trail of fire in my chest. I instantly sunk in the seat, my face growing red. I hatefully looked at Dale. But I was met with relief. Was I finally going home?

Dale waited until my mother disappeared inside of the building. He took a deep breath and stood from the car, leaving me on the seat beneath him. Then he leaned down with a child-like smile. "You're going to get married." He grinned.

Married. To who?

Everything inside of my entire body told me to run!

Run!

I refused to get out, but my body moved when he told me to follow him inside for the third time. I didn't want to move. My head was spinning. The crunching of the grass under my feet was enough to make black dots blur my vision. I had always planned to get married one day. I pictured Susan's drawings from when we were little. We had once imagined our husbands as princes. I glanced down at my old faded jean shorts and polka dot purple shirt. No pearl necklace and no long veil made of lace. Where was my beautiful gown? I didn't know how to connect the dots between my racing heart, stomachache, and the dizziness that made my knees weak. Who would I be getting married to?

We entered the door on the side of the building. It smelled of old people and sour cream and onion chips. I wondered if the building didn't have front doors, to keep people from running away. I couldn't run. The adults in the room shifted their gaze from me to him. They responded with slight, unwelcome greetings and looked away again. Like this was another old day of work for them. I pleaded with my eyes to make it stop. Nobody asked me what I wanted. I glanced around desperately looking for my prince, or even a frog. But all that stood next to me was Dale. His height three times the size of me, his hairline receding, and barely touching his wide forehead. His fuzzy beard trickled down across his face. He was a man. A grown man and I was still a child. They didn't ask my age. There was no preacher, no fancy flowers. Just the sound of Dale's hot breath and a kind of quiet that made my body cringe. The secret quiet when everyone sees something wrong but nobody is brave enough to stop it. I didn't like being this close to him in public, it set fire to my body. Mama didn't acknowledge me. I held tightly to the baby in my stomach to protect it from the evil in the room. I inhaled a deep breath and waited. The room spun out of control. If only Mama would run up to me with open arms and hug me. Pull me in and save me from this nightmare- give me just one or two teardrops. But nothing, she did nothing. She had the same blank face the day she dropped us off at Hawthorne. Full of relief. When the time came, Mama pulled my birth certificate out of her purse so quickly it nearly ripped in half. I inched away from Dale. My skin felt as if I laid out frying in the sun for three days on end. My heart raced and I tried to gather air in my lungs. Was this really happening or had I finally lost it? I focused on my younger sister, trying to figure out what made her the chosen one. Was she perfect? Was she good? Did she make Mama laugh? Was she everything I wasn't? I wanted to shout no, please someone save me. But the words, like so many times before, never came. I swallowed the growing frog inside of my throat- I hated myself in that moment as much and more than I ever had before. I was a stupid girl who couldn't do anything right.

Mama's hand held the pen, for a moment poised over the document. One signature and I wouldn't be her problem anymore. I stood there, blanched white from terror. Mama clenched the pen as she prepared to sign and paused. She looked up at me for the first time and she studied the grown man next to me. My eyes pleaded with her to make a decision that a mother should. But she hastily scribbled across the paper.

Then it was done. For the first time in my life, Mama showed up. She signed the papers quickly, as if she was selling an old car that she no longer wanted to be attached to. She staggered out of the room, unable to face me. I leaned back and sighed. Normal mothers don't let their daughters marry monsters.

I watched as Mama once again faded away, her heels clicking, pulling another little girl along her side. The girl ran fast just to keep up. She was quiet just as Mama had trained her to be. My little sister turned and faced me as if she was calling out for me, but they were gone. The heavy door pounded shut behind them. I gave up my last breath of hope for Mama as she turned and walked away from me, leaving me with him. The images continued to repeat in my mind, even on the long ride back. I said nothing, I barely moved. On repeat, a bad nightmare, but I was in the car awake. I was too scared to look at Dale, afraid of what he might do to me if he saw the terror in my eyes.

CHAPTER TWENTY-SEVEN

When a person gives up hope, it is similar to forfeiting war. Inside you feel nothing because things have been disintegrating around you for so long that all that is left is terror. I only had the clothes on my back and suddenly I was expected to be a house wife. At thirteen I should have been having the time of my life. A heaviness settled inside of me and hadn't left. I was married. I was married to Dale. There were literally no limits to what he could do to me now. I was old enough to get married but not old enough to get a divorce. I wasn't old enough to smoke cigarettes or drink but I was having a baby. I was scared because there was a baby growing inside me and I had no idea how it would come out.

When we pulled up to a green house, Dale grinned at me. "Welcome home, my wife."

His words repeated in my head and I wanted to slap him across the face. That was his way of expressing that he had won the battle. There was no stopping him. So I sat there and stared at the house, wishing I could set fire to it with my eyes. He continued…

"My sister lives here. We're going to stay awhile." I didn't look at him. I let the words pass through me. But when he said sister, I pictured little Emma and for the first time that day, I felt hopeful. Hopeful that this woman would see that I was a child and save me when nobody else did.

"No funny business… you got it?" Dale smacked the dash of his car and licked his lips.

I nodded my head and opened the car door. Crickets chirped and the tall corn beside us rustled in the wind. I could see so many stars filling the night sky that, for a moment, I admired the beauty until Dale shoved my back.

We walked inside. His sister sat in a recliner with a bowl of chips on one leg and an ashtray on the other. She took one long drag on her cigarette, eyed me from head to toe, and chuckled.

"You went through all of this- for her?"

As if somehow, Dale sacrificed so much to kidnap me. Instantly she became an enemy. I read her bad aura before the front door was even closed. Their mother must have bred pure evil.

"A lot younger than your last wife." She chuckled again.

I knew it right then. My chance at being saved slid right out the window with her cigarette smoke. The house was dirty and smelled stale and each day passed as slow as the mold that grew along the walls. Dale's definition of marriage was different. He instead used the word "marriage" to refer to the legal aspect of me making a contract with the state to remain united with him until death. I was surprised Jackie made it out alive.

Now I was his.

I didn't have a choice, and I never did.

Wives were expected to clean house. Day after day, I swept and did the dishes. Mopped the floors and scrubbed the mold off of the walls. I began slowly to teach myself to cook as Ima once had.

Wives were expected to serve their husbands. I made sure Dale's food was prepared at morning and at night. I crocheted baby blankets and little booties for his or her feet. I sang to the baby growing inside me. I liked that I was never completely alone.

Wives have sex with their husbands, whether they enjoy it or not. I continued to endure countless nights of pure hell. I was so good at going away in my mind- it didn't even physically hurt anymore. That's when I wondered if I were even alive.

Wives were to cook for their husband. I gagged as I cut fat off raw chicken. I stole corn from the field outside, and tried to be creative with what little food Dale brought home.

I was a child immediately expected to take on adult responsibilities like I never had. I was tethered to this green house before I had gained a sense of what I even wanted out of life. Everything changed for me that summer.

It wasn't until what would have been my first day of eighth grade that I realized just how many things I would never have again. *I actually missed my school uniform. The rainbow bottles and plants left behind in my window. The smell of the hallways on the first day of school. The plant from Rissy. Oh God, Rissy. Would I ever see her again? Did Susan think I died? What would they say to everyone?* I didn't understand it.

Nausea got somewhat better, but it never completely left. Over the months as my belly grew, Dale explained to me that the marriage went a long way toward legally turning children like me into adults. Children into adults? It didn't sit right. I had nothing left except one thing- books. I read every single thing I could get my hands on. That was the one nice thing Dale ever did for me— he brought me books.

From my books I learned that marriage should be a choice. For two people to bind together for all of time. But sometimes parents arranged marriage for their children. I thought of all of the other children like me, alone and afraid and robbed of their quintessential childhood experience and I felt sad for them. No more rooftop climbing or playing with dolls. No more taking risks like riding your bike a tad too fast on a gravel road, or running across the street with Susan while the cars rushed right towards us. Cooking, cleaning, and serving, oh and growing a whole human.

Dale made it clear to me that Hawthorne had agreed to let him resign. He wanted to insert that he still had control over leaving. The sad thing was that the school was more worried about protecting their money than saving my life. The school, my mother, my grandparents, everyone had failed me. It was so easy to believe that I wasn't worthy of love. And I did. So I curled up inside of myself and forfeited. I truly believed I deserved nothing more.

My feet were swollen, my stomach as big as a balloon- the skin underneath my shirt was rippled with pink and purple stripes. Like I had morphed into some kind of zebra. When I walked, there was immense pain on top of my pelvis. It literally felt as though a bowling ball was stuffed down my throat. The baby moved a lot and even though I thought I would never love something that I never gave permission to grow in my body, when I felt it move inside me, I felt a glimpse of hope. I knew right away that I loved that baby more than I loved myself. It was like my body absorbed every piece of the foreign DNA and the baby would forever be imprinted inside my heart. I wondered how, after having the baby, I could escape with it. It felt wrong to call my baby an it. And the last thing I ever wanted to do was to turn out like my mother. So instead, I called the baby my bean.

"Bean, you're up awfully early." I said to my stomach as I waddled to the bathroom in the middle of the night.

"Bean, you're awfully active tonight," I said as an aerobics class took place inside my uterus.

"Bean, I love you," I told it when I would cry because I was too tired to make dinner but I had to or else… But then he or she would kick to remind me they were there. I would get up and I would finish cooking dinner despite my swollen feet and tired body. I had to make it through to meet him or her.

The green house was a small house hidden in the cusp of the middle of nowhere. I didn't want to be a wife, but I forced myself to do as I was told. I often truly wondered what would happen to me if I didn't listen. As soon as he got a sense that I loved the baby, Dale had threatened abortion to me. He also tossed me across the room one night after drinking a half of a bottle of whiskey. I held my stomach tightly- not wanting anything to happen to the baby. I slept on the floor that night, tossing and turning, and replaying the day he married me over and over again in my mind. I wished I had shouted, said something—.

Can't you see I'm supposed to be a kid, Mama? But instead, I stood there, quietly fighting the nausea as Mama scribbled across the paper. I shook the memory from my mind. It had replayed constantly like a never-ending nightmare. I was so stupid, I couldn't even stand up for myself.

One week Dale brought me pregnancy books. It was his way of making up to me after he threatened to kill the baby he created inside of me. I read through each page believing that if I memorized it all then I would have to be a good mother. I had to have the mother gene that Mama was missing. But then I realized… I already knew how to take care of a baby.

I traced memories back to the baths I gave Emma in the sink. The times Mama was sleeping during breakfast and I cooked eggs for Emma when I could barely reach the stove. Or when Ralph's diaper became so full that he had a bumpy red rash up his behind. I made my own paste for him out of medicated cream and petroleum jelly. I knew the best way to rock Ralph when he screamed. I had helped raise them, but now it seemed so distant as if I were thinking of someone else. Who had I become?

Dale got home and found me reading the pregnancy and baby book. He took one look at me and sarcastically said, "Awe."

He walked closer to me and continued, "Bonnie, I know you are trying but being a mother is just beyond your understanding. I mean for God's sake, look at who you came from." He slapped my leg and squeezed it tightly. The words hurt but I no longer felt his touch. I blinked, and there were no tears, but my heart ached. I would be a good mom. I would.

By the time I could no longer see my feet, I wanted so badly for the pregnancy to be over. I could barely get out of bed without crying out in pain from the weight sitting on my pelvis. I could no longer reach to shave my legs or tie my shoes. It hurt to move. My feet swelled up three times the usual size. I no longer felt hungry, I was just tired. Tired of every single thing.

Dale's sister, Jody, was in some ways even more evil than he was. It was like no matter what I did to dance around her- she would find some way to create drama. If I cooked dinner, it was too spicy. If I made bread from scratch, it was too dense. If I scrubbed the floors until my knees bled, she would walk across them in her shoes after she collected the mail. I stood on my tippy toes to reach something, would ask her for help and instead, she would watch me and my big belly dangerously climb on the counter to get what I needed.

Dale left each day, but Jody never did. She just seemed to take up space in a room and veg out to television and watch me. It was no wonder her house had been growing mold before I moved in. Cleaning kept me sane and it gave me something to do. So each day, despite the pain, I woke and did chores. There was one phone in the living room. I had stared at it, longing to pick it up and call someone to rescue me. But I was so trained to believe that if I did something wrong, Dale could hurt *Bean*.

It was right in the living room where Jody usually sat all day stuffing her fat face with junk food. She ate so many delicious things in front of me, sometimes just the smell of a donut would make my mouth water like a dog's and send me into a pregnancy craving for anything sweet. But there was nothing sweet in the kitchen. Jody kept it all in her bedroom. Jody left once a month to collect money for disability. On that day usually Dale unplugged the phone and took it with him when he left. One morning, he forgot. For most of the morning I just sat there on the couch staring at it. Part of me was grateful that if I did go into labor at least I could call 911. But part of me knew it was a trick. One of Dale's ways of proving that I was a stupid girl. I was certain that if I picked it up, Dale would come flying in with petulance stamped on his face.

I exhaled my nerves and pulled the yellow phone up to my ear. The buttons rolled oddly in my hand.

It had been so long. The number however was fresh in my mind as if I called it yesterday. Less than one minute. That's how long it took me to recognize Mama's voice. Her voice momentarily stopped time, I grew clammy, my mouth dry. I had the phone pressed against my ear so tightly, sweat dripped down my ear.

"Hello?"

I placed my hands over my chest. Bliss tingled across my lips, my muscles tightened, and my heart pinged.

I started to respond, "Mama, it's me, Bonnie."

"Mammmaaa!" A child's voice echoed through the phone. I bit my tongue, my eyes widened. How had I forgotten?

"Jo, not now," Mama replied with the phone away from her mouth. Her voice, gentle, caring?

My blood rushed back to my head, but no tears came. It wasn't until I started to talk again, that the croak in my voice showed up. There was a kid at my grandparent's home with my mom. It took everything I had to fight back the tears that wanted so badly to break me completely. So instead of lashing out, I slowly put the brick wall back, piece by piece, until I mustered my voice back.

"I was hoping to talk to Ma-Maw…or Rissy."

"Rissy quit…and Ma isn't here."

"Rissy quit?"

"Yes. After she threw that fit with me… she never came back…"

I felt as though she left a lot of details out. But my heart longed for Rissy, and I wondered if I would ever see her again. It had to be Mama's fault she left. My nostrils flared. It seemed like the only thing Mama did was destroy things.

"Do they know?"

"Know what?" She asked.

"That you made me get married?" Tears spilled from my eyes and I sobbed.

"Bonnie, you wanted to be grown. Doing grown things. Well, the school told me everything. I thought if you married young maybe you would have a better chance than I did." I cried harder into the phone, not caring if she hated to hear me cry.

"Don't be such a crybaby. I swear, Bonnie, you're never happy. Running away, getting married, having a baby and all of this? This is why you needed to go. My good is never good enough for you."

Had I been the bad one this whole time? Was I not happy enough with what Mama had tried to offer?

I stepped back, the floor was rubbery beneath my feet. In that moment I let go of my mother. I let her drop to the floor with the phone. Her muffled voice faded.

The front door opened. My eyes widened. Heartbeat putters filled my ears. Dale stormed in. The door slammed. The house shook. His face was red. Another bad day, not another bad day. I crouched lower to the ground with my arms covering the baby.

"Get off the damn phone!" But I already was. It was still dangling from the base, nearly touching the floor. He slammed the phone back on the base and stepped towards me. His hand moved so quickly, a pain jolted through my body before I knew what even happened.

CHAPTER TWENTY-EIGHT

On the way to the hospital, each contraction that came made me shake uncontrollably. I held on to the side of the door until I could no longer feel my fingers. Nausea came and went in waves faster than I could breathe. I was going to die and never meet Bean, I was certain of it. Dale's mood had shifted. Anger faded away and he was jerky and anxious.

"You tell them you're eighteen."

His knuckles gripped the steering wheel and he leaned close to the windshield to look over at me. I couldn't think of anything I would rather hear less than Dale giving one of his speeches.

"But I'm not," I started but instead curled my toes under as another strike of pain hit.

"You're eighteen and we're married."

I closed my eyes and tried to focus on breathing.

He continued.

"You know after all I've done for you… you could at least just make things easy. Stop over-reacting. It just makes things more difficult that way."

I nodded my head just so he would shut up. Was he afraid? Would this be my chance to escape? The painful sensations in my abdomen and pressure on my pelvic area and butt made all my thoughts stop. I didn't care if I was 14 or dead. I just wanted the pain to stop. I didn't know it at the time, but child sexual abuse had become a public issue. Prior to that point in time, it had remained socially secretive. But Dale knew we looked suspicious, and he knew that if I were to be questioned, perhaps the baby would give me enough strength to break free for the both of us. I wished that were the case but years of manipulation had broken me.

"Do you have any marks where I hit you?"

I lifted my pants slightly to check. The spot where he pounded with his closed fist was still aching and a redness similar to that of a dying rose swirled across my thigh. He always chose places that weren't visible. He looked away from me and we made our way inside. Once again, I knew he wasn't sorry for what he had done. He only worried when there was a chance of being caught.

Dale made me refuse medication. He didn't want to bring any more attention to us. In the room, Dale was increasingly quiet, not because of guilt or worry for me but for the fear of being caught. Everything faded out of sight and nothing mattered more than getting my baby out. I didn't understand. That poor girl— she was just a kid having a baby. I look back and feel so sad for her. Perhaps I see her as someone else because it hurts so much to think of the physical pain and emotional abuse. But eventually my dark world shifted.

I held the little baby so lightly. Like he was an egg that could crack at any moment. My shaking arms had never felt anything so perfect. I was afraid I would break him. He was the smallest, wrinkliest and most cone headed baby I had ever seen. Nobody had warned me they came out like that. Not even my pregnancy book could have prepared me for labor. It was nothing comparable to any type of pain I had ever experienced before.

But when I looked down at my brand-new baby boy, there was no way to describe in words the feeling I got. For when we met eyes, he sang me every love song I had ever wanted to hear. He completed me.

"There you are, little bean," I gasped with tears in my eyes.

"Max, I will call him Max." I smiled and looked around the room. The doctors and nurses were busy and Dale said nothing as I named my son. It didn't matter. In that moment there was nothing that could take my smile away.

Until a few hours later, Jodi came barging through the hospital door. I held my sleeping son and looked up at her. She didn't even acknowledge me. Her eyes were icy blue and she surveyed the bed. Her eyes fixated on my baby. I hoped, just for once, she would give me praise, motherly love, anything.

But when Jodi saw the tears in my eyes, she bent down close to my face and snarled,

"You shouldn't have opened your legs if you weren't ready for a baby."

She snatched the baby from my arms and pressed her lips to his forehead.

I instantly felt torn because the human I grew inside of my body could be taken from me now. He was no longer safe in the womb. I lie alone in the bed with shooting pain from every part of my body and mind. Waiting for the moment to have my baby back in my arms.

At age fourteen, most girls were chasing boys, but I awoke with sore breasts, a stretched-out tummy and aching cramps. Nobody had warned me how hard breast feeding was. We were on the way home from the hospital. Each bump in the car sent shooting pain throughout my body. Outside we passed a field of cows.

"Now look, Bonnie fits right in over there." Dale had laughed. I looked down at my body and hated myself again. I thought my stomach would have shrunken back to its pre-pregnancy size. I didn't know I would still be blown up like a halfway deflated balloon.

Jodi chimed in, "She got herself into this." And she turned and looked at me. "Isn't that right? You made your bed— now you've gotta lie in it."

I learned how to escape them. I escaped to places in my mind. It was like when the two of them were together they brought out the very worst in each other. I explored my old fairy tales in my mind with Max next to me. I had something I was never letting go of. I would never abandon him the way my mother had with us. No matter what it took. No matter who I had to deal with.

Back at home things were different with the baby. I watched gratefully as some of the attention that had been focused on me faded away. At the same time, I never felt complete without Max in my arms. Jodi knew this and used every opportunity to hold him. She kept him close to her only shoving him towards me when he became frustratingly hungry, pooped or spit up. I resumed cleaning and cooking before my uterus even had time to shrink and heal. Blood left my body in clots and I walked in a waddle to avoid the pain. My body felt loose and sore and I felt sad and tired and so very alone.

Every Wednesday I was expected to clean around Jodi's bear collection. Porcelain, stuffed, button eyed, big and small. She collected bears of all types. They lined the shelves in the living room. Inviting smiles on each one and I longed to touch them. To squeeze one. But nobody was allowed. It seemed rather weird to me that a grown woman would be so amused by a collection of stuffed toys. It was hard not to while dusting around them. Especially when I still longed for toys to play with and there they sat with cute smiling faces- practically calling me over to them. She made something like a fluffy teddy bear that was usually so comforting distant and cruel.

Over the next few months, when Jodi watched me, I instantly felt on edge. My hands would shake and I couldn't get Max to fully latch. My breasts had become cracked spores that once belonged to me but were now just to keep Max full. They grew larger and plump. I lie across the bed crying while I fed Max. His hungry lips shot pain all the way down to my toes. Tears filled my eyes each time I fed him, the pain felt as though glass was dispersing through my nipples.

I liked to watch Max grow. His first smile made me feel so happy I didn't want him to ever smile at anyone else. He made me different, stronger. I thought maybe I was worthy of love because my own body was keeping a human alive.

When I tried to stand up for myself, they found another flaw to focus on to pull me back down. It was a constant game, like waves in the ocean, pulling me in deeper and deeper until there wasn't much fight in me left. I grew very emotional and confused in the months following his birth. I had trouble focusing and, in each moment, I was terrified he would stop breathing. I questioned my own thoughts. I would run over to Max and place my finger under his nose just so I could feel the warm air escape his nostrils. I tried my best for him, but it never felt like enough. Sometimes his cry was the only reason I got out of bed.

The days of being a mother and housemaid and personal chef for Jodi all blurred into a clump of losing myself. After Max turned one, I realized I was never returning to school, and it nearly broke me. I considered escaping many times, but I wasn't of legal age to apply for a divorce. Jodi never left me and Max together for long. She was always lurking in the shadows, watching me. When Jodi had guests over, I was made to stay behind closed doors. I would sit there on the floor with my legs crossed. My ear perched against the door. I listened to Jodi ooh and ah over my baby with friends as I sobbed into my hands. Each time the doorbell rang, I imagined grabbing Max and running. Tears dripped down my face as I listened to Jodi tell Marge that I was an awful mother. An orphan that Dale had saved. *Saved?* I shuddered. How could one family be so cruel?

"But look at my baby. My baby boy!" Jodi gleefully bragged. But he wasn't her baby and I knew I had to find a way out.

I just didn't know how to escape. It was like the more I wished to be free, the less motivated I was to leave. I had been trapped most of my life by this point. Even if the doors opened, I was a bird who had forgotten how to fly.

My days went on like this, not one any more significant from the other. Day after day I watched Max grow and purposely lost myself more and more. I cooked, I cleaned, and loved Max with all of my broken heart. I watched his little baby hands grabbing and inspecting every piece of anything he could. I memorized the mischievous smile on his face right before he threw a cup full of water at me. The beads of bath water on his forehead, and the way his body melted into mine when he was ready for bed. He was my everything.

As I became wiser of the situation, I began to realize that Dale planned this perfectly from the beginning. He worked in that particular place to control vulnerable children. He didn't save me, he trapped me. *How had I been so stupid?*

I had to pee so badly that I crossed my legs and wiggled around. I had been sent to my room while Jodi and Dale had a conversation. Max lie across my stomach. His eyes flickered in and out. His little hands reached for my face. I kept him as quiet as I could. I knew I needed to listen to this conversation.

My ears were perked and the urge to pee quickly left when I heard Jodi and Dale step out to the front porch to talk. I eased over to the window and slowly lifted. Just like Susan had taught me. The window shifted, heavy at first and then glided up. Quiet enough. I sank to the floor with Max heavy on my chest. I only had him to myself when they knew I couldn't escape. I smelled his freshly cleaned hair as they talked. I had an ability to hear things that I wasn't supposed to hear, better than most people. My childhood training had been good at preparing me for something after all.

"How many were there?" Jodi yelled. Dale spoke quietly. I couldn't hear him.

"What do you mean?" Jodi groveled. Her flat voice sent chills up my arms. This was something serious. I rocked my leg to keep Max from waking. The movement instantly lured him into a deeper sleep. I ducked low enough so I was concealed. My head awkwardly rested along the wall under the windowsill.

"What I mean… is that her mother gave permission. I didn't do anything wrong. She basically begged for me to marry her, Jodi."

I stilled and wondered if it was true. *Had it been my mother's idea all along?*

"I don't give a shit about her mother…what about the police? What about the others?" Jodi growled. I had never heard Jodi speak to Dale like this before.

"She was pregnant, I married her. They ain't charging me with anything."

"Statutory rape!"

"Marrying her prevented that." Dale's voice had a cockiness to it as he murmured. "Her mother wouldn't have known the difference."

"Well. You need to fix it. Hide any evidence. Get it together, and whatever you do, don't let her or them take our boy from us."

Jodi cracked the door back open, making me jump.

"Plus, if they know all the other documents were forged, it is going to be really hard to find another job."

What documents?

I scooted near the bed and lie across the floor. I held my breath. They knew it was wrong all along? I wasn't the only one. I was his secret. Dale's little secret was safe from the world, but not safe from him. He married me to avoid being arrested. Who marries a child to avoid being arrested? Someone sick? Someone cruel? How did that make any sense? How had I been so stupid not to see it? And my mother?

Oh, God. My mother.

Did she really believe this would be for the best?

Jodi came bursting through my door.

"Get off the damn floor." Max startled awake with a scream. She took him from me. She liked to be the one to comfort him after she made him cry. The door whipped shut behind her and I sunk back down to the floor even more alone than I had been before. My empty arms shook and I silently sobbed into my knees. What were they hiding from me?

For some reason, upon realizing Jodi and Dale were worried enough to have something to hide— my hope was restored. After being brainwashed and belittled for so long it was hard to know my own truth. I would be able to prove I was pregnant before we were married. I just didn't know how and I didn't have anyone that could help me.

I only had one chance to make it work. There was no way I would risk losing Max. So day after day, I did what I needed to. I kept planning and the years seemed to slip away right in front of my eyes. Max started crawling, walking, then running. I could barely keep up with him anymore. He spoke as quickly as he walked- with excellent pronunciation. My baby had turned into a little boy and I wasn't even an adult yet.

Some days I walked Max around the front yard. We looked for bugs together. Flipping rocks and moving leaves. Max had become quite obsessed with finding bugs- ants, roly-polies, caterpillars. I liked to think I was carrying on the love of Rissy's son, James. I just hoped that as he got older, he wouldn't put them in his pockets. I proudly grinned at his wondrous face as he pulled up a sweat bee on his finger to his eye level. It sat there, still as can be on his little finger as if it were his pet. His eyes glowed with excitement. I loved to see him grateful for the small things, finally another person who saw the world like me. We appreciated each type of life, no matter how small.

CHAPTER TWENTY-NINE

It was Max's fourth birthday. I wanted more than anything to make it a special day for him. Dale and Jodi controlled all the money and it was seldom that I got to go to the store on my own. But occasionally I would get to ride my old rusty bike four miles to the local grocery store. I made sure to get everything in line so I could go that morning. Jodi kept Max and sometimes he even cried when I left the house. I wondered what it would be like to leave your kids for a normal days' work, or to go out with friends. I held the small list in the palm of my hand the whole way to the store. I let the sunshine hit my face and the wind whip through my hair. I wore long sleeves to hide the bruises that lined my arms. I had made quite a lot of mistakes lately. I hoped I had enough money to cover baking a cake for Max. I had a recipe I had been saving for months that I ripped out of the newspaper. I was out of eggs and I needed sugar, flour, vanilla, and butter.

Jodi had requested lime soda and it used most of my budget. I was sweating as I carried all of the items up to the register. I had recounted the money in my hands over and over. Ten dollars wouldn't get me everything that I needed. The woman scanned the eggs, sugar, lime soda, and butter and tossed everything into a sack.

"That will be $12.36." She yawned from boredom. I twisted the two five-dollar bills inside of my hand wishing I could make them multiply. If I took any one of my ingredients off, I wouldn't be able to make Max a cake. This was part of their game. Control. Humiliation. Failure. Jodi had purposely sent me with not enough money because she knew I would put something back and not her soda. The bored woman stared at me and repeated herself. "That will be $12.36."

I looked back at my money then up to her. "I only have $10.00."

She stared at me with no emotion and glanced at the long line behind me. "What do you want to put back?" She did an exaggerated yawn.

I looked at the eggs, the sugar, the flour and the butter and I eyed Jodi's lime soda. The entire reason I came to the store. The man behind me cleared his throat. Before I could think another second, I pointed to the soda without making eye contact. The girl grabbed the glass bottle and tossed it to the side, re-tallied the price and as I handed her the money, I knew that I was gonna pay for it. My cheeks felt hot and I couldn't shake the feeling of dread.

When I arrived home, I purposely went into the side kitchen door. I took a deep breath and just ran inside with my bag. I could hear Max in the other room playing and heard the matches ignite from Jodi smoking. I pulled out the spaghetti meat I had prepared for dinner and boiled some noodles. As I did that, I measured out flour, sugar, butter, vanilla, and baking soda.

Max would have a cake for the first time.

Just as it began to lift in the oven and a wonderful cake fragrance filled the air, Jodi walked in. She opened the fridge and looked around.

"Where's my soda?"

I stood there for a moment, wondering what I should say. *I forgot it or they were all out or I put it back so I could bake my son a cake.* But nothing came out.

"You drank it, didn't you?" Jodi whipped around. It startled me enough to jump.

"Why you little…." She began but Max wondered in.

"Mama, what is that yummy smell?" He asked me with a wooden truck in his hand. I knelt down to him.

"I'm baking you a real birthday cake this year," I told him, smiling brightly despite the fact Jodi still glared at me.

"You're the best Mom!" Max said excitedly and I swear I watched Jodi turn red through the tears in my eyes.

"And you're the best bean in the whole world," I responded to him, and pulled him in tightly.

I checked the clock frequently to make sure I would have time to finish making dinner. The cake was almost done, the spaghetti meat was heated up, noodles ready, but I still had to make a salad. If anything would throw Dale into a tizzy that would be it. Coming home to a halfway prepared meal. No matter if it was his son's birthday.

I turned to face Jodi in the living room... I had grown so used to explaining my every move, it didn't even phase me.

"I'm running out to pluck some lettuce."

Jodi nodded at me and turned back to the television. Her silence meant she was brewing up ways in which she could take revenge for not having her soda.

"I want to help!" Max called behind me. Jodi stared at the program so I nodded, and hand gestured for him to follow. The moments alone with him were by far my favorite. By the time I reached the garden, Max was at my heels. I placed my hand on his back and breathed the fresh air with him. He was barefoot just like I was. It was another thing we both enjoyed together. The fresh earth beneath our feet. The garden was small, and I had struggled to keep it going with all of my other chores during the day. The lettuce had almost all turned into mush but, once I figured out it needed shade, I was able to pull an old fence over to protect it. I smiled when I saw our knobby, oddly shaped lettuce that was just as marvelous to Max. We both jumped up and down the first day we found our plants growing.

"We did it Max! We did it!" It had shown there was still hope.

It would also save a few dollars at the market and allow me to get other items we really needed. Max skipped ahead of me, heading straight to the lettuce. He loved the garden just as much as I did. It gave us our own sanctuary to escape to from the darkness of the home we lived in.

We pulled as much lettuce as we could and Max found a ripe tomato for us. This time I followed behind Max, carefully carrying our vegetables. I got so lost in the magic of our garden, I began to worry about the amount of time I had before Dale returned.

"Did you hear that?" Max called.

"It's just a bird, Max," I replied to him after surveying the area.

Nothing was out of place, but I saw a quick movement in the distance.

"Shoo!" I called to the feral cat who held a baby bird in his paw.

"Shoo!" Max copied as we raced towards the mangy cat. As we neared, the cat took off, leaving the bird in the deep grass.

"Don't step on him, Mama," Max said as he walked on tip toes. But just as we neared the flattened grass, the tiny, homely bird hopped towards us. He had large black eyes and stared up at us. He had little downy feathers sporadically growing on his back, a short tail and a few little wing feathers sticking out.

"Max don't touch— "I began, but Max already had the baby bird cupped in his hands and holding it closely to his chest.

"We have to save it, Mama." My heart swelled— I was raising a good human. It peeped again and Max giggled. Then the baby bird extended his mouth widely and waited.

"What's he doing, Mama?" Max asked curiously.

"He's hungry, Max. Why don't you look for some worms over where the garden is?" I dropped the lettuce and tomato into my apron pocket and scooped the baby bird carefully from his hands. The bird just stared at me— his mouth still extended.

"You're a brave little guy," I whispered to him. While Max dug for worms, I looked for a makeshift shelter for the bird.

"Let's call him Beaky," Max said after proudly feeding his new little pet a few insects that he collected. I smiled- we had worked hard to save little Beaky.

"This is the bestest birthday ever." Max giggled excitedly. I wanted to hug him, pull him into my arms and remember that moment forever.

But I heard the sound of Dale's car.

"Dinner, oh dinner- no, no, no." I turned and ran- motioning Max to follow me inside. We raced in and began washing our hands.

I ran water over it and threw the lettuce into a bowl I had just started chopping the tomatoes when I realized the noodles had sat so long, they were mushed together in the colander. I raced to get every-thing together as quickly as I could. Instantly I tensed as I heard the door open. The very presence of Dale in the home changed everything. Especially when dinner wasn't prepared. I had made this mistake many times before and the outcome was never good.

"Max, please go to your room," I whispered, ushering him out of the kitchen.

A shadow appeared over me within minutes, and I turned to face him. Dale had that look on his face. The one where nothing I did or said mattered. It had taught me to fear the silence worse than when he talked. It was like the air evaporated, suddenly hard to breathe- my mouth was completely dry, so I licked my lips.

"Can't even cook on time? I work all day to care for you and this is your thanks?"

Let it go through me and not destroy me, face it, don't fear it.

I clenched my muscles and felt the veins in my neck stand guard.

Dale smacked me across the face. Not as hard as he could have- but the tingle was still the same- burning. Pain that I no longer felt on the outside- instead it was stuck inside of me. Wondering around in there with everything else that was already lost and broken.

Just as Dale raised his hand again, I caught Max out of the corner of my eye. He stood in the kitchen, his body tensed up, afraid. His eyes were wide and I couldn't take my eyes off of the way his face pulled together as he watched. I didn't feel it, I just couldn't take my eyes off of Max. I stepped backwards, willing Max away, hoping he would turn and run and never have to see the things I let happen to me.

"Please don't do that. Please," Max mumbled as he took a step closer. Dale ignored his son. But still, little Max took another step. I glared at my sweet little boy and shook my head no- pleaded with my eyes for him to go back to his room.

"She was just helping Beaky!" Max shouted.

A look of confusion shot across Dale's face. He paused and turned to face Max.

His face a bright red, his eyes squinted.

I tried to draw the attention back to myself. "But it will be ready soon," I called, reaching out for his hand, pulling his anger back to me.

Dale shoved my hand away and bent down in front of Max. "Beaky? Who the hell is Beaky?" He growled at his son.

"Come on, I'll show you!"

"Max, no," I whispered but it was too late.

They disappeared out the back door. I quickly continued to re-make the noodles. I sighed relief as Max came back inside unharmed.

"Go to your room, please, Max," I called to him. This time he took the warning and headed back to his room, tears already forming in his eyes.

Dale didn't immediately come back inside. Grateful, I was able to have everything ready once he did. I leaned on the counter and let out a deep sigh.

I felt him come up behind me so quickly, I didn't have time to brace for it. But he didn't hit me this time, he pulled my body into his.

"That's more like it." He smiled, as if nothing had happened. As if I were the crazy one for not having his food ready. I managed to smile weakly. It appeared his mood shifted. Safety. I breathed a little easier, but his touch was repulsive.

I called Max and Jodi in to eat. We always sat together at the table—there was always this tension to pretend, just like we had at Hawthorne. It was typically awkward and silent unless Max wanted to talk. Everyone ate quickly and Max looked relieved his father was no longer red. After he finished eating, Jodi took him to bed as she did most nights to deprive me of those precious moments with my son.

"Hey, I want to show you something," Dale said to me and gestured for me to follow him out of the back door. I sat down the pot I was washing and followed behind.

The evening sun cast long shadows across the ground. The sky was ablaze with red and hazy clouds. I could already hear Beaky chirp, and I sensed the danger. I instantly wished he would go to sleep. Not to call attention to himself. Or that he would abruptly gain the strength to fly.

But it was too late— Dale was standing over the tote I had filled with grass and sticks and newspaper to make a makeshift nest.

"This bird matters more to you than me?" His voice shifted- it was jagged like a knife. In his hand was a single brick.

"It's not like that at all," I replied weakly, glancing from Dale to the helpless bird.

"It was only a few minutes behind, and I didn't mean to... Max cares a lot about this little baby bir--." I pleaded with Dale as I felt the warmth disappear from my cheeks. Beaky sat there still waiting- his mouth remained wide open and his big black eyes stared up at us.

He held the brick over top of the bird in a dropping motion. I gasped, the look on his face scared me more than anything I had ever seen.

Pleasure.

And as he dropped it- and I heard the crunch, it was the last ounce of heartbreak I could take. Beaky was no longer brave. He was no longer a survivor. He was nothing but a body, he had no chance and, if I continued to stay here, that's what I would be too.

CHAPTER THIRTY

"Doesn't it? Doesn't it hurt?" Max asked, pressing on the bruise in the shape of his father's hand that sat high on my cheek from the night before.

"It does when you press it like that," I said to him, wincing. But through all the cracks, and bruises, the hurt in my mind was so much deeper than the skin. I sat back and kissed his forehead gently.

"I'm fine." I put on a huge smile through my tears.

"I know it does. Doesn't it hurt when Pop pushes you like that?" Max leaned into me, closer, his voice as soft as velvet.

I blinked and cleared the tear before it trickled down my face. I looked into his little angry eyes and pulled him close to me. I breathed in that sweet little boy smell of wind and earth and of all things wild.

My heart ached for him as he ran outside first thing that morning to check on Beaky. When he reached the make-do nest, he found an empty space that once held an innocent little bird. I had cleaned up the blood that spattered, and the few remaining feathers that were scattered. I held the tiny crushed body in my hands. How could something so alive one minute simply be gone in seconds? Late last night when everyone slept, I buried him on the outskirts of the backyard. I used a spoon from the kitchen to dig so as not to wake anyone up. I cried for that baby bird as if he was one of my own. It hurt for me, and it hurt for Max and the memory that replayed in my mind- it hurt the worst. I was madder at myself than anyone. I continued to let all of these bad things happen.

I am so stupid. I should have stopped him. Stood up to him. Do something. Done something. But I hadn't, like always.

I didn't want to lie to Max. But I couldn't break his heart. It was too gentle and too trusting for that. I lie in bed all night and stumbled for the right words to say to Max.

But the next morning, once we got outside and he checked inside the tote, Max turned to me, "Mama! Can you believe it? Beaky flew away!" Max shrieked and jumped up and down.

"Why, it's a miracle," I said to him uncomfortably. "Now he's free, he can fly as far as he wants to."

Max's smile faded and disappointment filled every ounce of him. He had already considered Beaky a friend. I stuffed the sob back into my throat and ran to him. Hugging this little angry boy who I would do anything for.

"All babies have to learn to fly someday, Max," I whispered, kissing his forehead while staring off into the sky.

Why was I failing him? Why couldn't I stand up for myself? Face it. Face the monster?

Realizing that Max needed better changed everything for me.

I would have to figure this out.

I would learn to fly.

CHAPTER THIRTY-ONE

That night as I lie in bed, the question returned to me, over and over again.

Why don't you stand up for yourself? Do something.

Max's tear-filled eyes flashed through my mind and, in that instant, I knew I was ready. It was like all of those years crept by until I could no longer recognize myself or who I'd become. Somewhere among the brain washing and abuse, I had completely lost my courage. I managed to survive, I locked myself in a home at night with an abuser and his accomplice. Instead of locking the doors to keep them out.

I rolled out of bed and crept to the kitchen. I put the coffee on and, as it gurgled, I enjoyed the sun shining through the window. The resinous fragrance filled the air. In moments like that, I was nearly happy. The danger and darkness around me faded behind the hues that lit up the room. I was just a normal woman making my morning coffee.

I spent the first two hours before anyone else woke, like many other mornings, mopping, and dusting and scrubbing the table and chairs with polish. I had read in the paper that baking soda and vinegar mixed together could clean and also be used as mouth wash. The room sparkled and so did my teeth. I got lost in cleaning often, it was one of the only things that had been consistent throughout my whole life. And I was good at it.

Dale had begun investing and renting residential properties after he voluntarily resigned from Hawthorne. He traveled Wednesday through Saturday every other week. I enjoyed the breaks from him, but I also knew it might be my only way out.

"Wow, the trash can is still full," Jodi growled as she shuffled into the freshly cleaned kitchen. Her bare feet left dirty black tracks across the freshly cleaned floors. My body tightened; my skin crawled. I turned to face the sink to avoid letting Jodi know she still got to me. That familiar body ache when Jodi walked in the room. Her voice breaking through the quiet morning was enough to make me lose it all. To turn around and scream at this plump woman who was perfectly capable of taking the trash out herself. But I said nothing, again. I held back and took the bag from the trashcan and walked bare foot out the back door. The morning air surrounded me and I felt the tension fade in nature. The dew on the grass stuck to my feet, sending chills up my legs. I needed a plan. But how? I had these thoughts enough times to know there was no perfect plan that could free me. But now it wasn't just me.

I was constantly on guard, frozen in time, making sure I was safe, making sure Max was safe. More than anything I wanted him to know love. I sang to him, played with him any chance I got, and sometimes I would change his outfit into a new one just because- he was mine. I was able to see myself as a child through him and because of this, a new part of my soul was freed. I lived my childhood trying to be good enough for my own mother, so I wanted Max to know he was more than enough for me.

I longed to see something other than our little market. I even grew bored of the garden after so many years. Everything had just become work. In order to learn to fly I had to use the very same techniques Dale had used on me. I had to manipulate the way I was manipulated. The very same way I was taught to. So that day I decided, my only way out would begin with Jodi.

It was the week before Dale would leave for his next business trip. I had never gone on a trip with him before. But the idea of escaping was the only thing on my mind. Simply asking wouldn't work. I had to figure out a way to go on this trip.

I waited until Dale left the house. Until the floors were scrubbed, dishes wiped clean. Dinner was prepped and ready to be complete by the time Dale walked in the door. Finally, at nap time, the house was quiet. Jodi normally guarded the bedrooms from the dining room where she had a full view of the hallway and the front door. She used any opportunity to make sure I knew there was no way out. I joined her at the table, and she was taken aback at my closeness but didn't acknowledge me.

Jodi drank her tea, puffed her cigarette, and let out a loud hacking cough. I clenched hoping it wouldn't wake Max up. This was my chance.

I studied Jodi's aging skin and curls. I wanted to like her, to see something on her face that let me know she was human. But there wasn't one likable bone in that woman's body. I leaned in a little, just above a whisper.

"Why don't you ever go on trips? Dale is always going on fun excursions and you're here... Don't you ever want a break? I heard of women who get to travel, see the world and they're practically living the dream. Then here you are, here with us."

I emphasized *us* in a way that degraded Max and I to a chore.

I had to appeal to what Jodi wanted to hear. Jodi raised her brows at my statement. Her lips puckered together. I bowed slightly, had I blown it?

"Well, I know what you're trying to do. Trying to get me to leave so you can run away. But you got yourself into this."

Jodi took a long drag of her thin smoke, then exhaled as she continued. "But it ain't happening. I could never have kids you know. Body just wasn't made for it. And then someone like you seduces an older man."

I saw stars as I pretended not to be affected. A fire filled my body. It took every effort to control my muscles from melting onto the floor. That wasn't who I was. I didn't ask for this. I never wanted any of this to happen! I opened my lips to defend myself, but Jodi's words stung, ate at me like an infection but I mustered the courage to continue.

"I thought you would like it, that's all," I mumbled and stood. I began to walk away when Jodi began to speak. I grabbed a towel and began to wipe down the counters.

"I could use a change of scenery. That would mean you would have to come." I dropped the towel I was washing with. I calmly picked it up as I turned to face Jodi.

"It isn't right I'm here stuck with someone like you every day." Jodi coughed loudly, pushing her cigarette deeper into the ashtray. My heart did a happy dance beneath my skin but I managed to keep my face flat.

Somehow it all came together. Dale thought it might be a good idea to have us with him, he focused on how I could prepare meals for him. Of course, for his own selfish purposes but it worked. Later, while I packed for the trip, my shaky hands showed the parts of me who felt like I was betraying Dale. I had been brainwashed for so long, it was him I felt I needed to protect over myself. But then I thought of Max and everything within me stayed with the plan. I had this sense, somehow I knew it would be my last time in the Green House. I was certain of that. I loaded extra outfits for Max, tucked extra snacks beneath his toys. And in the very bottom of the bag, underneath my over-sized and holey clothes, I packed a screwdriver and a rope.

That night as I lie in bed, I reviewed it all in my mind. The items I packed, the plan for our escape. The dangers that existed, I pushed out of sight. Even if it killed me, at least I had tried. I felt a surge of energy running through my body. But I fell asleep surprisingly fast. For the first time in years, I slept peacefully. I had my first taste of freedom and I hadn't even escaped yet.

CHAPTER THIRTY-TWO

The car slowed in front of an old building. Oak grew along the sides and it was camouflaged amongst the other buildings in the area. I glanced around, but everywhere I looked there didn't seem to be any people. I expected it to be a busy place, filled with options for Max and I to escape. I fought a rising panic. And I was back at square one. But Dale turned away from the old building and onto a different street. I sighed to myself, relieved. The car rolled towards a tall hotel right in the middle of downtown. There were a lot of cars in the parking lot and nicely dressed people bustling by. A foreign smile met my lips.

Jodi got out immediately and reached in for Max, pulling him close to her. I clenched my teeth, perhaps it would all be over soon. I followed inside like the lost puppy I had been for so many years. I didn't join them at the concierge desk, but instead stood nervously in the back of the lobby, I rocked from one foot to the other as I tried to remember every detail of the room. Jodi stood behind me, close enough to feel her hot breath on the back of my neck. I had an urge to push her down and run with Max at that moment. But that would be too foolish. Even though I was no longer a little girl, my eyes darted and my hands couldn't stop fidgeting anytime I was in public with

Dale. I swear I could feel piercing glares even when nobody was looking at me. It began long ago when he had first began touching me while at Hawthorne. The guilt seeped from my body. It only grew stronger at the hospital when I gave birth to Max, while Dale growled in my ear to say I was older, pretend that I was an adult. That was one of the very few times that I saw Dale become nervous. Most of the time, he was very well put together and too busy convincing me that he was the good guy in this story. He told me his behavior wasn't harmful, that it was love. He always reminded me that I was the one who wanted this attention. I had wanted to be told that I was lovable and pretty. The way he talked me into believing that I gave him permission to do these things that were so wrong, it confused me into not knowing what was right for so long. This shame had uncontrollably followed me and became a part of who I was.

A woman walked up to greet us. She was beautiful in her business skirt and buttoned shirt. "Hello there, how can I help?" she asked, nearly knocking me off balance from the startle.

I felt she would believe me.

Jodi stepped in front of me. "No... we're being helped," she growled.

The woman stared into my eyes for a moment so I avoided looking at her again. I typically felt that I had to hide myself, and Max, from the world. Like I was less than a person. After she left, I managed to step out of Jodi's reach. I looked into the gift shop, glancing over all of the new things. I had never been able to buy something on my own. I inventoried each item slowly.

Shiny jewelry, candy bars, drinks, and a small collection of Teddy Bears. I smiled to myself, soon I would be free. Jodi talked loudly- just the opposite of me. The sound of so many people talking in one room caused my vision to go fuzzy. It had been a long time since I last interacted with anyone other than Max, Dale, Jodi or the market workers. I watched Jodi and Dale transform- in front of everyone else they were normal people. They smiled, nodded their heads, and appeared to be polite. *Did I have it all wrong? Was it truly me that caused people to behave the way they did?* Dale smiled at the woman who handed him the room keys and away we went to find the room.

"I want to push the button!" Max shouted racing ahead.

"Of course, you can push the button," Jodi said, patting his head. Max reached for me and nearly toppled over. But Jodi pulled him away, inserted herself in between us so he could no longer reach for me. The light on the button blinked as Max looked at it. I hoped we weren't too far up, it would only make things more difficult.

"Push seven," Dale said, reading over paperwork. He rarely made eye contact with Max, let alone spoke to him.

The room was simple- two bedrooms, small kitchen and one large bathroom smack dab in the middle. I didn't fall asleep that night. Hour after hour, I lie awake. Everything sounded so unfamiliar. The cars passing by outside, the sounds of doors closing and wind blowing on the busy street. I lie in bed next to the human that had destroyed my life so underhandedly, so purposely. I hoped it was for the last time.

Dale had threatened long ago, after Susan and I tried to escape Hawthorne, that if I were to run away again, he would find me and it would all be over. I thought of little Beaky in the bottom of that tote. I had no doubt in my mind that Dale would kill me. He could easily find a way to make another lie up. That was the one thing he never failed at.

I knew the key to our escape was trust and manipulation. They had to trust my stupidity and never-ending loyalty. They had to believe the lies they taught me all these years. I just had to wait until my opportunity came.

All the fire that ever lived within me was combusting.

CHAPTER THIRTY-THREE

Perhaps I was naïve in thinking that I could pull the entire plan off by myself. Had I gotten ahead of what I was capable of? Or maybe I finally gained the confidence that every adult in my life had helped to strip away, like one piece of wrapping paper at a time to eventually reveal the ultimate present. The moment I had I been waiting for. He snored loudly next to me. It would be the last morning I ever woke up next to a monster in bed.

BEEP, BEEP, BEEP.

My eyes shot open. It was go time. My stomach filled with butterflies and my heart flooded in panic.

Pull it together.

I rose out of bed as if today were any other day. But it wasn't any other day. I could barely keep the smile from curling across my chapped lips. My body was in the room, but my mind was elsewhere.

The gust of cool air and a door slamming brought me back. I blinked a few times. My world felt more alive than it had in years. Dale slipped out just like that- like he always had. Going and coming as he pleased.

Everything in my plan had to go right. I slid the screwdriver into my pocket. How meaningful simple things could become if they were the only shot of hope you have left.

It burned a hole in my pocket.

I became aware of each of my movements as if walking for the first time.

I crept to the window and watched behind the thick hotel curtain as he got into the car seven stories below. My heart raced. I could feel the pulse bulging at my temples. Sweat dripped down between my breasts. For a moment my vision went black. I pushed my hair out of my eyes hoping that would help me see clearer. I considered calling it off. The self-doubt returned. Wondering what he would do if he found me.

My vision turned to stars. As I took a step back, Max pulled on my shirt. I looked into his loving blue eyes, and it gave me the strength I needed. I held his hand as I watched. Dale smiled and waved at a woman getting into her car. I hated to see that side of him—the pretend one others got to see. The one I believed in when I was just a little girl.

Just leave, get out of here. I never want to see you again.

His door slammed. He started the car. Then as he pulled out without a glance in my direction, out of the parking lot, I stood straighter.

You can't hurt me anymore.

Jodi sat at the kitchen table, watching me curiously. She was always perched in a position that allowed her to watch all exits, to ensure there was no way I could escape. Waiting to place blame on any minor thing I did. Her eyes dissected me with every step I took.

I fidgeted with my hair. Anything to get Jodi's eyes off of me.

"Care for a walk this morning?" I asked Jodi, smiling.

"You can take one alone," Jodi replied, inhaling a huge puff of smoke. The curlers that remained in her hair reminded me of Cruella Deville. I smiled at the thought.

It was a game to her. It had always been a game. She liked waiting for a price to extract behavior that goes against her wishes. Her favorite was for me to lose time with Max or humiliating me in public.

For as long as I could remember, Jodi only suggested the opposite of what was sought after. If I held the slightest bit of hope, it was vacuumed away. She was the thief of joy. A black hole. But I was finally ready to play.

"I saw there is a collection of bears in the gift shop."

I glanced at the clock.

Jodi sat up slightly in her seat. "I haven't had a new one in a while." She tapped her fingers. "Well, I suppose we could walk down there." She pinched my arm tightly. "But don't you dare go out of my sight."

Thirty minutes later, the palms of my hands were more slippery than a salamander. I wiped them on my pants in order to have a better grip on the stroller. I knew I couldn't step away from Jodi with Max. So I waited patiently, counting each step we took until Jodi locked eyes with the woman in the gift shop. She liked to put on an appearance. As the older woman approached, my stomach lurched.

"Oh, how precious! How old are you??" The clerk called out, gesturing to Max. She knelt until she was just at his eye level.

Jodi smiled and turned slightly, taking her eyes off of me.

"He is four. My big boy!" A giddy, unfamiliar voice came out of Jodi's mouth.

I hated when she called him hers. Like he was an object.

My cheeks turned red when the woman glanced in my direction. "How about her, is she your daughter too?" I had heard this question many times before. On the rare occurrences of being out in public, people often questioned the girl who didn't look old enough to be a mother.

Jodi's eyes rolled slightly. "She's just the hired help." The woman's eyes empathetically flashed towards me. I shook my head in agreeance. Though I hadn't planned for one, an audience would be helpful. Jodi couldn't help herself when a stranger was around. It was her only chance to be seen as a decent human.

The woman engaged in a conversation that drifted onto other adulty things. The weather, good places to eat, museums— like we were actually here on vacation.

I waited, shuffling foot to foot, to make sure Jodi was so engaged in the conversation, she forgot about me.

"Actually, Jodi, can I please have the keys? I must use the restroom. Urgently." I stepped closer, inches away from the dangling key chain.

Two can play that game.

Jodi sneered at me, but was so caught up in her conversation, she handed them over. She knew I wouldn't go anywhere without my child. Neither would she expect a stupid girl like me had a plan. I took the keys in my hand. It felt heavy, like gold. I walked politely out of the store and down to the hallway and, as soon as I was out of sight, I ran with the key like I had won an award.

The elevator would take too long. I raced up the seven flights of stairs. It was the fastest I had ever moved. Stars blurred my vision. I huffed at the top and skipped down the hall. I fumbled for the key to fit and glanced back down the empty hallway. Nothing but the sound of my violent beating heart.

Hotel musk filled the air as I stepped in the door and shoved it shut behind me. I exhaled loudly. I bolted the door behind me. I raced to the bathroom. I only had a matter of what, five minutes? Or less?

The first part of my plan was working, could it actually work?

I glanced inside the teal-green bathroom that was filled with ceramic tile and flowered walls. I pulled the screwdriver from my pocket. It felt heavy in my hand. I had done this in my mind so many times I could barely feel the penetration of the screw twisting loose.

Four minutes, three minutes.

I quickly spun it in my hand. As I loosened each screw, I gently placed them on the floor, then finally, pulled the doorknob free. It was so satisfying,

"Thank you, James," I whispered into the empty room.

I spun the knob and entered the bathroom. Leaving the door propped open, I reinstalled it— backwards. I could sense Rissy in the room with me, or was it James? A soul rooting for me. After I tightened the last screw on the reversed doorknobs, I clicked the lock on the outside of the door. For the first time in years, I smiled proudly at my reflection in the dirty bathroom mirror. It is one thing to think of a plan, but a whole different feeling to be the plan.

I could hear footsteps approaching and I dashed over to the door. Unlocked the bolt, and flung it open more aggressively than I had meant. I swept my hair behind my ear. I tried to pace my breath. Max tugged at my legs immediately.

Jodi's nostrils were flaring. Her lips were curled.

"Too bad you left so soon. It's a shame. I didn't get one for you." A bright blue teddy bear was shoved in front of my face. Jodi laughed, and it triggered a trail of chills down my backbone. For once, perhaps I would have the last laugh.

I waited. I tried to form a thought but it all led me back. Back to the door. I forced myself not to stare at the knob. I could hardly wait until Jodi used the restroom. The things that I took for granted before meant so much in this moment.

I paced back and forth and cracked my knuckles. I busied myself with Max. My eyes willed Jodi towards the door, but she turned and entered the kitchen area. Jodi smoked a cigarette and ate a large donut at the same time. My stomach growled. The crumbs even looked tempting to me.

Three more cigarettes and a coffee later, Jodi finally stood to pee. With each step my muscles clenched. I held my breath to still the firework explosion of thoughts in my mind. But the door closed, and I heard it click. It was like the sound of that door locking was a button that was hardwired to my brain. Igniting a bomb that released the years of torture I had endured. I had to get to safety. This was finally our chance.

Another part of my brain took over, and I moved quickly. As if on auto pilot, I reached the stroller. I felt like I was watching a movie. I could see myself moving from outside of my body. In rapid speed—my mind was frozen but my body knew what to do. I grabbed the bag I had packed and placed it on my back.

The toilet flushed.

The water trickled in the sink.

I scooped Max up and put him in the stroller and I ran for it. Almost to the elevator, I could swear Jodi's desperate screams and pounds on the bathroom door could be heard.

Please let me make it out. Please.

First, we stopped at the 5th floor, the doors flew open and I wanted to run, but the woman who joined stepped in politely. After stopping on the fourth floor, I pushed the close button over and over. The woman looked over at me curiously.

"Sorry, in a hurry," I told her.

"Sorry," I told the businessman on floor 3. I hadn't thought about this part. I would have taken the stairs had I not had the stroller. Max was so quiet, as if nothing was out of the ordinary. Like I was just a mother taking her child for a walk. Alone.

We reached ground level. The elevator made a "ding" and the doors slid open. I expected to be caught. For Dale to be waiting as I exited. But there was no one. The lobby was quiet, empty. The only sounds were high heels clicking on the floor from the women leaving the elevator. I pushed the stroller slowly across the marble floors.

I was a mother taking my son for a walk.

Just a few more steps until I reached the door. Who knew how long it would take Jodi to escape the bathroom. What if she were already on her way down? I inhaled deeply and dodged outside. The wind felt fresher than it had in years. A man held the door for me, and I managed to thank him. The lobby led out past the parking lot to a sidewalk. Cars bustled by and I dare not look up at them. I kept my eyes trained on the sidewalk.

Bright orange, red, and dried brown leaves filled the sidewalk. The way they crunched underneath my feet reminded me I was alive. The crisp air swirled around my face, gently biting into my cheeks and ears. My heartbeat could be felt in my toes. Every car that passed looked like Jodi or Dale. Chills covered my arms. I walked faster and raced to the bus stop just down the street. Once on the somewhat empty bus and, almost in a whisper, I asked the bus driver if there was a way to transfer buses to go to London, Virginia.

"Yep- sit down. I'll get you to the transportation center," he smiled and within an hour, I was stepping outside of a run-down bus station. Once we boarded the next bus, I paid with all the money I had stashed over the past month. The money I had taken from Dale's wallet in one dollar increments as he slept. We took a long drive and transferred to one last bus. I held my breath as we pulled up to our stop. It was my only hope.

An old wooden sign hung crooked on the porch. **Shelter for**

Battered Women. I took in a deep breath of the afternoon air, thankful to be out of the stuffy bus.

We made it.

We made it!

I walked up the stairs to the porch in an adult body, but with a scared eight-year-old heart.

CHAPTER THIRTY-FOUR

I knocked several times. First, I pounded softly. Then I pounded harder, and one last time with an open fist. We waited. The silence greeted our tired bodies and wrapped a blanket of homesickness around me. Except it was for a place that didn't exist.

Please, please be here.

I peeked into the window and saw a light on. My body released a torrent of sweat despite the nippy wind. Max reached up for me. "I'm thirsty, Mama."

I ducked down to his level. "I know. We will get you something… I just hope they're still open,"

"Is this a restaurant?" Max asked. I didn't know what to tell him so I nodded my head no. I huffed out of defeat and tried the handle. It felt foreign in my hand. I knew I shouldn't but the old door slid open with ease. I cautiously walked inside, leaving our small bag of belongings and the stroller on the porch.

Automatic negative thoughts spiraled through my mind. *Would this place even take us? Would they have the space? Had I made a mistake? Why am I so stupid?*

"Hello?" I called out into the hall, and the intense fragrance hit me. It smelled cozy like a cashmere sweater and banana bread pudding.

"Hello?" I called again, my voice cracked this time, as I took a step into the hall. Straight down the hall was a silhouette of a person, I hoped they would notice me and come greet us, but they didn't. I began walking and the older woman came into view. She was crouched down over the TV twisting the big knobs A fuzzy gray screen blinked off and on. I walked closer, afraid I would startle her—that would certainly get us kicked out. The woman had disheveled gray hair and glasses that hung down off her nose. She wore a floral shirt, with large shoulder pads, and her face was filled with questions as she whipped around. I stared back at her, my eyes wide. Her forehead was furrowed and she stooped over to where I stood with Max hiding behind me. A wide smile spread across her crinkly cheeks.

"Hello there," she called, taking time to look and study each of our faces. Her eyes were kind, and glowing and her head had a slight tremor.

She gently reached out to touch Max's face. Her thin loose hands contrasted his smooth round cheeks. She embraced both of us in a big stroppy and very awkward hug. She held on with *two arms*. I closed my eyes. I didn't know the last time I was hugged in this way. Something about this woman made it feel like we would be okay.

But there must have been some mistake. Did this poor woman think we were someone else? Was she expecting someone?

"Um…I haven't called or been accepted. I don't even know if you will let us, but if you can please let us stay here…" I blurted out, awkwardly pulling back from the embrace.

"Well, that's an odd name," she smirked. "I'm Joan, like Jones but just Joan, not Joanne," she continued, making me smile slightly, "I'm the lead counselor and I also reside here." I felt my muscles melt like butter.

"Who do we have here?" Joan asked, gently rubbing Max's arms with her wrinkled hands.

"Max!" He answered loudly. His eyes looked more alive. Did he feel safer here too?

"I'm Bonnie," I replied, sticking my hand out awkwardly.

Joan refused to shake it.

"No, none of that business stuff. We do family here…It is so nice to meet you, please come in." Joan spread her arms wide open to share her territory.

"But we are already in," Max said, and Joan let out a laugh that filled the room with merriment.

"Well, my, aren't you a smart cookie? Of course, you're in. Come on over and have a seat." She led us over to sit on a couch. I sank into the couch and my skin crawled with goose bumps. The kind that made the hair on my arms stand and my back straighten. Not from being cold, or from breathing fresh air, but from the way Joan spoke to us, like we were real people.

Deserving people. In that instant I knew I made the right decision. We found safety.

CHAPTER THIRTY-FIVE

As the weeks passed, Max and I became used to the never-ending schedule that Joan encouraged. It was like a marathon- each grueling day I was training to be a better person. A normal person. I hadn't realized how much I had to learn. How different my life could have been if I was taught these things. If I was taught that I mattered. Through genuine and mutual respect in therapy I was able to actually see what had happened to me. I was shocked to find out there were more people like me. People who never were children because they spent their whole childhood just trying to survive. In each of the programs I felt included but also distant. As I began to understand what it was that I had been through— the part of me to let people in, closed. I didn't know if I would ever be able to trust or love someone ever again. My eyes were opened about my trauma and what it meant to be a victim of childhood sexual abuse. Hearing the very words brought immense shame to my face. For each time it was brought up, I felt debilitating pain, like I was the worst person and the only person who ever let it happen. It was crippling.

It was nice to have extra hands to help with Max. It was good to see him playing with other children and smiling from ear to ear. He never once told me he missed them. He never once asked me why we ran away. I knew that, despite his age, Max knew. He knew how humans were supposed to be treated.

Joan taught me of the high prevalence for those with childhood sexual trauma to be addicted to substances or alcohol. I had never tried a drug in my life so that part didn't worry me. It was discovering the long-term effects and the nervousness I felt inside my body each day. Feeling less than a person, unlovable and unworthy. Those things may never improve. The violations of children's bodies, especially by people who are responsible to provide care for them, protect them, are in positions of affection and authority, actually create deeply held issues with trust, intimacy, and dependency. *What did that even mean?* I would never love or trust anyone ever again? Would I never be able to be intimate with another person? Through the process of therapy, I was taught a new way to process what happened. I wasn't as stupid as I thought I was. It made me sick to my stomach that what Dale did to me was actually a process called grooming. It was a named process because it happened to other children and people and that's the part that broke my heart. In learning this, I felt completely alone yet surrounded by other people with patch-quilt souls. How did I not realize that I had been sexually abused? I never thought I would be believed. I was a little girl who didn't know any better. Especially not after Hawthorne just brushed it all under the rug. They didn't believe me or stand up for me, but then I sat in a room full of ladies who did. I guess most of all I felt so much shame about the things he did to me and made me do to him that I didn't feel I deserved to be helped.

Besides therapy, there were special events every week and, within four months, I had learned so much; how to sew, work skills and proper etiquette, how to handle money and finances, and I even became certified in CPR. I learned all of the life skills a girl's mother should have taught her before she left home. Even though I mostly felt safe, I continued to look over my shoulders. I constantly checked behind me. I thought that any day Dale would bust down the door and find us. The first few times, Joan had to rip Max from my arms. I was so terrified that if I let him out of my sight, I would never see him again. Joan made it clear that it was part of the journey. The journey to independence. She made it sound fun, but being an adult out in the world was actually terrifying to me. I hadn't even been a child out in the world and here I was learning all of this new stuff. I wasn't even sure if I deserved it. But Max did. He deserved everything and I had to be the best mother to him.

It was Tuesday, and that meant the dreaded group therapy. The wooden door was propped open already, so I walked in. I didn't like to make eye contact with anyone so I quickly chose the first seat I came across. The chairs in the room were arranged in a circle. I had already made it through quite a few group therapy sessions, as awkward as it was. That night though, I shifted in my seat and wiped my sweaty palms on my pants. I wasn't ready to talk about myself. The past 2 months I just sat in my chair and heard the terrible things everyone went through and I didn't say anything. I didn't want to share my story because if I accepted it— then I felt like I lost all the control I had.

I hesitated as each person went around the room.

"Stephanie."

"Evangeline."

"Josie,"

"Kate."

All eyes fell on me. I had introduced myself almost a dozen times before but I froze. My hands began to shake uncontrollably.

Why am I like this?

I couldn't get air fast enough. It was humiliating to tell my story out loud after it had been locked away in my mind for so long. I cleared my throat and my head felt unsteady on my body.

"Bonnie," I finally whispered.

"Thanks everyone," Joan paused and glanced around the circle. "Remember, we are here for each other, to support and to recognize that we are not alone. There is already so much darkness attached to trauma that sometimes it feels like keeping the pain within is safer. But it is an important step to recognize the abuse and become educated on trauma." The other girls nodded their heads at her. I couldn't really follow what she was saying, I was off in my own mind trying to figure out if I could just run out of the room before they got back to me.

As if Joan sensed this, her eyes fell on me. "I believe we will pick up with Bonnie," she said, smiling with an encouraging nod.

"Oh-kay… well um…"

I couldn't do it. I couldn't share something I had kept hidden for so long.

All of the reasons not to participate flooded my mind. I could get up and leave, run. But I couldn't move. The ladies in the room leaned in, waiting. Making my face feel as though I were a whoopee cushion expected to explode once pressure was applied. My pulse pounded in my temples. I had to participate to pass the shelter program. So, I sat up to try again… this time the words oozed out, voice unsteady,

"Since the age of 11— I was… I was raped by someone. A grown man. My house father at a home. At a home and school for children," I paused, not recognizing my own voice. Not wanting that voice to belong to me. Not wanting to be that little girl those things happened to.

The group let out a gasp in unison. Stephanie reached my arm and patted it softly. The way I had done when she told us she was beaten daily by her husband. I shifted.

"My own mother had signed a consent to let me marry this man and he is the father of my child. I don't know how I feel about sharing this and, um, I didn't even know the extent of my abuse until I came to the shelter. And now I just kind of …." Where was I going?

I froze. The room and the group members faces all spun around me. I could hardly breathe.

Saying this out loud made it so much more real.

My stomach twirled in knots and, little-by-little, the color faded from my sight, until blackness ensued.

CHAPTER THIRTY-SIX

Group ended early after I fainted. I swear I got bonus points from the other members because they hadn't wanted to be there either. Maybe they weren't ready to share with me when they did. For months I listened intently to their stories— the whole while I discarded how much courage it took to say the worst moments of your life out-loud. But they were right- a part of me was able to process my story in words from the group. The more you keep the truth inside, the easier it is to believe that it's not real. So much hidden pain for so long was exposed in a way I never imagined. I had people there who believed me. And when that happened, I think it was most validating.

I wasn't crazy. All of the terrible things happened and I couldn't change it. The groups' openness and ability to accept this made it easier for me to accept it too.

It helped me see that I wasn't alone. We all have good times and also go through bad times. No matter how good your life is— bad things will always happen. Some people rarely have good times but when you do, you learn to appreciate it. The situation doesn't define you. Your reaction and the way you respond to it does. No matter what- we are in control of our reactions. We get to choose how to respond to it. Nobody can ever take that part away.

Later that day, I sat at the kitchen table, Max was playing with his cars by my feet. Joan walked over and placed a steaming cup of coffee down in front of me, "Three scoops of sugar, and two ice cubes… just how you like it." Joan smiled.

"Thanks." I cupped my hands around the hot mug. Joan joined me with her own coffee. We just silently sipped our coffee. Joan kept her eyes on me as if she was waiting for an explanation of why I fainted in group therapy…but I had nothing to give her.

"I don't know what is wrong with me," I said.

Joan shook her head and leaned across the table towards me. She pulled my chin up until it completely faced her, as if I were a little girl again.

"Bonnie, it is not what is wrong with you." She paused and pulled my face back when I tried to look away.

"It is what happened to you, you had no control over it, and that's what we need to get out." My heart pattered, I knew that to the rest of the world I might be invisible, but Joan saw me, and that was just what I needed to push through. It's amazing how, through all of the darkness, just one person believing could bring the light back. Maybe I couldn't shake the horrible things that had happened to me, but I didn't have to spend the rest of my life hiding from my own nightmares. I wanted to show the world there was good left to give. If I couldn't show the world, at least Max would know. I never even considered that there was nothing wrong with me. My entire life I thought it was me.

I watched the others around me in the group home. There were so many damaged people who had been through terrible things. It was supposed to make you feel better— you know like… you're not alone, but I sat with this heavy feeling of defeat in my chest. Why did the world have to be this way? Why couldn't monsters stay a figment of our imagination instead of being visitors in real life?

I couldn't quite get comfortable at the shelter. It was too busy— people coming and going. Conversations spreading. Women who nearly healed and then faded into the gray once again. It brought me back to feeling really child-like versus independent. It modeled the same ways Hawthorne had run. Each week it seemed like just when I grew used to a new face— they would disappear again. Back to the person who they were running from. It was awful watching them return.

"You just can't understand." Stephanie told me the day I begged her not to leave. For some reason I had grown to like her. The one who always patted my leg in group. Stephanie, who smiled at me, but we never spoke on a deep level. The first one I watched resurface from domestic violence and turn into a new person. She had given me hope.

"Stephanie, I know you don't know me that well, but... you deserve a better life."

She had smiled at me that day- her eyes connected with mine as if she knew this moment would forever change her path in life. I studied her face- the freckle by her eye and her dingy brown hair.

"I'll be fine." She patted my hand and brushed hair from her eyes. The truck outside beeped for her but she turned back to me. For a minute-- she hesitated to leave. I hoped she would stay. But, as if a bug drawn to light, she flickered back to her abuser. That was the last time I ever saw Stephanie. Not even a month later— she was reported as a missing person. Joan showed me the article the following month after her remains were found.

Tears met my eyes as I re-read the article about Stephanie- who was once a person and now just a memory. One more person lost to domestic abuse.

"How do you keep doing this?" I asked Joan through my tears. I slammed the paper down on the table, but Joan looked as though she was in deep thought so I continued,

"She should have stayed. We shouldn't have let her leave."

"Bonnie...There is nothing you can make someone do when they want something else for themselves."

"But we could have..."

Joan interrupted me. "Shame is a powerful thing. It can be difficult for some to even admit they've been abused. It's never as simple as just leaving. Emotional abuse is never assumed to be as powerful as phys-ical because there's no evidence. Once your mind goes through it— it is hard to know the best way to escape it. It's hard to put yourself back together when you no longer know who you are,"

I stared at her unblinkingly- I couldn't figure out when we had moved from Stephanie to myself.

"I would never go back." I told her matter- of- factly.

"I would hope not, but Bonnie… let this be a lesson. It is hard to escape the cycle of control and remember— none of us are above making a bad decision." She took the paper from me and sat it back on the counter. As if getting it out of my sight would help.

I felt too strongly for other people. I felt too much- guilt, sadness, fear. Every emotion I had was so strong. I couldn't continue to watch people letting toxic cycles consume them. Because for so long they had consumed me and I let them. Still, the word victim was odd to me. It was hard for me to admit that I was one long before I ever knew what it was. It was hard to admit I was a person who "let" this happen to me. That I married a man who had abused me. It was more than shame. It was a sense of indifference- that I would never be equal to other people who made better decisions. An overwhelming rush of conflicting emotions —embarrassment, fear, low self-esteem, and the desire to be loved. A victim doesn't make sense to outsiders. They can't see why a person would be ashamed for something someone else has done to them. But it wasn't like that— there's so much more. The inability to stop it. The trauma leaves you feeling inferior and lost.

Joan said we were no longer victims, we were survivors. As I learned more and more about child sex offenders, I couldn't believe how blind I had been. How sick it was to allow it to happen and worry more about the school's reputation than a student's life. If I got lost inside of myself for too long— Joan reassured me that I was just a child when it happened. People told me that a lot. Like if I remembered that small little girl, maybe I could forgive her. But all I felt when I thought of her was immense and burning shame. Joan often told me that it was out of my control to save myself at that time. I had trouble believing her. The shame would block all rational thoughts from my mind, glazing over me like icing on a donut.

Since the house worked in steps based on progress, each month I got a little more freedom. I began to read again. I would venture out to the library with Max- grab a good book and cuddle up with it on the park bench while he played. There was a smile on my face as the wind whipped through my hair. I noticed the warmth from the sun's rays and the way the leaves fell gently from above. For the first time in my life, I was free to do as I chose to. This part was exciting and it was the first time I learned how to be a true adult. Learning to budget and eventually I found my first job. I ended up working at a place Max pointed out a huge sign of a tomato on our walk one day. "Mama, tomato! You love tomatoes." Luckily the manager of The Red Tomato, Frank, was short waitresses and hired me on the spot. Who was this person I was becoming?

CHAPTER THIRTY-SEVEN

Max and I stood outside of our new apartment. I paused before I put the key into the lock.

"Does this mean I'm really an adult?" I asked mostly to myself, but Max looked up at me with his brows pulled together.

"Mama, haven't you always been a grown up?"

"Not always!" I replied, sliding the key inside the door.

"Old people forget stuff really fast," Max mumbled with a smile.

"Hey now- I'm not that old yet," I teased, and I asked excitedly, "Are you ready?"

Max jumped up and down and reached his hand up to the knob. He twisted it and reached back for my hand as we walked inside.

It was dingy, and there were a few stains on the carpet. But there was a new paint smell over the layers of paint from the years before us and the sunshine crept in through the blinds. I glanced at his face in fear of disappointment shining back at me. But I met a starry-eyed smile instead.

"A home for just you and me!" Max ran excitedly from room to room.

"Mama! This is where we will eat!"

"This is where we will sleep!"

His voice became muffled as he ran in the bathroom. "Mama this is where we will poop!"

"This is where we will..." A knock at the door interrupted his announcement and Joan came bustling in with a large basket before I could even answer.

"We give out these welcome baskets to everyone once they get settled in, it has snacks, soaps, and essentials that can come in handy!" She maneuvered the basket onto the kitchen counter with a red face and turned towards us.

"Why, Max, what do you think of your new home?"

"Come see! Come see where we will poop." Max grabbed her hand and pulled her to the bathroom. I grinned and shrugged my shoulders at Joan and I heard her muffled voice.

"That is the best toilet I've ever seen, Max," Joan told him in the sweetest voice. And that's the moment I realized the reason Joan did what she did. Not for the heartaches or the ones who didn't make it. But for moments like this. For this feeling in that room. A new beginning. A magnificent new start. An empty apartment that would soon be our own. Broken souls turned into living humans. There are people out there who can help you, even if you're damaged... you can always find a way to come back.

Over the next two months, Max and I got into a nice routine. Joan stopped by every now and again, with hugs, cookies, and some pieces of furniture she found while thrifting. I visited her once a week for therapy too. I secretly loved that Joan was motherly to us. I had waited my whole life for that kind of attention. I continued to work as a waitress at the Red Tomato. It was my first job and I finally learned every item on the menu. The manager, Frank, was an older gentleman who was raised inside of the restaurant, so as long as I followed his rules, he left me alone. I was able to pick up day shifts, so I had time in between finishing work and picking Max up from Head Start. The shelter had given us roots to grow our lives on. I don't know what would have happened if it hadn't been for Joan and her kindness. It was fun saving money for furniture. We bought stuff from garage sales and thrift stores. I still went to therapy and the shelter still provided us with food and vouchers to the Salvation Army for furniture. Piece by piece, we turned our apartment into our home with furniture and items that had already been well loved. We had a puffy red couch with butt indentations that gave it just the right amount of worn-in feel that made you sink in a little. We found an old round kitchen table with mismatched chairs. It's funny how much the little things can mean to you when you go for so long without. When you've never had your own furniture or place that felt like home. That apartment became our fortress. Over time we moved our mattresses off the floor and onto bed frames. Everything just came together. Max turned the entire living room into a giant fort since we didn't have a TV. With a little bit of imagination, sheets, blankets, an old strand of Christmas lights, and couch cushions stacked up became our superhero cave, bear den, and pirate's cove. We played games and read books late into the night with flashlights.

"Everything is more fun in a fort!" Max had said. And it was. I had never experienced anything better than being alone in that fort with my son in those first two months.

My only real concern was the idea of Dale finding us that I couldn't shake. The apartment complex had taken on a small-town feel. Everybody knew everything about everyone. They talked and gossiped and I just tried to disappear. I kept quiet and to myself. When I did get approached, I ended the conversations quickly. Or when I ran into a neighbor in the apartment laundromat, I made an excuse and darted back home. When someone knocked on the door, Max and I would duck off into the bedroom. I was certain we would be found. Our closest neighbor, Amy had an apartment adjacent to ours. She often sat on the porch in a plastic chair, chain smoking cigarettes and being nosy. She had her nails painted in bright colors and wore a lot of makeup. Her clothes always seemed elaborate. No matter what time of day, I would find her out there and quickly avoid eye contact before she would start a conversation about the weather or gossip. Amy talked so much. She knew everything about every person who had ever lived at Ashwood. I was careful about sharing too much information from our past. I didn't mind that I wasn't making friends because it felt safer to be on our own. I didn't trust anyone. I did a pretty good job at staying to myself until one day when Amy caught me off guard.

"When you were a kid, what did you want to be when you grew up?"

I wondered if she sat there all day thinking of random questions to ask me just to watch me squirm.

I snuck past her and was about to escape inside but I turned to look at her instead,

"Are you talking to me?"

Amy had pinwheel curls that bounced around her face when she talked.

"Yeah… I always wanted to be a makeup artist."

"Oh… um, well that's a hard one… I'm really not sure but I have to go. "

"Oh hey…" She cleared her throat. Obviously, she couldn't take a hint.

"You should come to the BBQ this weekend. The whole complex comes together for us, every year! It would be a great chance for you to meet some new people." She exaggerated *new people...* I wasn't up for crowds and dark thoughts had been occupying my mind.

"I have to work, but thank you."

"Well, okay, if you want to be boring." An imminent frown crossed her face.

She actually looked disappointed so I smiled and added, "maybe next time" and slipped inside. I leaned up against the closed door grateful to be alone.

The rest of the week was uneventful until Friday. I barely made enough tips to cover my lunch and I couldn't shake the idea that Dale would find us. I was becoming paranoid. When I got a new customer with his back facing me, I held my breath until I saw his face and knew it wasn't Dale. My mind played tricks on me. I was jumpy and irritable. So I got to end my shift early since it was dead and all I wanted to do was shower and lie on the comfy red couch for a nap before Max had to be picked up. As I approached the doorway, I saw the familiar outline of Amy out of the corner of my eye. But she wasn't dressed up and she wore pajamas. I didn't mean to, but I stopped to study her for a moment.

"Oh, don't mind me… I was up all night with my nephew who decided to tell his mom for the first time…about his science project…." As she talked, I began to dig in my pocketbook for my keys. My wallet, *some gum, lipstick, scrunchies...* My heart picked up to a pace that was more familiar. But of course, she continued.

"Yeah… the night before his science project was due. So, since my sister had to work, we stayed up all night to finish it."

I let out a fake laugh, but I actually admired her for it. Maybe she was a good person. I sat on my knees and dumped every content of my pocketbook out. Amy moved closer. "Are you okay, *hun*?" I didn't want her to move closer because then she would see that I had started to cry. Dale's whisper shot through my mind.

Stupid girls do stupid things.

A prickle of fear danced down my neck. I felt Amy touch my shoulder, so I let my hair drop in my face to conceal my tears.

"I can't seem to find my keys…" I sobbed like a baby and my voice cracked. Any little thing could set me into a panic.

"It's okay- I do that all of the time. Really. it's not a big deal." Her brows met and she patted me again and picked up my wallet, Chapstick, old recipes, and set them back in my purse for me. I felt stupid for crying.

"Sorry- I'm trying so hard to keep everything together it just all feels really impossible right now. I don't even know who I am or what I'm going to do."

"It's okay- we can't be perfect all of the time, *hun*. Sometimes the bad things happen for a reason. Sometimes our minds just spiral and let us believe we need to be perfect. The past isn't meant to have you question who you are. You're just trying to align with who you're meant to be. Nothing that happened can tell you or define who you are. You get to decide that part, no one else."

I looked into her eyes and really saw her for the first time- staring at the freckles that trickled across her nose.

"See that old building right over there?" She pointed to the center of the complex by the playground. I nodded.

"That's the maintenance office. You go in there and you tell Jerry you locked yourself out. He will be up here in minutes. Tell him Amy sent you- he won't charge the locksmith fee like the office does." She used a genuine soft voice I hadn't heard from her before. The kind of person who stays up all night to help her lazy nephew finish a science project that should have been done months ago. There was this familiar, deep sadness in her voice. I felt an immense rush of guilt for avoiding Amy all that time. She had been nothing but kind to me. But I had been trained to look at everyone as a threat.

I stopped and looked her in the eyes again. "Thank you, Amy. Truly! I owe you one."

A proud smile crossed over her lips as if I had made her day instead of the opposite. She talked so much I hadn't considered the possibility of her being the lonely one. I assumed everyone's life outside of mine was perfect but I guess I was wrong.

I hopped over the small flower garden and made my way across the playground. The sky had turned into a full gray and it smelled of rain in the air, damp and earthy. I looped my purse back over my shoulder and reached the faded red door with letters lightly spray painted in yellow, **Maintenance Office,** and I knocked. It was metal and unexpectedly stung my knuckles so I tried the knob instead. Inside the entry was completely dark. It took my eyes a few moments to adjust.

"Hello? Is anyone in here?"

I took a few steps forward passing through two large rooms with one desk up front.

"Hello?" I called again but this time I jumped when someone replied, their voice grew nearer.

"What the hell do you want now, Jerry?"

An angry man stomped in from the other room.

He was the most handsome, angry person I'd ever seen.

"Oh uh— I'm sorry. I thought you were Jerry. Can I... help you?"

His cheeks turned red and he put his arm behind his head— revealing his defined muscles and arm tattoos. I stared a little too long.

"I am actually looking for… well, Jerry,"

A mutual smile spread between us and time seemed to stop.

"Damn Jerry. He's always causing me issues… I'm sorry to have yelled at you like that. He's like a gnat that I can't get rid of. Then when I need to swat him, he's nowhere in sight…I'll find him."

He disappeared in the back. I stood there awkwardly waiting and I wondered what the angry guy's name was.

He came back alone. I stood a little straighter once he joined me. Perhaps I had to just meet his gaze. He towered over me.

"Sorry…I can't find him." He was more relaxed. He smiled at me and his eyes were intense. They were dark brown with deep circles of caramel, like the sweetest chocolate. A foreign tingle crept across my entire body like the way warmth feels after you've been in the snow too long, like my body was thawing from years of abuse.

"Did you need help with something?" angry guy asked, holding his hands up. I noticed he was wearing a wedding ring. A wedding ring. That would be my luck- the first man I was ever attracted to was married. I blinked a few times.

"Well, yes. I uh…locked myself out of my apartment. My neighbor told me I could find Jerry here and that maybe… he would be able to help get me in?"

Angry guy raised his eyes at me. "Must be close to Amy? That woman comes in here like three times a week looking for him." He laughed, "I don't usually do this. That's Jerry's type of thing… but hold tight, I'll get you back in." He disappeared into the back room again.

The walk over to my apartment was awkward. At once, I was like a school girl again. Something within me zapped back to life when I saw him. My inner-teen and raging hormones that had been locked away.

Stop it- He's married. He's married. I told myself. The sad thing was so was I. I hadn't filed for a divorce out of fear it would lead Dale back to Max.

And it was a good thing he was married. I didn't need any more angry guys in my life.

Amy was gone when we reached my door, probably napping. He

pulled out his giant ring of keys and knelt down. I studied him as he tried the first key— he was tan, and everything about him was large, his muscles, his feet and a warm smile stamped on his face when he caught me looking at him. I tried to pretend I wasn't surveying his muscle toned arms, my cheeks warmed and I looked away. *Why did I feel so nervous?* I cleared my throat. *What on earth was happening to me?*

"Good old Jerry doesn't label the keys like he's supposed to," he said frustratedly.

"Oh. I see," I replied, trying to make words form together in a sentence was suddenly very difficult for me. Every time I looked at him, I turned to mush. He didn't seem to notice or care but he continued to talk as he tried key after key.

"Don't get me wrong. Jerry is a good guy. He's just really getting up there and I think it's time he retires."

"My son always says old people forget stuff a lot." I laughed. I don't know why I felt the need to tell him I had a son. He was off boundaries- taken.

"That's funny. My daughter says that too." *He had a daughter and a wife but yet I still hoped he never found the right key…*just being close to him was exciting to me. He looked up at me when he said *daughter* as if to study my reaction.

He slid another key in and my door was open. "There we go!"

He stepped inside to hold the door for me. I watched him survey the fort with an exuberant smile.

"Wow. Makes me want to be a kid again." He nodded towards it.

I laughed. "It takes up the entire living room, but I've been letting him keep it. I feel like he needs his own little place— just to process all the changes we've had."

"Are you just moving here?"

"Yeah... It's been um... complicated the past few months... I think kids just need to process in their own ways." I stepped inside but stayed facing him.

"Well, that's pretty damn awesome. You're a good mom. It brings back the nostalgia of being a kid." He nodded in agreement.

A giddy, flirty smile took over my lips and I had to force myself to look away. *What was happening to me?* He stared at the fort a little longer and hesitated to turn away once he faced me.

"Alright- see you around…." He waited for me to answer.

"Bonnie."

"Bonnie- right. I'm Tanner. Again, sorry for yelling at you and all…"

"Oh, no. Thank you for getting me in…Tanner— really."

"I'll make it up to you." He smiled at me - a true, happy smile, but there was something in his eyes that said he was familiar with heart break and that was something we both shared.

After he left there was this awkward child-like crush smile on my face that I couldn't get to leave. I reminded myself to stay away from him. But his words repeated in my mind.

I'll make it up to you.

There was absolutely no reason I should be looking at a married man that way. There would be no making it up. It was simple. He had to be avoided at all costs. I had to never see him again.

CHAPTER THIRTY-EIGHT

The next afternoon, Amy was on the porch waiting for me. She was fancied up like a doll - hair, make-up, clothes. Everything looked perfect, so I nodded hello to her and called out, "You look pretty today."

I watched her face light up and I truly meant it. I wasted more energy hiding from her than it took to just be nice.

"Thanks, Bonnie. I was thinking I could do your hair and make-up for the BBQ tomorrow?"

"Amy, I told you I wasn't going to it." She held up a finger and shook it at me, "Ah, ah, ah... you said you owe me one."

"But..."

"I know you don't have to work," she added, and I paused.

"What?" I asked spinning around to face her.

"You don't work on Saturdays, Bonnie. I've never even seen you leave the house on the weekend." A sudden bout of sadness hit me. I probably looked pathetic. I had been trying to blend in and disappear instead I called more attention to us. The loner mom and her son.

"Fine, Amy, fine." I let out a deep breath but then for some reason I pictured Tanner's brown eyes. Surely, he wouldn't be there. He would probably be on a date with *his wife*. I couldn't help but feel jealous even if she was the one married to him. I had to get out of my head anyway.

"Oh-Kay, Amy, I will go. Dammit, I'll go."

The smile on Amy's face reminded me there was no way I could flake out on her. Is this what it feels like to be alive? I let go of all the shadows, the fears and just focused on how it felt to say yes to a BBQ. I put my trust in her. As stupid as it sounds, it was the first time I ever agreed to plans on my own. How exhilarating the option to choose could be. I shrugged it off and decided that just for one night- I would try to enjoy myself. I could be social without exploiting our past. I put Max first in every moment of our short lives, I could do this one thing to be normal. Couldn't I?

The next night I sat down on the floor of Amy's bathroom and closed my eyes. It was odd to be so close to someone- my personal space was invaded. She had all kinds of makeup and eye lash curlers and lip sticks spread across the floor. Things I had only seen in stores. Max sat next to me.

"Will you make her look like a clown or a princess?" he asked excitedly.

"Definitely a princess." Amy smiled as she began applying foundation on my skin.

"Close your eyes."

"Aw I was hoping clown," Max said, picking up his action figures.

I kept my eyes closed and tried not to peek. I never had someone touch my face so gently and carefully before. Like it was a masterpiece in progress. It tickled and I could hardly resist the urge to scratch it. I focused on breathing opposite of when she did. She was *so* close.

Amy took it very seriously. "Stay still, Bonnie."

It felt like hours. Her standing over me, breathing in my face and tickling my skin. The makeup felt thick and moist on my face. I wondered how people could possibly apply this paste every single day.

"Okay, open up!" I blinked a few times, feeling layers of mascara on my lashes. I didn't even recognize the person staring back at me in the mirror.

"You look STUNNING," Amy said as her loud voice broke through my daydream. I continued to stare in the mirror. Maybe this is the way to be. Hidden, happily in front of a ghost of who I once was. Even if it included way more blue eye shadow than I ever had seen in my life, and even bigger curls. I smiled at myself in the mirror and turned to face Max.

"Mama! You really are a princess!"

I looked like an adult, a woman. Someone I could hardly recognize. When you've only ever seen a sad lonely person in the mirror, you realize just how good happiness looks on your face. I could be a real person. I could say yes and no to people. I could leave the barbecue anytime I wanted. I was refreshed- body and mind.

But I didn't want to leave. The night was beautiful, the sun setting gave everything a golden glow and a breeze whipped through like natures fan. The fragrance of charcoal, burgers, and grilled chicken danced across the wind. It was like I walked on to a movie set. I never fit into an environment so well without feeling like an outcast. I wasn't on the sidelines, left alone with cooties. I was greeted and introduced to and accepted. Families of all types sat together. Each person looked as if they knew the secret to life. I had never seen so many happy, nice people in one place. Each one played their role in making the community event happen. There were signs everywhere that said **Remembering Daisy** and I wondered who she was. I made a mental note to find out as I slid my rolls that I stole from work onto the table before anyone noticed. I glanced at all of the delicious foods lined up and covered from bugs. There were kids of all ages running across the playground.

Max was smiling when he looked up at me. "Can I go play?" His eyes pleaded.

"Go for it, bud!" I pointed. Tonight was for fun. Tonight was for being normal people. Then, with a tear in my eye and a smile in my heart, I watched my son join the other kids as though he had done this his entire life. The shelter had made him social. He wouldn't be trapped anymore- he had learned to fly. For whatever reason, I wandered right to the table that had nothing but alcohol. A young guy who looked like he could be a teenager stood behind it.

"Oh- hey, what can I get for you?"

I froze. I looked at the selections and all I saw was my mother. The colorful, inviting bottles all marking their unique tastes to make you drunk. I ran my finger along the bottles— thinking of the promise I had once made myself as a little girl. I would never become a drunk. I would be the best mother possible to Max. But tonight was for fun. Everywhere I looked, someone had a drink in their hands. The young guy cleared his throat and stuffed his hand in his pocket clearly growing impatient.

"You looking for something special?" He asked picking up a bottle of rum. I had no clue what to do, it seemed rude to run away and rude to politely say I didn't drink. I chuckled at the idea of telling him I couldn't drink because I promised my six-year-old self I never would. That definitely wasn't normal. Tonight, was for normal.

"I'm not sure... would you make me something sweet?" I forced a smile.

"Coming right up." He replied and began scooping ice and shaking a variety of liquids together. For some reason he reminded me of how I always imagined Susan's dad. Scientist like while pouring his concoction together. I wondered where she was at that very moment.

He threw some shriveled fruit on top and smiled. "Enjoy," he said as I took the disposable cup in my hand. He stared at me as if waiting for me to test the drink. So I took a sip and cringed, but instead told him, "Perfect- uh what is it?"

"It's called sex on the beach, doll." He gave me a proud smile and I disappeared into the crowd. After the second sex on a beach, it no longer burned all the way down. I enjoyed the numbness much more than I expected.

The mixture tasted bitter and sweet at the same time. Like fruits but then not. I kind of liked the way it made my mind at ease. It was the least anxious I had been in many years. The fuzziness brought me a calm feeling that I didn't know existed. For once, I didn't have to remind myself to breathe and act normal. I wasn't walking on eggshells, worrying about what my next mistake would be and I wasn't startled by anyone moving too quickly. Not tripping over each word to avoid saying the wrong thing. Each person who accidentally bumped into me wasn't evil- they weren't trying to hurt me. I didn't have flashbacks to the worst parts of my life and thoughts reminding me of the worst parts of myself. It was as though I took a nice break from the world I had known, and I had a nice view of Max with the other children the entire time. I was in some kind of other dimension where the nightmares that lived in my brain got to take a break.

"You started without me?" Amy smirked nodding her head towards my fifth devoured sex on the beach. I sat at a table by myself. I had been in a trance, staring at Max playing.

"It's beach on the sex... I mean sex on the beach... it is delicious." My voice slurred some and I didn't even care.

"You mean was delicious. Alright I'll catch up quick- be right back." She disappeared to the alcohol table. On her way there, I watched people gathering around her, giving hugs and patting her back. I wondered how she had enough energy to keep up with so many people. Just sitting at the table alone surrounded by people had me feeling drained.

I had secretly looked for Tanner a few times. I wanted to see him- to catch a glimpse of his wife. To see the way he treated her, like a husband should. To watch her with jealous eyes as his chiseled arms rested around her waist and wonder if she knew how lucky she was. But I couldn't find him anywhere.

"Alright- back." Amy sat down with one drink in each hand.

"I don't think I'll have any more," I told her.

"We'll this one isn't for you anyway... I said I was catching up." She let out a loud cackle. Laughter came easy to me and it was surprising. I was actually having fun. We laughed together as she began to chug her drink and then I spotted him out of the corner of my eye.

Even with all of those people there. Talking, laughing, chatting. Smoke blowing from the grills and cans popping open. He could look at me and it felt like we were the only two left in the universe. Surely, I imagined it. I had to stop making eye contact. *Is this what drinks did to people?* I turned back to face Amy but she had a stupid smirk across her face. As though she just witnessed the best gossip of the week.

"It's not like that," I told her, making a slurping noise to finish what was left of my drink.

"Mm hmm," she replied then she handed me her extra drink and said, "Cheers to new beginnings."

"Cheers," I said, and I meant it. If only she knew my past, she'd know how much this meant for me.

One hour later and I was completely drunk. I had stayed way later than I imagined I would. I had officially lost control of my brain and gross motor skills. Everything seemed funny. Everything seemed exciting. I didn't run from new people, I greeted and chatted with women in the park bathroom even. There were no more worries, just a type of fuzzy peace I had never felt before. I was afraid of nothing. But I was also aware of nothing. The darkness in my mind had evaporated with each drop of alcohol I consumed.

Amy and I sat down after getting the kids a plate, getting them started eating and then eventually we went back with our plates of food.

"This is so much fun! Can we do it again tomorrow?" Max asked in between bites of his corn on the cob.

"We just have it once a year," Amy told him with a mirthless smile. Her voice not quite as slurred as mine. It almost seemed like alcohol had the opposite effect on her. She wasn't nearly as cheerful as she was normally. As the sun settled in behind the buildings around us, I told myself to remember those moments. I had control over the things in my life, and I was surrounded by people who weren't out to get me. So that's what I did, I gulped down the music, the laughter, the children playing safely in the park. The smoke blowing by from the grill, delicious food, the gentle touch of Amy on my shoulder when someone told a joke, and the sparkling in Tanner's eyes when our gazes met.

"This is my husband, Jack." Amy introduced me to him, and I waved slightly as she continued to talk. "Mr. Jones eats spaghetti o's for dinner every night.

Sarah thinks she's with a good man, but I know he's cheating on her with..." she nodded across the way- "Bethany." I held back the urge to ask about Tanner's wife.

I followed along with Amy to please her. In all honesty I could not care less about the neighbor's gossip. The longer we sat there— the more anxious I grew from her negative mood. The only thing I cared about was keeping my business safe with me. I had to. It was my only way of survival. Amy didn't know what personal space meant so I had to be cautious and on guard even while I was wasted.

Max finished eating and threw his plate away. I wiped the sticky BBQ sauce from his face.

"I'm gonna go play catch!"

"Okay— be careful, it's getting dark soon," I told him.

"Okay, Mama." He huffed and turned to race away. I called for him.

"Oh, and Max— make sure you ask nicely to play," I told him and with that he disappeared. He asked kid after kid to play catch with him. And although I couldn't hear their refusal- I could see the disappointment on Max's face when they turned him down.

I chugged a few waters to try and fight the headache that had started. I was going to have to play catch so I went back for one more water. When I returned to the table, I couldn't find him. I paced and desperately searched for him. Hoping at any second I would see him playing with the other kids. But he wasn't by the slide and he wasn't by the swings. I ran down to the food to see if he was eating a snack. Then I ran up to Amy with panic setting in. As if in slow motion wondering if Dale had finally gotten to him. No matter how many drinks— how many days —it always came back to him. My real life monster.

"Sorry to interrupt but, Amy, have you seen Max?" I was out of breath and sweat had begun to collect on my hairline. She studied me for a moment and then pointed across the field.

"He's playing ball... with Tanner." She turned, smirked at me and went back to her conversation. I felt my heart tug in my chest when I finally spotted Tanner playing catch with my son.

He threw the ball and it slipped between Max's fingers. Tanner ran over to him and showed him how to hold the ball. Max smiled proudly the next time when he caught it. He bent down next to him and smiled as he talked. On his level. He treated him like a dad should treat his little boy. Something Max never had. A little girl stood near, waiting patiently for her turn. Then Max saw me and ran towards me. Tanner must have seen me too because my heart skipped a beat when he followed behind.

"Hi Bonnie, is this your son? He's got a good hand on him!" He said excitedly. *My God- he was even more handsome with sex on the beach pumping through my blood.*

I couldn't wipe the smile from my face. "Thanks for playing with him." My eyes lingered over his body, completely forgetting he was married. He was even more irresistible when I was drunk. And he was still wearing his ring.

"Yes, thank you! "Max added. "That was very fun."

"Anytime- anytime. Oh hey— Bonnie…have you met Sally?"

I nodded my head no and followed his gaze. It was his wife. It had to be- here would be the moment of truth. But instead, from behind him came the prettiest little brown eyed girl.

"This is Sally."

"Hi Sally, it is so nice to meet you!" I told her happily. The whole while my drunken mind was grateful it wasn't his wife. I had to stop… to get a grip on this crush. It was not okay. I wasn't ready and he… he was a married man in a healthy relationship!

"Did you know if you drink too much of that stuff it will make you throw up?" Sally asked me, pointing at my drink. I must have swapped out my water when I was panicking. I let out a giggle and poured it in the grass beside me. "Why, thank you, Sally. That is a great reminder."

"Yeah, my dad has too much sometimes. I don't know why he still drinks it if--."

"OH-Kay- that's enough of that." Tanner stepped in and pretended to cup his hands over her mouth.

"Dad!" She called to him playfully. They pretended to wrestle and I couldn't help but watch the gentle way he interacted with his daughter.

I made myself study his ring. My gaze fell back to his eyes as he looked right at me. I could get lost in them. I didn't know if it was the alcohol or fear but suddenly, I didn't trust myself to look him in the eyes one second more.

Sally tugged his hand. "Let's go, Dad. Before you get too *drunked*." She pulled him away and he waved to us.

"See you later."

"Later," I called and took hold of Max's hand. I would not be seeing him later. I had to stay far away from him, for real this time.

CHAPTER THIRTY-NINE

"I'm glad you came," Amy told me as soon as I reached my door after work on Monday. I had a great shift with larger than normal tips so I was already feeling excited. I whipped around to see her. I had been waiting for a time to ask her a question.

"Thanks for making me go, I did have fun." A smile crept across my face. "I felt pretty bad the next morning though."

"You like him." Amy shook her finger at me. "You do… I knew it!"

"Oh no. No, he's married." I stumbled on the right words.

"Was married."

"Was married?" I asked her.

"Bonnie, he's raising Sally on his own. His wife died."

"Oh God. Oh no," I sank to the seat next to her. I imagined his wife being beautiful, and perfect and very much alive. Now I understood the sadness behind his smile.

It had only been two days and I did stay away from him, but I couldn't quite rid the thoughts from my mind.

"Is it too soon?" Amy spoke in her motherly voice again.

"Well- yes. And no. Well… yes! I can't see anyone."

"How long are we talking?"

"Like ever again. I need to be the best mom for Max."

"Bonnie… you can be a good mom and have a date too… listen, I don't know your story but Tanner hasn't shown interest in anyone in over 2 years."

"What? You think he likes me?" I asked. My face blushed and I felt a warm, wax-like sensation harden my entire body. The idea of someone actually liking me. Someone like *him* liking me was even more terrifying. I had never been worthy of love.

"Heck, I don't know. That man is hard to read but you'll never know if you don't try."

Amy stamped her cigarette out as she stood, but hesitated to go inside.

"What… did your man die? Was he abusive?"

I was shocked from the invasive way she called him my man. I never considered to have a choice in the matter. But it being Amy I should have expected it. She just didn't have a filter.

"Um- yeah. He's not dead and it wasn't good. I had to run to get away and I'm afraid. I'm afraid of what will happen when he finds me."

Amy sat up and blinked her eyes. Pain crossed her face as if she felt what I had been through.

"Okay- say no more. I know everyone thinks I only gossip but I can keep a secret too. You say the word and I'd be there for you. It gets lonely with Jack traveling so much. I was honestly really happy to see you moved in."

"Thank you, you've been so kind- I've got to go pick up Max." I patted her hand, afraid I had said too much and slipped inside to change.

In that moment, I made up my mind. I would avoid Tanner for the rest of my life. I couldn't have something like this jeopardize everything I worked so hard to escape. He was too big of a distraction. Amy had said he possibly showed interest in me… and obviously I was like a darting minnow around him. Dale would be back and I had to be ready. My mind couldn't be cluttered with thoughts of Tanner while trying to rebuild our lives.

I walked down the block and crossed the street. Max was at his small preschool, The Wild Ones. I thought the name was fitting and they took my childcare vouchers. He liked it there and had even made some friends. He was as happy as ever to see me when I picked him up.

"Mama, I have a new pet." I briefly thought of that baby bird. The bird who saved us.

He ran to me and opened his hand. Inside he held a round rock with two scribbled on eyeballs and a big smile.

"Hmm. I like that he has a big smile."

"Yep- did you know you can keep a pet rock alive forever?"

I looked both ways. Behind us- in front of us. I surveyed each car that passed.

"Did you? Did you know they can live forever?" He asked again excitedly.

"I guess so." I felt distracted. I wasn't paying attention to him the way I should have been. I felt like at all times someone was after us. Every loud noise, every person that walked by- had become a threat to me when we were in public.

"Mama. do you think Dale will find us?" Max asked and chills raised along my arms. I don't even know when he stopped calling him Pa.

"Max- what? Why? Have you seen him?"

I held his shoulders a little too tightly and bent down to his level.

"No… I just don't ever want to be without you."

Oh, thank God.

"You won't be, Max- I promise." I knew I should never make a promise I wasn't certain I could keep but I would have the fight of my life for him.

We held hands on the walk back as we often did. I kept him closer than I probably should have but there was no way I was letting him out of my sight. I hated that he observed my paranoia, despite us never even having talked about Dale returning.

As we crossed the park, and neared our apartment, right away I noticed Sally. She had on mismatched clothes and a football in her hands. Her cheeks were caked with mud and grass.

"Hey- Max! Wanna play?" She asked, nodding towards her dad. My eyes met Tanner's and I resisted any urge of attraction and gave a flat wave instead. Even if he was a widow, I still couldn't accept that I was attracted to him.

Max looked up at me and I nodded at him. "Go ahead."

"No, I meant both of you." Sally giggled. I looked over at Tanner again whose gaze I was avoiding. But there he was coming towards me with a child-like grin on his face.

"You can be on my team." He smiled, then he motioned for me to join him.

You've got to be kidding me. But as if I lost control, I drifted towards him.

"You're gonna play, Mama?" Max jumped excitedly.

"I guess I will try!" I said uneasy but Tanner stepped closer. He was the kind of handsome that made me pause just to stare at him, it struck me to the core each time. He was perfect. His intense gaze and prominent jawline. I couldn't help but imagine how his lips would move in a kiss.

"Wait, you've never played before?"

His voice interrupted my thoughts.

"Nope- there's a lot of things I haven't tried." I brushed the hair out of my eyes. His smile warmed my soul. How was it that he could make me forget about all of my worries?

We practiced tossing it back and forth several times. I thought I could definitely catch better than I could throw the ball. Each time I tried it wobbled and landed either too short or way out of target.

I hadn't laughed that hard in a long time. Their faces, when I threw the ball and it wobbled to where nobody was, or in the bushes, were priceless.

"Alright- I have to show my teammate something." Tanner teased. He walked up right behind me and slid his arms around my shoulders. I couldn't focus on anything except his biceps being wrapped around me.

"Take the ball," he said in a gentle voice. I took it from him with both of my hands. He laughed at me.

"Gripping the ball is the essential part of throwing it," he said to me. "And you're cradling it."

"Oh," I said, unable to form words being this close to him. The heat radiated off his body and when he spoke close to my ear, chills prickled down every part of my body. He took my hand and placed it on the ball, moving slightly over my fingers. "Here- like this. Your hand should be more toward the top of the football."

I nodded and he traced my hand with his.

"Your index finger should be about this far from the top of the ball."

"Just make sure there's air between your palm and the ball." He smiled at me, turning to face me. We were so close I couldn't look away.

"Now you try. Your pointer finger should be the last touch of the ball." He stepped back and immediately I wanted his arms back around me. I held the ball up and watched in awe as it spun in the air landing perfectly in front of Sally.

"Yay!" She cheered for me and jumped up and down. Tanner gave me a childish high five. I felt carefree, and youthful, glimpses of what I had missed in my childhood.

But when I turned back around, Sally let go of the football and I watched it spin right towards me. It got closer and closer until my vision blurred. I tried to catch it. It slipped right through my fingers and slammed into my face— right into my eye and I immediately cowered to the grass. It had been my instinct since I was little.

"Pause!" Tanner called and jumped down next to me. "Oh man. I think you'll make it but we're definitely going to need a patch for your eye." His voice was low and he gave a cunning smile. He was so close to me again, right where I wanted him to be. Max and Sally stood above us. I sat up slowly.

"Mama you'll be a pirate!" Max added. Everyone leaned over me.

"I'm fine- I'm fine." I shrugged as the embarrassment heated my cheeks, then I noticed Sally standing there with wide eyes.

"I'm. So. Sorry," she whispered and cupped her hands over her mouth.

"It's not your fault, Sally. I'm fine," I told her and went to stand up. Tanner took my hand inside of his and pulled me to my feet. I swear I felt a wave of electricity pass from my body to his. I held on to his hand too long. We awkwardly pulled away. I was more paralyzed by the warmth of his hand than I had been from the football to the eye.

"Are you sure you're, okay?" Tanner asked and ran his fingers- featherlight-- over where the ball hit me.

My vision was blurry and my head spun. I truly didn't know if it was anxiety or a concussion.

"Sally- holy cow… you have an arm," I told her, smiling. But I wasn't fine. I stumbled forward. Tanner caught me. I could smell his salty skin and aftershave. It felt so natural to be in his arms.

"Let's get them settled at home, Sal."

Max turned to Sally. "Race ya there!" And they faded into the distance.

Tanner placed one arm around me and rested it above my hip. I tried to focus on walking. This was not staying away from him.

"I'm so sorry- if I would have known you never played then I wouldn't have invited you to be on my team."

"Ha- really?" I gave him a playful shove. We both laughed then- my head hurt even worse.

"Stop it. I can't even laugh right now," I told him followed by a slight grin that couldn't be suppressed.

Once inside, Max and Sally climbed inside the fort. Tanner got ice from my freezer and wrapped it up for me.

"You going to be, okay?"

"Yes- truly. I've had much worse." I moved the ice to my eye. He flinched when I said that and it made me realize what I said. I forgot being abused wasn't the norm for most people.

"I'm sorry, I had a rough childhood." I tried to explain but it looked like he was literally feeling my pain. I couldn't tell if he was just a good person or if he truly had interest in me. *How could anyone ever want someone like me?*

I didn't need to wonder. It didn't matter.

"Mama! Tanner… we need your help!" Max called for us. We turned to the kids and they held the fort doors open for us. Tanner looked at me with a smile and shrugged.

"After you."

I laughed, wondering how he would even fit inside. But he came in right behind me, looking like an overgrown kid.

"You'll be the king, Dad, and Bonnie is the queen." Sally dubbed each of our characters.

Tanner looked at me and grinned. "As long as the queen doesn't play ball, because that could put her in danger."

I shoved him.

"The queen shall do whatever she pleases," I responded.

"Well, the queen has to hold the king's hand." Sally pointed, causing Tanner and I to look awkwardly at each other.

"Yes," Max agreed. "I'll be the guard and, Sally, you can be the princess,"

"No. I want to be the kitty cat."

"Okay... then I want to be the dragon." Max put his finger on his chin with a large grin.

"Go on now, king and queen, hold hands." I hesitated but Tanner took my much smaller hand in his. He laced his fingers through mine in a soft grip. I thought my heart might beat out of my chest.

Max jumped up and started chasing the kitty cat. They ran outside of the castle leaving Tanner and I alone, in the fort, holding hands. It may have been the most awkward and best moment of my life.

"Aren't you going to go out and save the cat from the dragon, king?" I asked him playfully.

"I've taught the cat to fight her own battles... and how to catch." Tanner grinned. I nudged him with my knee. "You're never going to let me live that one down, are you?" He smiled at me and glanced down at my lips. I was certain for a second he was going to move in for a kiss. A sudden urge took over my entire body. I became aware of my hand growing clammy inside of his and as I leaned closer. Sally popped through the fort.

"Watch out! The dragon is coming." She jumped onto both of us, and Max crawled in blowing fire. He scrambled to us and we all fell into a dog pile on the floor, knocking down the entire fort.

Tanner didn't let my hand go until we found our way out of the deconstruction of blankets and pillows. My cheeks were blushed and I felt on top of the world just from holding his hand. When I realized they had to leave, I came back to reality. Everything truly was better inside of that fort. Just as Max had said.

After they left, I closed the door, locked it, and then peeked through the window until I saw them vanish into the distance. It was dark and Tanner carried Sally in his arms. I couldn't believe just seconds ago I was so close to having my first real kiss. In his presence I had no control.

"That was the last time," I said to myself.

"Last time for what?" Max popped up beside me.

"Last time… I play ball," I said, squinting my eyes at him trying to conceal my smile. "Now let's get you to bed."

CHAPTER FORTY

As my black eye faded over the next few weeks, I tried to isolate from the everybody knows everybody state of affairs. While I enjoyed the new faces and small talk, it actually was quite overwhelming to me. It took so much energy to pretend that I was normal. To fake a smile and act like I wasn't on the run from my abusive husband who married me when I was a child. I decided to take a step back and be more careful. I kept my blinds drawn tightly and dashed in and out to work when the coast was clear, avoiding Amy. Like a hermit crab I became only comfortable in my shell. The longer I stayed away from people, the easier it became to retreat back within myself. Just where I liked to be.

I spent all of my spare time just being present with Max inside of our apartment. Playtime, mealtime, bath time, bed. I gave every ounce of energy I had to him with no distractions. It was easier that way, being hidden together in our apartment away from people and problems. I could have stayed there forever with him. I didn't need love from a man. I had everything I needed right there inside of that apartment. The longer I stayed away from Tanner, the longer I could convince myself of that. I was able to forget about his brown eyes and woodsy smell and I convinced myself I could forget him completely. I would move forward until I was ready to try the dating world. If I was ever ready. I was convinced that, after Max grew up, I might spend the rest of my life in solitude. It didn't sound so bad after everything I went through. The more people you have to love, the more you have to lose. Sad that life was that way, but my life had been a series of losing everyone I loved.

Max and I became aware of what everyone did around us. Amy and her smoking. The couple that lived three doors down and the way their arguments made our glasses in our kitchen cabinets cling. The route Tanner took to the office each morning and when he worked long hours and closed shop at 7:30. I often watched around that time just to catch glimpses of him walking home. By the time we could finally afford a television, I knew that marked a new stage in our lives. We no longer had to observe everyone around us. No longer had to sense every vibration on our walls. Watching television together put us in a different place. There were many nights we slept side by side on that old red couch. Once Max fell asleep, I would flip through the channels, marveling at how wonderful and simple our lives had become. Trying to block out the thoughts of what life would be like with Tanner in it.

One night as I flipped through the channels a familiar face shot up on the screen.

"Are you shitting me?" My voice shook even in my head. I sat up and ran across the room. I bent down inches from the TV. It was Susan! She made it. She actually made it! Tears filled my eyes as I saw my beautiful friend who had grown into a woman. Susan's bright red hair was cut short and it was curly-- her eyes glowed on the screen.

"Susan— one of our first female meteorologists with the forecast..."

"Here is our official forecast for our area tonight- partly cloudy and mild. Look for a low temperature down to 55 degrees. Then for tomorrow it will be mostly cloudy- we'll call it that- with a 30 % chance of rain. Then look for sunshine over the weekend." She smiled brightly. When the screen flashed back to the commercial, I stayed there. Frozen in front of the television. Susan made it to the weather channel. I could hardly believe it. I pictured her all those years ago in our bedroom. She kept her promise. I ran to the counter to jot down the news station WYRT. I had to find a way to contact her.

The next morning Max followed me to Amy's door and we knocked. She looked confused when she opened it.

"Oh hey.. Stranger," she said with her voice still asleep. I could tell immediately she held a grudge from my rude disappearance and hermit behavior.

"Sorry, it's early. I just wanted to drop by before work to see if you had a phone book?" I smiled and gently offered her a coffee.

"What in the world? What time is it?" She leaned on the door and glanced around her dark living room.

"It's early. I'm sorry, I just really need to reach someone."

"Is it *him*?" She asked with slight anger trickling into her voice.

"No. Oh, definitely not. It's an old friend of mine. She's a weather woman. I saw her on the tv last night."

She grabbed the coffee from me.

"What channel?"

I glanced down at the scribbled piece of paper. "WYRT?"

"That's a Glendale station… that won't be in my book. I'll find out for you and swing by tonight."

"Thank you! Amy, thank you so much!" I wasn't a hugging person, but I could have pulled her in for a big one in that moment.

"You'll owe me one again." She smiled and closed the door.

CHAPTER FORTY-ONE

"Max be careful with the…"

The paper bag ripped in half. "Eggs." I huffed under my breath as I watched the entire dozen tumble and scatter. Hitting the concrete and splattering across our shoes.

"Max, I told you to be careful with that bag…" I was out of patience after watching him skip and hop and do everything that I asked him not to. I hated myself for losing patience with the one person who meant the most to me. But I wasn't perfect. We were headed back from the grocery store and the eggs almost made it back in one piece. The only bag light enough for him to carry just so happened to be the bread and the eggs.

"Look Mama, there's one left." Max smiled proudly, pointing at the single egg that rested in the grass.

"That will make a lot of food for us," I said sarcastically but he grinned at me, and I reminded myself it was only eggs. Not that we had money to spare but his sparkling little boy blue eyes took away my frustration.

"Alright. But now you'll have to eat spinach for breakfast," I told him, smiling.

"Mama, I'm not Popeye!" He smiled back and his face turned to disgust. "I don't need any spinach— I'm strong enough!"

I laughed at him and picked up the empty egg carton. I placed the one surviving egg back inside and, just as I stood, a shadow appeared behind me. My stomach turned inside out and I twirled around. My eyes met familiar brown eyes that poured warmth and calm over my worry.

"Tanner." My smile could be heard in my voice.

"Bonnie. Hi Max," He replied and wiped his hands on his work pants. I hadn't seen him since the black eye incident. I had purposely avoided him.

"Looks like you started breakfast?" He motioned towards the eggs with a grin.

Max's cheeks flushed and he shrugged his shoulders. Tanner kicked the eggs into the grass and took the ripped bag from Max. He folded it until it closed in over the bread and then, without asking, he took three bags from my left arm. I stared at the marks the handles left indented in my arm instead of looking him in the eyes. He slid the paper bag inside one of the others and followed behind us. He glanced back down at Max and added,

"The squirrels will enjoy it, don't worry."

Max grinned at the idea of it. I watched his worry disappear just as my own had.

Everything Tanner did was so graceful. Thoughtful. He somehow swooped in and made it look easy to fix mistakes and erase fear. Made it seem like I hadn't been purposely avoiding him.

"It's no big deal," he said to Max. I didn't understand how he coped with everything so well.

Once inside the apartment, I felt my cheeks flush as he carried my groceries in and sat them all on the counter for me.

"Have you been doing, okay?" he asked once he slid the milk into my fridge.

"Mhm." I nodded. "Thanks for helping, you really didn't have to."

"It's okay. No worries. Actually," he paused, glanced at Max and lowered his voice, "I've been thinking. Hoping to see you. Umm wondering... Would you like to hang out sometime?"

His question surprised me so much that I actually dropped the can of corn I was holding. *He really wanted to hang out with me? To date me?*

I picked the can back up and turned to face him. It was exhilarating.

"Tanner, I'm actually... um...I can't." The words escaped me before I even had time to think. The idea of getting hurt was more terrifying than actually going out with him.

"Oh. Okay. No worries," he responded and slid his hands into his pockets. The naked vulnerability on his face made my stomach drop.

"Tanner, I wasn't saying it like… like…"

"Mama! Tanner! The squirrels are eating the eggs already!" Max interrupted from the window. I watched Tanner attempt a smile for him. A smile to hide the disappointment. The disappointment that I had created. I never wanted to take his smile from him again.

"See? It's all fine, Max." His smiled slowly and his eyes stayed on me for a moment asking for an explanation.

All I could do was stand there frozen. Hating myself. Hating my words. I hated my fear and insecurities that made me the way that I was.

Stupid girls do stupid things.

"But I better get back to work."

His eyes were empty, defeated like on the first day I met him.

I watched him turn to leave. I wanted to tell him that I didn't know how any of this worked. That I was sorry. That what I wanted more than anything was to be close to him again. But I just watched him walk away.

CHAPTER FORTY-TWO

Every time there was a knock on the door, I had an urge to jump behind the couch and hide in a fetal position. I never got over the fear that Dale would find me. So, when the knock came unexpectedly, I froze in place. But with Max watching, I made myself inspect.

After peeping through the hole at her for an entire minute, Max and I finally let Amy in.

"I dropped by the library to find the Glendale phone book. I looked up the news station. And here you go." She dropped the number into my hand. She went out of her way to find this for me.

"I'm sorry for the trouble but thank you so much!"

"No trouble. But hey, Jack will be home this week and..."

"Jack?" I interrupted.

"My husband, Bonnie- jeez. It's like you live in a bubble." I met him once before, but I had forgotten. Clearly, she was frustrated with me.

"I'm sorry," I mumbled. She was lonely because he traveled for work. She paid me so much attention but I was always so distracted. I wasn't good at being a friend.

"Anyway, he's friends with Tanner and I was wondering if you could..."

"Tanner. No. Nope… I can't help if it has to do with him." I interrupted her again.

Amy studied my face. "He's been asking about you," she said back just as quickly. I smiled at that, one of those almost giggle smiles.

"You're blushing." Amy playfully shoved me.

I turned serious again. "He still wears his ring, Amy."

"I don't care if he wears a thong…you should hang out with us."

She flashed me her *you owe me* puppy dog eyes and I knew there was no way out of it. Unless… unless I told her my secret.

"Amy." I looked down at Max and gently patted his shoulder. "Go on and brush your teeth, please."

Once he disappeared into the bathroom, Amy turned to face me.

"He actually asked me to hang out already and I said no."

"You said no?" She repeated her eyes fixated on me.

"I didn't want to share this because I don't want anyone to know. I've never been on a date. I've never even had a real boyfriend. The entire thing is way too much for me right now," I whispered to her. Amy's eyes widened.

"But that doesn't add up. I mean you have a son," she said back, and I shushed her.

"I was just a kid and… he was an adult," I told her sheepishly, for the first time accepting this myself. I crossed my arms. Shame poured over me.

"Oh. Ohhh." Amy cupped her hands over her mouth. She froze. I could see the frustration directed at me escaping her mind.

"Okay. I'll save the favor for another time. No need to say more." She patted me as if I were an injured puppy and then she pulled me in tightly for a hug. After she left, I stood there with my arms still suspended. I knew that I wanted to go, but I couldn't. It was like my emotions were completely mixed up and turned upside down. There was this foreign feeling inside of me anticipating see Tanner and apologizing to him. It drove me wild. I had never felt so exhilarated at the thought of another person before. So why did I say no? There was a part of me telling myself to run. So, the more I thought of him, the more I told myself I was attaching to the first man that came after what I went through. The more I told myself to stay away.

After I carried Max to his bed, I sat down at the phone and pulled the number out of my pocket. I could actually talk to Susan but what would I even say to her? She had probably long forgotten the girl who she used to share chocolates with. I spun the phone as I punched in the numbers. The line rang and rang.

"News WYRT- this is Rebecka."

"Uh. Hi. Rebecka," I started and took a deep breathe. "I am trying to reach the weather woman, Susan?"

"Our meteorologists have all left for the night. Can I take a message?" Rebecka asked, laboredly.

"Yes. Please tell her it is her old friend, Bonnie, and I would like to speak with her."

"Alright, I'll get it to her." She took my number and Rebecka hung up before I could add any more. It didn't sound promising, but it was a start.

The next few weeks were quite the blur. Amy didn't ask me again about seeing Tanner that week, nor the next. I was surprised but also distracted. I anticipated hearing Susan's voice. I waited for her to call me. That was the only thing I had to look forward to. I obsessively checked my answering machine to see if she returned my call. Even if all I got was closure from my childhood friend, I still hoped for the possibility we could cuddle together and eat chocolates.

I went in and out of morning shifts and tried to spend as much time with Max as I could. Being with him was the most rewarding and difficult job there was— being a mother. Living alone came with new feelings. A mixture of satisfaction and a haunting fear I would screw it all up. The pressure was all on me to keep us alive. I felt the need to be the perfect mother for Max, but I quickly realized that just wasn't possible. Each day I pushed through the darkness inside of my own mind and found a new strength within myself. Something I hadn't known I even had until I had my own child. A motherly strength I feared would skip me like it had skipped my own mother. One night while we cuddled on the couch, Max opened his sleepy eyes and turned to me.

"Who needs a warm bed when you have a warm Mama?" He smiled and snuggled in close. I knew in that moment I was the safety net for my child. The net that held all of his feelings together after a long day. It gave me a sense of purpose during those long days filled with love and mistakes. Apologies and arguments with a four-year-old. The ups and downs and the highs and lows of raising a child. I forgot who I was and left the little girl behind in the darkness. I was now just Mama and the rest didn't matter. Even with all of the pleasure I found in dreaming of what Max's future held for him, I was still in denial that he was all mine, truly mine. And that scared me because I never wanted to lose him.

I tried Susan about a dozen more times. Rebecka clearly didn't care at all. I tried to explain to Rebecka the urgent situation of why I needed to talk to her. But she treated me as if I were just a fan girl, stalking Susan. No matter what I said, Rebecka never responded with any indication of interest. The only way I would be able to talk to Susan would be sending a letter to the news station. So that's just what I did the following morning.

I encountered long days filled with pirates and cowboys. Sometimes the laundry and cleaning were all I did on my days off. And as much love that I had for Max, often being a mother led me to wishing I had a mother of my own. Or an identity of my own. Someone to call when Max threw a fit when I gave him the blue cup and not the red one. Someone to take over meal prepping and laundry and allow me to take a bubble bath for just one day. Or someone to help teach Max how to ride his bike. But I did it all. At night I met sheer exhaustion from reading the copy of *Grimms fairytales* for the 10th night in a row and wishing Max would just fall asleep. Then when he did, I stared at his sleeping eye lashes and felt all of the mother guilt. Did I do enough? Play enough? Was I present? Did I give him a good life? Until I could no longer over-think and I would fall asleep myself.

The days went on as if each tiny minute part became one. Susan never called. I wondered if she got my letter. When I ran into Amy, I took more time to pay attention to her life. She had, after all, been thoughtful since the day I moved in. With time, I slowly began to open up to her. I didn't like spilling my deepest, darkest secret, but I felt as though I couldn't hold it in any longer. I gave her bits and pieces of the things that weren't completely suppressed. The idea of Susan had re-opened an innocent part of myself that I forgot existed.

Amy had to know why I was the way that I was. I shuffled my hands into my pockets and looked away anytime Tanner was brought into conversation. But my heart still raced just at hearing his name. I was certain he would be dating someone else by now. I missed my chance. Besides it was a stupid crush on the first man that came along. Right? I would get over it.

Finally on a rainy Saturday morning while Max watched a cartoon, I heard the phone ring and since I had only given my number to one person, there was a heavy feeling in my gut. I jumped up and ran to the phone.

"Hello?" I asked curiously. My heart raced.

"Bonnie." It wasn't a woman. Disappointment heightened the tone of my voice, "Yes?"

"Oh hey... it's Tanner. I hope I'm not bothering you but I just wanted to put myself on the line even on the verge of looking like... a stalker."

I paused before I answered and inhaled deeply with a smile.

"I'm good. Yeah, we're doing fine," I told him, trying to sound confident. Trying to forget the look on his face when I said no to going out with him. He had this way of making me forget how to speak.

"How did you get my number?" I asked.

"Okay well, I just wanted to check in. I came by last week and I was worried about you, your apartment looked all dark and... now it's beginning to feel like I'm stalking you and..."

My heart dropped. He really did care.

"Tanner, it's not you. I wanted to... I wanted to hang out with you. I've just never been on a real date before and it sounds... well, intimi-dating." My voice sounded like a schoolgirl's.

"Well... I know this is kind of weird. Uh... Amy gave me your number and all, but I thought maybe... maybe you'd like to hang out *with-out* the kids next Friday?"

"Is this like a date?"

"No. No, nothing fancy- certainly not a date. The furthest thing from a date, just us hanging out. I mean if you'd like to..." He mumbled and it made me blush. For someone like him to be at loss for words allowed me to feel normal. I glanced over at Max playing with his cars. My heart tugged at the idea of being away from him. At the idea of not putting him first. *Don't screw this up.*

"I don't... I don't know what to say. I would have to find someone to watch Max...

"I already did. Amy said she will watch them both."

"Did she put you up to this?" Insecurity crept back in.

"No. Sally has just been begging to play with Max and we wondered how you were and honestly I didn't like the way we left things."

"Yeah. Okay. I understand," I told him, keeping it business like.

But his voice changed, it was vulnerable and low. "And Bonnie. I wanted to see you."

My heart about beat out of my chest.

"You were thinking about me?" My voice cracked almost in a whisper.

"I feel like that's all I can do lately," he said back.

It feels like you're always on my mind too. But I can't bring myself to say it.

"Alright. Well, I would... I would like to hang out. But Tanner you must understand I'm not... I'm not ready for a relationship," I told him awkwardly, pulling back from what I really wanted to say. My voice, once again, sounding like a business transaction- flat and empty and not how I wanted to sound.

Silence on the line, but I could feel his smile through the phone. I resisted the urge to tell him I've been thinking of him. That I wanted to see him too. I wanted to know him. I wanted to be close to him. But nothing would come out. I dreaded hanging up. Part of me wanted to sit there all day, listening to his voice and not committing to anything more than that. I couldn't trust myself.

"Alright. Wow. I'll see you on Friday, Bon, for our *not a date. Friends it is.*"

I laughed out loud at that one. "Sounds like a plan." My smile met my ears.

I hung up swiftly. The idea that he called me Bon made my cheeks hot and I had no idea a silly nickname could make me blush like that. I wanted so badly to trust him. To be wrapped up in his strong arms like I had never been in anyone's before. And I sat there remembering what led me to this place. Why I didn't trust anyone with anything. All of the reasons why I had to keep resisting him.

I would not be like my mother. I would never choose chasing a man or booze over my child. One *not date* couldn't be all that bad. We could be friends, right?

CHAPTER FORTY-THREE

I twirled back and forth in front of the mirror. Gingerly, I reached down to caress the soft fabric with my fingertips. It was the nicest dress I had ever worn. It was tight fitting and concealed my chest, but with the slightest movement it billowed out around me. Amy asked me for my sizes and came back from the nearest mall with a dress and two pairs of shoes. I tried to pay her back, but she wouldn't accept the money.

So, there I was standing there with this beautiful princess dress trying to come to terms with how beautiful I looked.

"Are you sure it's not too fancy?" I asked Amy timidly. I didn't look like myself, I looked like a woman. Since when was I an adult? I reached my hands out to touch the make-up that glistened on my face.

Was I really about to go on a date? A date, date? A not date.

My stomach swirled and twisted just like my hair that was perfectly curled, thanks to Amy. I had an overwhelming weight in my chest- like my lungs had been hardened in concrete all day. It was hard to breathe and my heart was pounding. Skipping. I considered canceling for the tenth time as I tugged at a curl. It was so confusing to be rejecting something I wanted so badly, so fiercely.

Amy came in my room in her PJ's, holding high heels in her arms. "You're going to do just fine."

"Do you want black or tan?" She extended the heels out to me. A devious grin crossed her lips.

"I won't even be able to walk. Can't I just wear these?" I held out my old black flats that no longer had the brand inscribed on the insole.

Amy looked disgusted and shook her head no while taking the shoes from me. She passed me the black ones with a glare.

I sat on the edge of my bed and began to put them on.

"I'm nervous."

Ever since I agreed, I felt like what I imagined a teenager feels on their first date.

"Listen. You're just hanging out. It's not even a real date." Amy couldn't keep the smirk off of her face.

"I knew you put him up to this!" I hissed at her halfway playfully.

"He kept asking me how he could see you. I just helped him see you. I gave him your number...That's all. The rest is all him. Besides, where do you even go if it's not a date?" Amy pulled her brows together, continuing the silly grin on her face.

"I have no..." my sentence was interrupted by a knock at the door. I had a fleeting feeling to hide in my closet.

"Come in!" Amy shouted, then turned and focused on me and waved her pointer finger.

"Ah, ah, ah. You deserve this, *hun*." She gave me a reassuring pat on my shoulder. I stumbled in the heels and smiled at her as if to say, see I can't do this.

"I know, I know you don't want to ever do anything fun because you're a mom." She laughed, correcting my posture.

"I don't like leaving Max is all."

"You deserve to enjoy things too."

"I'm trying to be normal. Piece by piece." I held on to the dress again and brushed a curl from my face. While looking at myself, a large unfamiliar smile greeted me in the mirror.

"Okay, well enough staring at yourself. If you do that all night, he will surely wonder what's going on in there." She tapped the top of my head gently, then she whispered just what I needed to hear,

"You look beautiful. And he won't hurt you."

She paused, pulling me from the room.

"If he does, I'll kick his ass."

"Whose ass are you kicking?" Max stood outside of the door, with a cheeky smirk. He dodged me when I reached for him. "Mama and Tanner are going on a date!" He told Sally.

"Max!" I growled to him and then I met Tanner's eyes. We smirked at each other the way adults suppress a smile when a child says something they're not supposed to.

And as the heat filled my cheeks, every single worry I had faded away. It was as though he was the calm to my storm but also the thunder. He brought an energy with him that set fire to my soul. It was undeniable. That is why I had stayed away from him. Did he feel it too?

Max and Sally were already setting up a board game. The chatter from them took the pressure off us to say the right thing. Tanner and I walked towards each other awkwardly. A wobbly dance that showed we didn't know whether to act like friends or like that of two people going on a date.

"Guess what! Last time I played I scored eleven 60!" Max shouted proudly.

Sally cut in. "Well, I scored like a thousand!"

"Wow!" Max replied, both unaware his number was larger. I smiled to myself, wishing for that unknowing wonder that children have of all things in the world. Back when it all seemed so simple. Amy stepped closer to us like she itched to rid the awkwardness we set off. She gave me that 'I can take care of your child' nod.

"Go- off with you now." She motioned towards the door, shoved us to it and as we heard it lock, all there was left was silence.

"Well, what do we do now?" Tanner opened his palm and held it out to me.

"I don't really know. What do people do on **not** dates?"

Tanner laughed. "I have an idea- do you like ice cream?"

I smiled and nodded my head.

My hand fit neatly inside of his. I tried not to squeeze too tightly because mine were clammy. I was alone with him for the first time ever and I already never wanted to let go. There were more butterflies in my stomach than ever before. But they were the good ones. The kind that flutters all the way down to your toes. This giddy girl crush could not end well.

Thirty minutes later, the door made a loud chime as we walked inside the diner. Chatter could be heard all around. All of those people looked up at us. I felt like I was late for school. But when I looked again nobody was really looking at us. That fear of being watched I carried with me, avoiding eye contact, fear of being judged or found.

There was a large sign that stated **Seat Yourself,** so I followed Tanner to the booth like a well-trained puppy dog. I slid in across from him and felt the cool bench on my exposed legs.

"You okay?" Tanner asked, reaching across the table. Instead of taking my hand, he took the menu. I nodded at him but glanced back around, surveying the space for Dale. Stopping on each male figure in the room to confirm they weren't him. It was sad, this routine I had created any time I was in public.

"Hey. If this is too loud, we can go somewhere else?" he asked, reading my face.

"It's okay. I'm fine." I smiled weakly. *Act normal.*

A quick moving waitress interrupted.

"Hello…aren't you two cute. Welcome- *love birds.* I'm Betsy. What can I get started?"

"Um… I think we'll take a few minutes on the menu." Tanner smiled gently at me to make sure that was okay. I nodded but he turned back to Betsy.

"Actually… can you start us off with two shakes?"

"Dessert before dinner? My kind of people." She laughed and looked to me.

"Vanilla or chocolate?"

"Chocolate," Tanner and I responded at the same time.

"Haha jinx. You're so cute, it's like a romance novel."

Our eyes widened at each other. Her laugh followed her into the kitchen.

"Good thing this isn't a date because she would make things really awkward." Tanner grinned.

"Love birds." He mocked her and the way his eyes shined into mine made me look away. It was a soft gaze that seemed to lead into no return. I knew if I looked one second longer, I would fall for him. I would fall for him and completely lose myself. I just didn't know if it was really love or just my suppressed teen hormones raging at me. Everything changed when I was with him.

An awkward silence filled the air as we both read over the menu. I had no idea what sounded good. My stomach felt so nervous I didn't want food anyway. Tanner watched me read every item on the menu.

As if he could read my mind he asked, "Want to just start with shakes?"

I smiled and nodded at him. He had to stop doing that.

Betsy came back with our shakes- topped with whipped cream and cherries and slapped them down onto the table. I used my napkin to wipe the rim and edges that overflowed from her movement.

"Enjoy." She carried her tray to the next table. I took a large sip and the creamy chocolate flavor brought me nostalgia of being a child with Susan. I closed my eyes for a second and smiled.

"You have had a chocolate shake before, right?" Tanner asked, raising his brows at me.

A goofy grin covered my face.

"When I was young. I had this friend named Susan. She would literally steal chocolates for us and keep them. Anytime I was feeling sad she would give me one. Now every time I eat chocolate, I have this huge sensation of child-like happiness. So stupid." I laughed at how ridiculous I sounded.

"It's not stupid. I think it's cute," Tanner replied and closed his eyes while he took a large sip.

"I can see it now. Sally would do something like that."

"Max too." I smiled at the thought.

"What else did you and Susan do together?" Tanner asked. Memories flooded my mind. Probably the best times of my life.

"Well… we used to climb onto the roof of the children's home I grew up in. We would lie there under the clouds or stars and watch the world go by." I smiled but a tinge of sadness met my lips.

"Children's home?"

I nodded and took another sip. "Yes, she was my best friend there. My mother left me, my siblings there… it's a complicated story."

"Do you still see her?" Tanner asked curiously in between sips of his shake.

"My mother?" My stomach dropped. I hadn't thought of her in a long time.

"No, Susan."

"Actually, I just saw her on the news! She always wanted to be a weather woman and she made it. She really did it!"

"Wow." Tanner smiled. "What did you want to be?"

"Happy," I told him. "That's all I ever wanted."

"And are you?"

"Happy?" I asked him, my brows meeting.

"Yes."

"I guess. I am right now." We shared a smile again that seemed to freeze time and I realized all my nerves had dissolved. It was as though Tanner, and I were the only two in the diner. I had never felt more together with someone in a crowded room before. For whatever reason, I was able to let my guard down and feel happiness when I was with him. I didn't have to protect him in the way I had Max and I didn't have to protect myself for the first time in my life.

He reached across the table for my hand this time, his slid gently on top of mine.

"Me too. For the first time in a very long time," he said in a silvery tone, squeezing my hand gently.

"Can I get you anything else?" Betsy's sharp voice cut through our heart eyed gaze and Tanner pulled his hand back.

"I think I have everything I need." He told her, all the while never taking his eyes off me.

"I can't with you two love birds!" Betsy howled.

I turned red.

CHAPTER FORTY-FOUR

"Now I owe you two," I told Amy the next morning. I met her out on the porch when she finally woke up. I hardly slept at all. I lie awake in my bed replaying the night with Tanner in my mind. I sat on the plastic chair next to her, the sun already so hot it melted the skin on my legs.

"I told you… I had nothing to do with it." Her voice was still asleep and raspy.

"Well… it was like… Perfect. Like now what? Do I just avoid him forever?" I grinned.

"No, that is exactly the opposite of what you should do."

I thought of the night before. The diner, the milkshake, the night stroll we took along the river. The way the lightning bugs lit the sky around us, and there were no worries about the past or the future. We were just two people walking together on *a not a date, date*. He didn't touch me inappropriately and he listened with curiosity. He literally read my thoughts. He took my hand inside of his gently a few times. That was the only indication we weren't just friends. Each time I had dreaded ever letting go. It was different. I had been abused for so long I had no idea what it felt like to be treated with respect.

"Listen. You worry too much. The past, the future. You just need to focus on right now. We only have this one life, and look at you, you've barely lived it." Amy leaned to stand up.

Her words stung. I knew I had been too careful, cautious, but I was afraid. Afraid of taking the risk. Afraid of getting hurt. Afraid I wasn't truly capable of love after all.

"It just won't go away. The idea that I could be capable of loving someone in that way. I truly believed I would be alone for the rest of my life."

Amy was standing now and I looked up at her.

"Bonnie, now come on. You've been through some messed up stuff. More than anyone should have to go through. But you have to take some time to love yourself. You are what fuels Max. He needs you to have a life too. You deserve good things. You deserve love and happiness." Tears welled in her eyes.

I hadn't ever considered that me withdrawing us from harm also meant we were not living to our fullest potential.

"No matter what challenges we face, nothing is ever guaranteed." Surprise sparked through me as she became emotional.

"At any moment on any day you can literally lose everything you have. You can't be so afraid of losing that you forget to live."

I sat there, taking her words in. I was so closed in a box within myself I had no idea how to begin letting someone in.

"He already lost someone and he's willing to try again. How beautiful that is." She smiled but her eyes filled with tears.

"Bonnie, remember the BBQ? It was a memorial for Daisey. I lost my daughter. She died. And what that has taught me is that life is good, and life is bad- but in between that... the tiny gaps of little things- those are the things that matter."

"Amy, I am so sorry." I reached for her hand.

"I had no idea. I'm so sorry I hadn't known. I would have said something... anything..."

"Bonnie, there's nothing anyone can say. Death leaves us questioning how we ever believed we had time... Time to do the things we really wanted to. Your nightmare is over. You need to live." She smiled at me and I stood and hugged her. It was my first instinct and she awkwardly accepted.

"I didn't take you as a hugger."

"I'm not. But I am sorry I didn't take the time to get to know you."

"Listen, life isn't perfect. It's messy and from the moment I saw you… well I thought there was something special. A life that needed to be lived. A friend that was meant to be made." She smiled through her tears and nudged me with her shoulder.

"Okay. Fine. I will try to accept his kindness and really sweet gestures. Maybe I will just call him and tell him I had a really nice time?"

"There ya go!" Amy softly shoved me. "Let me know how it goes."

I waited until 8:00 pm because I knew Tanner would be settled in after working all day. It was all of the anti-stalking I had done when I was learning his schedule to hide from him. I picked up the phone and called him again holding a shred of a paper that Amy had scribbled on. Butterflies returned to my stomach and worry clouded my mind.

"Hello?" He answered— his voice made my heart speed up.

"Hi. Tanner. It's Bonnie. I just wanted to tell you that… that I had a really nice time with… you last night."

"Oh. Well thank you. I did too," he replied. I smiled when I heard the sound of happiness in his voice. I did that to him. I hadn't thought past that first sentence and I was left with no words. I felt hot all over, and stars danced in my vision. I wanted to tell him I had been injured. That I was broken. That I wasn't capable of providing a love that he deserved after he already lost his wife.

"I'm glad," I replied. That was all I had. My eyes darted around the room during the silence. I was relieved when he spoke.

"Bonnie, what are you doing tomorrow night?" he asked.

"I don't, uh, I don't have any plans." I mumbled.

"Alright... How about Sally and I come over for just a visit?"

"Okay that sounds nice… 8 o'clock?" I realized that I just spilled the fact that I knew his work schedule by heart.

"Sounds perfect- don't cook. We'll bring a late dinner."

I agreed and I had that stupid kid smile on my face again even after we hung up.

~

I worked a morning shift the following day and made sure that I picked up Max and had plenty of time to shower. I slid on metallic blue spandex leggings and a comfortable fringed shirt. I decided to refrain from the make-up since we were staying home. Amy had gathered up mascara and eye shadow she no longer used and given it to me. While tidying up, the pounding at the door put me into a frenzy. I looked over at the clock. It was only seven. Quite early for Tanner and Sally. I held my breath. I knew at any point Dale could come into my life and destroy everything once again. The knocking stopped and I made myself get up to look through the peep hole. Max cowered behind the couch. The terrified look in his eyes and trembling muscles brought me a new kind of sadness. Resenting myself for being this way. By now he knew what happened every single time someone stopped by unannounced. He was learning to be afraid just like me.

"I'm so sorry, Max. There's nothing to worry about. It's just Tanner and Sally." I stepped back and opened the door. I tried to smile but Tanner and Sally looked from both of us and seemed to sense the tension that filled the air.

"Is everything okay?" he asked.

I exhaled loudly.

"Yes… I think… Just startled us." I tried to smile.

"I'm sorry we came early but the burgers cooked quicker than I thought, and I wanted them to be hot still." Tanner carried containers of food in both hands to the counter.

Max and Sally ran off to play together.

"It's okay. I'm fine," I told him, feeling the blood come back to my face. I pulled down my mismatched plates I had picked up at the thrift store.

"Do you… do you get this way every time someone knocks at the door?" Tanner reached for me and rested his hand on my shoulder.

"Well… no," I mumbled.

He did a half smile at me and raised his eyebrows.

"Yes. Yes, I'm weird, okay. I just don't want anything… anyone to… "My voice grew shaky, and he put his other hand on my shoulder.

"You don't owe me one single explanation. Not one." He lifted my chin towards his and for a moment I thought he was going to kiss me.

A real kiss. But he left me in desperation to feel his lips when he turned away. Instead, he walked back to the door.

"When I come over, I'll always knock like this..." He reached over. knocked three times, paused two times and then three more. A smile grew across my lips until my cheeks hurt. He planned to come back again. He made it impossible to not fall for him.

"That's the sweetest idea. I love it." And with that burst of oxytocin I stepped closer and I reached for him. I placed my hands around his back and linked them together, resting my head on his chest. I inhaled the scent of him so that, if this was our last hug, I would never forget him. I felt his muscles relax like butter and he pulled me in to him. His strong arms wrapped around me and it felt more like home than any place I had ever been. After living at Hawthorne, I always assumed the desire for a home was a place, but it was a feeling. A person.

"Bonnie, is this a friendship hug?"

I let out a giddy laugh. The last thing I wanted to do was send mixed signals. I closed my eyes- a wave of extreme happiness and sadness both washed over me. The idea of the very person I held in my arms leaving me behind. I didn't want to love him because the more you love someone the more you have to lose. "Yes, friends," I said kind of sarcastically.

CHAPTER FORTY-FIVE

It was the best burger I ever had. A burger turned into spaghetti, and then I made us chicken and dumplings. Before I knew it, we were having dinner together every other night. It became a routine that felt so natural, I didn't have time to pull away. I began to wish I were with him all of the time, on dreary Mondays and Sunday mornings. When he was gone, it felt like a part of me was missing. Constantly, I wished he were with me, or that I was with him. Or even that we were together *anywhere.*

The next few weeks were perfect. *Too perfect.* I kept waiting for him to realize he was wrong about liking me. That he would grow tired of me and end things. But instead, it was as though everything I had ever wanted to feel was wrapped in a bow and handed right to me. Hours flew by like seconds.

The secret knock on the door. His smile when he walked inside. The way he glanced hungrily at my lips when we talked but respected my boundaries. Seeing his face light up after I had made a stupid comment and he laughed at me. Catching him staring at me while I cooked, and smiling before we both looked away. Or the way our bodies ended up being close to one another, no matter what we were doing. He became my favorite way to spend an afternoon.

Each night we ate together, we played a few games with Sally and Max. Or we went down to the park and let them roam as we sat on the picnic tables sharing jokes and smiles. We kept it light, small talk. We didn't focus on the rest of the world; we didn't put a label on the time we spent together. In those moments it was the four of us. I loved the way his laughter filled me with life. made me forget all of the bad things and when I did have a moment where I struggled to rid the past, he could see it on my face. He nudged me, soft and gently to make sure that I was okay. The way his eyes focused on me as if he could block me from all of the hurt.

Back and forth, we took turns cooking our favorite foods.

We kept it platonic. There was no more hugging. Just awkward feet touching under the table, a bump into each other here and there, and the space disappeared between us when together on my saggy couch. The way he placed one hand on my knee when he found something funny and it never strayed. His warmth sparked something inside of me each time, but it became harder to deny my feelings.

So we went forward, but did a slow dance out of friend zone without really ever addressing it. Eventually, I noticed a thin indention on the finger his wedding ring used to sit. The skin was pale and the sight of it being bare gave me the confidence to decide that night. Maybe one kiss wouldn't be all that bad? I would try and kiss him. It wasn't until Max and Sally had fallen asleep and we sat on the couch together. Our movie ended and as the credits strolled by, I knew it was my chance. I wanted to know what it felt like to kiss his lips. Someone I wanted to kiss. So I turned to him and stared into his eyes. Maybe I concentrated too hard.

"You okay there?" he asked me. I leaned back and laughed slightly.

"Yes, I was just thinking of you and me... and what we're doing..." I told him and avoided the fact that I was about to make the first move.

"I was thinking the same thing."

"Really?" I asked curiously. He took my hand in his.

"Bonnie, would you go on a date with me tomorrow night?"

"A date, date?" I whispered.

"A date, date." He grinned.

"I would love to go on a date with you, Tanner Goldstein." He gave me a soft, lazy smile with his eyes connected to mine.

"Let's hope Amy is free," I told him.

"Oh, she is."

"Wait, you were planning this?"

He grinned again. "Just waiting for the right opportunity to ask you when you couldn't deny me."

"I would have said yes… at any time. Whatever this is.. I've never felt…."

He cut me off. "It's happiness. Bonnie, it looks so beautiful on you. I would do anything to see your eyes light up."

Tears filled my eyes. The good kind. Nobody had ever told me I was beautiful before.

"Hey. Hey. I'm sorry. I never know what will make you upset, but I will try to make you happy every moment we're together. I want to kiss you. I want to be near you. Dammit. I can hardly keep my hands off of you anymore. The problem is that I'm afraid to make a move because I don't want to scare you. I don't want you to have that fear in your eyes. I hate whoever put it there." I pulled back slowly and crossed my arms.

"I'm still just trying to heal from the things I don't speak about. I don't mean to make things so complicated. I just… I'm afraid I'm the problem. That I'm going to mess all of this up. That I'm so screwed up, I won't be able to be who you need me to be. I worry that you're going to see through me and find that broken person and leave."

"Bonnie, I can take just one look at you, and it makes my life feel right again. I didn't think I would ever feel like this again. There is nothing you can do to make me feel any different."

Tanner leaned back on the couch and pulled me into him where my body fit perfectly spooned in his. He gave me a sheepish grin and an electric current shot through my entire body.

Warmth radiated from him, and I couldn't stop smiling as I leaned into him on my saggy couch. I listened to his breathing. It was slow. Felt his chest rise and fall underneath my face. I listened to his heart beating. As he slept, I lied there replaying his words over and over again in my mind. I was so damaged he didn't know what could set me off. He wanted to protect me. He cared about me. He wanted to kiss me too. Somehow, he took away every worry and my walls began to fall down. There was a door. And I could let him in past the broken bits.

This is it. This is what love feels like. It feels like home.

~

Tanner showed up right on time as always. He carried a blanket with him and a bottle of wine.

Amy had done my make-up and I looked down at my dress and once again unnecessary heels she forced on me.

"Bonnie, you look stunning," Tanner told me with a look in his eyes I couldn't place. "But you might want to change."

"I thought... We were going on a date? A real date?"

"We are... But you need to be comfortable for this *date.*" He exaggerated the word date proudly and held up the wine and with a cheeky smile.

I changed clothes and we made sure Max and Sally were settled in at Amy's. Of course, she shooed us away again and shut the door on us.

"I think Amy is insane." Tanner laughed and laced my hand inside of his.

"She may be slightly, but aren't we all?" I grinned. "Are you going to tell me where we're going?" I asked curiously.

"No. Just come on, I want to show you something!" I could sense his smile in the dark night. He carried a wave of excitement with him.

He led me to the side of the apartment complex right into overgrown shrubs. The sharp branches pulled at my pants.

"Hence- comfortable clothes," he whispered.

"Tanner, where are you taking me?" I asked again, gripping his hand. Now that I knew he wanted to be close to me as much I did him. I took notice of how my hand fit inside of his. Like the glass shoe fit on Cinderella. Like my hands were meant to be inside of his.

"You'll see." He pulled me past a few more shrubs and stopped when we reached the fire escape stairwell.

"You first." He laughed, and I thought he was joking.

"Go on. I'll be right behind you." His voice was serious.

He tucked the wine and blanket under his arm. I placed my hands on the cold metal rails and began to climb. The night was silent with only the clanging motions of us climbing up. He was right behind me. A barrier of his strong body keeping me from harm. With each level Tanner ushered us to the next one until we reached the very top. The very top of the building. When I stepped onto the flat roof and saw the entire city glowing around us, I gasped. He walked in front of me, ruffled the blanket out and smiled in the dim light. We marveled at the view— city lights, passing cars the size of ants, and a whole lot of stars up above us.

"It is beautiful," I said as I joined him on the blanket. The breeze brushed through and I shifted closer so that my back was touching him. The stars shined above us and I felt as insignificantly small as an ant.

"This is just what I needed." I marveled at the night sky aglow with the bright city lights and distant stars that stretched into infinity.

Tanner popped the wine bottle with his Swiss Army knife and took a drink right from it. He passed it to me and I did the same.

"Ever since you told me that story... about you and your friend, I've been trying to figure out the best way to get you up here."

"I don't know what to say...It is the sweetest idea." I took another long drink of the wine and this time let my body relax into his.

"Bonnie, I just wanted you to know that I care about you... and what you've been through... it makes me furious."

"You know?" Panic overflowed into my voice.

Tanner paused, and the brightness from the moon illuminated his face.

"Bonnie, I know a little, and that's the only reason I've been able to keep my hands off of you. I want to protect you. I want you to feel safe."

I sat up straight. A wave of emotions ran through me. The shame. I thought I should feel anger at Amy for telling him without first talking to me, but all I felt was a sense of relief. It was the one thing that held me back from him. I dreaded dropping my biggest darkest secret on him, but now I didn't need to. *He still wanted to be with me?*

"We don't have to talk about it, lie back down." Tanner gently glided me back to him.

"It's okay. I'm not going anywhere, ever."

Ever? But everyone I loved has always left.

I smiled and nestled my face into his chest. I never wanted it to end.

"I have a past too." Tanner held me tighter.

"Okay, it's your turn because Amy didn't save you." I smiled at him with curiosity.

"After all of those doors I unlocked for her…" he laughed.

"Wait- you mean Jerry, right?"

He chuckled again. "That's not the point. Okay, where to start. Okay. Here it goes. My parents were both alcoholics. I moved out of their home at 14. Lived in my car for a while. Sally's mom and I got together, and we had Sally…". His voice trailed off.

My brows tucked under and I rubbed his arm lightly. I wasn't expecting a life history.

"I'm sorry. You don't have to."

"No, There's more." Tanner wiped a tear before it touched his cheek.

"I tried. I tried to make her happy. I lost my way in drinking for a bit. She died of an overdose in our old home. It was ruled suicide and I… I couldn't save her."

"I'm so sorry, Tanner, I mean I can't even imagine how hard that has been for you and Sally."

I wiped his face and pulled his head into my chest. The same way I consoled Max when he cried. Instead of the strong man, I saw the vulnerable little boy that lived within him. Under the stars, the wind shifted slightly, ruffling my hair.

The air felt lighter once our secrets were exposed. Like everything that held us back dissipated. We both stared into the sky and then back at each other longingly.

"I stopped drinking so much after that. I knew Sally needed me since I was suddenly all she had. I still have a drink now and then, but not like I used to. And then I met you. You gave me another reason to live. Reminded me that my relationship with Sally was most important. That day I saw the fort… It changed everything. I barely touch alcohol now and left my pity party."

"I think it was like fate that led us here. So much pain, led us to this." I smiled and cupped his face in my hands.

"Do you mind… if we stay like this for a little while?" Tanner asked, holding me tighter than he ever had before. He let his body relax on mine and for the first time in a long time, I felt very safe and secure and comfortable in my own skin.

"I don't mind," I whispered squeezing him back. We sat there with our hushed breathing and feather-light touches staring up at the sky. Peace, serenity and acceptance. Marveling at the sky, recognizing how insignificant we were when the carpet of stars was spread out above us.

"What is it that you want out of life? You would have to be stupid to believe with all of these stars and all of these planets that nothing else exists."

"I just want a normal life," I said, not taking my eyes away from the sky.

"What is normal even?"

"Happiness? Peace? Just appreciating the small things?" I turned to face him. He was so close, the warmth radiated off of him like sunshine in darkness. The wine put a foggy distance in my brain between rational decisions and depleted my self-control to not make out with him.

"Happiness… hmm." Tanner repeated staring into my eyes.

I expected him to answer, but he didn't.

"What about you?"

"I want to have my own land, my own house. To prove to everyone that I made it. I can make it."

The idea sounded so perfect. The American dream, I couldn't help but picture myself by his side.

"Do you want a white picket fence too?" I teased.

"Why of course- that's what I want most of all."

I laughed, a carefree open laugh that echoed into the night.

"You want happiness and a normal life and I just want peace and my own land. I think together- we can find it all." His voice grew from firm to gentle.

"Find it all, huh?" I smiled and Tanner leaned in to me with his eyes fluttering to a close.

"I feel like I already have," I whispered right before our lips met in a soft and gentle caress. My first kiss. My first real kiss. He held my face gently, my lips and body ignited with a sensation of fire I had never felt before. All of the pain- past and present disappeared. Like we were the only two beings in the universe. The only two beings under the stars in that moment, with dreams and wishes, joined together as one. He kept one hand placed on my arm, and the other was laced with mine. He didn't wander across my body. I felt safe. In his arms, I felt like I already had it all. I had made a point not to do this- to not be in a relationship. I couldn't trust someone. But there I was and yet Tanner made me forget everything I had promised myself.

CHAPTER FORTY-SIX

When I wasn't with him there was this foreign feeling inside of me anticipating seeing Tanner. It drove me wild. I had never felt so exhilarated at the thought of another person before. No matter what I was doing, Tanner came to my mind. He was an invader in my train of thoughts, derailing me from focusing on what I was supposed to. The idea of getting too close to him, that's what scared me most. The fear of failing him. The fear of being left behind. A deeper relationship was so foreign to me- I didn't know how to accept it. I thought if I just danced on the edge of commitment then I would eventually fall in without doing any of the work. But I was wrong.

In group therapy it was brought up that childhood trauma can have effects on healthy relationships leading into adult life. If a child learns that it is not safe to be vulnerable, and the child is not well cared for or supported in an emotionally present manner, the child will learn to shut off feelings. Feelings such as sadness, anxiety, and hurt. Was I shutting out love because I avoided hurt? Possibly. But I didn't know how to fix it. I had learned to be defensive against love rather than being open to it. If I hid from it, I assumed I could keep myself safe.

"Bonnie, did you hear me?" I snapped out of it. Tanner was sitting next to me on the couch. I hadn't been present for most of his visit. There were uncontrollable times that darkness clouded my mind and I drifted away. Flashbacks and troubled thoughts consumed me. In an instant I was just that little girl who was lost and alone and I didn't know how to get out.

"No- I'm sorry what?" I asked.

"I said Max was calling for you, but it's okay, I got him a drink." He leaned in closer, intently and placed his hand on my knee.

"I'm sorry... it's just... I'm just..." he stopped me.

"No. Remember, you don't owe me any explanations, Bonnie."

He looked deep in thought. And I knew it. I had blown it. I had lost the chance to prove to him I could be vulnerable without the help of wine.

I turned to him then. Trying to form words out of the racing thoughts in my mind.

"I'm... I'm afraid of this." I pointed from him to me.

"Afraid of me?" Tanner asked arching his brows together. His voice grew defensive.

"No, no. I'm so worried about falling in love with you that I try so hard not to. I am afraid of not being who you need me to be."

He let out a deep breath.

"Listen... I had no intentions for any of this happening. I have no expectations of you. I never have. All I know is that each morning when I wake up, you're the first thing I want to see. You're the only person I've ever met that feels like sunshine in the human form. You bring me warmth and happiness, Bonnie. Before I met you, I had given up. So many bad things happened that I lost hope. But you reminded me it takes rain and sunshine to make a rainbow and there's nothing more invigorating than that."

He paused and leaned towards me and nudged me with his knee. I rested the weight of my leg back on his and he pushed my chin up to kiss me. His lips were warm and soft. The feeling I got always took me by surprise. As if my chest opened up to let him in straight to my heart. I didn't want to open up my heart and my chest to him. I didn't want him to get inside of my soul and mess me up. He did all of these things that made my life not my own anymore. There was this feeling of greatness attached to him. I didn't deserve it. Sunshine, warmth, happiness. It was all there.

"I just love to see you happy." Tanner brushed the hair out of my face.

"But, it's not... It's not your job to make me happy."

"I know. I know. But I want to," he said quietly.

"I'm trying to figure it out. I'm sorry. There are so many things that run through my mind." I blushed and pulled away from him, but he bumped his knee into mine again.

"There are moments where I can just see the darkness take over and I want to pull you out of it and never let you drift there again. I truly hate this person who did this to you." I stared at him in awe.

"And you do pull me out," I told him. I leaned over and rested on his shoulder. He ran his fingers through my hair gently, sending riveting chills across my scalp and down my arms.

That's when I realized the problem wasn't just me and my issues—it was that I was falling too deep for him. So deep that I didn't know if I could ever resurface unharmed. Being with him made me forget the terrible things that happened to me, and what it felt like to be sad. He made me want to take a chance and trust him. The problem was how easily he could just leave and take that happiness away with him. And that scared the living hell out of me.

CHAPTER FORTY-SEVEN

I knew I was becoming too dependent of Tanner cheering me up. It was like when I ran out of gas, he was the only person that had the right kind to make me run again. I tried to be thoughtful the way he was towards me. I tried to mimic every ounce of love he poured into me because I didn't know it worked like that.

But sometimes I would walk out and see him sitting there in my old red couch and it was like no other human I'd ever seen before. He didn't notice me, but I could tell he was thinking deeply. He had this way of shaking his legs when he was stressed out. He was still the most handsome angry man I'd ever seen. I smiled and watched him, transfixed. He was what I had been missing my entire life. The foundation to build my broken heart a home.

We were inseparable and even though Sally and Max fought a lot, they enjoyed each other's company too. I did Sally's hair and let her put on some makeup. Tanner taught Max all of the rules for football and how to flip a pancake. It was the simple, little things that helped time go by. Before long it was not normal unless Tanner and Sally were with us in my apartment.

One day he showed up early. A smile came across my face when I heard his secret knock on the door. I had just gotten home from work and showered. I still had two hours before I needed to pick Max up from school.

I flung the door open and Tanner stood there holding an entire armful of wild flowers. Purple, pinks, and orange blossoms in no order. An aw escaped my mouth as I looked into his eyes.

"Please don't be sad. I just plucked them from the medium in the middle of the highway." He smiled and stepped closer to me. I had no words to say, just pure infatuation with the way his brown eyes glittered at me.

"I know it's so cheesy, but the flowers called to me because lately anything wild and beautiful reminds me of you. I can't stop thinking about you, Bon. While driving, I wanted nothing more in that moment to see you."

I pictured him pulled over on the busy highway- watching the way the wind tickled the leaves and the draft of sweet and spicy wildflowers reaching him. *How did I get so lucky?*

"You picked these… for me?" My voice cracked and a flood of tears came to my eyes.

"It's stupid I know…" Tanner blushed and stepped towards me again when he noticed my tears. I sobbed as he wiped them away. Panic ran through my veins, and I had this strong instinct to run but my feet wouldn't work. It was my body's defense to love again, telling me to flee. But I put one step down closer to him. All I ever wanted was someone to love me. And here he was, and I couldn't even take the God-damn flowers from him.

Tanner tossed the flowers on the counter. I watched the way they separated, and it reminded me of the vase shattering into the wall when I picked wildflowers and Dale threw them that same day.

Tanner came up behind me. Gently wrapped his arms around my entire waist and crossed his arms over mine and held them over my chest.

"Shh. You're safe. I won't let you go," he whispered, rocking me slowly.

I started to push away, but felt my muscles turn to butter when I listened to his heart. I settled in to his warmth and tried to catch my breath. I nuzzled my face into his chest. He sunk us to the kitchen floor safely. As my breathing slowed, he moved the hair that stuck to my damp face and kissed my temple.

"If I would have known you hate flowers that much, I would have never brought them to you."

I smiled through my tears and laughed through my nose,

"I love them. It's just… I'm such a mess. I don't know how to accept you being so kind… to me."

"Hasn't anyone ever brought you flowers before?"

I shook my head no, and my hair stuck back to my matted face. Tanner brushed it away again, and kissed my salty lips. A gentle yet hungry kiss. He pulled away just a little and whispered, "I promise. I will never bring you flowers again."

We both laughed and somehow, he always knew just what to say to bring me out of the darkness.

CHAPTER FORTY-EIGHT

It was as though magnetic forces had been activated and I couldn't stay away. Each moment I would see something that led my mind back to him. Old historic buildings on my way to work. The big dipper shining in the sky when I took the garbage out to the dumpster. Even seeing a father and daughter at The Red Tomato made me grin.

I loved everything about him. The gentle touch of his hand. The pain behind his smile that matched mine. The thoughtful way in which he spoke to Max. Why was everything he did so perfect? Maybe it was just because I considered him to be too good for me. That I didn't deserve him. It was this fuzzy feeling when you know things are too good to be true. To shut out the good things before they even have a chance to break your heart.

"Bonnie, are you daydreaming again?" Frank, my manager, stood there staring at me.

"Oh, I'm sorry Frank." I turned to grab a refill for one of my tables.

"Well, I said there is someone waiting up front who wants to see you." He gave me judgmental eyes as though to remind me that I should know better than to have visitors visit me on my shift. My heart sunk to my feet.

Dale finally found me.

I desperately stared into Frank's eyes and every muscle in my body clenched together in knots.

"Did you hear me this time?" Frank asked obviously impatient.

"Frank... I cannot go out there. I can't," I told him in a weak whisper.

"Are you in some kind of trouble?" His tone was more patient, understanding.

"Well... no and yes. My husband was abusive and... I ran." I sounded like a child.

"Honey, you are as white as a ghost," Frank told me, taking the drink tray from my arms.

"Did he say his name?" Stars filled my vision.

"It's... It's a woman, Bonnie," Frank said with his brows perched together in the middle of his face.

"Did she say her name?"

Frank returned to his usual impatient voice. "I don't know. Let me go ask for you... didn't know I was a damn secretary now..." His voice faded as he left the service center. I stayed hidden in the shadows. In different circumstances I would have laughed at Frank. But there was no laughter left in my soul at that moment.

If he found me— I had nowhere to go.

If he found me— my life as it was would be completely over.

If he found me—he found *Max*.

Frank reappeared and he had a slight grin that made him look younger.

"Does Susan ring a bell?"

I placed my hands over my face. "Susan— Susan?" I spoke in a soft tremulous voice. I couldn't feel the floor beneath me. The panic had turned into exhilaration. She found me.

"I said Susan and that's all I'm asking." Frank was tired of putting up with me. "Just take a 30-minute break..."

I smiled and ripped my apron off and I rushed out to the lobby. Susan stood there— an adult version of my childhood friend. I knew she had to grow up the same way I had, but seeing her didn't make it feel any less bitter-sweet to have missed it. Somewhere between childhood and that moment we had become women. And man was she *gorgeous.*

"Susan…" my voice trailed and returned to the same child-like tone I used when I called her so many years ago.

"Bunny!" Hers was just as tender. She wrapped her arms around me and it felt like I could feel time moving beneath my arms.

"I just got your messages. I can't believe Rebecka never showed them to me. You would be happy to know that she was fired." Susan's woman voice was euphonious. Immediately, I felt my shoulders release years of tension.

She still loved me.

She still cared about me.

I saw Frank approaching out of the corner of my eye and feared he changed his mind. He gently waved at Susan and leaned in when he spoke to me.

"Bonnie, Charles offered to take your tables and your shift from you. I think you deserve a night off." His voice was gentle but it wavered.

"Are you firing me?" I whispered so none of the guests could hear.

"No. Just come back for your next shift please. Go on now- I think you got some figuring out to do." He patted my shoulder and it was the first time I saw Frank as a person instead of a manager.

Outside of The Red Tomato, I unbuttoned the top of my white button up shirt that smelled of deep-fried food. Susan just stared at me the same way I had her- watching time morph us into adults. "I can't believe you came to London." Susan smiled and tears welled in her eyes.

"I was hoping you would be here," I told her, smiling.

Susan and I made our way down the street to the same diner that Tanner took me to. Once again, the bell jangled as we walked inside. That time my heart didn't stop and I continued to breathe with the adrenaline pumping through my veins.

Once we were seated at a table, Susan pushed the menu aside.

"I literally can't believe all of this. You didn't deserve a single thing that bastard ever did to you."

I turned red and wondered for a moment if this was perhaps some crazy dream that I was having. Susan, adult Susan, was sitting right there in front of me.

"How did you find me? How do you know? Wait. You know what happened?" I asked her, totally perplexed.

Betsy appeared then. "Hi what can I get for you?"

We ordered food and an appetizer quickly so Susan could finish.

"I went to your apartment looking for you. I met your neighbor and don't blame her. I got so excited I asked her a million questions. She told me where you work and that you were looking for me. She told me what he did, what happened."

Good old Amy. I sighed.

I said nothing back to her. I could feel the familiar shame returning to my body as if it were on fire.

"You were a child." Susan sensed it and reached for my hand.

"A child." She repeated and wiped the tears from her face. "I hate that I didn't save you. It's my fault for telling and he got to just run off with you."

I reached back for her. "You were a child too, and you were trying to save me." And I gave her a half grin and squeezed her hand.

Her tone changed and she reached into her large pocket book.

"Oh, here, I got something for you." She smiled while handing me a box.

I knew instantly what was inside. Without another word, I opened the box of chocolates. I took one for me and held one out for Susan.

We opened them and placed them in our mouths. *The melting, and sugar, and creaminess.*

When I opened my eyes all of my adult problems were still there, but so was Susan.

We gazed in awe at each other for a few seconds as if somehow, we time traveled.

"Don't you ever stop and think about how far you've come from the events you thought would end you?" She asked me and a feeling of gratitude fluttered in my chest.

"Like you being a weather woman?" I asked her excitedly.

"Like you getting away from Dale." She replied to me.

"We saved each other." Susan and I said at the same time with an expression of both happiness and deep sadness pasted over our lips.

I knew then that I could make it through. I was capable of being a normal human. I could feel love and I could give love and it wouldn't kill me.

CHAPTER FORTY-NINE

After my two-hour visit with Susan, I took her with me to pick Max up from *The Wild Ones*. She couldn't believe how much he looked like me. Max was thrilled to know I actually had a friend which made Susan and I both laugh. Before she left, she told me she would see us again very soon. She had to get back to work but that it was one of the happiest days of her adulthood. I felt the same way watching her drive away. As if seeing her renewed the little girl in side of me back to who she was before she was broken.

Max and I stopped by Tanner's house on the way home. I rarely went after him first, instead I would wait until he wanted to see me out of convenience for him. Not believing in myself enough to think I deserved to pick a time to be with someone. I did his signature knock on his door and he looked surprised but happy when he flung the door open.

"Hello there beautiful, hi Max." He smiled at us. Having just showered, his hair was damp and brushed back. I could smell his soap and longed to be inside of his arms.

"Do you care if we come inside for a few?" I asked him, smiling. He looked at me like he couldn't place where this was coming from.

"Of course... is everything okay?" He held the door open for us and I put my things down on his living room floor. Max ran to Sally's room and I turned to face Tanner. With the golden hues from the sunset through the window, I noticed the light brown flecks in his eyes contrasting the deep coffee tones.

I reached for his hands. Both of them and held them tightly.

"Tanner Goldstein, would you be my boyfriend?"

Tanner stood there with a serious expression on his face until an awkward smile crept across his lips.

"Wait, are you serious? What's going on with you?" He pulled me closer to him with a quizzical stare.

"I am so sorry for being up and down. I don't want to let that man have another moment of my happiness. I love every moment of being with you. When you're not around, I feel like part of me is literally missing. I want to go out on many dates with you. In diners, under the stars, in a fort castle— I would go anywhere with you. I want to wake up next to you and I want to forever feel like you are my home. I was waiting for the worst of you to come out and gobble me up, but I can't find it. Not because it's not there. We all have demons… but I want every part of you." My voice shook.

He just stood there. Staring at me. Taking it all in. Every word I ever wanted to say to him came out at once. I felt all of the things I had been running from for the first time. I stood there feeling vulnerable and insignificant. I couldn't read his face. I was certain he would finally reject me. Then he pulled me in for a kiss. My entire body froze, not because it was the first kiss, but because it was the first kiss that I put everything I had into. I wasn't holding back anymore. Tanner pulled away for an instant and whispered, "Bonnie, I want nothing more than to be with you." He gently met my lips to his while sliding his hands through my hair. When our kiss was over, he locked eyes with mine, and let out a hoarse whisper, "Welcome home, Bon."

CHAPTER FIFTY

I never thought my smile would leave my face. For the first time in my life, things were falling into place. Weeks had passed and I fell into this balance of work and surrounding myself with those who I loved most. Tanner and I discussed moving in together. I spoke with Susan on the phone regularly. I actually believed this was my happily ever after. Tanner and I planned to go on a real date, for an entire weekend alone the following Friday and Amy offered to keep Max and Sally both nights for us. It was everything I ever wanted and more.

"Only six days to go," Tanner whispered to me. He had planned to take me to a fancy restaurant that overlooked the ocean. It was a two-hour drive but since we hadn't been anywhere other than close to home, this felt different, official, exciting.

"I think it will be the best day ever," I responded, as we walked back to the maintenance office. As often as we could, we would have lunch together on his break. I usually brought him some food from the diner once my shift ended. We both requested a full weekend off work so that we could escape and "be like lovebirds" like Amy called it. I worked a double shift on that particular night to make up for vacation time, so I had to return back to work instead of picking Max up.

I sighed when it was time for us to part ways. "I really don't want to go back to work."

Tanner pulled me in to him. "It will be worth it, I promise! Amy will pick Max up. You know she will take good care of him." He told me reassuringly. "I'm going to finish restoring garbage disposals and try and get some overtime, so I'll be thinking of you."

"I remind you of garbage?" I shoved him playfully.

"You remind me of everything," Tanner said, a sly lazy smile crossing his lips.

"Alright- I'll see you later." He gave me a quick peck on the cheek and I headed back to work. As soon as my shift started, I knew it would be a rough night. Everything I touched came crashing down around me. I spilled coffee down my white work shirt in front of Frank. Who, by this point, was no longer surprised by anything I did. I also dropped a glass of red wine off the drink tray, right into a woman's lap. After apologizing repeatedly, I offered Frank to stay even later to make up for it. He shook his head and agreed but thankfully, he didn't yell at me. So finally, when the restaurant closed, I sulked in the service room, rolling silverware inside of napkins. I tried to focus on the upcoming trip. Tanner's words replayed in my mind; *it will all be worth it.*

Outside, a thunderstorm ripped through, and I watched the lightning bounce off the walls while I replayed all of my mistakes from that evening. I blamed it on being tired, not used to working 12 hours. I even giggled a little when I thought of taking my customers drink for a refill and forgetting completely to bring him a new one. How could I do that? The look on his face. The spilled wine. The woman really shouldn't have asked for her drink first- I took it from the back and it threw off the balance of everything else on the tray. Frank's glare from across the room, but yet, he always let my mistakes slide since that night Susan came in. He had a soft spot for *sad people* he had told me. I never knew being a sad person came with perks. Even being patient with me despite him offering a free meal to both the drink guy and the wine lady. Any other manager would have fired me.

Stupid girls do stupid things.

Frank and I were the last two left in the restaurant and, as we headed to the door, he said, "Take this umbrella."

"Thank you, Frank. I didn't know it was supposed to rain tonight." I replied sheepishly.

"Bonnie, you probably don't even know what day it is today. I'm actually glad you're going on vacation." Frank told me as he locked the doors and we stepped out into the rain. I held the umbrella over him and smiled. "I know you want to get rid of me."

"I'll save money on free meals." He laughed back but patted my back. "Just a few more days. Hang in there. You deserve a break." I watched Frank climb into his nice car and dreamed of the day I would have my own. That was the next milestone I looked forward to, driving. The rain splashed beneath my feet as I tried to avoid the overflowing puddles. The night clouds blocked all of the stars and the rain muffled out the city noises. I made my way, holding Frank's umbrella over me.

I thought of standing in the rain with Susan. I briefly wondered if she were on TV at that exact moment, talking about the rain. I smiled at the way the cold water splashed me when I moved the umbrella. How different things were when I was just a child.

I imagined holding Max in my arms. I had never been away from him this long. By the time I reached Amy's door I was exhausted and wet. I rubbed my coffee-stained shirt and stomped the mud off of my shoes. I knocked on Amy's door lightly in case Max had fallen asleep.

"Hi there! Wow, you smell like food," Amy said, fanning the air and letting me in. That was my least favorite part about working in a restaurant.

Max ran up to me and I scooped him into my arms.

"See you guys tomorrow!"

We thanked Amy and walked back to our place.

"How was your day?" I asked Max after I changed into pajamas. The only thing I wanted was to fall asleep quickly.

"Good! I made another pet rock. This one is Dino." I inspected the rock like it were a diamond. On the bottom he wrote Mama with a crooked heart.

"I made this one for you. That way when you miss me you can hold it tightly."

"That is so sweet." I wrapped him inside of my arms, inhaling his scent-- my favorite, wild little boy smell. "I will always keep him with me."

"Can I sleep with him tonight?" Max asked me, his sleepy eyes becoming heavy.

"Of course, and then I'll take care of him in the morning." I replied. Max gave me a large hug and began to pick up his dinosaurs that spread across the living room floor from that morning.

"Max, you don't have to tidy up tonight. I'll clean it up for you," I told him and walked him to bed.

"Will you lay with me for a little?" He asked, holding onto my hand. I climbed into his little bed and curled up next to him, the ultimate feeling after a long day of work.

I must have fallen asleep in his bed because I woke up to loud bangs on the door. The sun hadn't risen all the way yet so the room was filled with a greyish hue of dawn. The thud at the door was impatient and loud. I tried to place in my mind who could be knocking like that so early, but my half-awake brain wasn't working yet. I stumbled sleepily to the door. It looked like a police badge in the peep hole. I worried something had happened to Tanner, or Amy.

I opened the door slightly and my heart sank to my toes when the man spoke. There were two officers.

"Bonnie Harper... We have a custody order that states, we, law enforcement, shall assist in the enforcement of this custody order and deliver Max Harper to the custodial parent. If you resist or interfere, we have the right to arrest you for detaining and concealing the child with the intent to deprive the full custodian lawful time spent with their child. It is considered a Class A misdemeanor, unless the child is removed and taken from one state to another, in which your case, it is a felony of the third degree. Now I know this is going to be emotional but you will be in a much better place if you just work with us. We don't want any trouble."

I couldn't process a word. I couldn't feel them when they brushed past me. I couldn't stop screaming as they took my sleeping son from his bed. I couldn't stop hearing his confused cry for help for me, "Mama! Mama please!" He wrestled in their arms. He kicked and scratched and bit the same way I had taught Emma to. I ran to him. I put my arms around him inside of the officer's arms and held him so closely. I squeezed him, hoping it would wake me up from this nightmare. The officer allowed it for a moment then he separated us as he walked out of the door with my son in his arms. The other officer had a frown on his face and waited until we could no longer hear Max screaming for me. My stomach felt like a pit of lava in a volcano, and I hoped it would erupt and take away my pain. He handed me a document and leaned down. "I'm really sorry Ma'am." I took the paper, despite my shaking hands.

"Please don't take my son. He's all I have left," I begged him. "He could be harmed there. We left due to abuse." I continued to rattle on, anything I could think of to get Max back in my arms.

"Ma'am, please calm down. It was ordered by a judge. Just between me and you, I see this all too often. Ironically, battered mothers flee in an attempt to protect their children, but if you didn't file for full custody, it's all used against you in custody decisions. The Judge always returns the children to the state they fled. It's considered his home state. The court prioritizes home- state jurisdiction. There's nothing I can do until you return to court."

"But how will I get there? What if I don't own a vehicle? Please, sir, please tell me how I can get my son back."

"A child custody decision will now be based on a court's temporary emergency jurisdiction. It can turn into a permanent custody determination if there is not a competing custody action in the state from which the woman fled."

"But I was hiding for a reason. I didn't file for a reason. I love my son, sir, and..." He cut me off.

"Ma'am, it's truly out of my hands. You must participate in the proceeding in your child's home state to preserve your legal rights."

"Oh. My. God."

"Good day," he said and turned to leave with a sympathetic look.

I would never have a good day again. The color drained from my face and I couldn't manage to breathe. Black stars faded in and out, my stomach lurched as if I might be sick.

How could this happen? How? Just when everything was so right, he came back like a never-ending curse. My legs wobbled beneath me. I spun around and threw up across the living room floor all over Max's dinosaur figures. Then I curled up like a crumbled-up piece of paper and cried like I never had before.

Please, God, let my baby be OK.

CHAPTER FIFTY-ONE

My door flew open and for the first time I didn't even care who it was. I was pathetic lying on the floor next to where I got sick after I let them take my son away. Amy leaned down and held me as I cried into her arms. She held me like the baby that I had always been.

"Shhh, I know. I know. I heard the whole thing. That asshole needs to pay." She rocked me back and forth. I don't know how long we were down there on the floor. I just know that eventually Amy cleaned my throw up, helped me change clothes and tried to get me to lie down in my bed. I refused and went into Max's bed instead. I climbed into where his body heat still remained underneath the blanket. I inhaled the scent of him as I sobbed into his blanket.

How could this happen, how?

I could hear Amy whispering to Tanner as he busted through the door. "Where is she?" His voice sounded angrier and more desperate than I had ever heard.

He crouched down next to Max's small bed and placed his arms around me. He repeated, "I'm so sorry Bonnie. I'm so sorry." But the words didn't register. They just swirled to the pit inside of my stomach and disappeared.

Stupid girls do stupid things. How could I not have thought of this. Why wasn't I prepared?

When I finally turned to face him, his face was bright red. He was unrecognizable. The cold stare in his eyes was frightening. I felt like I was living outside of my body, watching everything take place from the ceiling. The same way I learned to go away in my head when Dale did things to me. The same way I learned to go away anytime I was hurt, or afraid. This had to be a dream. A nightmare. *How can I make it stop?*

"Where does he live?" Tanner's words pierced into me, bringing me back to Max's room. I rubbed my neck. His voice was unfamiliar. He had a violent look on his face which was opposite of how it had always been. I hoped I hadn't ruined the soft side of him like everyone else.

I shook, but couldn't speak.

Stupid girls do stupid things.

I couldn't face Dale. How could I face him again?

Tanner's hand shook as he tried to comfort me. His arms were so secure around my shoulders, I wasn't sure if I would just topple off the bed head first if he let go.

"No. No, this can't be real. He needs me. I promised him. I promised him I would never leave him." My swollen vocal cords wailed. My voice was unfamiliar to me.

My body longed to hold Max in my arms. To watch him breathe. To watch him sleep. I was caged. Stuck— like the little bird I used to be that had forgotten how to fly.

I wasn't sure how many days I stayed in his bed unable to speak or eat. Time no longer existed for me because it had literally stopped the moment Max was taken. Darkness closed in on me. I tossed and turned and I went down memories of the dark path I had avoided for so long. Just when I had a handle on life, it broke. Everything came collapsing in around me.

CHAPTER FIFTY-TWO

It was Friday. The day Tanner and I were supposed to leave for our romantic weekend. I hated myself for ever agreeing to leave Max in the first place. I took every moment for granted even when I knew how much I had to lose. It was supposed to be the perfect day. The one we were counting down to. We had plans to take the kids to an arcade before we left. Plans to tell them we would be moving in together.

Instead, I stood there with tears in my eyes, next to Tanner. It hurt to face him. It hurt to love him when I didn't have Max with me. It was unfair. I studied the light brown flecks of caramel in his eyes. Salty tears escaped and rolled down my cheeks. He was always something so good to me, but I couldn't dare let myself feel happy when Max was gone. *Max was gone.*

It was the first time in days I stepped outside, the sunshine so bright I could barely look up at the sky without blinking. It literally burned my eyes.

"Are you ready?" Tanner asked and gently kissed my forehead.

"I guess." I went stiff under his touch. I don't know why he was still there for me. I wasn't any good for him.

He agreed to drive me the 10 hours back to Wallop so I could be present in court. Amy offered to keep Sally who was shaken and confused about why her best friend was gone. But I couldn't console her. I couldn't look at her without crying out in immense pain because to see her without Max meant he was really gone.

The hard chair stuck to my back. I hoped the Judge couldn't see the ounces of sweat that poured from me. The long car ride, being around people, my need to be someone who I wasn't anymore. I pretended I had an itch and separated my damp shirt from my back. The court room smelled of old books, stale coffee, and ink. I hoped if I just sat there, they would see the truth. They had to. Tanner was somewhere in the court room. My stomach filled with guilt when I thought of the quiet ride down. Every attempt he made to just make me smile.

Dale sat vertical from me. A cocky grin plastered on his face. For the first time I noticed the wrinkles that bore into his face. I saw him as an old man and I pitied the little girl I used to be.

So afraid. So timid. So quick to please.

Like a pop-up storm, the familiar thoughts returned to me. The shame, the self-hate. It all rolled in and disrupted my already broken soul. It was all too easy to forget the good and give in to the hate I felt towards myself in his presence. When asked who was representing him, Dale stood. I shook my head no. *That couldn't be right. It's not fair.*

The first time he spoke, his voice took me back to the darkest gray room, secrets and body aches. I couldn't focus on what was being said. I couldn't think clearly when I was in the same room with the man who ruined my life and continued to do so. My head spun and it all just sounded like I was holding sea shells up to both ears. Once I was placed on the stand, Dale cross examined me. From the beginning of the case, it was clear that Dale employed a strategy to achieve the ultimate goal of having the court terminate my custodial rights to Max.

He accused me of not being forthcoming. He belittled me. I knew he chose this as a tactic to break me down. His plan to recover what power he had lost when I left. I had to face my abuser and answer questions from his mouth, about the abuse he inflicted upon me. About how I was the monster who kept his son from seeing him. I could feel my muscles trembling, I was blinking too much. I tried to stay focused. I tried to tell them that I was thirteen when he forced me to marry him. My voice was unsteady. I came off as unstable, too emotional to speak clearly.

"Why didn't you report the abuse?" he asked with daggers shooting from his eyes.

I wanted to disappear. To fade into nothing.

"I don't know. I was scared," I replied weakly. I glanced at the Judge, waiting for someone to object this behavior.

"Scared, huh? Or was it because you have no proof of these allegations?" Dale asked me, raised his brows and looked around the court room.

"Do you?" he asked.

I stared at him, wishing I could set flames to him with my eyes.

"Do you, Bonnie? Do you have proof?" He repeated.

"No, but I have documents from therapy. I went to a battered women's shelter…"

"That's not proof of abuse," he replied.

I don't remember any of the other questions.

Everything around me faded as I made my way back to my seat.

"It had been almost a year since I saw my son. How is that not parental alienation?"

As the court discussed every single detail of my life, I faded in and out of awareness. "Mrs. Harper earns minimum wage as a waitress and has an adjusted gross income an estimated, $600 per month. She is currently renting a one-bedroom apartment. Mr. Harper is self-employed, carries a realtor's license and carries the adjusted gross income of $5,000. He currently owns a three-bedroom house."

He had half a life of a head start to become stable when I wasn't even born yet. I hoped they could see the fear on my face. Know that I was telling the truth. To believe me.

I distanced myself from his voice and, instead, replayed my last night with Max in my mind. I should have played dinosaurs with him or built a fort and read until we were too tired to keep our eyes open. I should have never worked a double shift on our last day together. The memory of holding my son in my arms and vowing to never let him go. I made a promise I couldn't keep. I got distracted with Tanner and I made the biggest mistake of my life. I let my guard down.

The Judge spoke and pulled me from my daydream. "Mrs. Harper fled the state with child, Max Harper. The court shows primary custody has been ordered to Mr. Harper in the child's home state. Mr. Harper has shown substantial evidence relating to the child's care, protection, training and his relationship. In this case… She did not file restraining orders, there's no previous arrests of the allegations, and she offers no proof of abuse. The Battered Women's Shelter was unable to confirm the abuse as she had no reports of injuries upon her arrival and some issues with confidentiality. At this time, the court finds full custody to be awarded to Mr. Harper. If seeking further visitation rights, with her history of fleeing, Mrs. Harper must participate in the proceedings to reserve her legal rights."

"But I don't live here, how can I afford to do that?" I nearly lost it. My public defender shook his head at me.

"Mrs. Harper, please don't interrupt me. Your financial state is not the responsibility of the court. There is no competing custody action in the state you fled to. In this circumstance, it sounds like you were close to receiving a felony charge, Mrs. Harper… detaining and concealing the child with the intent to deprive the full custodian lawful time spent with their child. It is considered a Class A misdemeanor, unless the child is removed and taken from one state to another, in which in your case it is a felony of the third degree. It is my understanding that you have engaged in an act of parental alienation. Perhaps you will take some time to figure out expenses and we will arrange permanent custody determination in one month. At this time, since you're out of state, we will postpone creating a visitation schedule to ensure the child has the opportunity to enjoy a meaningful relationship with the noncustodial parent until then. Sole legal custody and sole physical custody shall be granted to Mr. Harper until the final hearing."

Tears escaped me but inside I felt hollow. Clearly Dale had significant connections with the state. He planned all of this to happen meticulously. The smile on his face was enough to make me give up on myself but I would never give up on Max. "Court is dismissed."

Tanner held onto my hip and he opened the car door for me. The smell of him brought back happy memories and I wanted to cave into his arms and never leave. Instead, I climbed into the passenger seat and completely lost it. The combination between lack of sleep, stress, and hopelessness slapped me in the face.

I lost Max. I had to leave without him and it killed me. I failed him. I was now my mother.

"Bonnie, I know it seems like the hardest moment of your life right now. It's just so fucked up. There's nothing I can do to make you happy right now. It's okay to feel like giving up, but don't stay there. I'll be here for you no matter what. You always have my shoulder." Tanner's voice was shaky as he spoke. I could tell even he was defeated because, for once, he had no way to pull me out of the darkness. He didn't even try, he just sat there with me. He rested his hand on top of my hair, rubbing me gently. I tried to get it together, to thank him for being there for me, but the tears kept coming as I made a terrible sob.

"It was my fault. I wasn't ready for Dale and I should have been. Tanner... I have done what I said I would never do, just like my mother. I left him." I silently screamed and cupped my face,

"Oh God, I actually lost him to the one person I hate most in the world." How was I supposed to just wait? My son was gone, he was missing me. Crying out for me, needing me. Was he tucked into bed each night? How could he sleep without his favorite blanket? My body ached with fear. My muscles cried out for sleep, my empty stomach growled for food, but my mind raced with the worst-case scenarios. Would I ever see him again?

"Shh, Shh, Shh... Bonnie, there is no way you could have prepared for this, please give yourself a break. Come here, can you please, please just let me hold you?" I looked at him with tears in my eyes and snot rolling down from my nose. I was at my absolute worst and he still wanted to hold me. I realized in that moment, in order to fight for Max, I would have to give up the best thing that ever happened to me.

"Tanner, we can't go on like this. You know I will have to move. I can't be with you, dragging you into all of this and not really be with you. You deserve so much more than I have to give."

Tanner punched the steering wheel so hard that the car shook. I reached for him then, and took his hand in mine. I kissed where his knuckles were busted and without thinking, I crawled over the console into his lap, straddled him in the driver's seat, laid my head on his chest and cried and cried and cried. He rubbed my hair and comfort kissed my forehead over and over again. I don't know how long we stayed there, in the parking lot under the trees but it was the first time since I lost Max that I was able to feel again. His kisses trailed down my face and to my neck until every nerve in my body was tingling with anticipation. I sat back so I could look him in the eyes.

"Tanner. We shouldn't be. We can't. I just don't understand how this can be happening. I don't think I can be the same without you, Tanner. My heart has waited so long to be loved by someone like you." He threw his arms around me, pulled me close and kissed my lips soft and slow and when he pulled back, he whispered a gentle, "I love you, Bonnie," and followed it immediately with another kiss. When we were both breathless, I pulled away and climbed back to my seat. He really just told me he loved me at a moment like this. A moment where I couldn't even love myself.

"Bonnie, please... pulling away from me doesn't make this any easier on you."

I sighed and laid my head back on the seat.

"Tanner, I can't love you right now. I just can't do this right now. We never should have gotten together. I told you I wasn't ready and now look..."

"Whatever, fine. Blame it on me if you want, but that doesn't mean you didn't feel what we felt. I'm not like you. I can't just shut it off." He started the car and backed out quickly. His words repeated in my mind as we drove on in silence until he turned into a small diner. I didn't mean to shut it off, I just couldn't allow myself to feel joy without Max there with me. I couldn't even remember the last time I was able to eat a full meal. Hunger wasn't really a problem when you can't feel anything at all. I felt defeated, like a failure. I cared so much about him but when I looked at him, I felt empty. I couldn't remember any of the good times. I had to block them out. I had this cycle I went through to hide from the pain of failing, shame, anger, guilt, self-blame, self-hate. It was so hard to snap out of it.

I lost myself somewhere along the way of losing Max and when I had to look Dale in the eyes again. I wasn't really there; I was back to the detached little girl again. Just existing in survival mode. It didn't help that Tanner was fuming. He was angry and unlike the person I knew. It was hard to justify his anger when all I could feel was emptiness and shame.

At dinner, I watched Tanner down a few whiskey sours and I worried that this would break him too. Guilt consumed me just thinking about how different his life would be without me in it. I blew my chance to tell him how much I loved him. And I did love him in a way I had never loved anyone else, I just couldn't open that part of myself up at that time. I just moved my salad around in the bowl. I had no desire to eat. As we drove out of Wallop, I kept track of each mile marker that led me further away from Max. Tanner eventually calmed down and reached for my hand, but I instantly pulled away. I didn't deserve that. I didn't deserve him. I faced the window and cried until I had no more tears left. My worst fear had become true. I went back to basing my self-worth on what I could do versus who I had become. I forgot who I was and how I had grown. The only thing I knew was I had one whole month to sell everything I owned and move back to Wallop.

I hid myself inside of that apartment, everyone and everything was too bright for the shadows existing inside my mind. This continued for the entire week, the seclusion and pain becoming more intolerable with each day. I couldn't sit still, yet I had no energy to move. I considered showing up at Dale's doorstep, grabbing Max and running away with him. I was certain he would either kill me or try to charge me with trespassing. Or worse— kidnap me once again. I had no car, certainly not enough money to get back to Wallop. I hated myself for buying things for the apartment. *Why hadn't I been saving for this? Preparing for this to protect Max?*

Each second without Max was like a moment without oxygen. I knew the pain he felt. The ache in your bones for your mother to care enough to rescue you. I was suffocating in my own mind. I went from being completely numb to drowning in painful memories. I shut everyone out.

"I never stood a chance, did I?" I asked out loud to my empty apartment. I sank to the floor. The silence was amplifying my beating heart. I considered how much easier it would be if it just stopped beating. There was a lump in my throat that made it hard to swallow. The darkness ensued. It took me by the hand and drug me to the bottom of the sea.

I stopped answering the door. When Amy knocked, I felt guilty for ignoring her but I had no energy left to be nice to anyone. Tanner stopped by every night. I only knew this from his special knock on the door. Some nights, I could hear Tanner talking to me, begging me to answer. "Bonnie, please. Let me be there for you."

I was laying in Max's bed when I heard the keys jingle at my door. I stared at the ceiling, willing myself not to look. But her red hair caught me off guard. Susan and Tanner walked together into the room I shared with Max.

"Bunny, don't you dare ignore me. I know you're in there somewhere," she said. She knelt down next to the bed and tapped my head. I could smell her perfume and clean hair. For the first time I became aware of how badly I smelled. How gross I felt. My tongue was dry and stuck to the roof of my mouth. Susan leaned over me and squeezed me tightly, greasy hair and all. I couldn't find the words to say anything. My mind was fuzzy, like static on TV.

"We're not giving up on you," Tanner told me, spinning the maintenance keys in his hand. I glanced up at him and a sudden bout of happiness filled me.

"Did you really break in to my apartment?" It was the first time I wanted to laugh perhaps out of loneliness or delirium from not taking care of myself. I immediately hated myself for it. I shouldn't be able to laugh anymore. Susan giggled and Tanner raised his eyebrows.

"Tanner came to the news station and told them it was a family emergency. I'll be here all week. Now Get up, you have to shower". For whatever reason, Susan's voice and rather annoying persistence got me out of bed. I glanced at Tanner, ashamed of how disgusting I was, but happy he didn't hate me despite how terrible I had been lately. Dark circles surrounded his eyes like a raccoon mask. I didn't want to face him, to see myself through his eyes- the pain I caused and what I'd become.

"I'll start cleaning up." Susan turned and left Tanner and I alone. I wanted to apologize to him, do anything to see that smile of his. But I didn't, my head was spinning and it hurt to stand, my legs were wobbly beneath me. Tanner led me gently from the bed and into the bathroom. He held the door open for me and guided me inside. I stood there, frozen, not knowing what to do or say. I was a disgusting mess. He turned the shower on and turned back to face me.

"Do you need help?" I nodded as he began to help me undress. His woodsy smell and the warmth of his finger-tips radiated down my spine. It wasn't the first time he had seen me without clothes, but the silence in the room burned through me. I realized I had been waiting for the moment he couldn't take me anymore just like everyone else. *I always had been.* But he turned and just held on to me, held my shoulders and stared into my eyes, like he was recharging my soul. He opened the shower door, and cautiously gave me a push inside. His eyes never leaving mine.

"Tanner…You can leave me. They all do."

I felt the hot water against my skin and let the tears I hadn't known were left fall.

"I told you I'd never leave you. I'm not going anywhere."

He placed my towels on the hook and closed the door behind him softly.

I did feel better after my shower. Susan helped me get the knots out of my hair. She smelled nice. Her touch was warm, motherly.

"I don't want you guys to see me like this, Susan."

"Like what? Being a human? You don't have to avoid everyone when you're sad. You need to be okay with human emotions." Susan smiled at me, and lifted my chin, and with a voice like the first woman president, she said, "We're going to fix this."

I smiled for the first time in a long time. I wanted nothing more than to fix this. Susan extended her hand out to me and slowly opened it.

With tears in my eyes, I picked up the piece of chocolate.

"Do it for the little girls we once were. Remember, we can always forgive. You can forgive yourself too."

I unwrapped the chocolate and let it melt on my tongue. I went back to the girl I used to be for a moment. Before the hurt and the pain and the darkness. Back to the girl that chocolate still fixed her problems.

I leaned over and held on to Susan tightly, feeling as though distance and time never separated us at all. I wanted to ask her if she would run away with me again. But I couldn't. I had to face it.

The sun was extremely bright when I stepped outside for the first time. It was the day after I was supposed to be in court. I hadn't been able to come up with enough money for gas, hotel expenses, and the court fees on top of the bills I was still trying to get caught up on. I got out of bed slowly and Susan made me eat. She cleaned my dishes. She opened all of my bills. It was quite clear that I had lost my job and I was also being evicted. I even let poor Frank down again. There was no way I would even be able to pay for the next court date.

"That's it. You've had enough time. I know it's sad but this is what I think needs to happen…" Susan paused. I knew what she said next was going to hurt like hell. I braced for it.

"You're going to get your shit together and start saving. You can't let him win."

So somehow, I put one foot in front of the other. And that's exactly what I did. I went back to the Red Tomato and begged Frank for my job. He eventually agreed when two people called out on the same night and he needed me. The only thought I had on my mind was being able to save Max. I put on a smile. I did what I needed to do. Tanner and I had agreed to just be friends. It was hard to be near him but not inside of his arms. I had this ache in my body that needed him. But I wouldn't allow myself to feel any bit of happiness when my son was gone.

It only took me one month and crashing on Amy's couch to save up enough money to move back to Wallop. I had to say goodbye to everyone and the life I almost had that now felt like a distant dream. Once I got to Wallop, I would work my way into an apartment and save up for an attorney. Then I would go back and fight for Max. It sounded doable, complicated but possible. It would be even more years of my life given to Dale. But I could do it for Max.

I packed up the few things that I didn't sell and I bought my bus ticket down to Wallop. Tanner offered to drive me but I thought it would make the goodbye so much worse so I refused. Plus, it had been a whole month of not touching him, or feeling his soft lips against mine. I longed to crawl in his arms and never leave. The day before I left, I found a letter folded in half, slipped underneath Amy's door. It was addressed to me.

Bonnie,
Meet me under the stars, 8 PM.

I nodded my head at him even though he obviously couldn't see me. I would go be with him one last time and if he kissed me goodbye, I would let him.

~

I climbed up the metal rails on my own this time. I noticed how cold the wind felt on my back without Tanner there to protect me. By the time I got to the top of the roof, the wind rustled my hair and I was out of breath. Giving up on life and staying in bed was never a good idea. Tanner looked genuinely shocked. He smiled and took my hand. "I didn't expect you to show up," he told me with a sad smile across his lips. "Is it okay if I hug you?" he asked, and in that moment, I fell into his arms.

"I'm so sorry for everything I put you through. You didn't deserve this."

He wrapped his arms tightly around me and rested his hand on my lower back.

"You didn't put me through anything. You can't help that I fell in love with you." I nested my face into his neck, smelling him. I missed him so much. He loved me. He really did.

"Tanner, thank you for the happiest moments of my life," I told him, my voice giving out. I found myself wishing I had been with him every last moment that I could be. Soaking in the last moments we would ever spend together.

It escaped my lips before I had time to think. "I love you too, Tanner. I really do."

"Stay here, Bonnie. Make a life with me. I promise you— we will find a way to get Max back. We will find a way to make that bastard pay for what he did to you."

Tears welled in my eyes.

"I know it sounds crazy, but if you go back there, you are just giving him the control he wants. He's going to uproot you and destroy your life all over again…drag you through the mud just like he did in court. You have people here who love you. We can save every single penny and fight this."

Hope sparkled in Tanner's eyes like I had never seen before. It amazed me how much I meant to him, when he was the one who taught me how to experience intimate love. It saddened me to think of returning to a place where Dale existed, walking freely. And if I went there, I would face radicalism, evil, and I struggled to breath when I thought about it, but possibly even death. If Dale was capable of all of this evildoing, couldn't he kill me too? The threat he made so many years ago echoed in my mind. From everything he did to me. For every moment of my life, I suffered— like he had saved a reserve of straight evil that could only be used on me.

"Bonnie, please?" Tanner brought me back to the rooftop. To the endless stretch of stars in the sky. To the crescent moon that glowed and the wind that helped me breathe again. It wasn't the pleading type of stay— don't leave me. It was the look in his eyes of both desperation and safety. In that moment I knew that he was the only person I ever wanted to love passionately.

"Do you think... Do you think we can really fight this?" My voice grew weak as I spoke. How could I even consider this?

"I know we can. It won't make a difference if you're there or here. Together we can save up. We can get a lawyer. We can try to find proof of what happened to you."

I squeezed his hands and, for the first time, felt truly hopeful.

"And I will be there with you every single step of the way."

Here I stood at this crossroads. I could repeat history, or I could attempt to change it. Right in front of me stood my chance to put myself first, to love someone and be loved how I always dreamed of. But if I left, then I would have to face the person who created the worst moments of my life everyday- until who knows when. Would I even get to hold my son in my arms again? I was trying to walk away and hold on at the same time. How do you go back to hell when you have everything you've ever wanted standing right in front of you?

I heard Dale's voice play in my mind. *Stupid girls do stupid things.* The thought of seeing him sent a jabbing pain down my spine. My body froze and instantly I hated myself for the control I would allow him to have if I moved back. All of those years I spent being a coward... never standing up for myself. *Where would I live? Where would I work?*

"Do you promise?" I asked Tanner with defeat in my voice.

"You can do this. You can put yourself first to get prepared. I promise, Bonnie, you— we can do this." Tanner said as he cupped both of my hands into his.

"Bonnie, you just have to do whatever the hell makes you feel alive again."

He studied my lips and for the briefest moment I allowed myself to feel everything, every single feeling I had been hiding from. A moment so intense, when our lips met, I had never in my life felt entirely calm, but also buzzing with the most energy I had ever had. He paused and stared into my eyes in the darkness. With the yellow glow from the crescent moon on our faces, and endless amount of wonder in the sky, I made the hardest decision of my life.

CHAPTER FIFTY-THREE

When I was just a little girl, my mother told me she went to Hawthorne, a Home and School for Children. I didn't understand it. I couldn't bear to imagine a little girl like myself being ripped away from her mother. Even though I hadn't been alive even a decade, I easily read the pain in my mother's face. Right there, she transformed back into that little girl. The little girl whose mother didn't want her. I always knew that my mother would never leave me. She loved me and spoiled me from the moment I was born. She promised to never leave, and I believed it. That was…Until she did. She left me. She left us. She left the world. It was a week before I had my first daughter. Not a practical time to lose your mother. Although I don't think there ever would be a practical time to lose your mother. It doesn't matter if she is a good one, or a bad one. You need her, you love her and, if she is a good mother, she knows the answers to all your questions and how to patch up all your wrongs.

The world didn't move the way it always had. But it didn't slow, it didn't stop, it just kept spinning. Spinning and spinning as I dropped to the floor. My husband, Reid, held me tightly as all that was holding me up was his arms. I sobbed into his shoulder, and my son, Finn stood in the corner, chewing his nails. *Your mom isn't supposed to leave you.*

"What's wrong with Mommy?" Finn asked weakly.

His question went unanswered. The only thing that stopped me from completely falling into Reid, was my large pregnant belly that held our little girl. The little girl who was due within the next week. Due to be welcomed to a world that my mother no longer existed in. I clutched my stomach making sure I could feel her movement. Nothing felt safe anymore.

Your mom is simply there until she is not. As constant as the sun rising each morning. The moon glowing at night. What was life without my mother? The one person who knew all the answers left.

My mind repeated questions only my mom could answer.

Mom, how do I remove stains from a white shirt?

What temperature should I set the oven to bake cookies?

Mom, what were my first words?

What temperature is too high for a baby?

I am sick, what medicine should I take?

How do I fix my broken heart?

She answered each one- but she never prepared me for what to do when she was no longer there. And I hadn't asked. All the questions that helped me survive daily and I didn't even realize I took for granted— my mother with all the answers. There was a gut-wrenching pull, a lonely existence to have my baby come into a world where my mother no longer existed.

Everything changed when she was no longer there. It was as if the safety net that surrounded earth, the world I thought I knew, shredded, tore open. My protector, the barrier that kept me safe from all things bad. The air shifted, and I realized once that net opened up, at any moment, it was possible for anyone else I assumed to be permanent could be gone too. Once you lose someone you love, you realize just how much you didn't even know you had. So many things in each moment we let pass us by. Car rides, hugs goodbye, saying I love you after ending a phone call. The way my mother's hand felt touching my forehead to see if I had a fever. The last, tight squeeze she gave in a two-armed hug. Because in our minds, we are permanent and the things we love therefore, are permanent too. The way of the world as I knew it turned upside down and I never felt completely safe again. At first, I was angry, because how could my mother leave me? How could she leave me when I had a tiny baby girl growing inside me that was supposed to meet her? That was supposed to sit in her lap and be read to. A baby that would grow into a little girl who was supposed to hear her grandmother's beautiful voice when she sang, and go for bumpy rides in the stroller as she walked her favorite paths. I didn't know it was coming or perhaps I would have tried to stop it. But then again, I'm not certain if there was anything I could do. The pain that ran through my mother's blood had existed long before I came along. She just kept it hidden so well. Like a tiny vile of poison, she only gave to herself.

The next week was a blur. Life went on, but it was never quite the same again. The days passed, the sun rose, and the flowers were still thirsty for rain. The wind blew, the clock turned, early morning routines still existed. Responsibilities piled up, people still shopped for groceries and worked their 9 to 5. There were still jokes made, and airplanes, and traffic speeding by. The phone still rang, and bills needed to be paid. My baby was ready to be born. Why couldn't it all just pause? The sun should have left when she did.

I sat in the doctor's office waiting room. The small talk and conversation weren't appealing to me anymore. I lived in a bubble of questioning our existence on earth. I questioned every aspect of my life, of life in general, of impermanence and death. I didn't want to be at the doctors, I didn't want anyone touching me, or smiling at me. I just wanted my mom.

"Elowyn," the nurse called out with a large smile pasted on her face. I rose slowly because it hurt to move. The amount of pressure that was on my pelvic bone made me think it would snap at any moment. I could feel my body moving towards the nurse, and felt Reid following behind. It was like I was in a trance, so used to this routine I didn't have to think about any of it. Stepping on the scale and looking away, peeing in a cup and writing my name on it. The squeaky door that opened and made me think of all of the other people placing their urine in the same place. I washed my hands probably a little bit too long— I hadn't been alone in a while and the stillness in that bathroom felt nice.

Back in the room, I took off my clothes and wrapped in a thin, scratchy gown. Sitting on the end of that bench I felt exposed and bare. The same way my life felt without my mother in it.

The doctor reached inside of me to see if I was dilating, and I stared at the ceiling. I was numb.

"You're still 2 cm, so we will see you next week."

I sat up in a frantic panic. "But I was hoping to ask you... if I could be induced?" *I missed the funeral from being so close to my due date; I couldn't miss her memorial service too.*

"No. You still have plenty of time," he said with a large smile on his face.

I glanced at Reid and exhaled loudly. I didn't know how to say it.

"I...uh... well, my mother died." It came out jumbled, the words feeling foreign to my lips. All of my life I never realized how badly grief questioned the finality of all things. I was one of *those* people now. The people who realize that every single thing you have can be gone in one minute. The ones who live with grateful hearts on their sleeves because they've lost enough to know what they have. The people who talk about their dead parents with the hope lingering on their lips— hoping you won't take yours for granted too.

The doctor stared at me. He had been delivering babies longer than I had been alive. Perhaps this was actually a first for him. He wasn't usually speechless. He glanced at my husband and said, "Give me a minute." When he left the room, I wiped the tears that were layered in my eyes and got dressed.

The nurse came back inside with that big smile of hers.

"He wants you at the hospital by 8PM tonight."

Finally, something went right. I smiled and choked back the tears. I would be able to say goodbye to my mother even if I couldn't make it to her funeral. I had waited to meet our baby for nine long months, but now fear clawed up my throat. It was hard to think of adding a new life into the world that didn't feel safe anymore.

With no urgency, being at the hospital felt odd. My mind hopped from one anxious thought to the next.

Last time you were with me, Mom... Why did you leave me now? Why now?

I peed in a cup again, they checked me again, still 2 cm dilated. We were taken to a room. Pitocin was started while Reid unpacked enough food for an entire week. I was giving him evil eyes because I was no longer allowed to eat. He took a large bite of a cookie and noticed me staring at him. He swallowed quickly. It was the first time I laughed. He laughed with me. I could tell he was relieved to see that a happy part of me was left.

Pitocin worked quicker than they thought it would. The baby was born within an hour and, as I pushed, I kept my eyes focused on where she stood during my son's delivery. In the corner of the room, I could swear I saw my mom crying, jumping up and down like a cheerleader, cheering me on. A smile came back to my lips when I looked into my daughter's eyes. The colors in the room seemed brighter than they had. I pulled her closer and smelled her newness, and the nurse snapped a picture for us.

I didn't think my heart could crack open any more. The baby brought me a new feeling and hope. But later, right before I left the hospital, I received a bone chilling text message.

-'**I think I'm finally ready to meet our mother. Do you have her contact information?'-**

My stomach dropped to the floor and my skin had goosebumps on every inch of it. I stared into the picture of a face of a grown man who looked so similar to my mother. Max.

It was too late, Max. You were one week too late.

-'**I'm sorry but Mom died last week. I was pregnant and not able to make it to her funeral, but we are having a memorial service to**

plant a tree in her memory with her ashes. You are welcome to come.'-

Exactly seven days after my mother, Bonnie, died, Anastasia was born. The name Anastasia means rebirth- new beginning. I had a perfect new beginning in my arms, yet all I could focus on was the past.

CHAPTER FIFTY-FOUR

As a little girl, I held tight to my mother's hand as we crossed the street. I could look at her face and see the days where shadows were inside of her eyes instead of brightness. I wondered what I could do to make her smile. The way a little girl looks up at her mother is the sweetest and most simple thing there is in life. She could do no wrong. She was the fixer of all things. Super-woman. I looked at my mother like that. I laughed at her jokes and I preferred her over anyone else in the world. She was my safety net, where ever we were, she was my home.

The first time I had a school assignment about how many siblings I had. I remember asking my parents if I could share my "other brother," Max, with the class. The one I only saw in photos. Old photos in which he was still a baby or toddler. The one whose baby gown my mom still kept in a tote in her closet. The child who grew up without her. Year after year she tried to get him back but never succeeded.

She never forgave herself for that. When my older brother, Tristan, was born he helped restore pieces of her heart. The longing she had for so long was fulfilled, but not erased. There wasn't a day that went by that she didn't miss Max. One thing after the next passed until the days blurred together. I felt grateful to have a secret brother, and maybe even a little jealous, knowing my mom had a life that existed without me in it. I sat there that day watching everyone present their fairly normal families and it was the first time I realized something within my own was different. I became curious. Where did this little boy go? Why was he taken from us? I knew how much my mother missed her son. I hated the way her voice cracked when she spoke of him. Anytime she did, a broken part of my superhero surfaced and it couldn't be fixed.

On a day she was able to cope, Mom would pull out her old suit-case filled with pictures. She would talk about the hard times she went through. How she was just a teenager when she became a mother and how much she loved her son. How she sang to him and gave him baths in the kitchen sink. How clueless she was at that age- how lonely and afraid. She also talked about the day she married my father. They went to the town hall to get married. Her best friend, Susan designed her a wedding dress with pearls and lace. Her other friend, Amy did her hair and make-up in true princess fashion. This time, it was so special that she pushed the thoughts away of herself as a girl standing there with her mom next to a living, breathing, monster. She said it was easier that way— to pretend it didn't happen. Then she would sigh, take a deep breath and say, "Everything felt so right in a world where so much wrong happens." It was like she had a second chance.

I wanted to fix the broken pieces of my mother. To mend the cracks that were visible when she spoke of Max and her childhood. At that age, I thought if she didn't talk about it, then she wouldn't be sad. But instead of helping her feel better, I pulled away... it was hard to imagine someone you love living a life like that. A part of me jealous to hear her speak of another child in this way. An adoration, longing, loving kind of way. She was our mom. I thought Tristan and I should be enough to make her happy. Then I got really sad, when I realized Max probably missed our mom as much as she missed him. I could only imagine him as the little boy in the photos despite him being older than me. I felt bad for him missing out on the wonderful life she could have given him. The life she gave us instead. Still, she wanted us to know he existed. That a part of her puzzle that made her whole was out in the world and she would never be complete without him in it.

Other than Tristan, I had an older sister, Sally, and my father, Tanner, lived with us. Sally had a different mom and I didn't know much about that either. When I was about five, Tristan and Sally were older and already in school so I was lucky enough to go everywhere my mother went during the day. Appointments, grocery shopping, the library, planting in the garden.

I followed Mom up the stairs when her name was called. I sat on the floor of the dimly lit therapy room like I had so many times before. The only light, came from outside and a tiny lamp that sat in the corner. Mom often talked to this woman, Joan. I could tell it made my mom comfortable because she didn't use her hands to talk. Instead, I could see the tenderness in the therapist's eyes. It was like she collected the pain that came from my mother's words. The way she looked at my mom when she spoke. I would look up from the wooden blocks I was stacking and smile at my mom. Joan gave her a tissue and she wiped her tears away.

She addressed how much the trauma had affected her everyday life. Joan normalized my mom's self-hatred and self-sabotaging tendencies. She allowed Mom to see herself as a little girl again. To look back at that little girl and forgive her for what she didn't know. When she was done talking, she looked less sad, lighter. Some of the shadows that so frequently visited her face had vanished. I liked that Joan helped my mom to feel better. I liked hearing the woman remind my mother of how beautiful and strong she was— inside and out. Because that's how I saw her too. She breathed easier and her smile spread up to her eyes on the way home. I didn't know why my mother lived in a cycle of running from the shadows from her past. It was too complicated for me to understand. I didn't try to. I just soaked in knowing that I was loved. Because at that age, life is simply about you- you can't grasp that you're not the only one in the world. Every time we left the dim office, we held hands tightly. As if my mom was afraid,

I would get lost. She already knew the feeling of impermanence, long before I did.

Throughout our childhood, our mom feared if she let us out of her sight, we would be fully grown adults that no longer needed her. The truth was that she needed us more. Through the filter of our eyes- she lived for the first time. She let go of the guilt and anger and shame for us. She forced herself to move forward, and she reminded herself that it was the best she could do. There wasn't a day that went by that Max didn't run through her mind. My dad once told me it came to a point where it cut so deeply to even think of Max that she pushed it deep down with all of her other secrets. His memories didn't stay there but instead, stayed alive in her mind.

She lived for the moments she felt alive with Tristan and I. Back-logged dreams of Max always surfaced through our childhood and she told us. She brought them to life through us. Max had taught her how to be a mother, when she was still just a child herself.

Over the years, our mother took over every emotional fit with grace. She made herself suffer through each moment of spilled milk, and tugging on her shirt, and the constant demand of little children needing her at every move- rarely taking a break. She accepted this new chance at motherhood was like an ultimate marathon- long, grueling, and exhilarating, and worth the pain and effort. She believed she didn't deserve to take breaks. Every moment was dedicated to her family.

She gave us the life that had long ago passed by her. She repeated the same things for years on end. Being needed all of the time. Trying to keep track of every little piece that went to a play set. To keep the floors cleaned, the refrigerator full, and the never-ending worry that something would happen to us. Our mother was present in every moment with us. When we took our first steps, said our first words, and especially when we slept on her lap. My dad said she would sit there grinning at our perfect lashes flapping and our chubby cheeks falling slightly. The daily cuddles and physical contact were almost enough to make her forget the past. She had what she always wanted- love, a whole lot of it. It was the only thing that kept her heart sealed all those years.

As we got older, my brother and I managed to get into a lot of trouble, the normal sibling rivalry. Fighting with each other, the arguments, breaking her favorite vases or shooting each other with BB guns. Still, in trouble or not, Mom was there every step of the way. She helped us prevent our father from finding out all of the 'bad' things we did. I hadn't known she lived vicariously through us until I could fully understand her past. She read fairytales and many different books to us, rubbed our backs, and never let us suffer a moment in boredom. She told us words from when she lived down south, like *buggy* instead of shopping cart. *Pocketbook* instead of purse. She taught us to say guitar like *GI-tar* instead of *gah-tar*. Mom even threw the best birthday parties a child could ever want. As if she, herself, were still a child and reliving those experiences through us. Freeze dancing, homemade cakes, a lot of decorations. Treasure hunts, costume parties, and a whole lot of silly games. She would sit on the floor and hold balloons so kids could pop them with their butts as she held it in place, giggling along with us. She was one of us. Our happiness fueled her, as did our father's.

She loved my father with everything she had. They worked well together. He called her lovey dovey most of the time and when she was nervous, he was her calm. When she was angry, he was her punching bag and emotional support. It was a life of love and trust. Birthday parties, family meals, camping, and quality time. Everything my mother had longed for while she lived at Hawthorne, my father helped her give to us. So, in a way, my brother and I received the best end of this deal. Two people that had been beaten down by life, found each other and made something beautiful. I never had to wonder if I was loved. I never had to question if my parents regretted having me. Completely the opposite of what she had.

Our childhood was movie-like, happy, magical. I had no idea what hid buried beneath our joy. For all of the failures my parents experienced, they pushed to give us more. Unknowing to us at the time just how much our mother had overcome because, for years, she was able to pull herself together long enough to love us.

So, for a little bit, she did get her happily ever after. From the outside looking in, you would see a nice yellow home with flowers in the yard. You would see chalk markings on the sidewalk, and bikes leaning to the side that had been thrown down when a loving mother called the children in for lunch. You would see the perfect shaped butterfly sandwiches that our dad had mastered, pickle antennas, and pretzels over the wings, with small cheese flowers. You would see us children, outside exploring life through innocent eyes. Much of what my mother had missed is what she poured into us. She had this second chance and she wasn't going to fail. We ran wild outside and I always loved the rain. She wasn't like the other mothers, making you stay inside. She taught us to face the rain. We were never told we couldn't play in the rain, or that we had to wear shoes outside. She barely wore shoes herself. She taught us how to do a rain dance as we patted our mouths and spun in circles. She taught us to feel every moment in the moment. How important that is. The feeling of the cold pellets of water meeting my skin. The way the soft grass felt beneath my bare feet. Every now and again, she would join us. Standing there with her arms extended and her chin facing the sky, washing all of the darkness away from her body.

My mother suffered gravely when her grandmother, Ma-maw, died. I remember being curious to how we didn't even know the women who my mother cried for. We piled up, Mom, Dad, Tristan, Sally and I, in the car and drove 4 hours to the funeral. On the way there, my mom was in a buoyant mood. I think there was a spark of hope that maybe she could have a relationship with her mother after all of these years. Maybe she could fix parts of her past that were broken.

Dad was angry the entire way there muttering and complaining the whole way,

"Bonnie, this is ridiculous. We can't… We can't go back and change the decisions we made in the past. We can only live with them, and sometimes that means letting it go so we can be alive again." Despite being so against it, there he was once again in the driver seat next to her. He kept telling her she shouldn't give her mother the time of day because she was guilty for leaving Max.

"It wasn't the same thing, *lovey dovey*. She chose to leave you." My mother wasn't having it. I tried to back up my father. I didn't know much, but the only thing I did know about my grandmother was sometimes she got drunk and called after 8PM. I had a vivid memory of my mother sobbing after Ruby hung up on her and told her she was her biggest mistake. Her heart would remember how alone she felt, never being good enough for her mom.

"Mom, I think Dad is right. It is really sad that you even care so much of what *Ruby* thinks of you," I said, emphasizing Ruby because we never called her grandma.

"You don't understand, Winnie." She turned around in the passenger seat to face me. "She's my mom."

"Well, I get it but she's a bad one. You deserve better," I told her in my childish voice. I thought I could make her realize she deserved way more than what Ruby had to offer. But she had a soft spot for her mom because she believed if she faced the truth that her mom was a bad mother then she, too, would be labeled a bad mother because of Max. Because the one thing in life she set out not to do, she did and repeated the history she fought so hard to change.

I think deep down Dad knew what kind of pain Ruby would bring up from my mom's emotional reserve. I remember feeling odd as we dropped her off at the church for the funeral service. She hadn't wanted us kids to meet everyone at a funeral for the first time.

"Sally can watch Tristan and Winnie. I want to be there for you, *lovey dovey*." My dad offered.

"No. Tanner, I think this is something I have to do, alone." She told him and shut the car door. My stomach dropped, watching her enter the church. I felt like we were dropping her into a tank with piranhas and she might not come back in one piece.

After the funeral, we went to Ma-maw's house. Winding roads took us there and I had butterflies in my stomach the whole way. I would meet my grandmother, Ruby, for the first time.

Ruby was eccentric and had long gray hair that fell to her waistline. She was an older version of my mother, yet her eyes weren't quite as genuine. I stood back from her, she smelled of alcohol, but she did give me a hug. When she slid one arm behind me and patted me, it felt more forced than desired. Tristan whispered to me that she had dragon breath, and it was the first time I laughed that day.

Tristan, Sally, and I wondered around the house my mother had fond memories of. Away from all of the strangers, into the old green bedroom that had once belonged to Ruby. I studied every little thing, the decorations frozen in time, and tried to decide how it all went so wrong. It looked like a normal house. In the pictures they looked like a normal family. My father was not happy to be there and he made it pretty clear. But there was a part of my mom that was filled with both nostalgia and sadness. She told me about the rooster, Red, who attacked her. She led us to the washroom where she used to help Rissy hang clothes.

When the rest of the family arrived, the conversation bounced from past to future. Names were easy for her, she remembered all of the aunts and uncles from her past. It was like her mind separated into little folders. She had stored any bit of good information to outweigh the bad even after all of those years. Yet when she spoke to them, she felt like an outsider. She may have known their names but all their aged faces did was remind her what her life could have been.

Aunt Emma's arrival was my favorite part of that day. She was funny and told people like it was. I had met her a few times over the years and she greeted us with a genuine hug. She never wanted us to call her Aunt Emma, because that made her feel old. She was the one person my mom tried to remain relatively close to, but there was something missing between them that only heartache could explain. Emma grew up to have addiction problems of her own. She went on to repeat the same history her mother did. She left her children behind with their father and never looked back. She was too busy fighting her own demons to get them back. I think that scared my mother even more. She witnessed generations of abandonment and she wanted that to change. It goes to show how important being worthy of love is when you're a child. Pieces of their past couldn't be erased once they were abandoned.

Uncle Ralph was fortunate in that he adjusted well to Hawthorne.

He was one of the lucky ones who fell into a type of normalcy with supportive house parents since he was so young. I think all my mother saw when she looked at her siblings was her failure to save them and the deep feelings of being abandoned on those steps. She forgave her mother because she repeated history. But I never did. I never forgave her because my mother deserved better, they all did.

When Jo was introduced, you could tell there was tension. What made her different, for Ruby to raise her? Would it be the same judgment directed at me if I ever met Max? Or was it just the timing and things that took place that would forever change history? We're all made to carry different weight. All Mom ever wanted was to love and be loved. Ruby made a choice that forever changed lives.

Ruby talked about some of the seldom good times, as if talking about them could change things. I thought maybe she felt bad, perhaps it would be the closure my mother finally needed. Before we left, Ruby reached into her pocket and fetched out a ring. It was a platinum ring that Ma-maw gifted to her after her last daughter was born. It was Ma-maw's last attempt to have Ruby rekindle her role as a mother. Usually, a mother's rings celebrated the bond between a mother and her children. Typically, a mother's ring holds a set of birthstones relating to each child. I remember the look on my mom's face as she accepted the ring in her hand.

She said, "Bonnie, there is no way I can fix the past, but I hope you accept this as a symbol of my love and apologies." My mom twirled that ring in her finger all the way home. I could tell it made her feel as though she were that little girl again, whose mother thought she could fix things with a piece of jewelry. But another part of her felt special, she finally had something of her mother that she could hold onto. On the way home, she told us stories about being at her grandmother's house as a little girl. How much she loved Rissy, and how she taught her what love really meant. How she never got to see her again, but Tanner and her traveled to the old shack she used to live in, and she took clippings from the plants outside. Those clippings became plants that grew around my childhood home. The ring sat on her vanity, untouched.

We caught lightning bugs, and even bumble bees with old pickle jars that she had poked holes in the lids of. At the end of the day, we always set them free. Because, Mom had taught us that no matter how different or small a life is, it still has significance in the world and deserves to be free. I think this was one way she was able to forgive herself. She would watch with us as the groups of bees angrily dissipated into the air. "Everyone needs to fly."

She would say, "When a person cares about the happiness of others, that's what humanity is. Rissy always told me that."

I began to save earth worms drowning in puddles on the concrete during a rainstorm and my parents would stop in the rain and wait for me to release him back into the soft grassy dirt. The worm had value because the worm was a living thing. That's how I looked at everything and everyone— plants, people, animals. I thought everyone saw the world the same.

When we were at a store or restaurant and a person was nice- the worker, another shopper- my mom often pointed that out to me and my brother. "She's so nice, isn't she?" We began to notice when other people were nice too. It made us want to be nice people. She wanted to show us there was good in the world. How could she notice this after everything she endured? I didn't question that until after her death. That's the thing about time. You're in it every single second of the day. But somehow you forget the little moments. The small stuff. The little pieces of life that mean we're really alive. The way sunshine feels on your skin, the first bite of a warm glazed donut, the smile you can give to someone who really needed it. Life is all of those things. The mornings before school, time at the dinner table. The in-between moments are the ones we're rarely stressed about. It's everything else in the world that make us anxious and fearful or even regretful.

My father had a thing for saving and fixing damaged things and I like to think that's why they were meant to be together. He has a way with bringing back light to dark things. Constructing new barns from old wood. We watched as our father rescued turtles from the middle of the road. He would pull his truck to the center, as if he were Superman, stopping both lanes of traffic to save a turtle's life. He would confidently let the small critter go, back to nature, as if it also repaired a piece of his own soul. These small acts of kindness, however so small, were what I thought was normal. I was loved in a way that I truly believed everyone in the world loved the same.

Rust and mustard-colored leaves crunched beneath our feet, the air smelled of cinnamon apples, and it wasn't unusual to find my mother on the front porch with Aunt Susan in the mornings, coffee in hands. "It's autumn, Winnie. An ending and a new beginning. It reminds us that, even when we lose hope, there are changes and more beautiful days to come." Mom told me as soon as the trees began to transform and a golden hue filled the sky.

Autumn. It was always a special season. Our Aunt Susan came to stay for a few weeks each October. She called it her 'summer-break Meteorologist style' since summer was typically an active season for weather-related disasters. She traveled the US capturing natural disasters for the Weather Channel. All year she saved her vacation time for October, just to be with us. I loved Aunt Susan. I knew she wasn't my real aunt, but for some reason that made her even more special. I loved the way she put a smile on Mom's face- and how she nicknamed my mom, Bunny. Even though I don't think Mom was as fond of the name. I also thought the way she cursed in front of me was hilarious. Most grown-ups acted weird about that stuff, but not Susan. I had someone in my life who wasn't blood loving me as much as my parents did. Plus, we always had fun while she visited.

They told me that while living at Hawthorne, it was almost as if they watched the holidays through the eyes of others. Never having control, never being what they actually wanted to be for Halloween. That was another bonus of Susan coming. Each year my mom and Susan got to work on their favorite projects together. Designing our Halloween costumes. They had this secret between them about designing wedding dresses when they were little. My mom still kept her wedding dress Susan designed in her closet. They often pulled it out and told me the same stories about their crumbled-up wedding book dress over and over again, but I didn't mind.

Susan slapped a raggedy stapled construction paper down in front of me, "Check these out Winnie." I flipped through the brittle pages; afraid they would shrivel into nothing. I wanted to laugh, but the way their eyes met and shined revealed how much this little book meant to them. "Pretty cool" I had said, and so every year, Tristan and I worked together to come up with difficult concepts just to challenge them.

Mom hand-sewed Tristan and my costumes— Tinkerbell, Peter Pan, witches, and bank robbers, and even a bag filled with money that won a contest at the local YMCA. Susan was creative and inventive and hand drew and designed anything we could dream of. It allowed them to re-invent those days of idiocy at Hawthorne.

Normally, we took an annual family trip to the apple orchard with our dad too, but he decided to pick up extra work. "Alright kids, you're going unsupervised. No rooftops with Tristan and Elowyn," my dad teased the morning he left for work.

Later in the car, Tristan asked, "What was he talking about?" We were on the way up to Wayside Farm. Mom drove, Susan took passenger and Tristan and I were together in the back seat. Susan and Mom grinned at each other. Mom's face lit up. "Susan made me climb on the roof when I met her," she told us from the rear-view mirror. "Oh, come on, Bunny," Susan said shaking her head. "Your mom and I went rooftop nearly every week when we were little," she teased, "even though... she was quite a wimp most of the time."

"I was not." Mom laughed and gripped the steering wheel. It was usually our father who drove. "It was actually fun once you got used to the idea of not dying. But Tristan and Winnie, you better not *ever* think of going on a rooftop." Tristan and I grinned at each other. We loved knowing all of mom's secrets. At the farm, I overhead Mom and Susan talking about the time they ran away together with Ima and Harvey and their cats. I wanted a cat desperately, but the answer to pets was always a no. My dad didn't want us to have any pets until we lived out of the city on our own land. The smell of ripe apples from the tree's wafted through with smoke from the nearby fire. Both of their faces lit up watching us pick out pumpkins. Despite Tristan and I fighting over who had the best pumpkin, it was a peaceful fall day. By the time we filled the car with pumpkins and mums, I was ready to nap on the way home. But I couldn't because Tristan chomped his apple so loudly next to me. "Tristan, congratulations on letting the whole world hear you eat that apple," I yelled at him. He chomped on the apple again, this time right next to my ear. Mom told us to be quiet and turned the music off. She had become so dependent on Dad driving, sometimes she got really nervous. But right as I looked out the window to avoid Tristan, I saw a little puppy on the side of the road.

"Oh, look, Mom, a puppy!" I shouted out.

"Awwww," Susan called out.

"Mom, you have to stop," Tristan demanded.

"He is cute," Mom said then quickly added, "but we can't take him with us."

She smiled and nervously she pulled the car over to the side of the street. Cars passed quickly, not slowing so she demanded we stay in the car. My heart raced, because even though I wanted a cat, I would settle for a dog. She waited for an 18-wheeler to pass and climbed out. She took a few steps, calling out to the dog. I could tell the hesitant way she walked, she feared he would turn and dash into the traffic.

"Come here, boy." The dog backed away slowly.

"Give me your apple," she called through Tristan's open window. He passed it to her, and the dog waddled over to her. It licked her leg slowly and she realized it wasn't a puppy, it was a female dog.

"I want to hold it!" I shouted.

"No, I get to hold it," Tristan remarked, smacking me.

"Well, I can't hold it, I have to help with the maps," Susan added.

Mom ignored our argument and bent down to take the dog in her arms. She bowed to her and snuggled in her arms. Mom huffed loudly. Opened Tristan's door and sat the dog in his lap. I pouted and crossed my arms. Tristan shot me a told you so smile.

"We have to keep her, Mom," Tristan said, rubbing the sweet dog.

"We will take her home and see if she belongs to anybody. You know we can't keep her."

"Maybe Aunt Susan will take her," I offered reaching over to pet her.

"Oh, no, no- I have cats," she replied.

Before we even made it home, the dog had gotten car-sick and threw up all over Tristan. I was happy I wasn't the one holding her then.

That night when Dad arrived home, nobody said a word. He glanced down at the dog. His gaze shifted to Mom, down to Tristan, and over to me and lastly to Susan. We smiled but didn't make eye contact.

"Susan?" Dad asked turning to her.

"Nope. Not me this time." She looked proud- normally the bad, impulsive ideas were hers.

"We're just keeping her until someone claims her. We found her on the way home from Wayside," Mom explained with a child-like grin crossing her lips.

I held my breath and smiled. "Well, if someone doesn't, we will find her a home." We held back our rebuttal and, instead, scooted in closer to the dog as if we could change our fathers mind with love. He turned, "If not, Susan can take her."

"What is this? I am not taking this dog home to eat my cats."

Over the next few weeks, nobody claimed the dog. Susan eventually left refusing to take her. She became part of the family. We all called her Baby, except Dad, he called her 'fat dog' even though, when nobody was looking, I would see him petting her and feeding her left over scraps from dinner.

When Tristan was a preteen, he began doing normal things teenage boys do that can get them into trouble. I was still a kid and I often told on him when I caught him. This caused a lot of tension between us. But on that night, I was in the living room and Mom was walking through the kitchen. A flicker of light from the window caught her eye and she yelled, "Fire! Fire?" Small things sent her into a huge panic quickly. She jumped and ran towards the door. I threw down my

Barbie dolls and followed. As she rounded the corner, Tristan's eyes widened.

"Tristan!" She grabbed ahold of his arm, took the matches, and stomped them out. The fire had caught hold of several leaves and a tiny trail headed towards our wooden fence. She grabbed the hose and chased the trail of fire. She faced Tristan and threw the hose down.

"Really? Fire... what were you thinking?" Her face turned a crimson red. It was rare for her to yell at us. So, when she did, we had a hard time taking it seriously. That usually made her even angrier.

Tristan stood quickly and stuffed his hands in his pockets, his lips pursed.

"Follow me. Right now!" She yelled and stomped back up the steps and inside. She didn't hold the door open for us. She motioned for us to sit down at the table. Then she began digging in the china cabinet. Opening drawers, shifting things around. I stared at Tristan from across the table, he held in a smile and made his eyes big. I wanted to laugh too.

Had she lost her mind?

Finally, she laid a handful of objects on the table. A confused look crossed our faces as we studied the Christmas candles, votive candles, and matches. She turned and filled a bowl with water,

"If you want to play with fire, you need to learn the right way."

"Wait... what?" I said, I wasn't the one in trouble and this hardly seemed like punishment. Any time she came across a problem she wanted to teach us as early as possible how to overcome it.

"Winnie, you might as well learn now."

We watched our mother join us at the table. She struck a wooden match against the cardboard box. "You hold it like this, at the bottom so you're far away from the flame. Then you hold the box slightly sideways." She swiped it again, and we watched the flame that sparked to life.

"Your turn since you obviously figured out that part." She crinkled her nose at Tristan.

He took them with a big grin on his face now, and as he lit one the first try, his face filled with excitement. He tried a few more, lighting candles up across the kitchen table. I took the box, and after multiple strikes across the box, I heard the flame take off— like a rocket to the sky.

Over the next hour Mom taught us how to blow out the matches and place them in water without panicking to make sure the fire was gone. She prompted us how to sense when our fingers felt hot when the match burns too far down, so we knew when we needed to stop it before it got close to our fingers. She showed us when we held the fire lower it would burn quicker and to keep the flame above our hands. We lit candles and blew them out until the table was filled with flames and smoke. The putrid smell of the wick turning to smoke filled the kitchen.

Once the candles cooled, she let us dip our fingers into the warm wax and cover our fingers. She smiled at our faces. She enjoyed teaching us how to better judge and manage risks in real life situations. She trusted us and let us know if we wanted to play with fire, we could do it with her safely instead of behind her back. That's how she was with everything. Tell me and even if I do get mad, I'll be there and help you figure it out. The only thing she didn't prepare us for was living without her. Having a life without her in it.

When I turned eleven, my parents called Tristan and I down to the table, Baby followed behind us and laid down at our feet. Originally, we thought the dog was for us, but more than anything she became our mom's. You could see her face shift when the dog was nearby. A comforting presence. I smiled at the way my mother's eyes resurfaced any time Baby nuzzled her nose into her. The dog could sense stress and disrupted nightmares in her mind.

"Do you want to tell them, Tanner?" Mom asked and Dad nodded.

"We're moving."

"Wait- what?" I sat forward, squinting my eyes.

"We're *moooo-ving*, idiot," Tristan said loudly.

I swatted at him and pulled my shirt over my knees.

"I don't want--" I began but was stopped abruptly by my father's hand in pause motion.

"Listen, I know this isn't what anybody wants, but this is something we're doing."

"Great." Tristan slapped the table.

Our mother jumped and then composed herself quickly.

"So, we don't even get a say?" Tristan repeated twice.

Our parents exchanged glances. "We will be moving to the country. We will have our own private land." Our mother spoke in a matter-of-fact voice. She could make anything seem like an adventure.

"It is something your father has always dreamed of. He has always wanted his own property. Plus! Your dad brought you back something."

We leaned forward to inspect. He placed a cardboard box down. It had holes sliced into the top.

"Ew- it stinks," I said, scrunching my nose.

"Open it, Tristan," Dad gently shoved it towards him.

Tristan pulled the cardboard apart- first the sides and then the middle and gasped when he saw four little eyes looking up at him.

"Oh my! Lizards," he said excitedly and reached his hand in.

"They're called Anoles and they sell them here at the pet store for $14.99. How cool will it be to catch these in OUR own yard?" He smiled, tapping the table.

Dad could barely contain his excitement. I knew there was no way he was this excited about lizards.

"Wait, can we keep these as pets?" I asked and glanced down into the box. I was a sucker for anything that was alive. I instantly fell in love with the lizard eyes staring up at me.

"Of course, you can," Mom said, smiling because their trick had worked.

Tristan reached in and took his lizard out. It crawled calmly across his hand.

I reached in next and held my slightly smaller lizard close to inspect him. He changed a lighter green color right on my hand. "Wow!"

"Okay, that is pretty cool." Tristan smiled. "But will we have a club house again?"

"Even better- there's a large oak in the backyard that would be perfect for a tree house. I sprung up at that idea. "Yes! Okay I'm ready to move. Can I go pack now?"

"Sure but take your lizard with you. I don't want that thing on my kitchen table ever again," our mother called out to us.

I packed for a few minutes and made my way back downstairs. I sat down at the kitchen table. I just watched my mother as she cleaned, wishing, and wanting more than anything to be just like her.

I loved the way my mom's hand felt on top of mine. The way she laughed and teased me. Or the way that I teased her when she gurgled salt water and baking soda and we laughed at the faces she made because she knew I hated that sound. The stomps she made across the kitchen floor. The jingle of her voice carrying through every part of the house, her arm gestures when singing. The way she spoke of nasty things when it was time to eat. Like the time she discussed roadkill during dinner. Or the time she talked about a function of the human body during dessert. Her laughter was so contagious. Her silliness, and realness, and her ability to live in the moment.

I figured that most kids had a mom and dad who loved them. I didn't consider it to be anything special at that time. My childhood house was filled with love and laughter. Smiling faces and a lot of good food. We had toys, and we never worried about having clothes to wear. When we were bored, we simply went to our mother.

"I'm bored." And like clockwork, Mom created a new game we could play, or an activity we could do. If it wasn't a game, she made cleaning fun. Wiping down the counters and refrigerator. And sometimes, she would even let me and Tristan slide across the floor on towels to mop and call it ice skating. Water and suds splashed on every surface as we slid across the soapy floor like we were on a slipping slide. It seemed like our mother knew everything there ever was to know.

The day came that we had been waiting for. The land property went through, and Dad and Mom were about to be owners of their own land. There was excitement in the air when we loaded up the moving truck. Dad dosed baby with Dramamine, so she wasn't sick while we drove. It took all week but eventually we moved onto the property out in the middle of an old cotton field. Literally in the middle of nowhere. I remember feeling the disappointment when Tristan and I flipped a coin and he got the bigger bedroom. I remember the look on my father's face when we moved into our house. Accomplishment, happiness. It was something he always dreamed of. I remember the look on my mother's face when he built her a white picket fence and an arbor that held Lady Banks yellow roses with beautiful pale-yellow flowers on thorn-less branches that dangled from the trellis. Very much like in fairytales. My father hung a chandelier from the tree and lights went up around the white picket fence. It was an outdoor sanctuary where they would spend most of their time together, alone, on their own land and in peace. Susan came down to help us move in. She brought Mom an entire package of plants and seeds to start a garden of her own. Our mother repeated the same things for years on end. She embraced the identity of being needed all of the time. Sometimes, she even absent-mindedly placed things in places we could never find them. Like her keys, and her purse, and anything important. In a way, the past that haunted her had also forced her to heal for us.

Each night she would climb into bed, next to our father. As she fell in, next to his warmth, she knew he was exhausted too. Tanner worked in the heat of the day, physical labor. He often had sunburn and gashes on his hands that were covered in duct tape instead of band-aids. When he told her he was tired, she knew it wasn't a complaint, instead an honest assessment as to how his worn body felt after building all day. So, day in and day out they lived in the chaotic routine of raising children together. In ways much different than what they had experienced.

And each year life happened and there was never a right time to face Dale. Never enough money, never enough time, and never enough courage to go back. Mom got swept away in the life she always wanted. She allowed herself to feel happiness and everything that she ever deserved.

You could find her walking barefoot in the yard with a smile on her face. Or see her inside of her garden that somehow doubled in size each year. She removed each weed with anger. Plucking it from the soil and tossing it into a pile over her shoulder. The garden was hers- and hers alone. She hated things that intruded on her happy place. Her garden gave her more than the care and hours she spent tending to it. Not only food, but also a sense of safety. Other than critters and sometimes snakes, nobody could ever mess with her while she was gardening. It allowed her a space to clear her mind. To be that child she was all those years ago, following behind Rissy and copying every move she made. The sweet garden smell, of fresh earth and new life. Little daffodils shooting up, the bees buzzing, lipstick pink peonies growing in the yard, and pollen floating around like pixie dust. It was her sanctuary that gave her peace and she worked endlessly to give Mother Nature the same. Until we were teenagers it stayed that way. We had everything we ever wanted and more.

Being a teenager came with its own challenges. The day my mother warned me about happened. Bright red… it just appeared suddenly in my underwear. I was highly embarrassed. I had long, uncomfortable talks with my mom about having a period and she had prepared me, but I couldn't believe what I was seeing. I wasn't really sure what to do.

"Winnie, it's time to go to the lake." My mother called for me. I had locked myself inside the bathroom, inspecting my underwear and pacing back and forth.

"One minute," I called, after I tried wiping and wiping to make it go away.

How could I swim like this? My face felt hot, and I was angry- angry that my own body had betrayed me. Tears streamed down my face.

"Elowyn?" Mom called again from outside of the door. I sniffled and tried to respond, but nothing came out.

"Mom, can you come in?"

She opened the door and swiftly closed it behind her. Like she already knew. She took one glance at me, and began to dig underneath the cabinet, stretching for the very back. She resurfaced with two boxes. One with tampons and one with pads.

"I never got to have the period talk with anyone when mine started. It's OK, Winnie, I know it doesn't feel okay right now, but it will be." She sat the boxes on the counter and turned to me.

"I didn't have anyone to tell when mine started so I tried to hide it… mostly because it grossed me out but, I was also in denial about its impending arrival. Please don't use toilet paper. It's uncomfortable."

I wiped my nose with my sleeve. "I don't like this," I sobbed, holding my cramping stomach.

"I know. You will like the period talk even less." She shrugged with a smile. "I have one box of pads- they stick to your underwear. One box of tampons that take some time to get used to. I want you to read the box and see what you think."

I sighed and put my hands over my face.

"It's part of life, Winnie. These body changes are completely normal during puberty. Puberty is just a sign your body is developing like it should."

"Can you please stop saying puberty?" I whispered.

She laughed. She was always delighted to find words that people disliked. She enjoyed studying their faces and laughing until she cried.

"You can still go swimming if you are able to use a tampon. I know it's a lot, Wyn, but it happens to all of us women."

"I really wanted to swim."

"Read the boxes and we can figure it out. I'm going to tell Dad and Tristan to go on without us."

"Mom. Please! Don't tell them."

She squeezed my shoulder. "I won't." She smiled reassuringly and disappeared as fast as she came.

I stood there trying to read the boxes. I decided pads were best and stuck one to the new panties my mom brought me. I met Mom in the living room. Together we curled up on the couch. As if I were a little girl again, she brushed her fingers through my hair and rubbed my back. She brought me a chocolate bar, a heating pad, and a cozy blanket. She did everything for me that she never had. Almost as if she was reliving the worst moments of her life in a different lens. It brought her comfort and peace knowing she got to relive the loneliest moments, in ways she never got to the first time.

∾

By the time I was 17, my mother remained open with me. It wasn't the typical teenager-parent relationship. Same with my father. I would never leave the house without saying 'I love you' to my parents, even in front of my friends. As a teenager, I didn't understand why my mother didn't want to get her nails done. I didn't understand why she didn't like to be touched by strangers, or why she was so private. Why she didn't like to be the one sleeping closest to the bedroom door, so no matter where they moved, my dad always shifted the bed so he was the one by the door. I didn't know she was afraid of real-life monsters who crept into her doorway at night. Mom always valued her privacy, perhaps this is why she and Dad decided to move out into the middle of nowhere. But I did understand that I could trust my mother with anything.

When I lost my virginity to a not so prince charming and he broke up with me, it was my mother to whom I cried.

"Please don't tell Dad," I whispered to her. My mother rubbed my back. "I won't, but Winnie— It will be okay." She called out of work and crawled into my bed with me. She told me all of the things that nobody ever said to her. She never got to hear that it would be OK. That bad times were lessons. Of the proper way to start birth control and use condoms if it was going to happen. She sat there and shared her stories from Hawthorne. About Susan, and the roof-tops, pizza spins. But she would pause and share bits and pieces too— of the horror she experienced when the man who was supposed to be her house father began to rape her. How she never even knew she was losing her virginity. How someone took it from her and she hated herself for it. The pain she felt when she thought of Max spending his life without her. When she told me these things, it wasn't to make my situation seem less traumatic, it was to relate to me and share secrets she kept hidden for so very long. In a way I had become a space for her to fix the broken pieces of herself.

"Mom, you can't hate yourself for that. You were just a kid," I told her. Mom smiled at me, so I continued. "You will find him one day. You will find him, and we will tell him what happened and how wonderful of a mother you are." I gave her a big hug, forgetting all about my broken heart.

"Yeah." My mom smiled. "Yeah," she said. And I could tell she yearned to have that relief from the chains that Dale placed on her heart all those years ago. At that time, being a woman herself, she didn't understand how a mother could willingly leave her children. How a grown man could take advantage of a small little girl. That is why she chose to focus on the good. She unknowingly modeled all of the good things in the world for us. Together, her and my father created a space that would be unbreakable from the outside world's chilling grasp they both knew all too well, lived right beneath the surface of happiness. It was that same year I lost my virginity I decided I would go to college for psychology. I set out to be the person my own mother needed when she was just a girl. If she would have had someone who believed in her like I did, someone she could trust, then maybe she could have had an entirely different life. Every problem I faced, I never faced alone.

I watched as my mother's hair began to turn gray and she would just as quickly dye it. A putrid smell seeping from the bathroom and her walking around laughing at the way we all looked at her with her hair sticking to her head with a dark hue on top. I was eighteen and believed I would live forever and age would never catch up to me. Tristan was in his early 20's and he had his first serious girlfriend. My mother never pretended to be perfect by any means. So, when we had someone, we wanted her to meet, she welcomed them. She welcomed imperfect people into her life, and shared love with them. Usually when it came to my brother and I, it was by way of embarrassment. Perhaps intentionally, and perhaps not, she had a way to make other's laugh around her. She always said never to leave someone without first making them smile. It was how, after everything she had been through, she was able to endure the pain and bottle up the worst parts of her life with laughter.

His girlfriend was over for the first time and she pointed out the small white patch of hair behind Tristan's ear (that he was born with) and he shrugged away from her mockingly shouting "MOM!" while she, I and his girlfriend giggled. She did everything in fast speed, and was often rushing to do something else. Once she ran over Tristan's best friends' foot, who calmly stated, "Um, Mrs. Tristan's mom, you ran over my foot." She panicked and by the time she got the car off of his foot, the only thing we all could do is laugh and make sure he didn't need to go to the hospital. Luckily, he didn't but he never let her live that one down and it got her laughing every single time. Some would say she had a sick sense of humor. No matter what we were eating, somehow, she unintentionally brought up the most inappropriate and gruesome discussions. She appreciated these topics mostly for their humor value, but her favorite part was just to watch the uncomfortable looks and unblinking eyes as she continued to talk. She simply enjoyed being comical about the somewhat foul, fairly awkward and slightly unpleasant, especially at the dinner table.

Our mother never let a chance to spoil us pass her by. Even as we grew older, she continued to do things for us that we should have most definitely done for ourselves. Washing our clothes, and making our beds, and even getting us gifts on valentine's day- in every single way we knew we were loved. Even when Tristan was nearly an adult and had let his hair grow out, it was Mom who would help him put it into a ponytail before work each night. I would walk by mocking him, as I always did.

We had a hate-love relationship. We always fought for our mother's attention. We also enjoyed scaring her. The many times we could just walk into a room and she would go into full running mode, as children, was funny to us. We didn't understand the true meaning behind these actions, nor any signs to look for a psychological condition like Post Traumatic Stress Disorder. Later, I would think back to this and cry at the idea of this poor woman going through so much that someone walking into the room could scare her so badly. The four of us fit together nicely, I had a life that I thought everyone else had. I didn't realize until I grew up how lucky I was- the laughter at the kitchen table, the smile in my dad's eyes when he looked at my mother, the traditions we had and the togetherness.

Before we all knew, we had our last fight over breakfast one morning.

"Tristan and Winnie-- stop it," she called patiently while washing dishes at the sink. Dad walked in, scooting his slippers across the floor. Our dog, Baby, took the opportunity to steal bacon from the table.

"No physical contact," he would say with a grin on his face before stepping out to have his morning cigarette on the porch. Each morning he would survey his yard, the one he always wanted. I didn't realize how important it was to him. I waited until he couldn't see me and slapped Tristan on the back of the head. He kicked me back under the table. We thought we were sneaky and, although we managed not to get caught with several of our adventures, it was always our mother who found the BB gun pellets in the bathroom sink, or the broken glass knickknack we hid on a tall shelf.

Memories sat everywhere around that house. Moments we thought we would have forever, passed us by. As I got ready for college and Tristan left for the military, our dad continued to work and our mom was suddenly facing an empty nest with no idea how to survive without other people to take care of. She had a lot more spare time than she was used to. While Tristan was away in the Army, the house felt smaller. There was nobody fighting with me, and Mom had less clothes to wash and fretted over me more. Each Tuesday at noon, Mom would wait for the phone call from Tristan. Feeling relief as soon as she knew he was okay. On the fuzzy line, with loud noises in the background, she would talk to Tristan for as long as she could.

Social media was becoming really popular. So, we also got to chat with him online and play games with him in his down time. While getting used to the social media side of things, my mother had ample time to search for Max. Hoping that, one day, she would be lucky enough to catch glimpses of his life.

The day she was able to connect with Max, I remember the look on her face, of happiness and great regret.

"I know he's heard terrible things about me, but I'm going to tell him my side too," she said to me, but a part of her knew by doing so she had to return to that place she remembered all too well.

"How can you tell your son that the person who raised him molested me, forced me to marry him and nearly ruined my life?" Her muscles clenched and her eyes became wide. The feeling of something she created in her own body betraying her because of what they were taught. The immense guilt and shame rushed back from the shadows.

"I will tell him too. You're a good mom, the best mom and you didn't have a choice. If he can't believe it, then he doesn't deserve you anyway." I went to pack for college. I should have pulled her to the couch and hugged her the way she comforted me. I think back to those moments, is there anything I could have done?

She never did share their correspondence with me, but she did experience so many emotions, seeing him grown. It seemed to abruptly put her into a downward spiral. I noticed she was drinking each night, trying to forget the nightmares that haunted her. I could see every single hair on her arms stand up as she sat inches away from the computer screen, studying each of the pictures he posted with tears in her eyes late into the night. I sat down and wrote out a long message to Max. Trying to explain to him how much my mother loved him and how she was a good person. Maybe I shared too much, or maybe it was too positive. But I wanted him to have a clear description of the woman he was taught to hate. The mother he missed out on having because his father was a monster. I didn't say the negative parts as I believed that wasn't my news to share, but I ended the message with, 'She regretted every single day without you.'

I cried and cried for her, pressed send and I never heard back from him.

The day I left for college was bitter-sweet. I hugged our dog, Baby, goodbye. She had grown rather fat and old. My parents drove down behind me. Mom helped me decorate my dorm room. She chatted with my roommate, Jill, as she put my clothes away for me. It was easy for her to make conversation with anyone. My dad set up my lamps and hung my bulletin boards and calendars on the walls.

I could tell they were both happy and proud of me. I was more focused on what my mom would say to embarrass me in front of Jill, who I was already unsure of sharing intimate space with. She seemed more put together than I did. She had really expensive, matching sets of everything like it came out of a magazine. Her clothes in the closet were color coordinated and she had heels lining the bottom shelf. I felt a tinge of jealousy but her mother was not as nice as mine, she didn't seem to care where Jill put anything. I was relieved when Jill and her mother left for orientation. I breathed easier with just my parents. Everything of mine was mismatched and my parents worked hard to buy them for me. We found a place for everything eventually and I just sat on my new bed and gripped my new rainbow polka-dot fleece blanket in my hands. My mother was taken out of school at the end of her 7th grade year and my father had Sally at the end of his 11th grade year and started working. Neither one of them finished high school so that moment was bigger than myself. How confusing it could be to have the best parents who didn't have someone like them in their lives. *How lucky I was.* I tried not to cry.

The whole time, Mom had that look on her face- the vicarious and proud smile with tears in her eyes. I watched her peek out the window, study my new view of the campus. She sat an African Violet with tiny purple flowers and green fuzzy leaves in my window, and I think it was a symbol for the excitement of this new life I would begin. My stomach dropped watching her, she was so happy for me, but she experienced these milestones secondhand and it wasn't fair.

"I'm so happy for you, Winnie," she told me as she squeezed my hands and sat next to me on my bed. My cheeks burned at the idea of someone seeing me sitting there with my mom like a baby. I wanted my parents to leave but I also wanted them to stay.

"I think it's time to go, lovey dovey. Let go of her." My dad gently tugged at my mother. The looks on their faces as they drove away, and the shiny blue truck in the distance made me cry. I didn't know it at the time, but my magical life inside of my parent's bubble would soon be loose in the world, blowing in the wind until it popped. Seeing them drive away together leaving me in a strange city brought so many feelings at once. I told myself I had to grow up. I had to be an adult, and that meant starting college so I could live my own life. Besides, I planned for my future with my parents still playing a big role in my life.

You will have the rest of your life to spend time with them. You have to grow up someday. That's what everyone does, right?

CHAPTER FIFTY-FIVE

I tried to grow up, I really did. When hardships would meet me, I would drive the whole hour home on the weekends to be with my parents. Many nights crying in my mom's lap about the next guy who broke my heart. College guys were cruel. The months passed and visits home were less frequent as I began to make friends. I really enjoyed learning about psychology. The brain, the way it works, how amazing the way we perceive the world around us is. In my first Psychology course, I tried to write as quickly as my professor could speak.

Every. Single. Word. Circling notes, highlighting and drawing little explanations next to it. Somehow, I believed not only could I be who my mother needed when she was little for other people, but I thought I could take all that knowledge and help my mother cope with what she went through. I thought I could fix the broken parts of her with knowledge. As I began learning more about Post Traumatic Stress Syndrome, I remember highlighting each row of symptoms in shock. My mother had every single one of them in which turned into Complex PTSD. I wrote her name next to the criteria and I remember thinking— how did she pull herself together to give us a good life? I got so lucky that she gave me such a good life… I thought with me studying psychology, I was continuing something good that came from the worst moments of her life. I wanted to put goodness into the world, kindness and love like my mother had put into mine. I wanted to be who my mother had needed but to other children, to help stop the abuse and the hurt long before they grew up. Something terribly unspeakable leading to something beautiful.

It didn't start out like everyone would think it should have. It should have been noticeable. Like seeing a train coming straight towards you and knowing that you had time to jump out of the way? It wasn't like that. It was sneakier and came in like a bug inching towards the light. Slowly until it almost consumed my parents completely. Alcohol. Society's approved method to wind down. Alcohol is so accepted in society that when someone says drug, it isn't even associated with. Unfortunately, alcohol offered a way to ease the pain. My mother drank to deal with her resurfaced trauma, and my father was drinking to deal with everything else. Once we were all grown and had moved out, their home became more dedicated to being a sociable environment. Their house was dubbed a good place to go to have a few drinks. It became the norm to have drinks around the campfire while eating delicious food my dad cooked. This gave my mother a focus for it to become normal, a way to blend in her pain without being judged. I didn't think much of it at the time. Binge drinking was practically expected in college. Everywhere around me alcohol was available and socially acceptable- could even be considered a rite of passage for people my age. Nobody talks about alcohol addiction. The billboards, and commercials, only advertise the socially acceptable parts of alcohol. Not the parts that creep inside of you making you dependent on it. There's a heavy shame that's carried once the problem becomes noticeable. As if we were the only family going through it. The stigma, the shame, the loneliness and most of all, the denial. Because who wants to admit that a substance is powerful enough to destroy your entire life?

My mother was open about her drinking at first when there was nothing to hide. My dad would have a few drinks with her. It was social. Family gatherings, weekends, or having a drink after work. They used it to boost their moods in the normal times society advertises drinking for. The "normal" times that people "usually" drink so no red flags were raised. I thought they both drank to relax and unwind. To celebrate this new phase of their empty nest, to celebrate each other and how hard they worked. Alone time to just be themselves. *Too much* alone time after nearly two decades raising us. I was not as involved as I had been my entire life and Tristan was in the army actively fighting war in Iraq. I knew that got to her too. The idea that something she loved so much could be taken from her— again. I assumed it was like anybody else who needed a drink at the end of the day. It became normal in a way that should have never been. Alcohol just seemed to have positive effects on their moods, and when you're "celebrating" together, where is the harm in it? It is legal.

By the time I was a sophomore, I noticed on my visits that drinking at social events progressed to drinking earlier in the evening. The whole "It's 5 o'clock somewhere" was so advertised I began to believe that it was a normal way to unwind to deal with your emotions, to deal with the stress of it all.

You believe you're in control until you're not anymore. You would never become an addict because nobody believes they can become an image we are taught to hate. It's like there's an unsaid warning: It's 5 o'clock somewhere, but not if you lose control. Once you lose control, there is no turning back. Nobody thinks they will become addicted because that's not who they are. Nobody sets out to be an addict- an addiction takes over the person. The years continued to pass with the secrets hidden as well as the cans and bottles. We all accepted our new ways of life. Tristan came home from the army. My mom was able to stay at home. My dad continued doing construction. I was finishing school.

When it progressed from drinking at social events to drinking during the day, she hid it well. It was shortly after her therapist, Joan retired. Who had over all these years continued to unofficially work with my mother over the phone. Losing touch with her had caused a regression that she kept hidden. On a daily basis I was literally in class to learn about things she was dealing with. I learned all of the symptoms and signs of addiction. The stigmas, the ins and outs of substance abuse. I was taught about the deep, immense amount of shame related to any type of drug usage. The strong relationship between childhood sexual abuse and addiction. Drinking in response to trauma is literally self-medication. There's a stigma attached that even those who are deeply affected run from because nobody wants to represent the type of person we are taught to look down on. We all assume we could never become one. That our family member could never be addicted to drugs or alcohol. Our negative view of addiction prevents us from seeing it as a disease, a way to cope with pain versus a criminal offense. If only we could see the beginning signs as a call for help versus feeling angry. We refuse to confront the actual mental and physical health crisis that it is. I did too. Haven't we all? Alcohol is cheaper than therapy. Alcohol is more accessible than therapy. Alcohol hurts a hell of a lot less than therapy at first. Because as the time went on, she collapsed as a human being and found that alcohol helped relieve a lot of the pain.

My mother was exceptionally intelligent despite not having the choice to finish school. She also knew the symptoms and signs and knew what vitamins she needed to take to make up for any deficiencies. She hid it more from herself than from anyone else. She was in denial, and so were we, but the truth lay there all along. She drank every night to numb the pain and when she woke up, she began to drink during the day. She wasn't used to being home alone with nobody to take care of. She wasn't used to being stuck inside of her own mind for days on end. Left with the memories, the nightmares, the regrets. She literally took care of everyone from the moment she was born, but she had a hard time loving herself.

I think when it got to this point, she would have taken anything just to slightly ease the pain. She lived in survival mode. Being alone, she was left to encounter her altruism and childhood wounds, those dysfunctional coping strategies that helped her survive as a child, undercut her life as an adult. She enjoyed a drink after a long day of working out in the yard. Each night, she drank just one more, and those one more's didn't seem to add up at first. Her casual drinking was contagious and just as she had her first drink, Tanner would join in. They thought they had succeeded in life, raising their kids, owning their own land. They got everything they sought in life. He thought she was just handling her empty nest and trauma in the only way she knew how. They thought they had every right to relax under the stars, with a seemingly harmless drink. They were still very much a part of their grown children's lives. Coming to the rescue when needed, attending holiday events, graduations, and birthday parties. Slowly drinks began to trickle their way in everywhere. We were all in denial of what was happening, but the truth lay there all along. The more she drank, the less pain she felt until she woke and had an immense shame and anger at herself for drinking. Each night, she would have just a few more. Her nightmares returned. Suddenly flashbacks and diffi-culty trusting people returned. Each night she found herself defeated and pacing. The immense fear returned as if it had never left. She was that little girl again, lost in the world. The only thing that could numb her pain was a tall glass of anything that would make her feel nothing.

Hours later, she would awake with red eyes, and her mouth and throat dry, and she would roll out of bed and do her daily chores, all the while hiding the truth. Mom was smart enough she knew the dangers, but it doesn't matter how smart she was, addiction can take over anyone.

'One more day of this and tomorrow I will get it together,' she told herself.

After a while, I believe she became tired of chasing after herself. She made things so much harder for herself when she drank, she felt like she could never catch up. It was like she was chasing this idea of herself that she fought so hard for but couldn't quite escape the shadows that pulled her back under. But out of the blue— she re-emerged. Happy and as normal as can be, faking a smile to the outside world and pushing all of those feelings back down again. Dumping them into reserve and locking the door.

As far as she knew she had found her solution. For a number of years it worked, fairly well to the point where she could still function. She was present externally in life, but on the inside, she was that scared little girl again. Dealing with the abuse that happened to her all of those years ago. The shame and self-hate, suffering on a very deep level from childhood trauma. The trauma that over the years was stored there in her unconscious. She wasn't aware of it, it was discounted, minimized, forgotten until it wasn't anymore. The deep dark part of pain that came back almost as intense if not more as it was when it happened. Because all of those things she shoved down stayed there locked away. She was so frightened that if she allowed herself to feel those things she would fall apart, or the bottom would literally fall out beneath her. She used coping strategies that were developed in childhood in order to cope with and survive the dysfunction and trauma. She tried to build a new life for herself, but emotions that were never processed came back and prevented her from moving forward.

Addiction had heavy costs. Family roles were disrupted, everything spiraled out of control. As the addiction progressed, it disrupted life and changed how our entire family functioned. But the problem is that life didn't stop. We didn't have a pause button. No magic wand. So, we didn't focus on it. We waited until the mom we knew was with us, when the normal good parts of her shined through. It was easier that way-- when you watch someone you love slowly kill themselves. it is the most helpless and hopeless thing. But you can't forget there's still a person underneath all of those chemicals, a person who made the best parts of you.

Somehow, she did pull it back together. She had this way of coming out of a binge and convincing everyone around her that she would never do it again. She chose to heal herself, all the while feeling like her life was empty and meaningless. It was almost like her skin was livelier and sparkling but underneath, she felt empty. She didn't want to let the situation from her childhood control her anymore. She tried to focus on the yard, and her chickens, and the stories we told her about our lives. Secondhand experiences were her comfort zone. I know she apologized repeatedly in her mind but could never find the words to tell us. The action of admitting she was in too deep was more shameful than seeking help. She was fearful we would judge her and she would have to admit that she was repeating her mother's addiction. But she managed to pull it back enough for us to trust that was the last time. That she didn't have a problem. Somehow, she buried the childhood wounds again and pulled herself back to taking care of everyone. That's all she ever knew. So, I didn't catch it when I should have, we let it consume her longer than we should have. The insanity of addiction is that it can literally overtake anyone, but we all think we're immune. We think that it is something that can't happen to someone we love. It is not something that happens overnight. It's a poison that builds inside of your body and convinces you that you must consume it to survive until it breaks you down. By the time I was strong enough to admit to myself that it actually was addiction, it was too late. By the time we were able to figure out that it was going to kill her, it was too late. I asked her the hardest question. She answered, but I still wasn't able to save her.

CHAPTER FIFTY-SIX

ELOWYN—THREE MONTHS BEFORE BONNIE'S DEATH

"Do you want to die, Mom?" My voice echoed through the static line. I heard my words repeat so quickly I didn't have time to take them back.

"No. No, I don't," my mother replied. Her pronunciation was sheepish, like a child whimpering. I hated it. The sound of her being weak. She was the strongest person I ever knew.

"I want you to get the help you need." *Be firm.* I told myself. *This will help her.*

Silence responded, as if the whole world took a pause. She had begun binge drinking again. The cars rushed past me, the gusts of motion shifting me with each one that passed by. Bringing me back to reality, I had to get to work.

One, two, three.

I swallowed, trying to fill the void as big as the hole in my heart. The kind that exists when you are torn between real life and right now life. I wanted her to get better, but I had to get to work. To think of work as a bigger priority than my mother made me cringe. Work to pay the bills to take care of my child, but my mother's life was more important than money. If only life came with a pause button. I wanted her to get better, I wanted to see her, to jump on a plane and help her figure out what we could do. I checked the time again, and was about to give up, she responded.

"But they want me to testify, and I don't think...."

Perhaps I should have given her time. Time to get more of the words out. Words that I wasn't sure she had, words I wasn't sure I wanted to hear. But I didn't, I continued.

"Mom. Please. You have been THE best mother. You've been there for everyone, please let us be there for you. You were just a child; we can figure this out. I promise, Mom. Mom?"

More silence.

"Mom?"

With my heart racing, I checked to see if she was still on the line. She was approached by a girl she went to Hawthorne with. They wanted her to testify against Dale. This news had made her take a nosedive back into binge drinking. I was worried. We all were. I pulled the phone away from my ear quickly so that in case she responded I didn't miss it. As if that 20 seconds would matter.

Just as I placed the phone back to my ear, I heard her. She was back. In that strong, matter-of-fact voice from my mother that I've always known,

"You're the kindest person I've ever met."

My mom spoke, like her silence was because she was taking my words in and for a moment exhaled peace. *She needed someone to believe in her after all, because she was too tired and too ashamed to believe in herself.*

I smiled. "I have to get to work, but I will call you back later. I love you."

"I love you too. I miss you."

That conversation will forever repeat in my mind. The rawness of her exposed pain consumed me. If only she could see herself through my eyes.

In that moment I gave her the strength she needed to keep pressing forward.

I would have that phone call again, every day for the rest of my life, if I could have saved her.

The following week my phone rang late into the night. Instantly I knew that my mother was drunk and her words slurred. I remembered all the times she told me she wouldn't answer her phone for her own mother after 8PM.

"I married that monster and he did it to eight other *girlsss*… what kind of monster am I? I left my son with him. I left Max, Winnie. I am the worst person…"

"Mom, I know it is overwhelming, but if you could testify, I think…" My mind shifted to my own son and all of a sudden, I could barely imagine the amount of pain she felt when she thought of Max.

"Noooo." She sniggered lightly. "No way. I don't think I could. I don't think… I couldn't get up there… but I'll let you get off of here, Winnie."

"Are you going to be okay?" I asked with my hand on my forehead.

"Yes, Winnie. I'll be fine."

But she wasn't fine. She never was fine again. The very fact that this man who ruined her life had done the same to other girls ruined her. She could accept she was terrible and deserving, but she couldn't fathom other children going through what she did by the same man. The same man who she married and had a child with. It struck her to the very depths of her core. It was the deepest part of the darkness she could no longer forget. The immense shame and self-hatred for courses in life that she had little to no control over. So, she became distant. She pushed everyone away. The fuzzy effect from alcohol made her muscles relax like butter. She was completely numb- mind and body. No pain, no worries. Like a long-lost blanket draped over her. It took it all away as it had so many times before.

When my mother looked in the mirror, a feeling of sadness sunk in. She hated the person she saw staring back at her, disgusted with the reflection. She thought she had become the person she always said she wouldn't, her mother.

She would tell herself this was the last time. In the morning, hungover self would agree. Then, once the headache disappeared and the fire inside of her returned, she would do anything to extinguish the pain.

-Would you be willing to testify against Dale Harper? - These words burned her eyes as she read them across the screen over and over again.

There are eight girls wanting to bring justice.

Eight. Girls.

There were others.

There were other little girls.

She was the one who married this monster.

Then like a flash of light, the image of Max needing her, and his hands reaching for her. The hot air in a dark room and the sensations she never wanted. It all came back again just as strong as the day it happened.

I spent the next few weeks calling every single addiction hot line and rehab center I could. I just wanted to talk to one person who could help us. I thought there would be some magic wand that could fix her, there had to be. She didn't have insurance, and I was a therapist, but I still couldn't find her help. Unless you have a person who is willing to accept help, there are not many options. I called place after place. 'Please help me, she's going to die.' Over and over again it came down to insurance, money, and having a person who is willing to enter treatment.

I spent my days engulfed in other people's lives, offering therapy to my clients but I couldn't help my own mother. The days were long, and I enjoyed going home to my husband and son. But my mind was preoccupied. I would spend all night researching articles about alcoholism. Looking for options, trying to find her a way out of the hell she was in. As my belly grew, so did my worries. Over time she stopped answering my phone calls. She never responded to text messages.

I did, however, receive a letter in the mail from her. As I ripped into the letter, there was a small note in my mother's handwriting.

-I love and miss you. I want you to have this- my mother's ring-

It was the one thing her mother had given her, and it meant enough to her to pass it to me. I put the ring away and called her to tell her I would be sending it back. But her voice wasn't the same. There was distance where there used to be love.

"Will you go to the doctor?" I asked her. "Please, I don't want you to die, Mom."

"I'll be fine, Winnie." She had already given up. Alcohol had already taken over.

"Winnie, your mom is in the hospital." My dad called me, his voice sounded weak. "They're saying if she continues to drink, her liver will fail. I told them if they let her walk out of here, she will die but they won't listen to me." It wasn't often we got to see or hear my father cry. I hated it.

My dad told me he didn't need alcohol. "I was honestly drinking it to be able see her the way she was." He cried to me. "I was so scared of losing her. She said it was the only thing that helped, Winnie." Instantly I felt a sting of pain. I should have been there for them. I should have left work and went there and been there through their hardest times but life got in my way. That immense guilt I carry with me each day.

My dad quit drinking after she was hospitalized the first time. The hospital didn't educate them on her condition. Instead, she was condemned for alcohol usage, and left in deep shame. She was taken in due to severe stomach pain, malnutrition, and dehydration. Dad, he tried to oversee my mother's drinking. This became a difficult task for him. For even as he took the car keys, even if he took her debit card, somehow, she would manage to find a way to alcohol. That's the thing with drugs and alcohol. Once you're dependent on it, there is nothing you wouldn't do to stop the pain you're in. It's always a pleasure versus pain decision- getting drunk in that moment is better than feeling all the things, better than recognizing you don't know who you've become. Better than living in gray rooms with unwanted touches and flashbacks as real as the day it happened. He told her she needed to quit too, but there's a deep shame about seeking help. The alcohol addiction had come into the spotlight. By this point we all knew it was a problem, a big problem. I had learned about Wernicke - Korsakoff syndrome in school and I tried to explain to it anyone who would listen. I spent many nights re-searching. I knew continued alcohol use could cause a Thiamine deficiency and even though Mom had always been so careful, taking supplements and eating healthy food, it came to a point it didn't matter anymore. After you drink for so long, the stomach lining becomes agitated, even if you are eating healthy your body becomes unable to absorb the needed nutrients. Thiamine helps brain cells produce energy from sugar. When the levels fall too low, brain cells cannot generate enough energy to function properly. Unfortunately, few people know about the most serious conditions of alcohol abuse, like 'wet brain' or Wernicke-Korsakoff syndrome. These conditions can be treated if intervened early enough. This means that, if we would have admitted we needed help, maybe she could have lived. Addiction takes over and shame keeps you indebted.

It wasn't until she stopped drinking that everything took a turn for the worse. For the first time I became open about her addiction, grasping on any little string that could lead us to help and lead her to safety. Overnight, my dad had become her care-giver instead of her husband. He had to take her car keys, and keep the money with him, and watch her every moment. It was almost like her mind returned to a child-like state. He couldn't grasp how she had fallen so deeply into herself. The doctors told us her brain was literally the size of a child's. The alcohol had shrunk her brain. In many ways my beautiful, caring mother was already gone. Dad was able to stop drinking with no consequences, but it wasn't easy to watch my mother while he was trying to work. He left sticky notes for her all throughout the house. Trying to explain to her how to do basic tasks. She could no longer be independent and we tried to find an adult home that could watch her during the day. Without insurance, she wasn't accepted.

While in between working, I would sit on the phone with her for hours, the whole while she forgot that I had grown up. She forgot that I had a baby growing inside of my belly. The only things she could remember were from my childhood. A sacred piece of her life that was well preserved.

"I wonder when Winnie and Tristan will get home from school?" She would ask me and I would let her believe in that moment I was not her little girl. I wouldn't remind her that I was grown up and that she had forgotten. So, we focused on fond memories and I held back the tears. I remember holding the phone away from my face and sobbing because my mother had forgotten that I was a grown up. I remember hating the people who had texted her asking her to testify because it finally sent her over the edge. I remember wondering if those girls had troubles like my mom did too. It was like parts of my mother were there but in the same sense she wasn't there. She sounded like my mother, but she was no longer the mother I knew. I watched her slip away right in front of my eyes and there was nothing we could do to stop it. She didn't forget me as her daughter, she just lost me in a different moment in time.

So I would ask her questions about herself instead. "When you were pregnant did you have any cravings?"

"When I was pregnant with my daughter, Winnie, all I wanted was soda." I would pull the phone away and cry and cry. I wanted to scream, 'I am your daughter— it's me, Mom,' but I held it in. Feeling my daughter kicking me, knowing she would never know the woman I had known. The mother I had that had always rooted for me. And so, we had this way of connecting even though it was through her past. A way of connecting even though it broke my heart.

"When we hang up, you need to plug your phone in. Look for the post-it note that says phone." I would walk her through the steps of charging it. Take the plug and go to the end, find the place in the bottom. The simplest things, basic life skills she had forgotten. The saddest thing of all is even with all of that, she never forgot the pain Dale put her through.

There were glimpses of her and good days and bad days. Days where I would text her about which crib, I wanted for my daughter. Days she would be alert and tell me I should decorate her nursery in flamingo's. Then there would be days where she couldn't remember the end of her sentence, or she would have hallucinations and believe she was a child again. She struggled with memory and cognitive skills for the next three months. Until finally she was able to see that she was slipping. She came to the realization of exactly what was happening. She felt helpless and embarrassed and ashamed. She got progressively worse and we were powerless to save her.

Once my father revealed the extent of my mother's ordeal, we were all too quickly made aware of how badly it all had gone. It was too late. We struggled to come to terms with how quickly she declined. Dad had tried to internally deal with it, not wanting to pass the burden on to anyone else. Shame and protecting Bonnie from judgment kept him from reaching out. She had always cared too much about what other people thought. He preserved trying to manage on his own and had faith that the woman he had fallen in love with was still there, just shrouded by her relationship with alcohol.

After Mom was released from the hospital, she was never given an official diagnosis. The only instructions were to not let her drink anymore. No referral to counseling, no assistance in getting insurance. No assistance in finding adult daycare. The doctors allowed my parents to feel like frauds at the idea of seeking support for an illness which some may consider as self-inflicted from her alcohol usage. But instead, they should have assured them that alcoholism is an illness and she was just as entitled as anyone else to access support and services. Things could have been a lot different.

After returning home from the hospital, I knew deep down she was getting worse. On the phone, she had moments- bits of clarity but for the most part her mind was jumbled memories and emotions of a life she once had. The good times, the bad times, but not the recent times. She could no longer create new memories or do basic tasks. Her body ached with nerve damage, and she had trouble maintaining her balance. The doctors prescribed Thiamine and medication to slow down the deterioration of her brain but by this point, it didn't help. She tripped over her words and forgot mid-sentence what she was talking about. By the time my dad called me, he was relieved to leave Mom with me over the summer. Having been worried about her every day they set out to come the week my daughter was due to be born. But that day never came.

CHAPTER FIFTY-SEVEN

I picked up the note and twirled it in my hands. For the past month I had wanted to read it so badly, but I was filled with a devastating pain in my stomach when I saw her handwriting. I felt the warmth of her affection in the curves of her letters. I flattened out the wrinkles and used the back of my hand to swipe my tears that had trickled onto the thin paper. There didn't seem to be a profound message that would take away my grief. No hidden clues that offered closure. Just a glimpse of the mother that I knew and loved. The mother I had been grieving since the day she began to fade away. The one who died but stayed alive fiercely inside of my mind.

I don't know exactly how long it has been, but when I realized what was happening, I knew I wasn't strong enough. I used alcohol to get through the darkness but all it did was show me particles of light and take it back. It took everything from me. I failed time and time again to detox. Each time I thought it was easing the pain, helping me. I became aware I was losing my memory and that was something I had always feared. I knew better... the very thing I used to numb my pain was the end of me. You would think this would be motivating to hate alcohol. The poison I chose for myself, but the pain I was hiding for so long had surfaced so strongly I didn't think I had any other choice. I truly believed if I allowed myself to feel those immense memories, the bottom would fall out from beneath me. So, here I am having a good day. And even so, I am overwhelmingly hopeless. I don't have the strength to stand up and testify. I didn't even know he did this to other little girls. Jane, Felicity, every person in that home was consumed by his darkness. To think there are other little girls who lived at Hawthorne with ruined lives like mine. I always thought the problem was me. Maybe if I would have done something differently, it could have saved them. But I married the monster, and I left my son with him, and this is something I cannot get past.

Max, when I think of you my heart swells with love. You made me a mother. You are the person who brought me back to life and taught me how to stand up for myself and how to love myself. There is no better feeling than knowing that you were my son. I am sorry I am not strong enough to testify against your father and stand up to him for this last fight, but nothing can ever take away my love for you.

Mama, I forgive you. My biggest regret in life was losing Max, but I had to forgive you because I did the same to him. I hope that one day he can also forgive me and know how much I loved him. Some people get lost and cannot find their way back, I get it now.

Tanner, thank you for giving me the best years of my life. Thank you for believing in me and giving me the fairy tale, we always dreamed of. You have been my rock and I will forever love you. Live your fullest without me, for me. Alcohol isn't fixing things; it is only breaking you down. Together we found it all.

Tristan, please don't be angry with me. You allowed me to come back to life after the darkest moments of my life. I know this is not how we pictured life being. I wish I could be the same person I was for you growing up, but you will do many wonderful things.

Elowyn, please don't ever forget to love yourself. You were my last baby and will forever be my baby and I am so proud of you for pursuing your dreams. One day, you will realize that life is what you make of it. Don't make the same mistakes I did. You, Tristan, and your dad made life for me. You allowed me to fix parts of myself that were broken through your life. Thank you for that.

Susan, if I would have never met you, I don't think I would have survived Hawthorne. If only I had a box of chocolates big enough to fix this mess I'm in. Thank you for teaching me to stand in the rain and face your fears.

I loved you all, Bonnie

I set the letter down. I knew if I didn't, I would obsessively keep reading it over and over again. Trying to understand her decision, trying to see that she was no longer in pain. But nothing worked and nothing could change it. She was gone and there was no preparation for that kind of loss. I struggled to believe she was dead. Since I was 39 weeks pregnant, I was unable to travel to the funeral or to say goodbye to her. The day she died; Ruby drove all the way to the hospital to say goodbye. I felt torn in half that she got to, and I didn't. I thought perhaps Ruby had a change of heart. Maybe after all those years of being a terrible person, she came to apologize and redeem herself.

But instead, I later found out she rushed into the hospital room where my mother had died. As soon as my dad left the room to let her say goodbye. She turned and faced the nurse.

"Was she wearing any jewelry when she came in?" She stood there — next to my deceased mother and, instead of agonizing pain or apologizing, Ruby's only thought was about the ring. Her mother's ring I watched her pass down to my mom. The one piece of Ruby she ever held onto. The ring my mother went out of her way to have already passed down to me. The remaining link that was supposed to fix what was lost, she wanted it back.

"Elowyn, it's time." Tristan stood in the doorway, a sad crooked smile on his face. "I don't think… I don't think I can do this," I whispered.

"Me either, idiot, come on." For some reason the name calling was comforting. He had been unusually nice to me since Mom died. He dragged me by the arm outside. So many people. I saw glimpses of people I knew from my mother's life but I couldn't really see them. It was just too much to process. My mother was gone. We passed by Tristan's friend whose foot she ran over, childhood friends and their parents, many people whose lives she touched. But standing there in the background, the sight of him took my breath away. There he stood with the same striking blue eyes. My mother's face was melded into his and it ripped my heart out all over again. He wanted answers and I didn't want to give them to him. How do you tell your brother that his father was a living monster. A monster who never paid for what he did?

The yard was set up with tables covered in white lace. Memories and pictures of her life spread around the spot in the yard my dad chose to plant the tree. Since the funeral had to go on without me, it required my dad and Tristan to do most of the planning and communicating for the first time in their lives without Mom. Tristan was the one who came up with the tree idea, because of our mother's love for nature it only seemed fitting. So, she was cremated, and other than four tree necklaces with some of her ashes, her remains would be planted underneath a Royal Empress Tree.

We stood there and I had no words to say. Tristan nudged me. "You talk."

I shook my head vigorously. "No, you." Eyes from different walks of my mother's life studied us. My dad couldn't speak, the grief was too heavy for him. It was left to me and Tristan and all we did was shove each other back and forth in front of everyone. I don't remember what I said but it wasn't anything profound. In that moment it took everything I had just to stand up there. We couldn't form the words to talk about how wonderful our mother was. We couldn't find the words to explain addiction out loud. It was too shameful- as if people would think less of her, as if we were still protecting her image. Instead, Tristan and I fought about who would do the speaking. We argued about who would plant the tree, and in true Tristan fashion, he called me an idiot in front of everyone. I swear, it was just the way Mom would have wanted it. An imperfectly perfect goodbye.

After the service, Max approached us. There was no way to describe how it felt to look at him. So much of my mother stood right before me- in his eyes, forehead, and in his smile. Even the compassionate twinkle in his eyes. I couldn't tell him everything, I was too hurt from grief. I told him instead of how much she loved him. His face was filled with deep regret, having missed out on rekindling their relationship. He remembered bits and pieces of her. He remembered her holding him singing, the sound of her voice and most of all, her love. He hugged each of us and my father shook his hand.

When it was time for Max to leave, there was a part of me that wanted to keep him connected to us. To live out the dream my mom always had of us all being together. Dad asked Max if he wanted to take one of the memory necklaces that held her ashes. Then I watched as they went to shake hands and instead Dad pulled Max into him. I imagined the little boy he was so long ago, playing catch.

"I'll take her with me, everywhere I go," he said, accepting the necklace with tears in his eyes. He would take Bonnie with him everywhere he went. When it came time to say goodbye, he went up to the tree and placed his pet rock down. The pet rock he made her years ago, the one he clung to because it was his only reminder of her. The words Mommy with a heart that faded over the years like his memories of her. I like to think in that moment he forgave her and was at peace. It was always her biggest wish for us all to be together, and for a moment in time we were.

When I left to return home with my husband and family there was a lump in my throat when I hugged my father. I really thought I was going to lose him to alcohol too. After my mom died, he drifted away from us- consumed in the life of alcohol, he hoped if he drank enough, it could take him to be with her. He gave up. Tristan found him drunk and not taking care of himself, he completely lost it. They had an argument that my mom wasn't there to patch up. They fought and I believed everything was falling apart. I worried without my mother there to play the peacemaker that we wouldn't make it as the close family we always were. We all separated in our own forms of grief. The would haves, should haves. The guilt, the shame, and vortex of anger that swirled inside of us. The aching as big as the ocean, waves strong enough to create a tsunami inside of our hearts. There is no right or wrong way to grieve, but there are healthy and unhealthy ways. Once the tsunami takes over... you can either resurface or drown in grief.

CHAPTER FIFTY-EIGHT

It was the beginning of the school year, and the smell of crayons, books, and plastic filled the halls. My son, Finn, and I held hands tightly as we walked down to his new classroom. He was beginning first grade, not old enough to be embarrassed about holding my hand in public yet. When we reached the doorway, I bent down for a long hug. He hugged me back and we waved good-bye while I signed, I love you to his nervous eyes, the same way my mother had done to me. I crossed the hall and walked inside of my office right by the library. Bright pictures lined the walls, positive quotes, and emotional regulation tools. I liked being just down the hall if Finn should have needed me. I was where I belonged. New teachers, new rooms, new classmates. I smiled as the bell rang and I began to scan the list of names in front of me. The children I could potentially help. I was a school-based mental health therapist. My dream had come true. I was finally who my mom needed when she was little.

I knew Tony loved dinosaurs from last year and needed to work on anger management, and I knew Natalia would spend our sessions painting- it was a great way to process the grief from the loss of her mother, something about my sessions with her also healed me. There is nothing like the feeling in the room when someone has a safe space to share for the first time. Trauma can be healed in safe places. Aidan was shy and, in his sessions, we role-played conversations. He enjoyed drawing on the white board. Abigale was the last name on my list and my first to see that morning. I enjoyed sessions with her as she was usually goofy and enjoyed playing doll house as a means of play therapy. It was a light-hearted, self-care space for Abigale being the oldest sister of four.

Abigale was happy to see me. I was excited to hear about her summer. Once we were inside the safety of my office and got down on the floor with her next to the doll house. It wasn't as easy to get down on the floor as it once was but we did fall right back into sync like all of the sessions prior to this one. Right away Abigale picked up where we left off. She arranged the furniture in the doll house silently, smiling at me.

"I've missed you, Winnie."

"I have missed seeing you too, Abigale," I replied helping her stand up a man figure that had fallen down.

She leaned in with her quiet play voice. "Where are we going?" The adult man asked the little girl doll figure. Abigale smiled. "Let's go upstairs." She handed me the little girl.

The man dolls feet tapped each of the steps until he reached the top. Then she had me follow with the little girl. "You missed one." Abigale pointed out one of the steps, so I started again at the bottom.

Once I reached the top, Abigale took her from me and slammed her down. The adult figure picked up the girl and threw her against the wall. Abigale's' eyes were raised, and her lips curled inwards. This behavior was unlike her. I studied her as she made crying noises from the little girl figure. Loud sobs that sounded so real. It seemed to be reflective of something Abigale had seen but I didn't want to assume so I continued to let her play. I listened to the story Abigale was telling me without any words. When she looked up at me, she had tears in her eyes.

"I want to show you something." She exhaled deeply and looked at the floor as she continued. "Remember when you told me adults shouldn't keep secrets with little kids?"

I nodded at her, with a sinking feeling as she lifted her shorts to expose her thighs.

The bruises covered her thighs in places so purposely placed. Places that nobody would normally see. The purple and yellow hues on Abigale's soft skin contrasted so brightly. I pulled back slightly, pushing on the bridge of my nose to stop the hot tears from forming.

"You are so brave," I told her.

"I want to tell you something too… but… it is inappropriate," Abigale whispered.

"Inappropriate?" I repeated to clarify.

"Yeah. I don't like it when my uncle comes over. He hurts me and he tries to…. to tickle me in my private place and told me that it is inappropriate to talk about."

I tried to remain calm while staring deeply into Abigale's brown eyes.

"It's okay. We can talk about anything in here," I reassured her. "You are so incredibly brave to tell me. Have you told your mom?" I asked her quietly and saw the innocence of my own mother within Abigale's shadowed face as she shook her head no.

"It's not appropriate… To talk about and he said…" she closed her eyes, "nobody will believe me." Her voice was barely above a whisper.

"Well, you are the bravest little girl in the entire world. I believe you and I'm so sorry that it happened to you."

We talked about her bravery. I reminded her of her strength. I explained the steps we would take. We would call her mother and we would keep her safe. During the next 3 hours, we handled Abigale's crisis. Together we told her mother, and the principal, and we called children services to make a report. The mother called the police, and her brother-in-law was arrested. It took one day to stop this pain from happening. I knew deep down that not every case would be that way. Not every case would be justified, and many kids would slip through the cracks before they got help. But each one was a life saved. I thought of my own mother and how nobody saw the signs for her. I felt satisfied helping Abigale despite the long way she had to go. I thought of how big of a difference just one person can make. I was there in this position because of my mother's enduement.

CHAPTER FIFTY-NINE

I marveled at the view of the yard; the only place I could reflect back to that took me from childhood to adulthood. My mother's tree stood tall and purple flowers blossomed on each branch. The way the wind blew warmth allowed me to believe that a part of my mother was still there in that yard. So many things had changed since she left. Memories that I hadn't thought of in years returned to my mind as if on auto-play.

My mother laughing.

The sound of her voice.

The smell of her perfume.

The way she ran in place when she was startled.

The touch of her hand on top of mine.

I walked under the tree and looked up at the height. Taller than she had ever been. The velvety lilac-blue petals tinged with a sudden clash of pale yellow and white that burst from the center. I inhaled the sweet, vanilla perfume that surrounded me. She was still very much alive in my memories.

"It got big didn't it, kiddo?" My dad asked, stepping under the tree.

He still had to duck from some lower branches, but it made me think of all of the times he probably tended to this tree, watering it and caring for it like he always had my mother.

"It sure is beautiful," I told him, a smile curled on my lips as tears welled in my eyes. Looking at my father, standing there sober and in good health.

He came and stayed with us for a few months after her death and I was certain he would be lost to alcohol too after losing my mother. But something within him snapped back to life instead. He had a few drinks but it made him feel angry and hurt- the one thing they leaned on during tough times destroyed them. He had his yard and his property, now all he wanted was his lovey dovey.

Instead of holding on to hatred, losing the love of his life only taught him life was too short. Something changed and, for the first time, he realized he needed to live life while there was life left to live. The loss of his wife became his new reason for living.

"If I survived all of this— there must be a reason," he would say. So, he stopped drinking cold turkey. Slowly but surely, he came back to health. He became all of the good parts of himself and my mother combined. Being present in the grandchildren's lives, teaching me how to cook, buying presents for Christmas morning, and answering all of my dumb questions. Learning how to post the bills and do his laundry- all of those things she did for him. Without my mother, my father took over being my personal Google service. He was the link that tied us all together again. Without my mother to play peacemaker, my dad and Tristan had to communicate on their own for the first time and that only made them closer. Tristan joined us under the tree and, for a moment, it was just the three of us. "You going to speak this time, idiot?" he asked me, smiling. So I punched his arm.

Later that day, as friends and family members joined us under Bonnie's tree, we spoke for the first time. Since we didn't speak at the first memorial, my father stepped up to the microphone. The wind blew, and the warmth from the sun covered his face. He looked up at the tree above him and spoke directly to it.

"No one knows how much I miss you, Bonnie." He stopped to pull himself together and faced the crowd. I stood next to Tristan and his wife and children, Reid, and my four children and I looked out into the crowd too. So many faces of people who had loved my mother for who she was. Susan whose red hair stood out amongst the crowd stood with her arms crossed, the old raggedy book in her hands. So many lives she changed despite living through trauma.

"Thank you all for being here. You see, in life and death, there's one thing that is always true, nothing is guaranteed. Maybe that's where we get it all wrong. Maybe perhaps when a person dies, it is just one part of them. The physical connection may be gone. However, the love and life that that person had is never truly over. Bonnie lives within each of us. In each new plant clipping, in each smile we pass on to a stranger. She's with me when I watch the birds in the morning. She lies with Winnie when she rocks my granddaughters to sleep. She is with Sally every time she plays catch. She is with Tristan as he raises his sons and creates beautiful art. She is within each of us as we step barefoot in the grass. She is with Susan every morning as she announces the weather. She is within the laugh that her grandchild makes as she plays a trick on someone. Her story isn't just about trauma. It is about living the life that we have right now. It is remembering that each day is a new day, and no matter how dark the night gets, there is always a sunrise in the morning." Dad made it through without crying but had to excuse himself. He left Tristan and I standing there together and just as we were about to fight over who had to speak, the sky turned a dark gray color. It down poured onto all of us, right through the branches of Mom's tree. Tristan shoved me. "See? She doesn't want us to say anything!" I shoved him back.

"We'll resume in just a few minutes, feel free to go under the tent."

As I made my way back to stand under the tree, I wondered what I could say. I saw Susan speaking with a woman I had never met, and instantly it was as if I had always known this woman. I recognized her as Amy from the pictures they had taken on the day Mom married my father so many years ago. Both of their eyes were swollen with tears. I hadn't seen Susan since I was a teenager, but she looked like she hadn't aged. As they came towards me, I felt as if my mother were there too.

"I wish we could have met sooner, Elowyn. I'm Amy." She reached out for me but instead of shaking my hand, she held it inside of hers, tightly.

"You look so much like your mother." Amy smiled, a tear escaping her. "We were young, but I never forgot your mother and Max. She was the reason I finally went to beauty school, and she gave me hope after losing my daughter." She released my hand. I smiled slightly, so many people loved her. Susan reached for me, and I had an urge to pull her close. To grasp on to anything that once made my mother smile.

"It's so hard, I know. When you lose your mom, it is your first lesson of life. It's like suddenly everything before this moment was just a dream." Susan spoke finally. Everything faded from around us her words rang so true.

"But how is it a lesson? How do I ever move forward?"

"Well, Elowyn, nothing helps you understand the fleeting beauty of life more than death. It teaches us to grab onto everything that makes our souls happy because we can only then truly understand that *nothin'* lasts forever." Amy spoke, took a deep breath and reached for a cigarette.

Susan nodded. "After I lost my parents, it was Bunny, your mom, who concreted my feet back to the earth. She taught me the greatest meaning of life, even as she was a child."

I sighed, waiting impatiently for more. "What? What is it?"

After wiping tears, Susan continued. "To live to feel the power of impermanence. To accept that bad things will happen no matter what you do. But you are not at fault- you didn't choose this. You didn't ask for the bad things- the things that hurt. But you can choose how to respond." I calmed my breathing, brushed the hair from my eyes. It didn't make sense.

Amy leaned in closer. "Each day that you're alive- the power of your mother's love can see you through the dark days. You have an opportunity to create a life with purpose and meaning."

My lips parted and I reached for their hands, as if it all suddenly was clear to me.

"Death... death teaches us to live fully?" I asked finally.

Susan smirked as if I passed the test. Amy nodded approvingly.

"Your mother isn't gone. She will live on in our hearts, our minds, our dreams, and far beyond the physicality of this world. We just have to grab on to the ones we love, life is fleeting."

Tears rolled down our cheeks. Amy stepped back to talk with my father.

"And sometimes, Elowyn- we need to stand in the rain, dammit."

Susan took off her shoes and I flipped mine off. We stepped out from underneath the tree together. Water washed over our skin so strongly, the world felt lighter around us as our clothes grew heavier. I could see people from under the tent questioning our sanity. Together in the grass, with our bare feet pressed onto the earth, I realized nothing, not even death, can take someone you love, because Bonnie was still there in every moment we lived. While someone leaves the world in one form, there is one thing that always remains, the power of love.

We were the continuation of her love.

Tristan motioned for me to come back to the stand and laughed. I made my way over there with Susan.

"I wonder how she did that."

"Did what?" Susan asked, curiosity filling her eyes.

"Lived every moment *in the moment*. She took this terrible thing and made it the reason why she fought through for so long. Long enough, to pull herself together for us."

"Yeah," I said. "She was everything to us. She taught us how to do everything, except how to live without her." Tristian extended the microphone to me and I wiped my wet hair and rain from my face. I stepped towards the microphone for the first time, with Susan and Tristan by my side.

My thoughts spun out of control, but I spoke into the microphone,

"There's this sense of dread and insignificance that comes with death. A moment when you know life will never be the same again. When you figure out your parents didn't take you camping because they enjoy the great outdoors. Or to the ocean because they wanted to bathe in the sun. When you find out all of these little things happened, it was because they were trying to give you what they never had. The magic of Christmas morning, Santa Claus. The easter bunny, and tooth fairy. It was her; it was her all along. Thank you for being the best

Mom I could have ever asked for." I passed the microphone back to Tristan.

"We're not without her though, that's the point, isn't it? She lives on through us," he spoke.

"The love she gave will last all generations to come. She did it. She broke the generational trauma anyway." Tristan smiled. We were proud of her.

"This is how she did it," I said, once again taking my shoes off and walking into the yard. My tears mixed with the rain. I pulled my children out there with me and Tristan followed with his children. Susan grabbed hold of my dad. Amy pulled Sally out to the center. We spun and danced around in the rain until the mud was up to our thighs. All of us, barefoot in the grass without a care in the world. There, in that empty space, lived our mother. Every person she touched, every smile she sparked, every single lesson she gave and sacrifice she made. Love is always the one thing that continues, and no one can ever take that from you. As the rain slowed, I felt the sunshine on my face. It peeked from behind the clouds and was a reassurance that Mom was there after-all. I held my children's hands tightly and as our bare feet left trails of mud and earth behind us, I thought of the love they would eventually pass on to their children too. I glanced up at the tree, the purple flowers were covered in droplets of rain and it glittered in the sun's rays.

My words blew into the wind, "I am because you were, Mom."

The End.

*The horrific actions portrayed by the character Dale have never been brought to justice in real life. *

AUTHOR'S NOTE

Dear Reader,

I can't thank you enough for reading my debut novel. It took me around 3 years to craft this story and it came straight from my heart. Stories give us the ability to learn about different ways of life and to bring forth empathy and understanding for others and their situations.

Even though topics such as childhood abuse, child marriage, mental health, trauma, grief and loss, and addiction are not always easy to read, they are still exceptionally important. Stories of this nature can appeal to our emotions and senses in a way that not many other things can. Books allow us to read about people we may never be and go on adventures we may never have. Bringing awareness to difficult topics is essential for the general public to develop a sense of empathy and understanding that could potentially save lives and work towards change.

Child and marriage are two words that should never be said together. Were you surprised to learn that child marriage continues to exist not only across the world, but even here in the United States? Look it up, the statistics may surprise you. Addressing child marriage requires us to look at why and how this continues to happen, so we can move forward with focus on social, policy and legal change.

Mental illness is NEVER something to be ashamed of, but society has let us believe it is. So often people turn to drugs and alcohol because it's easier to access than therapy. Addiction stems from trauma and mental illness. It's not about the alcohol or the drugs used to numb the pain. It's about that lonely person deep inside who would rather feel nothing than accept that the floor gives in when trying to comprehend what happened to them.

It's about the pain that's buried deep within. Locked away in a case that holds a bomb of emotions. With an explosion more powerful than giving up. An explosion so enormous that day after day they choose "pleasure" over pain. A heart-breaking truth when accepting what happened and moving forward is harder than becoming one of those people that society has given up on. Let's not give up. We can still make a difference by bringing awareness to childhood abuse of any form and take immediate action against child marriage that continues to exist. We can still make a difference by spreading awareness about sensitive topics and normalizing mental illness. If this novel inspired you to help or even seek help, please see the resources that follow.

Finally, when writing a book, you always want to get feedback from readers. Getting feedback on my writing is incredibly beneficial and integral part of the writing process. It enables me to continue to grow as an author and specifically from you as a reader. So, if you've read this far, I would love to hear your thoughts and if you loved it, please reach out to me or share your kindness by posting reviews across your preferred reading platforms and social media.

Maybe you can't share your feedback in person, but you can find me on

- Instagram: @lovelessica.writer
- Email: authorjessicaloveless@gmail.com

Both authors and fellow readers feel gratitude and appreciate your feedback.

Together we can make a difference!

Thanks again from the bottom of my heart.

RESOURCES

Unchained At Last is the only organization dedicated to ending forced and child marriage in the United States through direct services and advocacy. Unchained provides crucial legal and social services, always for free, to help women, girls, and others in the US to escape. Unchained also pushes for social, policy and legal change; the organization started and now leads a growing national movement to eliminate child marriage in every U.S. state and at the federal level. If you need help escaping a forced marriage, or to help women, girls, and others escape forced marriages visit **unchainedatlast.org**

There are ways you can help stop child maltreatment if you suspect or know that a child is being abused or neglected. If you or someone else is in immediate and serious danger, you should call 911. Or contact your local child protective services office or law enforcement agency. There is also, **Childhelp, a National Child Abuse Hotline** (Call or text 1.800.4.A.CHILD [1.800.422.4453]). Professional crisis counselors are available 24 hours a day, 7 days a week, in over 170 languages. All calls are confidential. The hotline offers crisis intervention, information, and referrals to thousands of emergencies, social services, and support resources.

If you, family, friends, or someone you know would like to get support for alcohol use disorder you can contact the following resources:

National Institute on Alcohol Abuse and Alcoholism (NIAAA): Phone: 301-443-3860

Alcoholics Anonymous helpline: Phone: 212-870-3400

Substance Abuse and Mental Health Services Administration (SAMHSA): Phone: 1-800-662-HELP (4357)

National Suicide Prevention Lifeline: Phone: 988

You are a valuable person. Alcohol does not define who you are. Don't hate yourself for the ways you tried to erase the pain.

ABOUT THE AUTHOR

Jessica currently resides in Indiana with her husband, 4 kids, and their dog. When not writing, you may find her listening to true crime podcasts, or Taylor Swift. She enjoys spending time with family, baking cupcakes and reveling in nature. She enjoys the ups and downs of motherhood. She also loves photography, rainy days, and the small things in life. Jessica is a huge advocate for Mental health. She relishes the chance to make other people's day better with kindness. Prior to becoming a SAHM & Author, Jessica was a Mental Health Therapist.